THE CAPTAIN OF
Kinnoull Hill

For the Tennants and the Alexanders, who led me to Perth in the first place, but especially for my father James McEwan Tennant 1941–1995

CHAPTER ONE

"Hey! No take drug! I call police!"

Dennis Duckworth woke with a start, as if he'd stumbled in his dreams.

"Hey! In there you!"

In where? Where the hell am I? For a moment, his lids held shut, as if his eyes were filled with half-set glue. As his eyelids came apart, a yellow blur appeared in the dark. Gradually, the blur settled into shapes, letters, words—specifically, the words *please insert token.*

"In there you!" An accent, not an American one, accompanied by a stuttering series of dull thumps—someone knocking on a door with the fleshy part of his fist. "No needle drug! You watch movie!"

Oh yeah. That's where I am.

"Shoh'kay." Dennis lay sprawled in the dark. He struggled to raise his buttocks off the faux leather seat, in order to fit his hand into his pocket.

"No take drug, I call police!" More thumps.

"All right, all *right!*" Getting his hand in his pocket was hard enough; getting it out was worse. When he finally yanked his hand free, he fumbled briefly with a token before snapping it into the coin slot with a flick of his thumb. Blue light flickered away the darkness and filled the cubicle with heavy breathing and the occasional ecstatic curse.

"You hear that? No needle drug, I watch *movie*, okay? Leave me alone!"

The thumping stopped.

"Asshole," the non-American accent muttered.

Dennis sighed and rubbed his eyes.

The city that never sleeps won't let me sleep. How goddamn fitting.

New York. New-Goddamn-York-Goddammit-City. Cleaner and safer than thirty years ago but still a reek like sweaty garbage. Like someone had pissed on the rocks in a sauna.

Karma was one mean son of a bitch.

*

Dennis Duckworth's trip to New York City had included several agenda items, but sleeping in a Times Square porno both was not one of them.

The original plan was simple. Dennis would fly U.S. Airways from O'Hare to LaGuardia. On the airplane, he would scan his notes and prepare for his meeting with the Universal Music Group. He would meet with the brass—no more A&R boys—at two pm. He would finally have face time with the various VPs and VIPs who held a record deal just over his head, teasingly, like the ball in a game of keep-away or bullies who had stolen his baseball cap.

Dennis wasn't used to these kinds of meetings. First of all, he was representing the band *in absentia*, which didn't seem right. The Random deserved to be here. Back in Chicago, meetings were held at the 5/4 Records office—one room, eight desks, unfinished walls. The artist was present at every spirited, shouty meeting. Not shouty because of arguments—though there were plenty of those—but shouty in order to be heard over the racket in the rehearsal space next door.

The shouty days were over. The rehearsal racket was now muffled by soundproofing, new walls, and new doors on the newly renovated conference room. Now the only racket came from the new espresso maker. The Random had brought silence to the conference room, because The Random had made 5/4 Records a boatload of money.

That boatload was about to become a shitload—which Dennis assumed was bigger than a boatload, based on the emphatic nature of the word—so Dennis suffered these strange, arid, artist-free meetings in New York. They went as planned, almost to the minute—minus some talk of the band's newest music. Jack McGinley had started with that, a request to hear the latest demos, which he quickly brushed aside, much to Dennis' relief.

"That's an issue for another day," McGinley had said. "It's time for dinner."

And so the agenda items continued to check themselves off. Smiles. Handshakes. Dinner at a Spanish restaurant and a trip to the lower east side for drinks. Beer and an assortment of whiskies rotated in and out of Dennis' grasp. Late-night Chinese food followed. Just before he left, he cracked open a cookie to reveal an unlikely fortune. "You are the master of every situation," it read.

Dennis agreed.

I almost got my band signed to a major record deal, and I got fed and shitfaced for free. I am the master of every situation. This is some true shit right here.

From the grim confines of his video booth, Dennis noted that it all went to hell at about that moment. The moment hubris entered the picture, the gods scrapped his agenda and drafted up a new one.

The lobby of the hotel, at 45th and 8th, seemed more "laden" with marble than constructed with it. It seemed too heavy, as if it weighed the room down. Dennis heard it had been renovated, or was in the midst of renovations, but saw no suggestion of that in the lobby or in the price, which was the hotel's most important feature. When the ink on the record deal was dry, Dennis could stay in better hotels. The ink wasn't dry. It wasn't wet. It was still in the reservoir.

Dennis tapped his credit card against his palm, impatient. A few young Asian tourists talked quietly by the front doors. Ten yards away, an elderly African-American man in a blazer rocked slowly in a chair, half-asleep; both the man and his blazer were rumpled like the legs of an elephant. In the lobby, invisible speakers leaked Muzak, or the satellite radio equivalent thereof. In the office behind the counter, a tinny radio or telephone speaker played "On The Horizon," the latest *song du jour* by some British kid named Kit Carson, a skinny white boy with tousled hair and a voice that sounded improbably reminiscent of Teddy Pendergrass.

When the desk clerk finally appeared, Dennis glared at her, held his card out silently and proffered what he hoped was a withering glare.

"I arranged a late check-in."

The clerk exhibited no signs of withering, making instead with the usual pleasantries as Dennis eyed the impressive staircase that led to the mezzanine. "I'm sorry, sir, but your card isn't working."

And with that, the agenda derailed completely.

"Really? Try it again."

"I've tried it three times already, sir. It looks like it's been cancelled. The machine doesn't really tell me."

"Doesn't really tell you?" The girl was probably twenty, her hair black at its roots and tips and the colour of trampy in-between. Her name tag read "Hilda."

"Well, Hilda, if it doesn't really tell you, you can't know what you're talking about. Try it again."

Flustered, Hilda swiped the card again. Dennis frowned intently at the machine until it beeped. Hilda, clearly unhappy with that beep, spoke to the floor.

"Sir, it isn't working. Do you have another card?"

"Yes, Hilda, I have another card." He flipped his wallet open and thrust another card at the uneasy desk clerk. She swiped the new card. The bottom of Dennis' stomach began to drop away, and it seemed like ten minutes passed before the machine inevitably beeped again.

"Sir—"

"Look, don't tell me it's been cancelled, okay? Try it again." Dennis watched her face flush crimson as she stood motionless.

"Try again for Christ's sake," he snapped. "Is something wrong with your head or—"

Somewhere in his head, Dennis thought he could hear laughter. A cruel, condescending laugh that he had never known until a few months ago.

Sylvia.

"Hilda." Dennis spoke her name like a sigh. "I just…listen, I don't want to overshare, but my wife just left me. I'm a bit…cranky. I'm sorry I lost my temper, I'm just a bit stressed out and upset. Can you hang on while I make a call? I need to call my credit card company and straighten this out."

"Yes, sir," Hilda replied, unimpressed with his soul-bearing admission. "Is there somewhere semi-private I might go?"

"Yes, sir, around there by the elevators, there's an alcove and some payphones."

Dennis took the two cards out of Hilda's hand and offered a decent approximation of a smile. "Okay. I'll be right back, I promise."

He would not be right back.

*

"Dennis, it's two in the morning."

"You're not fucking sleeping, Sylvia."

"Having a problem checking in?"

"What the fuck do you think?"

The laugh again, distant over the miles, diminished in the tiny speaker of his cell phone. The laugh had been louder in his head.

"Those cards are all in my name, you bastard," snickered Dennis' soon-to-be ex-wife.

"You knew I'd need these, Sylvia." Dennis struggled to keep the volume meter low. "You know I have no cash left in the account, because you took it all. Why are you such a bitch?"

"And why are *you* such a *saint*, sweetie?"

Sylvia's sarcasm rained heavy drops that hissed and steamed like acid, like Alien blood, melting the telephone's earpiece.

"Save your life, Dennis," she said, "because you've only got one."

"That's a Smiths quote, and it's out of context."

"Fuck you, Dennis."

And she hung up.

"Bitch!" Dennis kicked his carry-on suitcase and winced at the unexpected pain.

You just kicked your laptop, asshole.

As he reached to cradle his toe, his cell phone slipped and hit the floor. Simultaneously, he wobbled, tilted, and righted himself with his sore foot—which came down on his cell phone heel-first. Dennis heard the crunch and watched the life go out of the tiny screen.

New-goddammit-York-goddammit-Sylvia-goddammit!

*

No money, no hotel. Welcome to the Adult Video.

Times Square had long ago shed its 1970s squalor, and the Adult Video was one of the few such establishments left in the area. He hadn't considered that Farooq Fahri, the recent Turkish immigrant who worked the night shift, might have ousted six transients and four drug users from his booths since June. The Adult Video was a time machine, Farooq Fahri would tell his friends; in there, it was still 1977, and Times Square was still a seedy, pre-Giuliani experience.

So, to appease Mr. Fahri—whose name and ethnicity he did not know or care to know—Dennis was forced to keep the screen alive, as if somehow porn watching and needle drugging were mutually exclusive. Ordinarily, Dennis had a certain enthusiasm for adult entertainment, but sleep dep and roiling fury did not a sexy mood create. On screen, the actress was having a horrible time, despite her protestations otherwise, and her voice felt like a sharp-mandibled insect in his ears.

Dennis turned sideways in the seat, hoping that he wasn't putting his pant leg into a gummy glob of something disgusting. It improved his physical comfort, but the volume of the film still dug into Dennis' brain. There was no visible volume knob, but there was a box of tissues on the arm of the chair.

Thoughtful, like a pillow mint or complimentary champagne. Wipe yourself up, on us! We hope you enjoyed your stay!

Dennis tore up a tissue and rolled the strips into earplugs. It smoothed out the grating trebly edges created by the tinny, crackling speakerbox, but the audio remained a 2 x 4 full of nails to his skull. The tissue merely removed the nails.

When blessed blackness returned to the screen, Dennis felt about in his pockets. They were empty. He couldn't deplete his cash reserves buying more tokens. No more watch movie. It was time for the last resort.

No, I can't. I can't sleep at the airport.

It should be noted that Dennis Charles Duckworth, born and raised in Chicago, was not easily spooked. He had no phobias, no apprehensions, no fears—not spiders or heights or airplanes—except for one. What loosed the centipedes into his veins was the thought of falling asleep in public. Being unconscious, unprotected, unaware, submerged in a sea of strangers, no walls or sheets or doors, just him asleep, open, vulnerable, powerless. He'd rather sleep in a peep show booth. A peep show booth had a locking door.

"Hey!"

Dennis jumped to his feet—an awkward jump restricted by the tiny space and the carry-on luggage at his feet—and flicked the latch to pull the door open. He had hoped to fill the doorway imposingly, but his luggage blocked the door. It opened three inches. Dennis stepped backward, lifted the luggage onto the seat, and leaned into the doorway, the process of which eliminated anything remotely imposing. Farooq Fahri—a short and saggy man who resembled a miniature version of that McDonald's character, Grimace, with a bushy black moustache—looked more amused than threatened.

"Okay, you little bastard, don't worry. No needle drug. Now fuck off." With one arm he shoved the titular little bastard against the booths. "Get out of my way."

As he stormed towards to door, the little bastard, a.k.a. Mr. Fahri, shouted in a foreign language, words that were likely curses (and indeed were, albeit of the Turkish variety, which tend to be less foul and sexually insinuating than those in English). To Dennis, they sounded, quite literally, like curses. Gypsy curses. They suggested a deeper, more ancient anger than Dennis' casually-dropped F-Bombs ever could. His desire for drama still burning, Dennis leaned one shoulder into the exit door to storm away with a physical flourish. Instead, his head bounced off the glass. The door opened inward, not outward; twice in sixty seconds, the direction of door hinges deflated his show of righteous rage.

If it wasn't for that bitch I'd be in a hotel right now. Dennis felt his face sink into the rancid soup of Manhattan air. *I'd be a bedbug buffet, but at least it would be a safe, air-conditioned room.*

Shoulders slumped, visibly defeated, Dennis wandered off towards Broadway, carry-on in tow. From behind the half-naked neon woman in the window, Mr. Farooq Fahri glowered after Dennis until he and the carry-on were well out of sight.

*

Sylvia hadn't always been cruel. The mean streak may have always been there, though, hidden like sharp claws beneath soft, fuzzy paws.

Not the most apt image, he supposed. She had never been soft and fuzzy. Soft and fuzzy did not appeal to him. Oddly, bored and sarcastic *did* appeal to him. To his aesthetic. When he had met her, Sylvia had snappy one-liners, impeccable taste in fashion, irreproachable taste in music (despite his constant attempts to reproach her, due to his vehement hatred for French pop and current hip-hop, both of which she adored), and unbridled ambition. When Dennis first met her, however, she kept it all tucked away neatly beneath an intriguing surface shell of contempt and *ennui.*

Dennis liked that. When the shell cracked and exposed her inner self, he was surprised to learn he liked her even more.

In the early weeks, Dennis had assumed the divorce would proceed smoothly. They had nothing over which to argue. They did not own a home, they had no children. Yet her freshly unearthed spite seemed empowered by this lack of boundary. She even suggested that she was coming for future earnings—it was Sylvia, after all, who first took him to see The Random. She'd discovered them, not Dennis.

She doesn't really want my money. Why would she cut off my credit cards and potentially fuck up the Universal deal if that's the source of the future earnings she's going to take?

Sylvia had been talking about future earnings as if it were a sport in the pantheon of Divorce Events. X-treme Alimony. Now he saw that it was never about money, it was about hatred. That's why he was drunk and alone with nowhere to go in the middle of the night in Manhattan. The depth of her vitriol was impressive; admittedly, he almost had respect for her. Except for the fact that the vitriol was largely his inspiration. What with the extramarital sex and all.

July in New goddam York. It felt as though his sweat was already filthy *before* it trickled from his pores. Chicago could be plenty humid in the summer, but it never gave him the same grimy feeling New York gave him.

Darkened windows reflected the bright lights of the Times Square businesses still open at this ridiculous hour. Forever 21 beckoned tourists to buy dresses in case a sudden occasion presented itself at 4 a.m. Dennis doubled back along the street and considered the YMCA, but if someone was even at the front desk, he knew what he would get—one hundred and ten degrees and a shared bathroom. He'd stayed there before, and the place had been a cockroach sauna. From the moment he had lain on the mattress, keenly aware of the undesirables who had likely lain their heads on the same pillow, he'd begun to sweat through what would prove to be a sleepless night.

Dennis continued to wander instead. Plastic suitcase wheels ground against the gritty sidewalk, and the sound followed him like a gravelly trail. Knots began to form in his frontal lobe and the pain ricocheted off the back of his skull. The airport, in all its horrible reality, was truly his only option.

Nopenopenopenope

Several blocks ahead, at the point where Broadway angled to the west, a yellow light drifted in the dark. Despite a frantic, jittering sweep-like wave of his right arm, the light sailed past him and into the night.

Dammit, I look like a crazed parade Santa. Bad idea to look any kind of crazed anything in Times Square—even a post-Giuliani Times Square—at 4 a.m. When he spotted the next taxi, Dennis merely raised his arm straight, fingers splayed, hoping for maximum visibility. The taxi slowed as it approached, seemed to consider his presence, sped up, slowed again, and finally pulled up as its driver side window slid half-way down.

"Where you goin'?"

"LaGuardia. Terminal for U.S. Air."

"Shit, yeah. Get in."

Thank *God.*

Dennis yanked the door open hard enough that it bounced on its hinges. In one motion, he tossed his suitcase and himself onto the sticky vinyl seat. Leaning back, he rubbed the bridge of his nose with his thumb and forefinger and allowed a tiny smile to creep onto his face.

"Shit *yeah?*" Dennis asked.

"Shit *yeah,*" the cabbie repeated. "Even with all that construction on the parkway, this time of day? An easy ride, brother. Make me better money takin' you to LaGuardia than takin' another asshole back to the lower east side."

"I was on the lower east side myself tonight."

The cabbie said nothing.

The lower east side. Dennis could remember watching Wayne/Jayne County and the Electric Chairs at some random club on the lower east side in 1994. Or maybe that was the lower west side. He thought to mention it to the driver, but reconsidered; judging from his demeanor, his ball cap, and his age—clearly under thirty—he wouldn't have a clue who Wayne County was.

It hardly mattered. No one knew who he/she was. In the real world, almost no one knew the bands Dennis loved. They were the heaviest lightweights; the tallest midgets, as it were. Not that it bothered Dennis.

Fuck 'em. The real world has contemptible taste in music.

Dennis began to drift into semi-consciousness. At one point, he felt vaguely aware of acceleration. The next moment, he felt the taxi slow and stop as the cabbie turned his head toward him in the dim.

"We're here, man. You said you wanted U.S. Air, right?"

"Shyeah." Dennis mumbled. "I guess I was dozing."

"Don't gotta tell me, brother. You was actually talking in your sleep." The cabbie laughed and slapped the meter off. "Kept sayin' the same thing over and over."

Wordlessly, Dennis reached into his pocket and pulled out the ever-thinning billfold. The driver stared at him with a half-smile on his face, clearly amused by something.

"You don't wanna know what you said?"

"Do you want your money?" Dennis blinked at the driver, who gave him a moment's consideration, laughed to himself, took the bills and started to make change. He slapped a few quarters into Dennis hand, looked him in the eye a moment, and smiled.

"Look, man." Dennis hoisted his suitcase with one hand and cracked the door with the other. "If I wanted to know what I was saying, I would have said it while I was awake."

Dennis knew it made no sense, but the cabbie liked it, and laughed deeply.

Not awake but in motion nonetheless, Dennis went through the familiar process of checking in. It was now after five, and his flight was not for another three hours. The waiting area was deserted; he double-checked his flight pass again. LaGuardia to O'Hare. U.S. Airways Flight 6751 at 7:55 a.m.

Whatever you do, Denny, don't fall asleep.

The next few hours passed by as if he were a drunk in mid-blackout. He would raise his head sharply every few minutes. Dread filled him every time. *I can't fall asleep here. I can't fall asleep here.* Slumped over in the plastic seat, legs splayed outward, shirt damp with sweat, jacket rumpled from trying to sleep in too many ungodly places and positions, he knew he must have looked twitchy and unsettled. An exhausted part of him pressed, *just go to sleep, you'll be asleep you asshole you'll never know what's going on around you*, and then the fear would grip him with fervor and wrench him awake again. At times, he felt as though he were dreaming; at others, as though he were awake in another reality. People were watching him, he knew; he could feel it. Yet when he lifted his head again, he could see, though his disorientation, that no one gave a rat's ass about his presence.

But someone is watching me. The minute I sleep, they stare. I can feel it.

Finally, through a cottony haze, he heard someone's amplified instructions for all passengers. This was their final boarding call.

Dennis half-stumbled to the gate. He held his boarding pass up weakly, received a quick nod in return, and sleepwalked down the ramp into the already-stale recycled air inside the craft.

The near-eternal shuffle behind the slow-moving procession of passengers, the heat, and lack of sleep drained him completely. It took all he could manage to hoist his luggage into the overhead compartment. Fatigue overcame fear, although his fear had lessened immensely; somehow, an airplane was less a public space than an airport. Dennis dropped into sleep even as he fell into the aisle seat. Neither the announcements nor the motion of the aircraft during take-off—not even the complaints of his seat partner, as she clambered over his unconscious body to reach the aisle—brought him back to the surface.

Hours passed before Dennis felt his consciousness crawl slowly from its hole. The aircraft shuffled subtly from side to side, sailing through some mild turbulence, causing his head to nod as it hung limply from his neck. With a stifled yawn, he stretched his neck from side to side, rubbed his eyes, and adjusted himself to sit up straighter. How long had he been out? Chicago was just over two hours from New York, but they still seemed to be at a fairly high altitude, judging from the clouds outside the window. He squinted through the small opening, his vision thwarted by a blazing sun and the stark white glare of the clouds. He glanced to the front of the cabin to see if there was a display on-screen that might be tracking their progress.

Indeed, there was a multi-coloured map on a screen at the front of the cabin. It displayed the coast of the United States, the Atlantic, and Europe. There was a dotted arc across the ocean, and the digital representation of an airplane almost at the apex of the arc.

The dotted line led from a clearly labeled origin, New York, and ended at a clearly labeled destination. Glasgow.

What the fuck?

Dennis rubbed his eyes again, certain he'd misread. New York. Glasgow. The more he rubbed his eyes, the clearer the word Glasgow became. The problem was not his eyes. The problem was his brain. He was dreaming or he was insane.

No. I'm just on the wrong flight.

It wasn't possible. It wasn't fucking possible. LaGuardia was a domestic airport, wasn't it? How was he on a flight to Scotland? How could he mistake the gate, and then get past all the checkpoints with the wrong boarding pass? Someone would have noticed. Someone.

Dennis jammed his thumb against the call button repeatedly until a flight attendant approached him with a practiced forward lean.

"Yes sir, how can I help you?"

Pause. Sigh. Glare.

"Well, ma'am, you can explain to me why I'm on the wrong flight."

The practiced lean was accompanied by a practiced look of pleasant helpfulness, but his statement made her eyes shimmer briefly, as if some kind of ghost had passed through the machine. Dennis made note of her name tag—Rochelle.

"I, uh, sir, I'm not sure I—"

"Then let me explain it to you." He sat up straighter, wide awake now, wide awake and pissed off. A thousand half-thoughts swarmed in his head like gnats—wrong flight, fucking idiots, Sylvia—but his eyes were clear and furious.

"I bought a return ticket from Chicago on U.S. Airways, and I was supposed to be on Flight 6751 to Chicago. According to your helpful display screen, I am clearly not on a flight to Chicago. So what I would like help with—what I would like to *know*, Rochelle, is how the fuck a man can actually walk up to a gate with a boarding pass that says Flight 6751 to Chicago and be allowed on a plane that's going to a foreign country. Hmm? Would you like to explain that to me? Or perhaps that's a little beyond your scope. Perhaps there's someone else on the flight that might be able to tell me how you guys could fuck up this extremely?"

The ghost passed through Rochelle's machine again, but this time kicked the machine off-line entirely. Rochelle looked confused, and marginally worried—not about the mistake, but about Dennis' tone of voice.

"Sir, I assure you, that can't happen under normal circumstances. We're very careful with security since—"

"Yeah, I'm sure you are, since, you know, people started hijacking airplanes." His voice began to rise, and a few people nearby shifted in their seats, noticeably uncomfortable with his choice of verbs. "That's another reason I'm getting so pissed off here. Could someone tell me what the hell is going on? I am supposed to be on a flight to O'Hare. That's in *Chicago*, as I think you oughtta know. And here on my boarding pass it *clearly…*"

Dennis produced the boarding pass from his jacket pocket and glanced at it. He blinked. He blinked again.

New York. Glasgow.

Another attendant, some sort of superior to Rochelle, approached from the rear of the plane and stood silently, poised as if ready for trouble. Dennis' glance had locked into a disbelieving stare.

"I…some…I was issued an incorrect boarding pass." He had checked the boarding pass. It had said New York to Chicago. It no longer said New York to Chicago. It was New York to Glasgow.

"Is there going to be a problem here?" the supervisor asked in a mild Scottish brogue. There was an uneasy stillness to the air, and Dennis realized he was suddenly the kind of passenger for whom air marshals were hired.

Deal with Rochelle. Deal with the hole you just dug. You can deal with this other impossibility later. Time for improvisational games. Theatre sports. Fake your way out of this, Denny.

"Oh. My God." Dennis acted as if he'd had an epiphany. "My God, I don't believe it."

"What's the problem, sir?" The supervisor asked.

"I…I didn't mean to freak out like that. I just…I guess I was dreaming. I must have been dreaming. I mean, look…"

He held up both his boarding pass and his ticket for Rochelle and her supervisor to see.

"See? Obviously I'm on the right flight. For some reason I thought I was going to Chicago, I don't know why. I'm from Chicago and I must have been dreaming. You can ask my seat–mate here, I've been totally asleep until just now."

Dennis' seat-mate had no desire to join the conversation, but submitted a reluctant nod. Dennis looked up at Rochelle, his expression earnest. "I didn't mean to swear at you. My God, I never behave like that. I'm mortified. Is there something I can do? I promise, I'll behave more acceptably the rest of the way. There's nothing wrong with me. It was just a strange moment. I assure you I'm not insane and I'm not here to make any trouble."

"Where are you headed, sir?" The supervisor wanted nothing more than to believe him and be done with him, but there was still doubt in his eyes. Dennis scrolled frantically through his mental files, struggling to keep an apologetic expression on his face. The pause was almost imperceptible.

You're on stage and the game is still on, Denny. You can do this.

A snippet of music came to his mind. Something from the hotel lobby hours before.

"Scotland." Dennis cocked his head sideways as he talked, trying to project a casual air while his brain hastily assembled a story. "I work in the music business and I'm going to meet with a singer named Kit Carson. Heard of him?"

Music trivia knowledge had never had much application in the real world, but here he was, using it to avoid an incident in international airspace.

"Kit Carson?" A small smile touched the supervisor's lips. "He's fabulous, Kit Carson. 'On The Horizon,' that's a wonderful tune."

"It is."

"So you know where he is, then."

Dennis arched an eyebrow and held what he hoped was an enigmatic expression. Thanks to the internet, Dennis was able to talk about all sorts of things he didn't care about, able to hold entire conversations about artists he'd rather not think about, let alone listen to. The daily deluge of information was usually a bane, but today, a boon—it rose from the din, the memory of some U.K. music blog, something about the "disappearance" of Kit Carson. On the eve of his first BBC television appearance, he was a no-show, and no one had seen nor heard from he or his parents since, leaving behind a black hole, a swirling galaxy of rumours.

"No," Dennis replied, "but I'm going to meet some people who know some people, etc., etc. In other words, I'll know where he is soon enough."

"Ah. Some people think he's gone off to the U.S. or is hiding in London," said the supervisor. "Me? I think he's just gone home."

"I'll let you know," smiled Dennis.

Thank you, skinny white Teddy Pendergrass.

"Well, sir." Rochelle was apparently bolstered by her supervisor's reaction. "I think we can accept your apology and move forward. You haven't been drinking alcohol or—"

"No, no, ma'am, I'm completely sober—just a little stunned from waking up this way. You know those moments when you wake up from a dream and don't know where you are, or who's with you, or what's happening?"

Now Rochelle allowed herself a smile. "Yes, I do. Well, thank you, sir. I'm sorry for any misunderstanding."

"No, no, thank you for understanding."

Rochelle and her Scottish supervisor smiled fully now, and made their way back to the rear of the cabin again, chatting softly. Dennis' seat-mate, who had leaned as far up against the window as possible, now fixed him with an incredulous look.

"You didn't even really apologize," she said.

The well-practiced fake embarrassment dissolved.

"I don't apologize."

Dennis looked down at the ticket in his hand. New York to Glasgow, one way.

It wasn't possible. It just…wasn't. Yet no matter how often his eyes flitted back to the words, they continued to read New York to Glasgow. One way.

Maybe it really is a dream—because if it isn't, I may be going completely insane. I've been let down by everyone and everything I've encountered in life, but never by reality. Reality was always what it was.

Now he wasn't so sure.

CHAPTER TWO

I really need a damn beer.

Tray tables had been ordered into the upright position, and the aircraft had begun its descent. It was too late for a damn beer.

Somewhere around twenty-three thousand feet, a brilliant pain had exploded above his left eye, at once dull as a headache but prickly as pins. He pressed the heel of his palm into his eyebrow and winced. There were no signs of discomfort in the blubbering infant on the lap of the woman across the aisle, or the doughy middle-aged passengers engrossed by the trans-fat porn, otherwise called a cooking show, on the postcard-sized televisions ahead of them, or the members of the Girl Guide troupe on their way to toss cabers or do whatever-the-hell a New York girl guide troupe would do in Scotland. The agonizing barotrauma was his alone. It was also his to endure in silence. After his impressive performance as Potential Threat, and his Inappropriate Post 9/11 Passenger Behavior, Dennis had been loathe to ask U.S. Airways the unreasonable favour of finding him a Tylenol.

From the moment Rochelle and the Scot had turned their backs on him—making immediately with the conspiratorial glances and hushed conversation that certainly meant a future filled with Scottish authorities and cavity searches—Dennis craved a drink. In truth, he craved eight or nine, to flood his brain and drown the real question: Why in hell was he on a flight to Glasgow?

It was impossible, nonsensical; no error he could imagine explained the situation. Perhaps someone had traded boarding passes with him while he slept at the boarding gate. It sounded reasonable enough, but what would have been the motive? And how did he get on board with the wrong boarding pass? What about the gate—hadn't he been at the proper gate?

Dennis envisioned his pocket as a locked cabinet; he envisioned no pocket at all. Anything to fight the urge to pull out the flimsy cardboard ticket again. It would only cause another confused sensation of free-fall and confirm that he was, indeed and inexplicably, on an aircraft making its final approach to a country nowhere near his own.

His eye blossomed, as if a thousand new needles had been pressed into his flesh. As a distraction from his predicament, the barotrauma was a terrible, excruciating one, but it was a distraction nonetheless. Thanks to his ever-lovely soon-to-be-ex-wife, he had no credit cards, and only about forty-seven U.S. dollars left in his wallet. That couldn't be much more than twenty pound sterling.

Dennis pressed his palm into his forehead, against the pain, and listened. The muted drone of engines. A steady hiss of recycled air. An infant snorting and gasping in the stages between crying and calming. It was, in a way, like listening to music; the overlap, the interplay, the layers of sound that found a rhythm in ways many people never noticed. He longed for real music, but his music player was his phone, now a cracked and useless handful of plastic, wire and chips. The promised "music channels" on the flight were entirely silent, save for a barely audible fizz/sine wave combination on channel six. Channels seventeen and eighteen were the Spanish and English soundtracks to the flight's chosen film, something from Adam Sandler, which, well, just no. He would rather listen to an entire Fall Out Boy album than watch this drivel.

Fall Out Boy. The name alone made him bristle. Some people in Chicago called The Random a "second-generation Fall Out Boy," which at one time was dismissive but not entirely wrong. Fall Out Boy had a new album slated for early autumn, and Dennis had heard it. It was good. It was going to be huge.

The Random were better, but the world wasn't going to agree. Dennis' envy was extreme, even if it was premature, so he had taken to denigrating

Fall Out Boy every chance he could. Listening to Dennis, you'd think Fall Out Boy was responsible for "Who Let The Dogs Out."

Well, The Random don't sound like Fall Out Boy anymore. Which might be a point of contention vis a vis this big record deal you're trying to sign.

Music was Dennis' business, but he hadn't tired of its magic yet. Rarely did he venture into the world without music. He often still used a Discman—in his business, polycarbonate plastic discs still flowed like wine on a day at the lake with Jesus, and even the songs on his phone were usually ripped from CDs. He had no moral objection to downloading music; downloaders were the kind of people who would buy T-shirts, concert tickets, and, occasionally, albums they had already downloaded. They were music fans—the ones who actually gave a shit. If he didn't get promo copies all the time, he'd probably download, too, but as it was, someone was always sending him the newest release by somebody. It was almost always something indie or indie-minded; in the last few months he'd received discs from a dozen bands known almost exclusively by him and his fellow music geeks.

None of that was available to him now. There was only confusion, anger, and a pain that grew denser with every thousand-foot drop. He found himself staring numbly at the screen and at the digital aircraft on its arc, having passed Newfoundland, and the city of Godthab, Greenland, an island Dennis had assumed was entirely without cities.

Then, through the muted roar and steady whispers of the cabin, something like music appeared in his head. It wasn't a memory, and it wasn't a sound. It wasn't coming from outside. It was a melody, an unknown melody...*in his head.*

Before he could even ponder what auditory hallucinations could possibly mean, it disappeared, along with the metaphorical beating of that blunt, spiny object on his eye. Dennis closed his eyes and set his teeth. The sound of people filled his head and swelled into his sinus cavity, but the music was gone.

What in hell was that?

The anger that had begun to burn like acid against the insides of his veins, to muddy his perception of time, alternately stretching and condensing it, also began to fade, and by the time he disembarked, his limbs felt loose, his head disconnected from his body. In this state of depersonalization he grabbed his suitcase, lumbered off the airplane, and began a dreamlike journey through the airport. He saw it in visions caught in the spaces between blinks. Wall murals in the corridors advertised a nation with ten-foot photographs of men holding lobsters and swinging golf clubs; conspicuously absent, Dennis thought, were men holding bagpipes or feasting on haggises. Customs, too, was a blur, a question or two answered with a lie so natural he almost came to believe it this time; he was on his way to meet with Kit Carson.

"You know where he is!" the customs officer said, more of an exclamation than a question.

"Well," Dennis offered, "Some people think he's off to the U.S. or hiding in London, but the odds are good that he's just gone home."

"That's what I've been saying?" This time, the officer's exclamation was more of a question. "I do suppose it's hard to hide in Crieff, though. Small place."

"Sure is."

"Right, then. Passport?"

"Of course." Dennis never travelled without his passport. It was a holdover from the days when, on a whim, he and Sylvia might decide to go up to Canada and visit her parents.

Great. Now I have Sylvia to thank for saving my ass.

Traffic flow was sluggish, but eventually the crowd carried him out into the tiny arrivals concourse of Glasgow International. The rotunda at O'Hare was bigger than this entire airport. He checked the exchange rate against the contents of his wallet. If his brain function still allowed him proper math skills, he had almost twenty-four pound sterling. He had twenty-four pounds to see him through to the time he could call someone, get help, and get back on a plane headed for home.

There is no one to call, Dennis.

And there wasn't. The moment a list of names appeared in his head, an angry red X appeared beside each of them.

Sylvia, for obvious reasons, was out. Her reaction would be sarcastic disbelief. She'd simply assume he'd made up some cockamamie story to make her reinstate his credit cards.

Disbelief is going to be the common reaction to this story, Denny.

His hand strayed to the inside breast pocket long enough to feel the sharp edge of the boarding pass, and he fought the urge to see if it still said Glasgow. It no longer really mattered, after all. Here he was. How in the name of all that is holy…

Before he could convince himself not to think of it, he heard the melody again, like the faintest wind in the grass. At first, it added to his sense of disbelief and confusion, but when it disappeared after a few bars, he felt oddly calm.

What in hell…?

Dennis returned his attention to the situation at hand. Two days ago he had spoken to his mother. For the fifteenth, perhaps twentieth time since the announcement of the Universal deal, she had showered him with praise and we-knew-you-could-do-its; he imagined his father, ten feet away, pacing the kitchen floor as he nodded his head slightly, yes, yes he has, he has done it, finally, not the way we'd hoped, but finally found the success we wanted for him, even if it took him a decade and a half.

Richard and Elisa Mae Duckworth still lived in the house they had bought on Bernard Street, the year before he was born. Whenever Dennis spoke to them, he imagined the interior of the house, the exterior, the entire Irving Park neighbourhood, streets shielded from the sun by rows of trees. Out in the yard, sun streamed through branches and kindly touched each blade of grass. She smiled, his father paced and nodded, and beneath the praise and the pride, he felt, more than anything, the buoyancy of their relief.

Now, the scene as it would be after this phone call: the way his father would shake his head, as indiscernibly as he nodded it, and flip through his wallet to remove his Mastercard for yet another bail-out. His mother, sighing "Oh Dennis, how could you make this kind of mistake." Disappointment and a disconcerting lack of surprise, as though every disaster—failing algebra, being caught with half a joint by the principal at Schurz, doing nothing with his University degree, ruining his marriage—had been purposefully created to disappoint her. Richard and Elisa Mae did not deserve to be tied to another weight, when one had so recently been lifted.

It was Sunday, so the 5/4 office was closed. Though he knew his staff phone numbers by heart, no one had signing authority on the bank account (the ATM card for which had been stolen and summarily cancelled months before), and there was no corporate credit card. He couldn't ask any of them to front him the money for a one-way ticket from Britain. At Christmas he had given them advance copies of the Random's rough mixes. Crappy versions of an album they were all going to hear anyhow. Some of them already *had* the rough mixes. Attached to each had been a card, with a photocopied note that read *This will be responsible for next year's Christmas bonus.* An ill-advised statement of good intent from someone whose good intentions were inherently suspect. No, his staff was not likely to be sympathetic. He rested one palm against the cool steel of the payphone.

By this time next year, my staff will think differently, but for now, they're out, too.

Parents, staff, ex-wife…no.

Paul?

Yes.

If there was one person who might help, it was Paul. His oldest friend wouldn't question or scoff. He'd simply try and help.

From the day he had graduated from Schurz, on the summer road to college, Dennis' high school friends had begun to disappear. After one month at U Chicago, he had lost touch with them all, with little compunction. Paul, however, still called every few weeks, to talk about this record or that record, this movie or that movie. For years, Dennis didn't see him—Paul had moved to Iowa and only returned after Dennis and Sylvia had married—but they always spoke. Dennis wouldn't admit it, but he was thankful someone was still with him, and especially thankful it was Paul. The rest could go fuck themselves.

Just after his final college exams—he did not attend his own graduation ceremony, much to his parents' dismay—Dennis moved in with three classmates named Shelley, Joe and Max. For the next nine months, alcohol and testosterone dictated most of his decisions, causing him to lose touch with many college friends. The rest he alienated—including Shelley, Joe and Max, largely over the Afterparty Incident, as it was dubbed, in which at least two dozen people, all of whom had made Dennis' acquaintance no sooner than ninety-two minutes prior, had invaded the house and did not depart until the toilet was broken and all household condiments had been carefully dumped into a pot, boiled, and poured onto the living room carpet.

Paul, however, continued to call, every few weeks. It was Paul's very absence, most likely, that kept Dennis in Paul's good books. Paul never changed, and he never asked you to change, either; if you did, he seemed to accept it without judgment. Paul never judged anyone.

Conversely, Dennis had begun to hone his judgment skills when he met Paul in grade ten. It was a defense mechanism that Paul somehow skirted, or burrowed under. Perhaps Paul was simply unusual enough to stymie Dennis' new-found hypercriticism. Paul had an ovoid face framed by fine blond hair, the ends of which clung close to his chin. The aroma of marijuana clung to him just as closely, but he never seemed high and he didn't "party" like Dennis' other friends did. Instead he smoked weed, brewed a pot of tea, and, at fifteen, read Hesse's *Romantische Lieder*. By sixteen, he was reading *Krieg und Frieden*—after reading many of the works in-between, in chronological order. When asked why—and only Dennis asked him why, as only Dennis even knew about it—Paul replied, "I dig Hesse."

Such a weirdo. Thank God for Paul.

Dennis scanned the dialing instructions on the boxy metal telephone and fumbled with the round plastic buttons. A somnolently accented woman guided him through the collect call process. The phone rang. Twice. Three times. Dammit!

Click.

"Hey. Me. Message. Go."

Beep.

"Paulmaniminarealbadsituationandneedahandbuddyimstucksome-whereandhavent-"

Two beeps, and then a pleasant automated voice told him that no one had answered his call.

"Fuck you," Dennis replied.

*

"Celtics or Rangers?"

A bead of condensation slid down the side of his glass. Dennis furrowed his brow in its direction.

"You might as well ask me Cubs or Sox, man."

Three other brows furrowed in unison.

"What the fuck's that?" asked Sick Boy.

"That's baseball." Dennis raised his hands, palms upward. "What the fuck does an American know from football? We can't even make the ball the right shape."

Laughter burst upward from the table like fireworks. Sick Boy swallowed almost half his pint glass in one pull, while Renton belched loudly, igniting another gale of laughter.

These were not, of course, their real names, but real names were never given, and Dennis could never meet a group of strangers without affixing mental name tags to each. *Trainspotting* was probably lazy of him, but Renton really did bear an uncanny resemblance to Ewan McGregor, were McGregor red-haired. Sick Boy could very well have been the guy who played Sick Boy, as far as Dennis knew, though he appeared a few years too young. Spud, sadly, didn't look a damned thing like Spud. Vince Neil after a botched nose job and a mayonnaise diet, perhaps, only with shorter hair and younger features. The pudginess, however, did lend a certain suitability to the nickname Spud.

At Glasgow International, Dennis had been faced with a dilemma. The calm brought on by the phantom melody prevailed, though a haze hung like close clouds around his head. His anger felt as though it had been burned lifeless by its own fire, replaced by a void of Zen Buddhist proportions. In this Zen state, he decided he knew what to do. He would go into the city. His only real hope was Paul, and Paul was known to disappear for days at a time. He would not spend those days in a fucking *airport*.

In Glasgow, there was likely to be a consulate or an embassy or even just a cheap hostel sympathetic to his plight. There would certainly be more than rows of scuffed plastic chairs and the endless scuttle of luggage-laden travelers. In the city, he would find a way to Master this Situation. This insane, bad Kafka rip-off of a situation.

The bus brought him to Glasgow Central Station. The enormous antique clock, suspended from one of the high steel girders, read 7:32. Trains hissed and spat at one another on the other side of the gate. He was in Glasgow, on a Sunday evening, with nothing to do but wait until morning.

Out onto the street he wandered, around corners, down a wide cobblestone promenade. Suitcase wheels ground hollowly against the stones, with a repeated clack-and-pause, clack-and-pause, as they coursed along the uneven surface. Near-ancient facades cradled darkened storefronts. Eventually a red-paved square, scattered with gardens, benches and statues, opened to his right. Achromatic heroes on horseback, and a gentleman named Robert Peel, standing, as it appeared from this angle, with one hand in his pocket. Someone had placed a red and white traffic pylon on Mr. Peel's head, giving him the appearance of a giant, lumpy crayon.

Dennis dragged his suitcase from the square. Another train station, less impressive than the first, dominated the block. Just as he was about to wander around the corner, the Trainspotting crew called out to him from behind.

"Oi, tourist!" one of them shouted, and Dennis gave them a "guilty as charged" expression that elicited laughter.

Apparently, Sick Boy had spent several months in Chicago, though he was obviously drunk the entire time, or very drunk now, to have missed the prior Cubs/Sox reference. Either way, it seemed like a bonding moment to seize. A block upon which to build another improvisation. In other words, he hoped to befriend them and have them buy him the beer he so desperately needed.

It worked. Dennis thought of them as good ol' boy types, albeit of a Glaswegian variety. Lads? Punters? He didn't know the lingo and it didn't matter. He simply tried to be someone these guys would *like*. So far, his improvised charisma seemed to entertain them. They laughed—although they seemed to laugh too hard, as if trying to win him over.

"What do you do for a living?" asked Spud as a dribble of beer escaped from the corner of his mouth. "You're a businessman?"

"Not really. I run a record label."

Renton raised an eyebrow and tossed an inscrutable glance at Sick Boy. "Should have known, with the black jeans and the black shirt. A fuckin' music guy, yeah? Lots of great bands in Chicago. D'you work with anyone I've ever heard of?"

"Not likely," Dennis admitted. "We've got a band called The Random that you might hear about some time soon."

"Don't know either of 'em," said Spud, which confused Dennis, given that he had only mentioned one band. Spud's dribble became a rivulet as he leaned back and folded his arms.

"No? What do you listen to here, anyway?"

"Don't listen to much music," replied Renton. "Whatever's on the radio or at the club I suppose. Disnae matter much to me."

"Really? There's so much great music here, though, so many great bands have come from Scotland. Jesus and Mary Chain, one of my all-time favourites."

"Eh?" burped Sick Boy.

"Jesus and Mary Chain? Belle and Sebastian? Teenage Fanclub? Frightened Rabbit? Biffy Clyro?"

Blank stares between.

"Franz Ferdinand…?"

Ahs of recognition now, followed by a strangely inscrutable glance between Renton and Sick Boy. Spud seemed to watch the glance as it crossed the table.

"Yeah, of course, we know them, yeah."

Spud cleared his throat and spoke in a way that sounded oddly precise.

"Well lads, this place is probably closing up soon. It's Sunday. Let's go find a club somewhere maybe?"

"A grand idea, Billy," Renton grinned. "Chicago, you're with us?"

"Sure." Dennis was thankful for the possibility of a few more hours with something to do, and with the idea of more alcohol—hopefully funded by more Scottish hospitality. "Don't see why not."

They announced their departure with groans and the thick chalky slide of pub chairs on hardwood. The bartender doffed an imaginary cap with a small nod of thanks, but something in his expression, something unsettled, caught Dennis' eye. The three Scots, clearly a few pints ahead, wobbled to the door like a gelatinous mass, as the movement of one somehow pulled at the movement of the others. As they turned down the hill back towards the square—George Square, or so claimed the tin sign bolted to the corner building—they resembled a condensed white version of the Fat Albert gang, a thought that made Dennis giggle. Sick Boy glanced over his shoulder, gave Dennis an oddly girlish wink, and turned to whisper in Spud's ear.

Something's weird.

It was an absent, errant reflection, thanks to the alcohol, but there was undoubtedly something odd as he followed the Scots diagonally across the square. Their unsteady amble had stiffened and slowed, as if they were walking into the wind. Sick Boy slowed further and stopped in order to cup his hands and block the mild breeze as he repeatedly thumbed a lighter to no avail.

"Oi, have you a lighter that works?" Sick Boy tossed his to the ground and spat after it.

"Sorry, man. No."

The trio had stopped in their tracks now. Dennis, oblivious, nearly walked into them, when suddenly he noticed movement on his right. What felt like the sole of a combat boot connected with the back of his left knee. The movement to his right turned out to be Renton's fist, and it connected with Dennis' right cheek.

Dennis stumbled and barely registered that he had tripped over his suitcase before the back of his head bounced off the red paving. With every blow his vision flickered on and off, a succession of tiny blackouts that kept him unaware of who was hitting him and where. A whoop and a shout obscured Dennis' gasps as one of them began to kick him in a lower rib with a field goal kicker's precision; Dennis pushed his left arm inward, trying to tuck into himself, as Renton's face loomed above, visible between flashes of blackness and blossoms of pain.

"Fucking Yank!" His fist connected again, the blows no longer a flurry; each had started to take on its own weight and power as Dennis' surprise was replaced by icy comprehension.

"Fucking…" Hoof. "Hipster…" Hoof. "Yank…" Hoof. "Yeah!"

"That's what your friend already said," Dennis spat through the bubbles of blood in his mouth.

"Fuck you!" The foot slammed down harder this time, and Dennis swore to himself he heard a crack. A meaty slab of fingers pulled at his right arm, trying to move it aside to make room for another boot in the ribs. For one brief moment, hardly even an instant, Dennis could see all three of them, faces at varying distances above him, speckled with dirt and sweat, open mouths pouring yeasty breath over him, smiles, drunk yet sharpened eyes. Scary, fucked up, wild, beating-the-shit-out-of-you-for-fun eyes. Dennis pulled his hand from his side of his own accord and reached quickly into the breast pocket of his blazer, now ripped down no less than three seams and covered in grayish dust. With one sinuous move of shoulder and wrist, he brandished his only weapon.

What are you going to do, give 'em a paper cut, Duckworth?

The boarding pass cut the air in a cursive motion, a perfect short arc that passed a breath away from Renton's hovering face. The Scot's smile jittered, trembled and fell into a howl as he fell back out of Dennis' line of vision.

"*New York to Glasgow, motherfuckers!*" Dennis shouted.

Dennis pushed himself upward and backward, spun towards his suitcase, and snatched it with two hands before he stumbled forward into a sprint. Even as he ran, bloodied and half-aware, he felt a crazy urge to laugh.

You gave him a paper cut. To the eye.

At his back, shouts and the muffled scrape of rubber on asphalt, the sound of Renton's buddies scrambling to his side, all beneath an agonized wail peppered with inventively vulgar curses. It would be a few seconds, at best, before one or both of the standing Scots beat a trail after him, caught him, and proceeded to pluck out the eye they were owed. Ahead of him loomed Glasgow Queen Street Station, and he made directly for its doors.

"What's the next train?" Dennis was at least twenty yards away from the ticket window as he shouted, his voice filling the vast interior of the space.

"What's that?" The ticket salesman eyed him warily—more warily as he approached, and, as he finally arrived, with unmistakable apprehension. Voices burst into the air like startled pigeons, a cacophony of *but he fookin you should fookin see what he did to our MATE!* somewhere in the room behind him, followed by a quieter but somehow more authoritative pair of bass voices.

Understanding washed over the elderly employee's face. Dennis felt soaked in what he was sure was not sweat.

"The next fucking train, man, anywhere, I don't care, get me out of here."

"Next train's in about one minute, lad, you'll have to—"

"How much?"

"Ten pound an—"

Dennis tossed a ten pound note and a few coins on the counter and rolled his finger forward in the air to suggest speed. The clitter of the printout machine slowed to a crawling clack clack clack in Dennis' ears as time nearly disappeared entirely.

"Here you go. Headed to Perth."

"The where doesn't matter, my friend. Only the when."

There was no need to wait for the platform information, as only one train sat idling, ready to depart. Dennis jogged for the gate, with a pause to slip the ticket into the automatic gate machine. A shout arose from behind.

"There he is!"

Another shout arose, a more authoritative bellow, and Dennis flinched but did not look back. The gate clicked open and Dennis was on the platform and through the door, which whished closed behind him. With his breath hitching in his chest, he took a moment to look back through the window. At first he saw only the rest of the platform and his transparent reflection, misshapen and blackened with blood. Just beyond, as the earth shifted slightly and the train began to shudder forward, he spied Spud and Sick Boy, drunkenly negotiating the gate themselves, trying to lift their legs over, while two blue-shirted security guards grabbed at them from behind, hindering their process. Sick Boy made it over and dashed for the tracks, but it was too late. The train was in motion. Dennis reached his right arm forward and leaned against the door, suddenly weak.

I got the characters wrong, he thought. *They were all Begbie.*

A second or two later, he collapsed.

CHAPTER THREE

"Sir."

It was more of a statement than a question. An imperative, somehow, as if telling him there was something he should be doing, or something he should stop doing. A solid flat heat, like an electric blanket, lay across his cheek and neck. His eyes were pushed deeply into the crook of his elbow. Sun. He was laying in the sun.

Oh, Jesus. I'm sleeping outside.

When Dennis tried to raise his head, pain assaulted him on all fronts—a blast of light against his eyes, a searing sizzle against his left cheek, the sensation that a concrete-laden trowel had been buried handle-deep between the tendons in his neck. If the pain had not stopped his breath short, he would have cried out. Either way, it was painful enough to block out the dread that had risen immediately in his head.

I've been sleeping outside!

"Sir."

Again, not a question, not quite a statement. A demand of sorts.

Dennis tried to blink away the glare, but his eyelids, sticky with sleep, refused to cooperate. After a moment, he realized it probably wasn't sleep, but blood. The owner of the voice, judging by the soft gasp the voice now made, confirmed his realization.

"Sir, are you all right?"

Lengthy pause.

"Yyyy. Yyyy. Eah. Yeah. I'm okay."

A spike passed through his left side, pinning him to the strange, rough surface on which he lay. It felt oddly like Astroturf.

"Can I help you up?"

Dennis managed to prop himself feebly on one arm and used his free hand to rub at the semi-congealed substance in his eye sockets. Dried crumbs came free between his thumb and forefinger, and one eye opened. The voice, apparently, belonged to a redhead in a blue golf shirt. A uniform. A parks uniform. Behind her, suspended on a silver chain-link fence, was a red rectangle. Something jogged sideways in his head. *Putting—Crazy Golf.* That was what the red sign said. He'd had to lean his face within an inch of it to read it in the dark, after he'd staggered out of Perth Station. Now he remembered everything, almost instantly, as the sign set off his synapses like falling dominos.

"Sir?"

That time, it was undoubtedly a question. Dennis steeled himself and pushed his torso upright; the word "ffffffffuck" escaped him as a hiss, without the vowel. He blinked and saw he had been laying on a kidney-shaped mini-putt hole, surrounded by dirty red bricks and dark green bushes with yellow flowers. The fenced-in "crazy golf" area (not "mini-putt," he noted, *crazy golf*) had seemed fairly secluded, he recalled now, better than a bench and better than the dirt under the bushes. Sleeping out in the open, where cats or rats or kids or cops or junkies or anyone might come near…Dennis was shocked he'd passed out as quickly as he had.

"It's okay." Dennis turned his head and spat, mostly to see if there was blood in his saliva. There wasn't. "Just a sec."

With a low, rattly grunt, Dennis pulled his feet underneath him and stood. Something cracked somewhere, but it didn't feel like bone. Which was good, he supposed. *Fucking Begbies. Fucking Scotsmen.*

"What happened to you?" The woman's face was freshly freckled, like a person who, in recent days, had seen more sun than usual.

Dennis stepped towards the fence, stumbled, and braced himself against the chain link with his hands. It took a moment for him to catch his breath.

"What the fuck do you *think* happened?"

Redhead McFreckle, as he'd already dubbed her, appeared unoffended.

"You look like you ran into some trouble. I thought you were a homeless person, but the way you were dressed looked—"

"Where am I?"

"What?"

Pause.

"Please tell me I don't need to repeat such a simple question. Where the hell am I?"

"You're on the South Inch."

Pause.

"What the fuck's an inch?"

This time, she was offended.

"Sir, calm down. I'm only trying to help you. You're on the South Inch. The park. You do know what city you're in, don't you?"

Dennis smiled to himself grimly. Redhead would have described it more as "gruesomely."

"Yes, I know what city I'm in," he said, though it took him a moment to remember the name of the city. Perth. "And you know what?"

"What?"

Pause.

"I *am* homeless."

She eyed him disapprovingly a moment.

"Your attitude is unnecessary, sir."

"So's your help," Dennis spat. Redhead McFreckle, flustered, stood awkwardly, leaning back slightly away from Dennis and his undoubtedly unpleasant odour of beer and blood.

"If you're waiting for an apology, you're not getting one." Dennis turned from her and scanned the ground for his suitcase.

"You were talking in your sleep," she said, and turned to walk away.

How to win friends and influence people, Dennis. Being a dick isn't helping you, so maybe you might want to think before you yammer?

Easier said than done, Dennis snapped back—to himself, he supposed. He had been nice as possible to the Trainspotting crew; how had that worked out?

Nice? Bullshit. You were running a game.

That, of course, was true, and what burned him the most—other than the actual, horrendous physical agony—was that they'd turned the tables on that game. Free beer had been the pursuit, and free beer had put him in a better headspace. He'd even begun to feel slightly—*slightly*—guilty about the fact that he was, indeed, using them for beer. He didn't care about their stupid jokes and their stupid faces, to which he had affixed stupid nicknames. Then he discovered it was he who was stupid. They'd been running their own game, planning to kick the shit out of him all along. Dennis knew the look in their eyes. They were just violent maniacs who had picked him as the evening's suckerpunch.

Every time I trust someone, I get burned.

*

The tropical jacket and two pairs of matching pants were navy. 55% Dacron, 45% wool, according to the tag. Made by a company in Venice, Florida. Two rows of three gold buttons lined the front of the jacket; golden embroidery decorated the sleeves above the cuffs. The white shirts, three of them, were short-sleeved, with epaulets, striped with four gold bars, an anchor above them. On the white and blue cap, some kind of leaf insignia, with more embroidered squiggles on the navy brim. A navy tie and clip. A pair of well-polished black brogues. After that, nothing more.

This was definitely not his fucking suitcase.

He was definitely not mastering the situation.

Dennis rubbed his forehead gingerly. He had heard the phantom song in his head, felt light-headed and disconnected, and taken someone else's suitcase. Looking at it now, it was identical to his, which had been new and unfamiliar. Sylvia had given him a bright yellow and purple striped ribbon to tie to the handle.

"That's stupid," he had said. "I'll recognize my own bag."

Spread out before him was a man-made boating lake, greenish water brushed with silver-blue ripples. Bright, primary-coloured boats lay tethered to a long dock; seagulls crossed the sky above, and their droppings stained the gray walkway at his feet. Dennis sat alone, though even at this early hour the park was beginning to fill with wanderers, soccer players and children. It was as hot here as it likely was in Chicago.

I have to get off this bench and go somewhere. I have to figure out what to do. I have to call Paul again. He's the only one that can help me. Correction: he's the only one that will. *Second correction: he's the only one I even want to know about this.*

Dennis placed his palms against the wooden bench and stood tentatively, braced against whatever new misery his body would inflict, ready to fall backward if necessary. Stiffness was more prominent than agony—but agony was likely to set in after another night on a fucking mini-golf green. Even the bench seemed out of the question; McFreckles had been ready to oust him until she'd seen the gore smeared on his face. Even now she watched him, from across the tiny lake, as she swept the dock behind the gently undulating boats the colours of children's toys.

Dennis gazed across the South Inch at the gothic spire of an ancient church that parted the trees in the distance. The sea of green between himself and the steeple seemed to counter the nightmarish red that kept flashing in his mind—seeing red, red blood, red pavement. He stared every few seconds, a throb pulsing out from various points on his face and body.

Sitting in the park was pleasant enough, but he had mere pennies in his wallet, cuts and bruises on his body, and, well, he was in *fucking Scotland*. It was time to Master the Situation.

Some yards behind, a woman in low-rise jeans and a tiny black top with spaghetti straps strolled across the common. A tattoo, indistinct in design but bright red, flashed in the sun that lit on her shoulder. A duck honked behind him, its tone caustic, as if chiding Dennis for staring.

Logic has obviously fucked right off, so I might as well just follow the hot girl.

Hot Girl—perhaps his least imaginative nickname thus far—strolled towards the Inch's edge; judging by the sun that was to the east. Dennis' mind briefly boxed the needle as he set off down the

41

pathway after her, someone else's suitcase in tow. The woman led him past the borders of the Inch, where hedges broke to reveal grayish-brown stone homes, squat, rectangles cut by rectangles with the arched pediments of doorways. It all seemed very Scottish, somehow.

Hot Girl crossed the road and continued east as Dennis stayed on the opposite sidewalk, just behind her. They passed white garage doors, ducked beneath a train trestle, and came upon a cluster of traffic lights on short poles gathered on a cobblestone island that floated in the intersection. A red, white and orange bus passed ahead of him; as he watched it disappear, he noticed Hot Girl had disappeared as well.

For a second—less, really, an immeasurable instance of time—he felt something he had not felt in a while. It was both wistful longing and true sadness. It used to come whenever Dennis saw an attractive woman on the El. He would wonder, what if she didn't get off at this stop? What if they simply sat there, riding the train back and forth across Chicago, until something prompted them to speak? Maybe even one more stop would be enough for him to screw his courage to his chest and…

Then, a few years later, he stopped feeling that. He had lost his fear and would probably have spoken to the girl on the El. Or in the club. Or wherever it may be. He had lost his fear, because for the most part, he'd just stopped caring. There, on the cobblestone island, he thought he might have been happier with the longing than with the girl herself. It was a troubling thought, and he shook it off with a physical shrug.

All around him, sleeves had been peeled away to reveal more tattooed shoulders. Women wore halters and even bikini tops, regardless of whether or not it the fashion choice was sympathetic to their body shape. Sweat gathered on Dennis' brow and stung at the gashes there; every few seconds, he squeezed his eyes shut. Injuries, reddish black flakes of blood on his torn, dirt-dusted clothes—he was a real, honest spectacle. Eyes followed him longer than they normally would, and he started to notice.

The street was crowded in the pre-lunch rush. He could see no public toilet, no anonymous McDonalds or KFC with a bathroom painted anonymous white. It was a Monday morning in small-town Scotland and there was nowhere to dab at his wounds and wash away the congealed blood. Pubs opened for lunch, however—this much he knew—and dominating the corner before him was four stories of gray/brown brick with a sign that pronounced it the *Rat and Raven*. Vermin and a bird that represented death; Dennis, in his blackened mood, thought the name a *good* omen.

Though the pub was clearly closed, the door was open. Dennis stepped inside with an assuredness he didn't quite feel until the third step. He always felt it by the third step. It was a trick he'd learned. If there is a threshold you're afraid to cross, simply cross it without a thought. Bully your way past your own reservations. Once you're past the doorway, there's usually nothing left to fear.

"We're not open yet."

The voice was matronly, but somehow young, its owner buried in a shadowy gloom. Red drapery and dark wooden tables seemed to absorb any errant streams of light. The soft vibration of refrigerator motors smoothed out across the room, an almost calming sound; the pensive sound of public spaces not yet public. A glass tapped against hardwood and as his eyes adjusted to the dark Dennis saw a woman, dish towel in hand, lining pint glasses along the top of the bar.

The woman looked at him with a lopsided squint. Her face, like her voice, appeared young and old at the same. Young in feature, mature in demeanor, Dennis thought as he yanked the suitcase over the saddle of the doorway and let the door close behind him with the bright tinkle of bells.

"I understand you're not open, but I've had a bit of a...a bit of an accident, you might say, and I was wondering if I might borrow your washroom and clean myself up a little."

She was already walking towards him, still behind the bar, and her lopsidedness evened out. Her eyes widened at the sight of him but remained oddly flat with caution.

"It's okay, I'm not any trouble, and I'm not *in* any trouble," he said. "I promise. I wasn't even in a fight, really. I was jumped by some lads in Glasgow last night. I haven't had a chance to clean up since then."

Pause.

"Did they rob you?"

Dennis thought about his empty wallet.

"Yes, they did that, too," he lied.

"So why you?" A smile brushed the corners of her mouth but her eyes remained flat and keen.

"What do you mean?"

She spun on one heel mid-stride, turning to face the back wall in a strangely balletic motion. She was younger than her manner suggested.

"Well, you must have done *something* to make yourself a target."

"I didn't do anything. All I did was be American."

"Hooray for capitalism, we're winning the war on terror and such, yeah?"

"No, ma'am, nothing of the sort. Just sat there, politely but innately American."

"Ah, well, that's good enough reason, innit?" On the mirror-lined wall, Dennis could see the reflection of her smile flicker and flare at the edges, if only briefly.

Yes. I am Master of Every Situation. Even one this stupendously fucked up.

"I'm innately American, but I'm not innately caked in blood—and I don't usually smell like an August slaughterhouse. It's really taking away from my charm."

"Is your charm as innate as your American…ness?"

"It is indeed. If you'll let me use your bathroom a minute, I'll come out fresh and tell you the whole charming, bloody American story."

In the mottled mirror her smile flickered again, but this time it caught like a pilot light and a warm glow rose to illuminate the rest of her face. Eyes to the floor but in his general direction, she spoke over her shoulder.

"Straight down the bar, just to the left, through the second door. Don't leave bloodstains on the porcelain."

"I'll do my best, ma'am." His voice, filled with artificial sunshine, sounded as bright as the late morning outside.

*

Underwear was the only problem. Even if there had been a pair in the suitcase, he wasn't about to wear some other guy's gitch, and going commando in someone else's pants felt almost as disgusting. Once he wiped away an unsettling gluey sensation with some paper towel, however, Dennis could stand the three-day-old underpants. The rest of the his new apparel, as ridiculous as it looked, was at least clean and free from rips, tears, scuffs, and bloodstains. Incredibly, every item fit, even the tropical jacket and cap. He stood before the mirror in full regalia—the new brogues, the shirt, the jacket, the tie, the cap. Face freshly—albeit gently—scrubbed, he looked almost uninjured and, from a distance, could pass for a regular tourist. At close range, however, the bruises, small cuts and three days' stubble told another story. An unsavory story.

I'm dressed like the Captain, on the white piano behind Tenille. But who am I? What's my story? Where's this improv gonna go?

Good question. Was he some kind of seafarer, recently attacked by pirates southwest of Indonesia? Possibly. Dennis could spin bullshit into golden yarn, and had done so to spend the night with more than a few women. Today, though, the idea of inventing an entire life—one that involved sailing the seas, especially—seemed too much effort. Dennis was more at ease using his improvisational skills (aka his bullshit) to charm women than he was using it to, say, get free beers from Glaswegians or talk his way out of getting arrested on airplanes, but it still required the same attention to detail. Detailing adventures on the high seas? He hadn't enough energy.

Dennis deconstructed the outfit, breaking it down backwards from its full glory. He removed the hat and the tie that marked him as captain of a ship he would never command.

There. Sylvia would roll her eyes at navy pants and a short-sleeved dress shirt, but now you look like a normal tourist. He imagined Sylvia's mouth gaping in horror and laughed to himself.

The pubkeeper's reaction was not of horror but bemusement. She had turned up a few incandescent lights behind the bar and stood beneath them—a safe distance from Dennis, he noted. She didn't trust him yet.

45

"I know, I know. The clothes aren't mine. Picked up the wrong suitcase."

"You've had a lot of luck this trip, have you?" Tiny wrinkles stitched the corners of her eyes, but now that there was enough light, he could see she was no older than he was. An ability to estimate age was necessary for a successful approach; it dictated the tone of voice, the truths to tell and the truths to avoid, the pop culture references to make. How best to impress. She wore no make-up, and looked as though she rarely did. Her nondescript brown hair was pulled back, but loosely. A black golf shirt clung to her outsized chest, flattening breasts that obviously longed to be free. She was attractive, in a way, and that triggered something in the centre of his brain as surely as that bell made the Russian dogs drool.

She doesn't trust me yet, but she let me use the washroom—so she wants *to. Game on.*

"Do you mind if I have an ice water?"

"Not at all." A pause, the tinkle of ice. "This has to be the hottest weather in recent history."

"Scottish history, I presume."

"Naturally."

He took the water-beaded glass before she could reach it with the lemon wedge. For a moment, her hand hovered uncertainly in the air, long enough to note that the hand, her left, was free of rings or wedding bands.

Though he'd offered to tell her his story, he didn't offer again. He moved three seats farther towards the corner, near the bathroom, and stirred his ice.

"I honestly do appreciate you letting me come in before you're open."

"Oh, it's nothing really. It's almost time to open anyway." She stared at Dennis. He pretended to survey the signs and mirrors on the back wall, pretended not to see her making a series of decisions about him. One of these decisions, apparently, was to pour him a pint of stout, which she slid towards him with a nod.

"Still, I believe at the very least you owe me a story," she added.

And so he began, almost truthfully. No woman was identical, and tales always had to be tailored. The first matter at hand was to keep his implausible story straight, and to make sure that he left out the details that damaged his story—one such detail being that he had no real reason to be in Perth. The truth about the boarding pass made him sound forgetful at best, utterly fucking crazy at worst.

Don't forget the music, Dennis. The phantom music kind of suggests the latter over the former.

There were no interruptions while he talked, save for the occasional sigh, gasp or one-word acknowledgement. At first merely interested, she eventually became engaged. He exclaimed when necessary, self-deprecated frequently, laughed occasionally. Leaning over the bar, she eventually forgot the glasses and the rag and the gummy concentric circles, minted the night before. When he reached the red square, she shook her head, frowned, and moaned an "uh oh" for effect; shortly after, she came around the bar to sit with only one empty stool between them. One stool was polite, not cautionary. Game on, indeed.

When he mentioned Kit Carson, she smiled.

"You know his stuff?" Dennis asked.

"I know *him*. Or should I say, I've known him. I worked as a teacher for a spell. He was my student."

You're fucking kidding me.

"You're kidding me!"

"No, no, not at all. I mean, I was a substitute, only taught him English a bit, one half semester. He stood above, that's for certain. Charismatic and haunted at the same time. Handsome, all the girls loved him, but he had no ego about it. Sweet lad, nice girlfriend, a wholesome sort. And that voice! If I'd not seen him perform at the school I'd never believe that little fellow could have that soulful voice come out of him."

"It's almost a Rick Astley thing," Dennis said.

"It is!" she laughed. "His own music is good, but I'd love to hear him do rhythm and blues. Imagine him backed by Amy Winehouse's band!"

"The Dap-Kings aren't *really* Amy Winehouse's band—" Dennis began, but cut himself off. It was no time to argue music minutiae.

"—but yes, that would be something."

"He's so very talented," she continued, "but even I could see, he's so very anxious and insecure. I imagine he had no idea how to deal with fame and that's why he's disappeared."

"Ah, yeah." Dennis tried to keep several trains of thought on parallel tracks. "Yeah. So, this was in Crieff, I guess?"

"Yes."

"Ah. It's…not far from here, of course."

"No, it's not even twenty miles."

Perfect.

"It's such a small town, isn't it?"

"Yes, it is."

"Much smaller than Perth."

"Certainly."

"Which is why I'm staying here, not there," Dennis said. "Don't want to draw to much attention."

"So he's in Crieff, then?"

Part of the game, of course, involved using new information for further improv, the way Theatre Sports enthusiasts took suggestions from the audience.

"I'm not at liberty to say."

"Well," she replied, "that would be a surprise. I heard the Dunlops moved and no one knows where they've gone. You know that's his real name, yes?"

"Of course. Dunlop. Kit…Carson…Dunlop?"

"Indeed, Carson Dunlop. I don't know where the Kit came from."

"I do." Dennis pretended to look up at the ceiling. "But again, I'm not at liberty to say."

She laughed and swatted his thigh with her damp dishtowel.

This is Second City-worthy material. I should have been on 'Whose Line Is It Anyway?' That was a BBC show too, wasn't it?

When the story was finished, she mock-applauded and Dennis knew that it was time to cut out. If he looked too keen, too desperate, she might back off or begin to think him some kind of freak. No, the only way to gain more of her trust was to cut. Now.

"Jesus, I've been going on forever. You probably need to finish setting up or your customers will think the place has gone to the dogs. Or to the rats, as it were."

"Ah. A vermin joke. Never hear *those* around here."

"I didn't say my material was great. You sure wouldn't put me on *Whose Line Is It Anyway.*"

She looked over her shoulder at the clock on the wall and sucked air through her teeth. She was late opening; offering to leave of his own accord made him seem more thoughtful. Well played. As always.

"Well…I was supposed to stay with the Dunlops, but we called it off last-minute. The attention, like I said. The place they're living now is just too small. Actually, I'm afraid it's got me in a bit of a spot. I didn't budget very well for this trip. I'm not even sure there's enough space on the company credit card for a hotel room." He kept his eyes to the floor and his tone sheepish. "Especially now. I'd guess it's high season. Is there, I don't know, a bed and breakfast you'd recommend? Something I can walk to?"

There was, indeed, a row of them across the River Tay and up the hill. "You can take a walk up there," she said, "perhaps find one for yourself."

"Is it a long way to drag a suitcase, if I don't have any luck?"

"Oh, well, you can leave that in the back, if you don't mind coming back for it."

Dennis grinned. "Sure. That would be great, thank you. I can come back, maybe grab dinner, and I can let you know if I made out all right. I know you're going to be worrying about me all afternoon."

He laughed. She replied in kind.

"Ahem," came a voice from across the room. It wasn't a throat-clearing sound, but literally the word *ahem*, as if read aloud from a script by an actor who was unaware it was supposed to be onomatopoeic.

In the doorway stood a slightly paunchy but nevertheless fit-looking man, at least six four, in a tailored suit. Improbably, he held a motorcycle helmet beneath one arm, and wore an equally improbably out-of-date moustache. He resembled John Cleese circa Fawlty Towers. Nicknaming completed, Dennis looked back to the woman, who also looked up at the doorway. Briefly—like a barely-visible wisp of cloud making a shadow on the ground—her face darkened.

"Just a minute, love," she said to Dennis, and went to the doorway. Dennis sipped at the remnants of his Gillespie's and pretended to stare at the surroundings while he tried to eavesdrop. There wasn't much to hear, as they were keeping their voices low, but there was an intensity in the frequency that Dennis recognized. He especially noted the quick flicker of an eyebrow on the part of Fawlty, clearly intended as a subtle nod in Dennis' direction. She was less subtle, as she turned her head in his direction and back again. Knowing the topic of conversation now, Dennis was able to make out bits and pieces of her highly truncated explanation. Fawlty looked unconvinced. This, he imagined, was the husband or boyfriend.

When she returned, the wisp of cloud was more of a thunderhead, but she did her best to smile through it.

"Husband or boyfriend?"

She scrunched her face into a Mr. Yuck expression and when her face relaxed, the darkness was gone.

"Neither, thank God. He's the landlord. He…well, he fancies himself the potential boyfriend. He's not shy about making one have a drink with him, and if one's into him for a couple months' worth of the let, one tends to concede."

"So he manipulates you."

"Aye, like a professional."

Dennis said nothing.

"I'm Margaret, by the way."

She gave her name first. He extended a polite hand and inwardly congratulated himself.

"Margaret, nice to meet you. I'm Dennis. Thanks for the beer. And the washroom. I feel a bit more confident on the streets without the gore, even if I am dressed like I'm ready for yachting."

Margaret's laugh, sharp and bright like a bell, followed Dennis outside, where the heat flattened itself against his cheeks once again.

Smug satisfaction filled Dennis as though he'd inhaled it from a cigarette. Tonight he would return to the pub, eat dinner, sip a few pints "on the house," and after closing she'd take him home. He'd bang her, sleep, and in the morning, he would decide whether to stay or to go. Like always. Though he had to admit, this was a little different. He had never had to seduce a woman for shelter, for chrissakes. In fact, the fuck was secondary; maybe he'd just sweeten her up enough to let him sleep on the couch. Keep himself distant. She'd be willing to help him out longer that way. Then again, it would be nice to get laid and fall asleep on fabric-softened linen instead of prickly green plastic grass.

In the back of his mind, he considered that the fuck might even be tertiary. Margaret, after all, seemed sweet. Maybe—

Yeah, right, Captain. Have you noticed the situation you're in?

He pushed the thought sideways. It was almost as if he were watching a film. To enjoy a movie fully, one has to muster a willful suspension of disbelief. The boarding pass was gone, left behind damp and bloody on scarlet pavement…but he was still in another country. He was still, somehow, unable to get home. Every time he started to feel disconnected, surreal, even frightened by the strange goings-on, there was the music. He no longer heard it—he simply remembered a snippet of the melody, vaguely Celtic—and he felt inexplicably disinterested in the impossibility of the last two days. As if the music were saying, shhh, it's all right.

Yeah, as if the music isn't completely freakshow too.

The row of bed and breakfast places was on Pitcullen Crescent, she'd said, just across the Perth Bridge and up towards Scone. None of these proper nouns meant a damn thing to him, but no matter—he'd go, he'd register the names, he'd perhaps even knock on a door or two and gather a little anecdote from one of the proprietors. Later, when he explained to her how every place had been full for the night—this being high season, and all—the details would come in handy.

Downtown Perth was smaller than any given Chicago neighbourhood, including his own. The Rat and Raven was on South Street, clearly one of the only large roads in town, lined with unfamiliar shops and subtle differences from home. Storefronts were "to let." Tesco was a grocery chain. Cobblestone was less annoying when you weren't pulling a suitcase full of uniforms.

Dennis passed a bank of phone booths. It was Monday. The kids were back in the office. He was expected back first thing; it was probably 6:00 a.m. back in Chicago, maybe 7:00, he wasn't sure. There was enough change for a short phone call—he could leave a message, tell them he got waylaid and that he'd explain later.

So he did that.

One block to the north, High Street ran in a parallel direction. Every British city had a High Street, he supposed, as surely as Main Streets could be found in every burg across America. Part of this High Street was cordoned off from traffic, paved with smooth grey stone and dotted with bronze sculptures and phone booths—phone *boxes*, he supposed. On the sun-baked common he noted more than the usual per-capita-share of attractive women under thirty. This was decidedly unexpected.

High Street came to an end at Tay Street, the river road lined by some ancient but stately government building with a steeple that looked up the river and possibly clear into the highlands. Black iron fences and stone walls lined the riverbank. The Tay appeared almost still, but flowed gently southward under the spans of bridges that stitched the city together. Near the horizon, an island split the Tay in two but failed to stop it in its tracks. It wasn't a swift river, nor was it very wide. Perhaps a hundred yards across, he guessed. As he walked, heavy iron railings appeared, sprayed with the diaphanous designs of spiders, webs weighed down by what appeared to be hundreds of flying insects, now stilled in the early afternoon sun.

A large stone bridge to the north, the Perth Bridge, spanned the riverside road as well as the Tay itself. Unfamiliar makes of automobile passed through an impressive archway, guarded by a tree whose green radiated and shimmered when set against the reddish gray of stone.

Wandering up a slight incline, Dennis crossed the bridge. The waters rippled and skipped along the edges, but the middle of the river was a darkish looking glass, somehow alive, that meandered along to the green and brown slopes where the Tay turned eastward.

On the other side of the bridge the roads split in several directions; most led up into hills. A low stone building was sunken into the earth on his right. To his left, some kind of convenience store, and beyond, Main Street—according to Margaret—led to Pitcullen Crescent and a row of near-identical refurbished homes.

A mild murmur crept up the banks from the river behind him. Softly and self-consciously, he started to sing. Something half-remembered, his version vague in melody and more mumbled than sung, but it picked up his spirits as he headed north, up the incline of Main Street, to find bed and breakfasts where he would have neither bed nor breakfast.

*

It was only a Monday, but the Rat and Raven was, if not exactly raucous, at least *alive*. An acoustic duo were set up in one back corner, playing the occasional top forty hit peppered with traditional Celtic songs; Margaret's first words to him, when Dennis slipped into the room after his faux-lodging-search, had been to direct him to the corner on the opposite end.

"Don't sit too close to the band," she'd said, though it wasn't exactly a band, per se. "They're likely to get people up dancing and you'll have their arses in your face all night. And sorry it's so bloody Scottish, but at least they're not singing shortbread tins. They're actually pretty good."

So bloody Scottish? They were in the midst of performing "Sick Bed of Cuchulainn," an Irish tale sung by The Pogues, who were English. Dennis refrained from setting her straight. Women didn't like to be set straight on these sorts of facts, especially not women you'd just met and were hoping to get to take you home. Most women weren't impressed with the arrogance that came naturally to many music nerds, and even if they were impressed with your knowledge, they wouldn't be impressed by it in a corrective capacity.

Dennis spent most of his evening thumbing through local newspapers (The Perth Advertiser was apparently the town newspaper), sipping pints (provided with a smile, presumably free of charge, by Margaret, who barely escaped from behind the counter without dropping a sentence or two in his direction) and watching the duo who were, indeed, pretty good. They focused on '80s and '90s alternative mixed with Celtic and Pogues tunes; presumably, they were Dennis' age, and though it was cheesy pub music, it was at least familiar cheesy pub music, and that endeared them to him.

Later in the evening, as the third pint began to shift the weight of his brain forward, the duo were on a particularly smarmy version of Bush's "Glycerine"—not the high point of the set—and the room was appropriately (or at least politely) hushed when the heavy oak door abruptly opened, slamming against the alcove wall. At first only hoots, indistinguishable hollers, and a gale of louder-than-necessary laughter tumbled into the room. Shortly after, a small, wiry man in a soccer jersey followed similarly, literally tumbling through the door and collapsing in a heap on the floor. Another burst of laughter followed as the lad picked himself up and presented the doorway with a double-fisted middle-finger salute.

"Fuck you, cunts!"

The cunts themselves then made their appearance—four other men, all dressed as though fresh from a rugby match, followed by the man Dennis knew as Fawlty. He'd dressed down for his pub crawl, donning a bright red soccer jersey and jeans; he had not, however, shaved the mildly ridiculous moustache. The shape of his face—the heaviness of the nose, the prominence of the brow—seemed to rest entirely on top of that moustache, as if it needed the support. He wasn't unhandsome, but appeared unformed—possibly not fully evolved—and his expression lent to the primitive quality of his face. It was the alpha look. The look that dared everyone to challenge his status, so he could prove it; nothing made guys like Fawlty happier than reminding everyone who was in charge.

If Dennis were a musician, he would have been one of those correct-but-annoyingly-self-righteous ones who stopped performing mid-song to chastise a chatty audience for their disrespect. The duo here had seemed incredulous when the interruption began, but once Fawlty came through the door, they shifted their eyes nervously to the floor, soldiered on through their ballad and wrapped it a verse early. Fawlty and crew gabbled and guffawed their way to the table next to Dennis. Margaret scowled in their direction, the scowl deepening as Fawlty motioned for her to come over.

"Oi! Maggie!"

Margaret dropped her bar towel and dashed in their direction, her body stiff, her posture reflecting her barely-contained contempt. The mood in the entire room had changed; hairs on necks stood straighter, charged by a low-grade current of tension.

Dennis' arm shot out and tapped Margaret's wrist as she headed back towards the bar. He motioned for her to come close.

"What's up with the landlord, anyway?"

"What do you mean?" Margaret seemed agitated by the question.

"Beyond being a rude son of a bitch, he seems to have scared the shit out of everyone."

Margaret glanced down at him and shook her head almost imperceptibly. "He's nothing," she said quietly, "but he thinks he's something because he has money. He's a mean, self-absorbed bastard, and you'd do best to pay him no mind. He and his friends, they're not so…well, they're a bit prone to the physical, if you know what I mean."

Dennis ran his fingertips lightly over one of the welts on his head.

"Yep, think I do."

"You see that jersey?"

"Yes. Rangers, is it?"

"He wears it on purpose," she said, "instead of St. Johnstone's. That's the Perth team. He just wears it to tick people off. He's especially happy if it ticks them off enough to start a fight. Just so you know the type of fellows we're talking about."

Margaret went off towards the bar again, but her conversation with Dennis had drawn Fawlty's focused yet feral eyes in his direction. Fawlty didn't even pretend to look away; his was the sort of bullying power Dennis had seen many times. Fawlty was the sort who asked, "What are you looking at?" even when you were looking in the opposite direction.

"Oi." Fawlty frowned and motioned forward with his chin. "What's yer name?"

"Dennis Duckworth."

"Dennis, eh? Looks like you've had a rough day, Dennis."

Fawlty stood and walked over to Dennis' otherwise unoccupied table. He made a performance out of it, pulling out a chair, raising it in the air and stamping it to the ground loudly before collapsing his considerable height downward into the seat.

"Rough day, eh?" Fawlty asked.

Dennis blinked.

"Naw. Today's been pretty great. Yesterday, on the other hand, was a bitch."

Fawlty guffawed, a false, bravado-powered laugh, but he seemed to decide that, for the moment, Dennis was a good enough egg not to crack.

"Saw you earlier today," he said, "You were talking with Maggie. You know Maggie?"

"No, sir, I'm new in town."

"Och, aye. I can see that. Especially with the costume you've on. What's with the outfit? You sail here yourself?"

Someone at Fawlty's table heard that and found it funnier than it was.

"No." Dennis was glad the jacket had been tucked back into the suitcase. "Mix-up at the airport. Got the wrong bag. Probably look stupid, but I'd look stupider naked."

"Aye, that ye would!" Fawlty banged his glass on the table, and proffered his hand.

"Bruce McKee. I own the building."

"So Margaret said."

Bruce raised an eyebrow and his hand wavered, as yet unshaken. "Yeh? And what else did she have to say about me?"

"Nothing you'd want to hear." Dennis meant it to be friendly—jocular, a nudge-nudge between two men, you know, about how women are.

"What'd she say?" A reddish hue crept from Bruce's hairline downward across his forehead to meet the already crimson blush of his cheeks. His hand fell to the table, now forebodingly clutched into a fist.

"No, nothing—it was a joke. You know. Women. All that."

"No, I don't know. All that."

From a good egg to scrambled in one sentence.

His face now entirely flushed, Bruce McKee stared at Dennis.

"She didn't say anything, Bruce, I was only joking. She told me you were the landlord."

"And why were you here before the pub was open anyway?" Bruce demanded. "Serving patrons before opening time is against the law."

"Is it?" Margaret had appeared at Dennis' side. "Is it really, Bruce? I don't know if that's true."

"In my establishment, it is."

"This isn't *your* establishment," replied Margaret, visibly reddening herself. "And I'd like you to remember that. Now sit down and enjoy your drink."

As she whirled away, Bruce stood unsteadily and was half-way back to his table before he seemed to remember Dennis. He spun towards him as if Dennis had been planning a surprise attack from behind. He eyed Dennis suspiciously a moment before a strange smile came to his face and he raised his glass. *The last people to raise their glass to you had meant to curb-stomp your Yank ass, Duckworth.*

Dennis raised his glass in return anyway.

CHAPTER FOUR

The stereo was a low-rent box of cheap plastic and shoddily soldered wires. On top of it lay a copy of *Get The Knack*.

Uh-oh.

Dennis believed that certain tastes in music were good, and others were bad. This was not subjective, but entirely objective, empirical, logical. Some music was great, and some music was shite. The Knack, however, were both and yet neither.

So, did she have *Get The Knack* on CD for the right reasons?

There were plenty wrong reasons. For example, "My Sharona." A perfectly decent song, but the wrong reason to own *Get The Knack*. It was in that stupid *Reality Bites* movie from the 1990s—but then, if she were a fan of that movie, she'd be more likely to own the soundtrack than an entire Knack album. Maybe she'd heard "My Sharona" at a dance club, where it would appear in the always-incongruous "rock segue," when the generally dance-music-top-40-oriented DJ tried to appease rock fans with the likes of "Smells Like Teen Spirit" and "Brown-Eyed Girl." The only connection between songs like these was that you could spin them and not clear the dance floor entirely.

Maybe she loved the song because—and this was the worst possibility—she was just an unoriginal shithead who didn't really like music. Like the college girls in Chicago who cheered when "Paradise by the Dashboard Light" came on at the pub, who then joined in the singalong (the guys with Meatloaf, the girls with Ellen Foley) as everyone swilled back Miller High Life only to release it into gutters and toilets by two am.

No, "My Sharona" was the wrong reason to own *Get The Knack*, even if it was a good, solid pop song. It wasn't just what you liked, it was *why* you liked it, or—more concisely and abstractly at the same time—it was *how* you liked it. Maybe she sincerely loved the album, bought it in her teens, when she would sit in her bedroom and listen to "Frustrated" or "Good Girls Don't." Dennis recalled hearing "Good Girls Don't" at the age of ten. He didn't know what sex was, or what it was that she did and good girls didn't. Still, he felt some kind of inexpressible, pre-pubescent arousal when he heard it—despite the fact that the version he'd heard was recorded by The Chipmunks on an album called *Chipmunk Punk*. What genius had suggested they record that for a children's album, given the lyric "An in-between age madness that you know you can't erase / 'til she's sitting on your face?"

During his years hanging out with his old gang—Robbie, Jason and Mike, first at Belding and then at Schurz High—no one knew he liked The Knack. The Knack were, inexplicably, considered "new wave," along with Split Enz and Joe Jackson. Joe Jackson wasn't cool; hell, he sang a song about faggots and queers, so maybe he was one himself, and the cool kids weren't down with that. Not suitable listening for a group of preteens who lionized Motley Crue, Helix, Rush, Zeppelin and Ozzy. A group who could never hear the Schurz motto—"A Block Long And A World Wide"—without adding "just like my dick" and bursting into obnoxious laughter.

Robbie, Jason and Mike did not understand, but Dennis did. It was how you liked it. How did she like The Knack? Out of context, it was impossible to tell. In context—the context of her music collection as a whole—it was a different story.

Dennis couldn't know what mp3s she had stored away, but a CD tower stood in the far corner of the room. He tossed an arm over the edge of the single futon mattress and patted the carpet until his hand found underwear amongst the pile of hastily abandoned clothes from the night before.

Margaret lay on her side, face towards the flaky whitewash of the windowsill, breath even and gentle. She looked older in the stark morning sunlight, wrinkles not deeper now but more sharply defined. The morning sun really showed her age, so to speak. Still pretty, though—and she had been good in bed. There was something to be said for older women. The last girl he had taken home had been meek and passive. Margaret, on the other had, had no problem telling him how to fuck her, had moaned and howled at him, hands clenched around the corners of the futon above her head. She had shouted some seriously nasty shit. A nice bonus, considering he'd picked her up not for sex, but to score a place to sleep.

Dennis crawled out cautiously, slipped on his underwear and crossed the room. One record told you nothing. A whole collection told you everything.

"Hey," said Margaret sleepily.

"Hey." Dennis was already standing beside the CD tower. He was annoyed that she was awake.

"What are you looking at?"

"Uh…nothing."

"Looking at my music?" Margaret asked. Again, Dennis felt irritation creep its way inside him, carried by the sound of her voice.

Shut it down, Dennis. She's done nothing to you. Don't be a—

"Not much of a music fan, are you?"

Margaret, still half-asleep, seemed confused by the statement.

"What's that?" she asked.

"You've got less than, like, forty discs here."

One of which is the Best of Sting, which is never a good sign. Dream of the Blue Turtles maybe, but The Best of Sting, no. It was like a wishy-washy commitment to a wishy-washy artist. Then again, maybe she was a die-hard Police fan. That would take some of the sting out of it. Hah hah.

Margaret sat up, a frown twitching on her lips. "Good morning to you, too."

"I mean, two Westlife records, a Take That album, and a Robbie Williams CD? Robbie's cool, I met him in Chicago a couple years back. Nice guy. We talked about Scrabble. Still, all your stuff is old. Nothing new. Nothing recent."

Who cares, Dennis? Stop.

"And what's this, the *Commitments* soundtrack?"

"Dennis, are you making *fun* of me?"

"No."

Yes.

"You're going to have to get out of here."

Dennis blinked. "Beg pardon?"

Margaret was fully awake now, leaning on one arm, rubbing the bridge of her nose with the same hand.

"Mindy will be here soon."

"Mindy…" The name passed unrecognized between hangover-loosened synapses.

"You remember Mindy."

Ah. The other waitress.

"Remember, we're off to Aberdeen today. I don't want her to know I had you back for a shag, if I can avoid it. All right?"

There was no apology in the statement, not even a "no offense" disclaimer. Almost curt. Different than the usual, though not in a refreshing way.

You just insulted her—to her face—because of a film soundtrack, and you're hurt when she throws you out? I'd throw your sorry ass out, too.

"Oh. Yeah. Well, yeah." As he sat on the edge of the futon to pull on his socks, he half-expected her to roll over towards him, throw and arm around his waist or nibble at his back, but she simply laid back and rubbed her eyes into wakefulness.

"Sure, whatever." He was going for a terse indifference, but she had thrown him off-balance, and he sounded petulant instead.

British chicks. Shit.

"Your suitcase is over by the door," she said, not unkindly, as she wrapped the sheet around her breasts and crawled off the futon. "I guess you'll be on your way out of town soon, too."

Cotton/polyester blends have the strangest sheen, sometimes, he thought as he buttoned some unknown sailor's shirt.

"I guess that's likely the case," Dennis replied.

"After you meet Kit Carson, of course."

"Of course."

"Hmph." Margaret rolled sideways and closed her eyes. "Well, enjoy your stay. Don't forget your suitcase."

Pause.

"Oh, and by the way, you talk in your sleep."

*

She couldn't see me out the door fast enough. And what's with this talking in my sleep shit? I've never talked in my sleep in my life. I mean, whatever, who fucking cares, but…

Dennis had no real bearings in Perth yet, but the walk from Margaret's apartment was mostly a wide arc that lead down towards the centre of town. The slope was carved with the swirls and spins of narrow streets lined with grey brick bungalows. Hedgerows created vibrant green frames for blocks of white and ash. The road eventually straightened, and, with a few zig-zags from street to street, he found himself back in the town centre. It was not, as he previously imagined, such a small town after all. It still measured in the tens of thousands, not the millions, but his initial images of colourful locals and films like *Local Hero* faded as he dragged his suitcase through town searching for a payphone.

"Hey. Me. Message. Go."

"*Thatlastmessagemustaseemedweirdreallyneedhelpillcallyouwheni-haveanumber.*"

Click. Sigh.

The phone booth smelled of old plastic and stale gum, but he stood a moment nevertheless.

Just call, Dennis.

"Good morning, 5/4 Records." It was his publicist, Stephanie.

"Hey. It's me."

"Hey!" replied Stephanie. "Where in hell are you? Are you still in New York? I thought you were back Sunday night."

"Uh, yeah," he replied, embarrassed. "I'm…still there."

"There?"

"Here. I'm still here. In New York. I got waylaid."

"Waylaid? That's a weird choice of words."

"Yeah, well, anyway, I'm still here, and it looks like I'm going to be here for a few more days at least. You guys holding it down okay?"

"Sure, yeah. Business as usual. A few messages for you. Are you checking your email?"

"Um…I, um, I could, yeah. Forward anything that seems important." Dennis' laptop was likely on a yacht somewhere, with the rest of his clothing, but there was surely a public library in town, or an internet café.

"Well?"

"Well what?"

"You just had a meeting with Universal, Dennis! Jack McGinley sent a message this morning, and it sounded pretty promising."

"A message?"

"Yeah, he sent you a message and cc'd us."

"Anything important in there?"

"Aren't you checking your email, Dennis?"

"I, uh, I haven't today, no."

"Well, nothing too important. He did say his boss changed his mind about the demos, though, and that he'll need them after all."

Oh. Jesus Christ.

"Did he say when he wanted them?" Dennis did his best to sound nonplussed as he steadied himself against the ancient telephone.

"Labour Day is apparently about the longest they can wait."

Gravity doubled, trebled, reached upwards and tried hard to buckle his knees.

Stay with us, Denny. Master this. Goddamit. Master this!

"Okay." Dennis closed his eyes and concentrated on forcing thoughts into this larynx. "Okay, well, let's not tell him the demos are already done. Who knows what the boys might want to do—they may want the next few weeks to re-record, or remix or something. So just don't mention they're done. That way he won't rush us, and he won't rush the band."

"Makes sense," agreed Stephanie.

Yes. Of. Every. Situation. You magnificent bastard.

Dennis said farewell and stared through the cloudy plastic at nothing in particular.

The Random demos. Damn, that was close.

Universal, it was understood, were not simply going to sign The Random. They were going to give 5/4 a big-ass bonus to buy the contract. They might invest in 5/4 as a subsidiary or who knows? Maybe even buy the label outright. Either way, they would remain semi-autonomous, free to make decisions, free to sign deals. Free within reason, of course. Just like The Random were free to record their new album as they saw fit. Free within reason.

Dennis left the booth and turned towards the High Street, waggling fingers through his pockets and listening for the faint chink of coins. He felt the thickened ridges of one pound, swiped off the bar at the Rat and Raven, part of someone else's tip that Dennis had pocketed. Even while he secreted the coin away in his pocket, he told himself it was unintentional, as if he could fool himself with his own bullshit—which, sometimes, he could.

The Random were supposed to be the meal ticket that meant no more pocketing tips like a two-bit magician. A guarantee not only for him but for an office full of people, more than a decade younger than him, who barely scraped by on minimum wage. After he and Sylvia had refurnished their apartment, Dennis stopped inviting his staff to visit, feeling too self-conscious. The widescreen television was worth more than what he paid Stephanie in a month. Far more.

Soon, though, his staff would get paid what they deserved, all because a drummer named Rick Jackson had bumped into Sylvia Duckworth at a shop in Wrigleyville. Sylvia had had a full-fledged design career by that time, and some of her new designs racked on consignment, and Rick was killing time, waiting for the booker at the Metro to arrive so Rick could introduce himself. Rick played in a band called The Random Effect, he told her. Sylvia mentioned her husband owned a label called 5/4 Records.

Jackson had heard of 5/4, not because of the music, but because of James Iha, former guitarist for the Smashing Pumpkins.

"I don't think Tangerine has anything to worry about," Iha had said, referring to a preeminent Chicago label, "but 5/4 look like they have promise."

When Sylvia related the story, Dennis was impressed, mostly because Iha's muted compliment was a surprise. Dennis knew Iha and Billy Corgan, too; the Smashing Pumpkins members had worked together in a record store, years before they had become famous. In high school, Dennis would wander in, eagerly talking shit about music, rehashing Paul McDermott's intelligent-sounding opinions about the Minutemen or Tom Waits, while the two future rock stars stared at him blankly. They knew each other well enough to nod "hello" on the street. Dennis got as much mileage out of the almost non-existent relationship as he could. He was never one to invent relationships, to lie outright, but the people he had met—Iha, Corgan, Steve Albini, even those fuckers in Fall Out Boy—remained close at referential hand. He never avoided an opportunity to clock an extra nod or wave. The greetings were wordless and ephemeral, but valuable all the same.

Regardless of their ambivalence towards Dennis, James Iha and Billy Corgan had been fans of one of the label's first signings, a kinetic freak-show of rock'n'roll energy known as Snack Donkey. Snack Donkey's singer had a problem with alcohol and safety limits; while some singers climbed the monitors or the stage rigging, C.K. was known for falling off of them. It had made them a novelty act in the Chicago area, and thus, the Pumpkins members were aware of 5/4 Records. Albini, on the other hand, claimed Snack Donkey was only a sped-up version of his band Shellac, which was true, although Dennis would never admit it. Jackson, somewhat starstruck by Iha, assumed that 5/4 had to be some kind of big deal, and according to Sylvia, he almost danced around the store when she told him she'd happily pass along a demo to her husband.

The demo was fantastic. Back then, it had reminded him of another band in town, Fall Out Boy, and indeed The Random Effect and Fall

Out Boy had been friends before the band's two singers, Pat Stump and Rennie Dolling, wound up in a fight, probably over a girl, probably involving alcohol. Who knew? They became enemies, the bands became rivals. Dennis went to see The Random Effect play The Empty Bottle on the very day they shortened their name to The Random. They were fine songwriters, and the live show, though it had a few slippery spots, was fairly together. Dennis cornered Jackson and Dolling after the show, and by the end of the night, they were as good as signed.

It didn't take long after that for word to catch on, with the local indie media even playing up the rivalry. Fall Out Boy were much farther ahead and signed to a major label; their latest record had sold some stupid amount that Dennis didn't care to calculate.

Universal creamed themselves over The Random's debut, *Fantastic Time For You*. The album made them a Chicago critic's pick for best new band. Universal came knocking, tentatively at first, as noncommittal as possible, but over time, they warmed.

Then, The Random took a left turn.

Jackson and Dolling brought their new songs to the office on their iPod. When the music started playing through Dennis' computer speakers, he didn't recognize the band, but he liked it.

"This is kinda cool. Who is this?"

"That's us," Jackson grinned, and Dennis felt his heart sink.

Their music had become wiry and jittery, still melodic but strung through with jangled nerves and paranoid twitches. "Kid Who Hates Eggs," the last track Dennis heard, sounded like a Minutemen/Television mash-up, which was weird in and of itself. Maybe Fall Out Boy were fans of both groups, but they sure weren't trying to sound like them. The problem with the new material—which, eventually, Universal would want to hear—was that it was amazing. From the first second, Dennis could hear what they were going for, and was stunned. The guitar sounds were taut, like piano wire in gloved, murderous hands, while the drum and bass popped around one another in strange, syncopated rhythms. Yet Jackson's melodies were the spoonful of sugar; everything

The Random was writing was catchy, insistently so, and given a chance, it could be huge.

But not huge enough for a major international record label.

It was likely that Universal wouldn't give it a chance, Dennis was sure. Hell, the general public probably wouldn't give it a chance, and that's who bought Universal's records.

The general public is full of assholes.

Universal was on board to release a reworked version of *Fantastic Time For You*, with a few new, poppy, "normal" songs for added value. *Fantastic Time For You* would see wide release, Dennis had no doubt, but one sale-able record would not result in a major contract. Of course they wanted demos of the new material. New material they would hate.

You have to get back and convince The Random to write more pop songs.

They'll tell me to go to hell.

You have to get back and convince Universal just how visionary the new material is.

They'll tell me to go to hell.

You have to get back.

Dennis stared through the window of the Tesco beside him.

Universal wants Fantastic Time For You, and you're about to give them "Kid Who Hates Eggs." Christ.

Through the glass he could see a display of chips—er, "crisps"—with names and flavours he had never imagined. Beside a row of shopping carts lay several bundles of rapini on the floor. The Tesco doors slid open as two grandmotherly women struggled out with large bags of groceries. They stopped momentarily to secure their grips on a large bag, held between them. As they stood in the doorway, something came to Dennis—not from the depths of his mind, not from misfiring synapses. The melody—now familiar—wasn't a stress-induced hallucination. It was playing on the sound system of the grocery store.

You have lost your fucking mind, Denny.

Yes. Yes, perhaps. His eyes followed the walls inside the supermarket, past a row of liquor bottles, a cash register, and came to rest on a bulletin board, framed with blue and orange plastic. Tacked squarely in the centre was a white index card. Most of it was unreadable at this distance, but the red letters across the top, somehow slanted in both directions at once, were plain and simple.

Help Wanted.

Dennis, you have to find a way to get home. You have to get back. Call your parents. They'll get over it. Call Stephanie. She'll get over it. Try Paul again. Just, Jesus H. Christ in a sidecar, don't go into the Tesco.

So Dennis went into the Tesco.

*

Oh man. Man oh man. What have I gotten myself into?

Dennis was seated in a prefab office chair, the near-industrial kind found in governmental agencies around the world, in the office of one Gillian Gent.

"Call me Gigi," she said, in a thin, high-pitched and cartoon-like voice. Her mouth wormed sideways when she spoke, wriggling oddly beneath strands of mottled-together hair, not quite dreadlocks, not quite dirty, but somehow clumped and streaked with grey. Gigi's cardigan was a different shade of the same colour, covered in loose stitches picked outward, long loops hanging as if she were regularly climbed by cats. Her glasses, her shoulders, and her belly were round; she was apparently pregnant, though Dennis thought her to be forty-five at least.

"I'm forty-one," she said, as if she could read his mind, or at least feel his eyes on her abdomen. "Probably a little old for this I know, but my husband and I just wanted one more."

One more, according to Gigi, would make six; this, apparently, was part of the reason there was Help Wanted, part of the reason Dennis was here at the Scottish Forestry Commission, answering the strangest want ad he had ever seen. Inside Tesco, he read:

Help Wanted
Night watchperson needed
Sleep on site (camping)

Contract length uncertain
£20/day
Possible REWARD included, details at interview!
Contact Gigi at 01350 727284

"So lovely someone's come!" Gigi said. "Did you see the note at the Tesco, then?"

"Yes ma'am."

"Lovely, lovely, lovely! Are you interested?"

"I'm afraid I don't know what I'd be interested *in* yet, ma'am."

"Oh, of course not. You don't sound like you're from around here, either. Are you?"

"No, ma'am."

"Oh, that's fine, that's fine, in fact lovely. It's under the table anyway. Oh, but I'm getting ahead, far ahead."

Gigi's government-issue office seemed confused by her presence. Her desk was topsy-turvy with files and folders, and it leaned to one side where a leg was broken. The drywall behind her was splattered with a rainbow spray of coloured paint and a few lopsidedly hung photographs of what appeared to be the ruins of a castle, taken from various angles. Behind her, on the computer screen, the screensaver was one of the same shots at dusk.

With both hands, Gigi parted her hair like a curtain and smiled through it. Odd, yes. Nuts, no. Her eyes brimmed with a calm enthusiasm, but they were lucid. There was only one crazy person in the room, and that was the American in nautical pants.

"It's lovely that you've come." Gigi had used the word "lovely" at least fifteen times since Dennis called, and they had only exchanged about ten sentences. As she said the word, Dennis watched lower lip pull downward in the middle, creating an almost perfect "U" as she said it, brogue thickening her thin girlish voice. "Loo-vleh."

"I certainly didn't expect someone such as yourself to apply," she continued. "You seem an upstanding citizen. Which is lovely, aye, can't very well give the job to teenagers or troublemakers. It's teenagers or troublemakers we're out to stop! But that's all I've seen, three applicants since I posted the ad last week. One looked like he'd not seen the sober sun since 1976. The other two weren't even born in 1976! And maturity? Not a speck! Imagine, if you will, that some downtrodden soul were up there in the midst of it all, and decided they were going to toss themselves into the abyss. You know. Jump off the hill. You think these kids would have the maturity to handle such a predicament?"

She pronounced it "matoority."

"Not that it's likely, don't worry, don't worry," she reassured Dennis, who still had no clue what she was talking about. "I tell you! No. Oh! I should have written it on the advert. No teenagers! No troublemakers! But this, this is lovely. Yes. Right. So. What do you need to know? Of course, of course. Yes. Well, it's simple. For twenty quid a day, we…well, it's not we, really, it's me, mostly, but my husband, he's involved, so there's the we… we want you to live on the hill."

"The hill?"

"Yes, yes, Kinnoull Hill." She gestured out the window to an escarpment Dennis had barely noticed as he had trudged along the Edinburgh Road. It was a white-grey cliff, steep and mottled by tufts of green moss. Trees lined the top, and silhouetted against them in the teeming sun were the remains of the castle found in all of Gigi's photographs, a grey slightly darker than the cliffs themselves, with some kind of cylindrical tower standing tall above crumbled walls.

"Live atop the hill."

"That's right, yes." Gigi stood, smoothed her sweater against her rounded stomach, and sat again. "Up there, on the hill. At the top, by Kinnoull Tower. We've had a few problems, you see, vandalism, kids we think, teenagers and troublemakers. Punters in training. Fires and beer cans, that's nothing new, but lately, some nastiness, nasty people, maybe some kids listening to heavy metal music, I don't know, but there's blood. They're killing rabbits and there's blood everywhere."

"Killing rabbits?"

"Not just that! Stabbing them with knives! Blood everywhere. Who would do such a thing? The Rangers didn't realize it was blood, you know, in the day, when it dries, blood looks dark, kind of browny, yeah? They sussed it out when they found the carcasses, just ripped up with knives and tossed over the side of the hill."

"So." Dennis paused and looked at the excitable hippie in front of him. "So you want someone to be like a live-in security guard and try to catch the culprits."

"Correct. And if you do, the one thing I did get the Perth and Kinross Council to agree to was a reward. Get these youths to the police and we'll get you five hundred quid. Five hundred! It's a fantastic reward! Really, it is. Except they only offered two hundred. I might have talked my husband into, you know, perhaps, expanding the amount a touch. Just a touch! Pitching in just a wee bit, to make it five hundred. Just enough to make it truly something someone would want to do. Like you!"

Five hundred quid was a ridiculous reward, and it was also enough money to get him home. It was unorthodox, a bit

...fucking stupid...

A bit fucking brilliant, thank you, in that he was now able to save face. With everyone. No one ever had to know about his magical misadventures in air travel. He'd come to this office because of a promise, certainly, but...there was something else. There was something that drove him that he didn't understand. It was as if he'd had a premonition. A premonition that led him to this hippie dippie wacko's office, and now that he was here, this: a reward. Over a thousand dollars, and he could avoid admitting he'd fucked up, avoid prostrating himself before his parents yet again, and still get back home in time to sew up the deal.

Master of Every Situation!

"So you want me to live in a tent, deter the troublesome teenage troublemakers, and if it comes up, talk people out of suicide."

"Oh, that's not part of the job, no no, but if you were to, you know, see someone, you know, about to jump off the hill, perhaps it would be a fine idea to ask them to stop."

"A fine idea."

"A lovely idea, really."

"You don't think that would be best left to a professional counselor?"

"Oh, you're not a professional counselor too?"

Dennis gazed out the window at the tower, stately in the sky atop the hill, and imagined people leaping to their doom one at a time like orderly lemmings.

"Gigi," Dennis began, "Mrs. Gent, Gillian, listen. I've been polite, and I'm still interested, but I don't know if I can go any farther without being honest with you."

"Please, yes, please be honest." She leaned forward a little, a look of expectation hidden behind the grey curtain of her hair.

"Honest. Okay. Great. Well. Keeping in mind that I absolutely want this job…you do realize that this is entirely, completely, inarguably fucked up, don't you? Stupid. *Ridiculous*. What kind of organization asks random strangers in the supermarket to come and sleep in a tent for a couple months? What about the kids? What if they're actually really bad kids and beat the shit out of your watchman? Or if he falls off the cliff and dies? Are you insured for this kind of thing? What the fuck would I do if I caught someone, politely ask them to stop? Would I be armed? Do I have to take a crash course in fucking *suicide prevention*? What kind of government organization is this?"

He had tried to contain the sarcasm, but if he was going to continue digging his own hole of crazy, something had to make sense, somewhere, at some point. After boarding passes and red squares and phantom music, a foothold in reality would be nice.

Amazingly, Gigi flung her head back, the curtain parting once again to reveal a wide smile. She laughed aloud and, even more amazingly, applauded wildly.

"Yes!" She suddenly stopped laughing and looked pleasantly relieved. "Yes, it is crazy, isn't it? I'm a complete nutter! Hah! Crazy old hippie, everyone knows it, everyone says it, everyone. See, I'm so happy you said that. I know I'm a nutter, oh, lord, I know it, but I'm harmless, really. I promise! I'm not clinical, clinically insane, but I'm always making choices that others think are erratic, eccentric—bizarre, yeah? So for you to question me about this crazy job proves you're not crazy, that I can trust you. Follow?"

"Um…I can't believe I'm saying this, but yeah." Something about her reaction, so unexpectedly pleased, immediately buffed away some of the barbs he'd felt rising along his tongue. "I do follow. I'm glad you approve of my skepticism. I still need to know what the hell the deal is before I say yes, though."

"Of course, yes, of course," she replied, still beaming. "Well, let's see, now. A deterrent, yes, is mostly what we want. A flashlight and a 'who goes there' would be fine, just fine. People have seen at least one of them, a very short boy, they've said, a short boy in a red cap, but never his friends, so maybe he hasn't any, yeah? If we thought there was actual danger, that they were going to cause you real trouble, we'd never ask. We're not insured for anything whatsoever, of course, because it's not the Forestry Commission, it's just me, me and my husband, who work for the Heritage Trust. This is all rather, well, not rather, completely, all rather completely unofficial. There's no money in the budget, no one at the Perth and Kinross Council willing to approve something like this, something so, as you put it, so fucked. I mean, they proffered a bit of the reward, sure, but Crimestoppers would do no less. No, my husband and I, though, we took this awfulness personally, you might say. It's not just the job, working here, yeah? It's where my father proposed to my mother, up that hill. My husband, when he wasn't my husband, when he was my boyfriend, he thought it was a romantic story, so he did the same, proposed there, yeah? In fact…"

Her voice trailed off as she dropped her eyes to the floor. "In fact, if I can say it, you know, something so personal, but that's where my current son, I mean the son we're about to have, he was begun there, shall we say. Little Eddie. Eddie!"

Her hands clapped again. "It's very completely unofficial. That's why the advert in Tesco was so vague."

"So, this is an independent endeavor."

"Independent endeavor, what a lovely way to phrase it! Yes, yes it is. We're just horrified by what's been happening, and my husband, bless him, he's willing to indulge me, even in a scheme such as this. I wanted to do it myself, can you imagine? My husband nearly lost his mind. A pregnant forty-one-year-old sleeping in a tent! Leaving five children to the care of one man, wonderful as he is! Madness. So I came up with this idea."

A lone white wisp floated in the blue above Kinnoull Hill. Dennis regarded it silently for a moment.

"Okay," he said. "Okay. So your husband and you will pay me to live in a tent and stop kids from killing rabbits in the ruins of an old castle."

"Tower. Kinnoull Tower. Built by Lord Gray of Kinfauns."

"Yeah. Of course it was. The ruins of an old tower, then." Dennis rubbed the bridge of his nose with his thumb and index finger. "Jesus Christ, this is fucking weird."

"Odd!" Gigi agreed. "Bizarre! Off-kilter! That's part of why it's so lovely. But you're still here, and you said you're still interested. Which means, Mister Dennis Duckworth, that something about you isn't afraid of a little bit of strange, yeah? Willing to dive into something rather mad, no? Yeah?"

Dennis chuckled humourlessly, but the smile that followed was sincere.

"Gigi, the truth is, I'm very far from home. I have nowhere to live and no money whatsoever. I don't even know how I got here. Even though I can tell you the entire chain of events, there are gaps in its narrative logic that you could drive a truck through. So in a nutshell, I'm homeless, broke, and temporarily insane. How can I say no?"

*

For Dennis Duckworth—Chicago resident and owner of the 5/4 Recording Company—patience was an ephemeral thing. This trip to the Forestry Commission, this pow-wow with Gigi, all of it now seemed like a momentary lapse of anything akin to reason. Upon learning of the reward, he'd decided he was again mastering the situation; now, he wasn't sure such a situation could be mastered. He was on a prolonged tour of a bad neighbourhood in Crazytown.

It wasn't a tour he could slip away from, either. Strapped into the passenger seat of a rusty red Fiat, he scanned the horizon as they sailed along a narrow, curved road towards the top of Kinnoull Hill. In his head, the voice of Sylvia. *Having fun, are we Dennis? Such a good idea, taking an under-the-table job as a...a camper? A night watchman in a tent? Bra*-vo, *Mr. Successful, I can't wait to get my hands on half of this fortune.*

Fuck off, Sylvia. It's your fault I'm here in the first place.

Now, plagued with second, third and fourth thoughts—as well as the voice of Sylvia Duckworth, it seemed—he had to withstand a barrage of lovelies. Lovely, lovely, lovely, fuck. She had the strangest vocal ticks he had ever encountered, and in the rock business, you met some kooks.

When she offered to drive him to Kinnoul, he was hardly surprised to see her car already stocked with amenities—sleeping bag, pup tent, bottled water, camp stove, dry goods.

"Can you imagine?" She'd clapped her hands together after she'd opened the trunk with a flourish. "Can you imagine? It's all there, lovely! Just perfect, peachy even, peachy and lovely! Couldn't be better prepared. Good for you, I suppose, with nowhere else to go, yeah?"

Dennis thought he could feel his right eye begin to twitch. It had never twitched before, but sweet Christly Jebus, if he were to develop a facial tick, now would be the time.

You agreed to this, sweetie, he heard Sylvia say as they sped along what proved to be a blessedly short route. Gigi continued to drone, spitting lovelies at him with every opportunity as she recounted the immensely uninteresting history of a hill named Kinnoull.

One of Dennis' shortcomings, he believed, was an inability to tune out the human voice, no matter how insipid or stupid the content of its words. As a result, he now knew that the Tower had been built by the 9th Earl of Kinnoull and Lord Gray—though some historians disagree—after Lord Gray visited the Rhine Valley in the eighteenth century. The tower was built to mimic the look of the crumbling yet regal castles that line the German river. As they turned out of the parking lot and onto the motorway, Dennis could see Kinnoull Tower and even from a distance it appeared to be falling in upon itself.

"No, no, it's all lovely," she insisted. "The rubble is artificial. It's a folly."

"A folly?"

"Yes. Built for no reason except to look nice. And it does! It looks like the ruin of a real tower, doesn't it? It's lovely, really."

"Folly. Stupidity. Idiocy."

"Oh, yes, but that's not what it means in this case."

Yes it does.

"So the tower has no historical value."

"Well, no, it disnae, technically, but it is an important landmark."

"But it isn't anything. It's just there."

"Well the Empire State Building's just there, isn't it? Does it have more historical value because there are offices in it?"

The land and the Tower passed from private ownership to public when it was granted to the Perth & Kinross Council in 1924 by Lord Dewar, she told him as he pondered why in hell he would ever need that information.

"The park is lovely, yes, it's a wonderful place for walking, and all the botany and geology and historical finds, yeah? They found gouge there just twenty years ago, a socketed gouge, probably late bronze age, can you believe that? That and the heathland, there's all sorts of calcifuges plant species, you know, and the cliffs, the andesite, exposed andesite, and that's hardly it either! There's evidence of a dyke, a big one, an intrusion of melted rock that goes back some sixty million years—lord, can you imagine, sixty million years!"

Dennis kept his face to the window. What he presumed to be the highlands rose in the distance, the haze giving the hills the illusion of translucence, as if they were but shadows on the horizon. Below them, from this elevation, much of the countryside was visible, pools of golden brown in puddles between the rich green of trees. Beside him, Gigi continued to prattle. By now she was rattling off geological terms at a heady clip, and she didn't pause as they spun the car into a roadside parking spot. He looked through the windshield at a gentle slope of fuzzy grass, dotted by brown patches that appeared worn like spots on old velvet. A cluster of tall purple flowers, which he presumed was the legendary plant of Scotland, lay half way between the car and the treeline.

Gigi stepped out of the car by stretching her legs out the door one at a time with a low, protracted grunt. She bent down as if to grab her ankles, surely impossible in her swollen state, emitted a quick bark-like squeal, and stood.

"Better!" She pulled open the trunk and started unloading its contents.

"There's a lot in the boot here, and I'm in a bit of a state, as you can see." Gigi rubbed her belly as if it would be the first time Dennis noticed. He blinked at her, not comprehending.

"I mean, could you take something for a pregnant woman, Dennis? You don't expect me to haul it all up myself?"

Dennis blinked again and relented, taking the tent, bag of food and water, and a duffel with unidentified contents, leaving Gigi with only the sleeping bag. Without a word, she stepped up onto the slope with a short grunt. A path wound behind a small cottage and then tilted upwards off into the wood.

"Is it far?" Dennis had assumed they had driven to the top.

"Oh," replied Gigi, "Not so far at all, really."

Not so far my ass. Dennis wiped away the sweat that had begun to pool in the creases of his face and sting his eyes. Gnat-like insects buzzed into his ears and nose. He slapped and swatted, wiped his eyes, and saw the specks of former bugs smushed onto his skin like a paste.

They walked for at least fifteen minutes, though if someone had told him it had taken four hours he might have believed them. The trails of red earth were well kept and easy to negotiate, even where they were salted with needles and twigs, but the climb sharpened with every yard, taking them further upward into the bug-pocked heat.

Gigi was clearly part machine or so crazy she didn't feel pain. Admittedly, the most hiking Dennis did was from the bar to the upper balcony of the Metro. Still, Gigi was well into her third trimester—that or giving birth to a three-year-old—and she traipsed along the path as if she were skipping through the lilies. Dennis panted and wheezed, quietly thankful he had stopped smoking, even if it was at Sylvia's insistence.

Now I'm sweating, being eaten by insects, and thinking about Sylvia again. Thanks for a lovely, lovely fucking afternoon, Geege.

The trees seemed to grow taller as the trail crossed others, split apart, rejoined, and finally turned up to the right where suddenly the trees darkened into a silhouette against a brilliant white sky. A crumbling wall was visible at the top of the hill.

"Here it is!" Gigi skipped into the clearing in front of the tower.

It was difficult to determine what parts of the façade had crumbled away and what parts of it were merely designed to look age-worn. A whitish-grey mortar filled gaps between stones, but the original stones were a darker shade of grey; the mortar was obviously new repair. Against the painfully bright sky, shades were difficult to perceive, and the tower looked nearly black. The light created a halo around the structure, and blasted through rectangular windows filled with steel screening to dissuade people from climbing through and falling seven hundred feet.

A tall cylindrical stone stack—the tower part of the Tower—rose at least forty feet from one corner of the half-fake ruin. The part of Kinnoull Tower that actually resembled a tower was ringed by rusty metal bands that Dennis thought might help keep the aging structure from crumbling apart. He squinted at the edifice for a few more minutes, cocking his head from side to side for Gigi's benefit, reading the details on a sign entitled CLIMBING PROHIBITED. Eventually, though, he felt himself lose interest in feigning interest.

"It looks so—"

"Lovely?" The light ached and pulsed in his skull, so he began to study the browned grass, scuffed away to dirt in places like an old, cheap carpet. A small fire pit lay to his right, near the tower. A wooden bench sat in front of a grove of trees Dennis could not identify, though he was quite certain that Gigi could.

"You can put up the tent in there, I'd think, yes, that'd be perfect for you, don't you think?" She was gesturing to a small clear spot in the grove, where some sort of green foliage gave way to a forest floor lined with the reddish remains of fallen needles and leaves.

"Better than out here," he agreed. "Don't much like the idea of waking up to some schmuck watching me sleep."

Gigi's smile disappeared into itself.

"You've changed your mind, then?"

"No." The reality of sleeping in a tent now rushed in at him like a dam had burst, and he fought to stay calm as that mild terror began to pool around his ankles. "I need to make some money, get back on a plane, and get back to work so I can sign an important contract and make me and my staff some goddamned money. I'll still do this stupid-ass job."

Instead of looking offended, Gigi looked sheepish and oddly disappointed.

"Its unorthodox, but it's not stupid," she said. "It's important to me. There's no reason to be mean about it."

You're mean, Dennis.

Dennis felt a hitch in his chest, unexpected and alarming.

"Gigi, let me tell you something." He squinted at the silhouetted tower, the sky behind it so bright Dennis felt as if he were staring into the centre of a star.

Life made you mean, Dennis.

"I'm not a very nice guy," he said suddenly, surprising himself. He stood a moment, uncertain, and then flopped backward onto the wooden bench. "I don't know why, Gigi. I get angry. I have no patience. I don't want to be a jerk, but I don't…I don't think. I don't even know if that makes sense. People don't really like me. At best, I'm a prick. At worst, I so thoroughly offend people that they can't get rid of me fast enough. My soon-to be-ex-wife is the most recent in a long line of people who would agree."

Were you always this way, Dennis?

"My staff thinks I'm a son of a bitch. My parents think I'm a fuck-up—and at my age, I shouldn't care, I guess, but I do. I can't even begin to explain how I got here, to Scotland, except that maybe it has something to do with karma. Do you believe in karma, Gigi?'

Gigi didn't respond.

"Well. I don't know if I do, either. But this sure looks like karma. My ex-wife screwed me. She screwed me because I screwed her. More succinctly, Gigi, I screwed some stupid twenty-year old girl back in Chicago.

An eye for an eye, at least figuratively speaking. And then some...some... *strange* shit happens, and here I am in Scotland, on top of a hill with a woman who thinks everything's lovely, and I'm thinking that none of this, not a second of it, is reasonable."

He felt her sit on the far end of the bench.

"But you're still going to do it."

"Yes."

"Why?"

"I thought I just explained that to you. I don't know."

"Because maybe it's not karma, it's fate. There are powers that we don't understand, Dennis, and they work in mysterious ways."

"It's not something I want to consider."

"Why not?"

Dennis wiped his brow. He felt exhausted.

"Because it doesn't make sense." He looked over at Gigi, with her face tilted upwards, squinting at the sky.

"Oh, Dennis Duckworth," she replied, "what the bloody hell does?"

CHAPTER FIVE

His first night in the tent was terrifying.

The sounds that rose and swirled around him were unlike anything he had ever heard. Vehicles on the distant motorway were a comfort, but at this hour, that faint, friendly whoosh was infrequent. Instead, he felt he had been cast into the heart of the rainforest. Night, he now understood, was twice the party out here. It was when the forest really came alive, and only a sheer yellow nylon wall protected him from that life. At one point the hiss and growl of some unknown creature startled him; it seemed to come from above his head, as if the beast was poised to rip through the tent and claw out his eyes as he lay. Dennis steeled himself with logic—there was nothing in these woods, no bears, no wolverines, no mountain lions; in fact there was more dangerous wildlife in upstate Illinois than there was here in Scotland—but the continued rustle still made him feel small and foreign. Alone, there was no need to feign courage. The sound of tiny footsteps in the fallen leaves, even if it was merely a rabbit, scared the shit out of him. There was no way he was going to fall asleep tonight.

Dennis was a city person. A *Chicago* person, to be precise, but he presumed he would survive well enough in Seattle or Toronto or London (though New York and L.A. were out—they weren't cities, they were meccas for assholes and idiots). The number of times he had been camping in his life totaled two. One of them was with Paul McDermott—*Hey. Me. Message. Go.*—in southern Ontario and had revolved around weed and Ween cassettes. The other time was with Sylvia. Sylvia, despite her cosmopolitan conceits—the outfits, the in-crowd, the Lexus, the lattés, the vinyl collection, the iPad—had once been an avid camper. So off they went, the back of her Lexus piled high with coolers and camp stoves and sleeping gear, and headed out to Beach State near Zion. It was hardly a portage, but it was still too rustic for Dennis. They lasted an entire twenty-six hours. Somewhere between Dennis' complaint about the spaghetti (too *al dente*, which in retrospect was reasonable over a propane stove) and his complaint about the late-September morning chill, Sylvia's expression changed. The rounded curves of determined optimism sharpened and her face hardened; it no longer expressed, but tried to hide expression.

"What the fuck made you think this would be fun, anyway?" he had spat. "Half the time you don't like dirt under your nails. You scream if you see a spider. Why in hell are—"

Sylvia stood and stomped toward the tent.

"What? Come on. Fuck."

At the fly she whirled around. Her eyes were black embers and the edges of her mouth trembled like the arms of a fatigued power lifter about to drop the weight. Her tone, however, was even.

"You're mean, Dennis. Did life make you mean or were you always this way?"

Dennis turned away, listening to her unzip the tent and the soft rustle of sleeping bags. She didn't bother to pack or roll. She simply bundled everything into her arms and marched it to the car.

"Once you got going, I knew it," she said over her shoulder. Her voice remained cool. "I knew if I sat quiet long enough, you'd go from just bitching to actually saying something mean. You always do."

Dennis stared at the ceiling of his tent, barely visible in the darkness, and remembered. Yes. Yes, he always did get around to saying something mean. Eventually.

"What in hell am I doing anyway?" he asked the pitch black that hovered over his head. By now he should have regained balance and perspective. He should have arranged for his return to Chicago, and he had not. Why not? Nothing made sense.

Oh Dennis Duckworth, what the bloody hell does?

Only one thing, Gigi darling. You might be right. Part of me thinks I am supposed to be here.

Outside, another ripple washed through the leaves, the footfalls of some animal. Yet the footsteps were...*wrong*, somehow. They were strangely solid, but not heavy; the footsteps of a small child in iron boots. The more he listened to the rhythm of the footfalls, the more it seemed the visitor was walking on two legs.

Dennis pushed himself upright. He patted his palm blindly against the tent floor until his fingers closed around the mag light. He tried to unzip the tent flap quietly, but all the other sounds had now disappeared, leaving the clearing still; in the silence, the zipper roared like a jet engine and he stopped after only a few inches.

The footsteps stopped, and in the stillness that followed, he could hear the occasional smack and slurp, as if someone were eating a particularly messy hamburger with no regard for table manners. Then, after a pause, the voice of a man, humming. It was throaty and gruff, a melody grunted out by a Tolkein dwarf, growly and slightly off key.

Dennis found his shoes, slipped them on, and crouched by the tent flap, one hand on the flashlight and the other on the zipper. His heart pounded. It may be a teenager or something even more benign, but he was frightened nonetheless.

Go.

If the zipper hadn't caught the sheer nylon on its way up, he would have managed to emerge in one fluid motion. Instead, it hitched half-way, and Dennis had to jiggle his fingers until it came free. When the zipper hit the top he bounded through the tent flaps, snapped the light on and shouted.

"Hey!"

The round end of the beam landed against the bottom of the stack, illuminating the narrow slit of its doorway. There was a flicker in the corner of his eye, a figure that was gone as soon as it flashed before him. The sound of footfalls, galloping eastward. Dennis tried to follow the kid with his flashlight beam but failed.

It had, most definitely, been a kid—a boy, probably no older than eleven or twelve, possibly far younger. A boy in a red cap, as Gigi said, though it wasn't a baseball cap as he'd imagined; it was more like a red beret. Tendrils of straggly hair spilled out from beneath it and across the collar of a brown jacket.

"Hey, you little fucker, come back here!"

The footsteps and breaking of branches disappeared quickly, off down the hill, and the night sounds resumed.

Whoever he was, he was heavier than his slight frame suggested, judging by the unearthly clomp of those feet. Yet still he had been fleet, quick to dodge into the trees and make his way through the brush. Dennis, on the other hand, had hardly been able to get the hell out of the tent. Dennis wondered if the kid would ever bother coming back, knowing now that someone was onto him. Maybe in a way, he had screwed himself out of the reward money that would take him home.

Sylvia, and now this situation with Universal…yeah, I can't wait to get home.

Dennis marveled at how, implausibly, he withered himself with his own sarcasm. Behind him, the moon had risen and the tower took on a new kind of darkness, skeletal white in places, shadows brooding in others. He walked across the clearing and into the inner corner of the ruins, towards the entrance of the stack. It was a narrow doorway, top slightly arched, just tall enough for him to pass through without ducking but not wide enough for him to stroll through confidently. Inside the stack was entirely black. Dennis flashed the light at the circular floor, perhaps five or six feet across.

"Oh, *Jesus Christ…*"

The floor of the stack was covered in dirt, dry, brown grass, potato crisp bags, a couple of bottles, what appeared to be half an old shoe, and a few cigarette butts. In the centre lay the carcass of a grayish brown adult rabbit. Its bottom, also grey but edging towards white, was slashed by a crimson gash, out of which spilled bits of red and black meat. Blood darkened the grass around it.

An urge to gag rose and fell. Dennis nudged the animal with his toe, to ensure it was actually dead, and looked back over his shoulder.

"You little sicko," he said aloud. "What in hell are you up to?"

Click.

"Hey. Me. Message. Go."

Beep.

"Hello, Paulie McDee, this is your old friend Denny Ducky. What's up, man? Sorry about those last few messages, I was calling collect and trying to say as much as I could in the two seconds I had. I have a hell of a story for you. Some seriously fucked up shit is going on and I really need your help. Let's just say I'm in Scotland, and..."

Dennis gazed at the horizon. The late morning sunshine was so perfect and clear, creating the illusion that the horizon was somehow closer than usual, as if the light folded the distance back over itself. He felt as if he could reach up and touch the furrowed fields and irregularly measured patches of green and brown. As if he could dip his toe in the Tay from here.

"...and things are weird," he continued. "But at the moment, I'm on top of the world. Though more literally than figuratively."

Dennis flipped the phone shut. It was Gigi's personal cell; loaning it to him had been her idea, its boon only devalued slightly by the fact that it did not play music.

Kinnoull Tower stood flush with the cliffside, and one could not pass it without doing some hardcore rock climbing, clinging to unstable surfaces that looked as porous as an Aero bar. The tower stack itself was set back several feet from the edge, however, and a small earth ridge led around it to a craggy outcropping of stone. Dennis sat at its edge, where it formed a natural seat, like an outlook floating above the trees; here, with his back against the tower, he felt as though he were perched in the sky itself. Dennis brushed the occasional ant from his pantleg and watched the river gleam golden in the sunlight.

Behind him, he could hear the hollow clomp of hooves on the path. The first day someone had come through on horseback, it had surprised him; that he was still capable of being surprised was a surprise in and of itself.

Gigi had forgotten to mention the horses, though she certainly hadn't forgotten to mention much else. She'd returned in the morning with more historical information, including the fact that Kinnoull Hill had been clear-felled during WWI to supply wood for the war effort. To Dennis, the trees didn't seem so new. They seemed as old as the hill itself, *part* of the hill itself, like tufts of hair or freckles or fingernails. Dennis raised his eyes and stared at the stack, which rose ominously above his head, black against the bright, the tallest thing in the world, the only manmade object rising into the sky. Light sank into his pores and charged his skin. Absently, he pulled his freshly purchased black t-shirt up—purchased, along with a long distance phone card, after his first payday—and lay his tanned arm against his pale stomach. He looked like he had spent a week in Mexico, not the United Kingdom.

It was Dennis' sixth full day on Kinnoull Hill, his second week in Scotland. Back in New York, Universal was making its final decisions about 5/4 Records. He could imagine what was going to happen if they went ahead with the plan. It would involve plenty of contractual ifs, ands and whens. They'd want to pay nothing for The Random's back catalogue. They'd want to hire new producers for Leven, the solo project from the former MC of the Future Fighters, the label's only hip-hop act. Universal would like Leven's flow but hate his beats. They'd insist there was absolutely no way they could market Snack Donkey, but would they consider changing their name anyway? Asking Dennis as though he was the artist himself. As if Dennis ran the bands.

As if Dennis ran *anything* at this precise moment.

The last five days—the days since he spotted the wee psychopath in the red hat—had been oddly restful, though it was a tenuous, unstable form of rest; any errant thoughts of home blasted holes through the calm like buckshot. It wasn't a thought he could avoid. He'd called the office again and lied to Stephanie—that he'd decided to celebrate the near-completion of the deal with an impromptu trip to the United Kingdom. To Dennis, this amounted to a half-truth; he was, indeed, in Scotland. Despite years of sarcasm and shitty bonuses, Stephanie and Dennis were something akin to friends; she would be pissed, but she would take his side and defend him against the rest of his sure-to-be-irritated staff. In the end, the office would be fine. As far as they knew, there was no reason to believe The Random record deal was in jeopardy.

Dennis, of course, knew differently. He continued to have the same fruitless circular arguments with the voice in his head, over and over, until his esophagus tightened and his stomach churned. He debated himself, cajoled himself, invented and acted out various scenarios in his head, and yet every time it could be reduced to the same sentences he had thought the day he went into the Tesco.

You have to get back and convince The Random to write more pop songs.

They'll tell me to go to hell.

You have to get back and convince Universal just how visionary the new material is.

They'll tell me to go to hell.

The entire *deal* was going to hell. Universal, like Stephanie, had heard a story in which only the important details were accurate. There were songs they had not heard, songs like "Kid Who Hates Eggs." They wanted another Fall Out Boy and Dennis was on the verge of giving them another Fugazi. The fact that Fugazi were monumentally more important than Fall Out Boy would fall on deaf Major Label ears.

You have to get back.

For what? To lose two separate arguments?

You can master this.

How?

If…

The idea came swiftly and all at once.

They don't have to love the demos. They just have to hear that the band is going to continue in the same direction. You deliver the new demos, and it'll be like when Lou Reed recorded Metal Machine Music. Well, okay, maybe not that drastic, but same idea. The record label will lose their collective minds. They want to hear some new music that sounds similar, that sounds saleable. So don't deliver them the new demos.

Deliver them some old demos.

How would they know? The band would never know what recordings Dennis had sent to the label. The label would never know they weren't new recordings. It would be no more than a fib, a little white lie, a band-aid to patch up the situation. Universal would be satisfied with their investment, they'd release *Fantastic Time For You*, and the future would work out one way or the other.

Situation mastered.

The band would never approve, and neither would Universal, but by the time his trick was revealed, it would be too late for everyone—and they'd all be thankful for it.

Dennis stood and stepped forward to the edge of the cliff. Here, on this spot custom-carved by nature, on this outlook shielded by the tower and exactly one tree, he had solved the last problem that stood in his way. He smiled to himself as he sat down again with his feet dangling above the trees hundreds of feet below.

It was clear why some threw themselves off this cliff—though Gigi had said it was probably only two or three in recent years. It was quiet and peaceful, but an overwhelming call came up from the trees below, that macabre pull people feel when they stand at the edge of high places.

Now that his genius had mollified the situation on the homefront, Dennis began to ponder his present location. Over the last few days, the terrifying night sounds began to wash through him, to blend into a soothing drone. Knowing nothing about local wildlife, he invented his own sources for every sound; a chipmunk here, a squirrel there, though he wasn't sure; maybe there was no such thing as a squirrel in Scotland. He began listening to the sounds the way he listened to Japanese improv or noisy, avant-garde music. When you listened to LaMonte Young or Glen Branca recordings, you could only appreciate it if you listened to it differently than you did rock'n'roll. You had to engage it half-way, and with some velocity. It was active listening. Dennis recalled when he first heard Merzbow. It sounded like jet engines being scraped across God's blackboard. Eventually, he figured out how to listen for nuances, swells, rhythms and textures. Downtown Chicago sounded like rock'n'roll, with a backbeat of El trains and car horns; here, it was a soft sine wave and a fluttering chirp, it was a record by Sachiko M. He listened closely to the forest, and that way, found its rhythm. It did not escape him that for the first time his obsession with music had become a useful survival skill.

Hands in the pockets of his yachting pants, Dennis walked back to the clearing by the tower. The horse had disappeared, but a boy and a girl ran playfully back and forth from the door of the stack to the far faux-crumbling wall; as it stood, the remains of Kinnoull Tower basically had three sides left, though Dennis was pretty sure there had never been a fourth side, nor a roof, for that matter. Folly indeed.

He peered into the stack, reached up above the door to check his handiwork, and smiled. Tonight he would catch a killer. A rabbit killer. He would reap his reward and be off to save the day.

Despite the stiffness—it felt as though his veins were filled with pipe cleaners—sleeping in a sleeping bag on the forest floor had not been so horrible. He stayed up late, in order to keep watch, but nevertheless rose somewhat early to spend the morning doing little more than relaxing. His terror of sleeping exposed was metered by the fact that, in a little tent in a cocoon of darkness, he could convince himself he was well protected. With some of his meager pay advance, he'd also bought a used paperback copy of Slaughterhouse Five, and just this morning, he had finished it on the outlook, under the arc of the warmer-than-usual Scottish sun.

"Dennis, oh my, you cannae stay up the hill the entire time," Gigi told him that first morning when she had returned. "We aren't paying enough for that, no, we're not even paying enough for what you're doing as it is, you know, clearly, you've nothing to worry about, head into town, go. People will leave your things alone."

The only possessions Dennis had actually belonged to Gigi and some unknown sailor, so ultimately, Dennis left his goods unguarded and went into town. He had even forged a routine, which provided an unexpected feeling of comfort.

He trudged back down the red-earthed path, through groves and over gullies spanned by short wooden footbridges, until other trails merged with his and led him to the fuzzy green/brown hillside above the small parking lot on the Corsiehill Road overlooking the hills to the north.

The walk into town took about thirty minutes, down the incline beneath the overhanging boughs, past the cottages and homes of Brigend along the Bowerswell Road, or so he thought; street names changed two or three times along his journey, though he never seemed to leave the same road.

Today was also unreasonably warm. Gigi had claimed, as Margaret had, that it was the "hottest weather in history." He donned the Captain's hat, tilted slightly to one side as if to suggest a certain amount of irony. It looked asinine, but then again, so would sunburn on his nearly shaved head.

As he reached the Perth Bridge, he felt into his pocket for the remnants of the advance he had secured from Gigi. As he had done every day for four days, he stopped into the shop on the corner and bought a copy of the Perthshire Advertiser and two bottles of water, opening one bottle as he strolled through the sunlight and across the Tay. On the other side, in the shadow of the council offices and the steeple, he sat on a bench and flipped through the paper, marveling at what passed for news here. Complaints about drunken punters terrorizing the Ropemaker's Close. Horse race results. A headline regarding a shooting raised his eyebrow, and he chuckled when he learned it involved a BB gun. In America, this would be a hick town, but here it made Perth seem…quaint, though "quaint" was not a word Dennis had ever used without sarcasm.

After finishing the paper, which only took a few minutes, Dennis wandered towards Mill Street, where he had already stopped by the Tourist Information office and procured several street maps, a map of Kinnoull Hill, and Woodland Park. He would wander through a new street once a day, and today was no exception, but he always landed on South Street and made his way to the library and an hour of free internet time.

The A.K. Bell Library was impressive, aged and stately, with puzzling doors and stairs and ramps leading every which way. It had taken him a few attempts to discern which door was the main entrance.

"Good morning, Dennis," said Meaghan Behind The Counter. Dennis thought of Meaghan Behind The Counter as a rolly-polly little bat-faced girl, a description he lifted from Paul Simon.

"Morning, Meaghan. You're looking spunky this morning."

Meaghan Behind The Counter blushed and clutched at her bright pink sweater. "It's a bit bright, I know."

Goddawful, actually, bat-face, but it won't improve your day any for me to mention it.

"Oh, this library could use a bit of brightness, don't you think?" Dennis grinned, and the library brightened simply from the flush in Meaghan's cheeks. She handed him his ticket and he went to a computer to check his inbox.

Nothing from Universal. Another "Mail delivery failed: mailbox is full" bounceback from Paul's account. Hardly a surprise—Twitter, Facebook, text, emails, all tools that Paul had in his possession but never checked, used or logged into whatsoever.

Dennis considered checking his Facebook, but it was littered with photographs he had yet to remove. Photographs he'd rather not look at today. Instead, he cut his hour short and visited the sandwich shop on High Street for the sixth time. He ate the sandwich on another bench, watching the crowds stream down the concourse. What did people in Perth do all day other than wander the High Street? Everyone looked calm as they wandered about, with almost feline satisfaction, in the midday sun.

Across the road was an almost unmarked mall entrance, modestly tucked away in a large business complex. It was the kind of small-suburb mall he'd drive miles to avoid at home. Instead, several days ago, he'd headed inside after he spied a three-letter word in a familiar pink font. "HMV."

HMV was the kind of chain he'd also drive miles to avoid back home. Dennis was a boutique record store snob—the more obscure the stock, the better. The record shop in *High Fidelity* wasn't too far off from some of his favourites in Chicago, though most were far smaller. This HMV was now part of his daily routine. It was the standard-issue franchise, with racks of CDs down each wall, despite the media's dwindling sales. Dennis was now well familiar with the U.K.'s top forty. A row of Fall Out Boy albums slapped him hard just through the gate and he blinked at them, willing them to disappear the way the band had once disappeared, but they remained in place, defiant. He concentrated harder and squinted his eyes, imagining the cover of *Fantastic Time For You* instead, but the colour scheme was all wrong, and his brain wouldn't assist in the optical illusion.

There weren't too many people on staff in the afternoons, and in three visits, Dennis had identified only four employees. There was ManagerMan, who looked for all intents and purposes like your average franchise-retail manager. There was Skinny Munster, who looked like a pale, thin Fred Gwynne might have when he was twenty-four. There was Italian Girl, who looked entirely out of place in Perth, let alone behind the counter of a record store, with her long, carefully sprayed hair. Each tendril appeared to have been individually waxed and placed to dry in position for hours before she could move from the bathroom mirror.

It was the remaining employee, Abby, who intrigued him the most. She was the only one who defied a nickname. He considered McNose Ring, but it was a stud, not a ring; it matched the other stud that clung to the bottom of her lower lip. Her hair was slightly shorter than a bob cut, dyed the same black as her clothes, but she didn't seem goth. She was a standard issue indie rock chick, but she carried it well. He was about to settle on Alterno-Girl, which was not particularly inventive, when Italian Girl called her by her real name, and it stuck.

Dennis wondered if he'd finally found a like-minded person, a human of similar spirit. He spent his days talking to a wacko hippie and smiling at hikers. Any kind of real conversation might suffice—but his first two attempts at conversation had gone unutterably awry.

"Excuse me."

Abby had looked up, her eyes like lenses tightening into focus. Dennis envisioned her point of view as infrared, with figures and stats in a sidebar, as if she were *The Terminator* or *Iron Man*. Her analysis was brief but its conclusion visibly concrete. With one glance, she'd decided she didn't like him.

"Yes."

Not a question or an offer to help, just a "yes." It reminded him a little of Sylvia.

"Do you guys take requests?"

"We're not a DJ service or a radio station." She looked back down towards her magazine.

"I was just being funny. I mean, if I asked you to play something in the store here, would you? So I could hear it?"

One of her arms waved indistinctly towards the back of the shop. "We have listening posts."

"I don't want to hear what you've got on the posts. I want to hear this."

Abby looked back up at him tiredly. "Okay, sure. What have you got?"

Dennis handed her a copy of the last Sonic Youth disc. Sonic Youth, that band was going to be together for an eternity, he had been sure. Abby looked down at the cover of the disc with mild bemusement.

"Yeah, this I can handle. It's pretty good, actually. They don't disappoint much."

Finally, someone he could talk about music with. She turned from him, magazine in hand, placed the disc in the CD player, and flipped open her magazine with her back to him.

"Thanks," Dennis had called.

"Yeah," she'd replied.

Uneventful, true, but better than the following attempt. He'd expected Sonic Youth would do the trick—he knew the type of girl who liked Sonic Youth, or at least had some knowledge and/or respect for them, and figured it might at least prompt a comment. The next day, however, he miscalculated.

"Dashboard Confessional."

"Yeah."

"I'm sorry, mate."

Dennis blinked.

"Pardon?"

"I'm not putting that on, man."

"Oh, come on. I just want to hear if it's any good."

"I'll save you time, mate. It isn't. Aren't you a little old for emo, anyway?" With that, she flashed him a glance so contemptuous it sucked the air out of his lungs.

"He was better when he stuck to the acoustic guitar anyway," she finished, face back into the magazine.

The next day, on Friday, he had marched in to prove himself, but after twenty minutes she did not appear. Unwilling to ask ManagerMan where she was, he stormed out, as if her day off was a personal slight. Elsewhere in town, he found two other record shops, small independent places filled with the smell of cigarettes and old vinyl. Neither of them were good, overstocked with classic rock albums of varying degrees of awfulness.

Lacking music, Dennis had begun to burst into snippets of song as if it were a nervous twitch. He tried to remember the phantom melody, and occasionally he'd hum it to himself in his head, but when he opened his mouth to give it voice, it disintegrated, dispersed like vapour. He needed a disc player, an iPod, a radio, anything. He'd asked Gigi, not particularly politely, if she had one, and she had merely shrugged and gestured as if to say *wasn't the cell phone enough?* It was not the type of cell phone that played music, so to Dennis, no, it wasn't enough.

Abby was behind the counter today.

"Hey there," Dennis chirped. The enthusiasm was false, but he had decided that trying to outcool Abby was going to be impossible.

"What is it today?" Her voice was so limp it barely registered as a statement.

"Something local."

Dennis held out the latest Belle and Sebastian album. Abby took it and studied the cover, blowing a strand of hair away from her eyes, before she looked up with a look that bordered on disbelief.

"Are you desperately trying to impress me, or what?"

How in fuck did she call me on that?

"I wasn't trying to impress you. I'm married." It jumped out reflexively, surprising him.

"Oh, I see. I've never been hit on by a married man before."

Dennis dropped his smile so quickly it almost made an audible sound. "I'm not hitting on you."

"Oh, please." Abby held his gaze, her look hardening from indistinct disbelief to mild disgust. "You work in the music business, don't you."

Again with the statements that ought to be questions.

"Yeah, you do," she continued, "I can tell. You're loitering in a record store in the middle of the day. You've read every bloody magazine on our rack from cover to cover. You snickered when Len played the Joe Satriani record—you didn't roll your eyes, you *snickered*. You've got that cooler-than-thou air about you. So I can only assume you work in the music business."

"I'm not sure what your point is, Ab—"

"And that's another thing. You know my name. I'm not wearing a name tag. Are you stalking me? Is that it? Because it's not particularly charming. Which makes you not particularly charming. Verging on charm-free."

Scottish women are fucking brutal.

"You know what?" Dennis reached over the counter and snatched the disc back out of Abby's hand. She didn't flinch. "Forget it. Thanks anyway."

Dennis turned on his heel to make a dramatic exit, but realized he had the CD in his hand. Swearing under his breath, he walked half-way down the middle aisle, replaced the disc, and headed back for the door, drama deflated.

"Hey," Abby called. Her voice was different now; not softer, but smoother, less jagged.

"Yes?"

"You work in the music business," Abby repeated. "The Belle and Sebastian record came out in February. You didn't pick it out because you wanted to hear it. You've already heard it."

*

95

Of *course* he had already heard Belle and Sebastian's new album. He sure as hell hadn't expected her to figure that out, though. She had no way of knowing an American would give a shit about a fey Scottish pop group. She had no way of knowing he was in the music business, either, but there you go.

Life would be so much easier if he could just strike up a conversation in a polite way, something akin to a normal human being. Instead, he was coming on to Abby, and though she was kind of cute, he wasn't in the market—*hey baby, wanna come back to my tent?* The sincere approach was unthinkable. *Hi, strange person. I'm lonely. Wanna be my friend?*

On his way back up the hill, the gnats buzzed up against his eardrums and eyelids. Embarrassed and agitated, he focused his attention on indirect revenge. Karmic revenge. On the rabbit killer in the red cap.

After the long, sweaty climb, Dennis went back to observe his handiwork inside the tower. Looking straight upward, he could see the sky through the top of the tower, blue settling into itself, sunlight fading over the hill to the west. It was like looking up from the bottom of a well. A mossy grass grew over the edges of the hole above, and the circle of sky was divided into six uneven sections by three metal support bars. The bars appeared rusty but nonetheless sturdy, firmly in place. A length of twine crossed over one of them and disappeared over the lip of the opening.

It was a trap. A horrible, poorly designed trap, but the best Dennis could do, having had no experience trapping things in Chicago. He'd tied a fairly heavy rock to one end, along with a large bundle of sticks and brush about five feet in diameter. Inside the tower, Dennis pulled the twine and hoisted the rock and bundle of sticks up the side of the stack. It crawled and tumbled upwards like a spider on the water spout until it hung suspended a few feet above the outside of the doorway.

The kid had been back twice since that first night, and left rabbit carcasses as proof. Sad-faced park rangers shook their heads and carted them away, but made little reference to the hill's new resident; Gigi had quietly informed them, hoping they would look the other way, which they had.

The next two nights the kid came back Dennis hadn't seen him. For two nights, Dennis heard nothing but the seething of the forest, and thought perhaps the presence of the tent had scared the boy away. A normal kid would find another place to get up to his little freak show, but no, this kid seemed to prefer skulking about the tower. Saturday morning, Dennis found another rabbit, deposited dead and bloodless on the floor of the tower stack. It made no difference how late Dennis laid awake, listening for footfalls above the nightly din—somehow, the little bastard managed to arrive after Dennis fell asleep.

There was always one rabbit on the straw-strewn floor of the stack, but never much blood, as if the kid did the bleeding somewhere else and only used the tower to dump the evidence.

The weight of the rock and bundle were not much, a few pounds at best. Dennis had tied a twig to the other end of the string, and he now pushed said twig firmly into a small gap between the stones. This stick was part of the trigger mechanism and needed to stay put if the contraption was going to work.

The idea had come to him in the Bell library, and the instructions on how to build a snare were easy to find online. However, half-way back up the Corsiehill Road, passing the sign for St. Mary's Monastery, he realized actually *trapping a child*—even a sick and twisted one—would not be smiled upon by Gigi, her employers, the boy, his family, or the lawyers that would inevitably be involved. He didn't want the boy dangling from a tree anyhow. He merely wanted to detain the stealthy little bastard a few seconds.

Too much of a breeze, or an errant squirrel (if they had them in Scotland) could send the whole precarious mousetrap crashing down, but tonight was a test run more than anything else. The trigger itself was merely a strand of black thread, quintuple-looped for strength, fastened to a wooden post in the dirt; the thread was also attached to the twig jammed between stones. The concept was simple: the kid would trip the thread and pull the twig out of the wall, and the rock and the bundle of bramble would fall. The sound of the rock would alert him (he had lain some empty soda cans in a pile where it would strike the ground) and the bramble would block the doorway. It was by no means a trap—one kick and the tangle of leaves and sticks would be gone—but it could delay escape by a few seconds, especially if it scared or confused the boy a moment.

Rube fuckin' Goldberg territory, he thought as he stepped out onto the rocky outpost. *But it's going to get me a sick little fuck, and I'm going to make a citizen's arrest.*

The sky had slowly lost its colour, its blue draining out over the horizon, drawn downward by the sun. Ants mingled in the dirt; occasionally one would strike out on its own erratic path and disappear into a crevice or the grass that tufted out from the base of the tower, circling it the way a tonsure circles a monk's scalp. Soft breeze tickled away the dampness from his brow. All day, he felt like a grimy, soupy mess, but evenings were better. After sunset, the temperature dropped quickly.

Some nights after sundown, he read by flashlight. Others, he wrapped himself in his sleeping bag and watched the dwindling lights that flowed along the motorway. Most nights he simply retired to the tent.

I can't believe I'm not fucking completely insane. Dennis spread his sleeping bag out, reaching inside to remove a balled-up pair of socks. Marks & Sparks, £3.00 for five pair. Tomorrow, Gigi would arrive with his remaining money for the week. He needed to buy clothes or have Gigi do laundry—the cotton yachting pants were rank and smudged with dirt. His black jeans and black shirt had been caked in blood so long that they were permanently stained. "Turned my wash brown and red," Gigi had laughed. "It was, you see, just disgusting, yeah?"

You could also take that money and get the train back to Glasgow.

No. Not yet. He had a job to do first. He wasn't going to take a train back to Glasgow unless he was also taking a bus back to Paisley and a plane back to Chicago, and that meant waiting for his mousetrap to fall.

The last flashes of yellow burst and fell to the west. Though he no longer dreaded the silent, furious roar of the forest at night, he had found new, even uglier realities to ponder. Like his ex-wife.

You've been sticking your little dick where it doesn't belong. That's what she said when she confronted him. Right? Hadn't she said that? Had she?

His brain felt warped like a vinyl record left in the sun, and he didn't trust memory as much today as he had last week, in that other life of his. It was simpler to focus on his amateur trapping skills, on the jeans he might buy tomorrow, on smoothing things over with Abby at the HMV. Simpler to focus on finding Paul McDermott. He would not focus on his boarding pass, New York to Glasgow, New York to Glasgow, New York to…

The hollow clatter of cans cut through his reverie, and Dennis was moving before his eyes had fully opened—already in his shoes, flashlight in his hand, tent door unzipped. It worked. The little fucker was right there, thirty feet away.

In the dark Dennis could hear the brush rustling, along with incoherent, guttural exclamations from the boy wrestling to move it out of his way. Dennis reached the tower door, his brain flashing and absent, and he flailed one hand blindly into the bush, grasping a thorn somewhere in the cluster of brushwood but paying it no mind. He yanked the whole thing aside and his right hand flicked at the flashlight switch.

A face burst into the blackness, illuminated from below like a child making scary flashlight faces—but the face wasn't that of a child.

It was a man. An old man with withered, leathery grey skin and a dark red cap. Dennis' heart seized, then lurched forward again with a thump. Blood had gathered in the recesses of the man's gums, gums that sprouted wizened, wicked teeth like fangs, and in his eyes something licked and danced like red fire.

"Dè fo Dhia a tha thu a' dèanamh?" it exclaimed.

"Jesus Christ!" Dennis felt fear smother him as if he had fallen headlong into water—but even as he felt his lungs fill, there was a soft sound, like a still wind, and the little old man with the fire in his eyes vanished.

CHAPTER SIX

I know the difference between dream real and real real. That was fucking real *real.*

He could tell by the way the traffic sounds washed over him like distant waves and the way the wind blew across his face. He could tell by the dead rabbit, stomach again split open like a haggis on Robbie Burns Day. Blood oozed from the fatal wound this time, as if he had interrupted the boy—the man, the thing—before it could drain the carcass dry.

A few inches from the rabbit lay what appeared to be a sharp stone or crude arrowhead. Dennis sank down on his haunches, breath quicker than even the rabbit's had once been, head swimming, his heart threatening to jostle his ribs out of alignment. It was no stone, natural or shaped by man. It was a tooth. Grayish, as if carved from old bone, razor-sharp, appearing sickly yet strong. Dennis reached out and picked it up by its tip to examine it in the flashlight beam. The tooth had the density of lead. It wasn't an incisor, or a canine, or even bloody *human* so far as he could tell. All he knew was that it came from the mouth of the long-haired little man.

He had been no taller than Dennis' lowest rib, maybe shorter; the size of a very young boy, seven or eight at the oldest…but his teeth had been long, vampiric, crookedly gathered like a fistful of bent nails crammed into his mouth. This tooth was whole, its roots attached, as if it had just dropped from the man's mouth as he disappeared into thin air.

Disppeared into thin air! Jesus, how about *that* little detail? He *had* disappeared into thin air. That wasn't possible…but neither was that face. It was no child in a latex Hallowe'en mask. The crooked spikes that filled its maw had been attached to blood-red gums, which had been connected to a mouth connected to lips connected to the rest of his leathery face. Even in the dark, Dennis could see it was no mask, and if it was, it was part of a six-hour Hollywood make-up job.

"You daft bastard!"

Startled, Dennis fell forward, the tooth in one hand and the flashlight in the other. Without hands to brace himself, he slipped on the slick rabbit blood and struck the wall; stone gnawed at his forehead and he cried out.

The little man in the red cap stepped forward and filled the doorway, inasmuch as his miniature frame would allow. Dennis raised the flashlight beam to the man's face; the man squinted and raised his hands.

"Och, have you not done enough already? *Cuir dheth an t-solus!*"

Dennis tried to swallow but his throat merely convulsed.

"Oh yeah, yeah, yeah," the little man said in English thickly accented with sarcasm and a Scottish brogue. "You will nae speak the Gaelic. Turn off the bloody flashlight, then. It hurts my eyes. I've already got a hole in my mouth, so could you at least do me a favour and not blind me as well?"

Dennis clicked it off without thinking, and when the weak, urine-coloured beam was gone, darkness swelled inward. Dennis tried to swallow again.

"Och, don't you worry, I'm not going to hurt you," the little old man said. As if to prove it, he stepped backwards, with a hint of bounce, and bowed slightly. When he motioned politely for Dennis to come forward, Dennis hesitated.

"Come out the tower, you idiot. I'm trying to prove I dinnae mean any harm. And I dinnae, I promise—but you've got to do me a favour."

Dennis blinked in the dark. "Favour?"

"Aye, favour. You're familiar with the concept, yeah? Something you do for another person's benefit? Out of the kindness of your heart?"

A sarcastic Scottish vampire midget, thought Dennis. New York to Glasgow in-fucking-deed.

"What's the favour?"

"Could you watch your mouth?"

"What?"

"I'm asking you not to swear again."

"Swear?"

"Swear. Curse. Use the big fellow's name in vain. It worked, you got rid of me. There was a day I'd have come back to rip out your guts—it hurts like a right bastard to lose a tooth that way, you know. But I no longer harm humans. You must believe me, I've only come back to ask you not to do it again."

Dennis watched the man's mouth as he talked. Were he to yawn, with those teeth, he would look like an angler fish.

"Do what again? What's your tooth got to do with it?" Dennis squinted at the man but could only make out an outline against the moon. He was tiny, but stocky in a way that children are not—thickset, stump-chested, with short legs. Dennis watched and waited as his eyes adjusted to the dark. Soon, he could see the man's face, craggy and ashen in the moon-light, like dead flesh, or at least the dead flesh in George A. Romero films, zombie-shaded and loose. Grey hair hung limp and ragged from beneath its cap, which was like a well worn, misshapen beret. In the moonlight, a patch of the cap glistened with something horrid and viscous.

"What's your tooth got to do with it? Losing it 'that' way—what way?" Dennis insisted. He was certain the freak would lose patience with him, leap at him, sink his deep-sea-predator's teeth in to his neck. "What did I say?"

"You said the name of—you know, not the father, the son, J.C., I'll not say it myself. You swore, lad, did you not do it on purpose?"

Dennis shook his head in the dark. The man cocked his head to one side, like a curious animal, and regarded him.

"You're not from Scotland, are you, lad?" More statement than question.

"No."

"And...hmm....you've no idea what the bloody hell I am, do you?" Another shake.

"Well, I'll be buggered!" He slapped one palm against a thigh. Dennis noticed his hands were small and crooked, with talon-like fingernails at least three inches long.

What in hell is with this guy? I don't believe in fucking midget fucking vampires.

There was a pause, a second where the disbelief and shock intersected with Dennis' brusque internal monologue. The intersection was where Dennis could stand, for a moment at least, without running, screaming, or losing his mind.

"Well?" Dennis said.

"Well, what?" replied the man.

"Well what in fuck *are* you then?"

There was a pause, followed by chuckle that burbled into laughter.

"What in fuck am I?" He laughed, coughed dryly, and laughed again. "Oh, lad, where do I begin?"

"Begin with why saying Jee—"

"Ah, fer heaven sakes!"

"Okay!" Dennis held his palms up and stepped backward. "All right! Why did swearing make you lose a tooth? And where the hell did you go?"

"One thing at a time, lad," the man replied. He now regarded Dennis with more curiosity, eyes darting up and down his frame, head still cocked. "You're a Yank, right?"

"American, yeah."

"Ah. You've got next to no folklore then, have you? You know all about pixies and faeries, I suppose, but little else, and what you know you got from movies."

"Or books."

"Americans read?"

"On occasion."

"Good. That makes it simpler." The man paused. "I'm a sort of… goblin. They call me a red cap."

Dennis laughed, but part of his mind believed the old man, and he choked the laughter back down.

"You're….you're a goblin. So, stealing babies, guarding bridges, standing on the wings of airplanes, that sort of thing?"

"I've never stolen a baby or been on *The Twilight Zone*, but you've got the idea."

"So how does a supernatural being catch a pop culture reference?"

"By watching movies, how do you think?"

"What do you do, sit in the back wearing a human costume?"

"Oh, you're a witty one, you are," said the red cap with a curiously melancholy smile. "You're saying you don't believe me, then. Hmm. I suppose you've no goblins in America."

"Of course not."

"Not many left here, either," the red cap sighed. "No one really believes in us anymore. There's a few—despite the dubious advances of modern technology, there are still people who believe. Distantly, deniably, but they do. That's why there are still some of us around—that, and sheer numbers, of course. Law of averages would state we'd still be around. Lord, you should have been here a thousand years ago. Back in the day, one might say. Everyone believed in us. Everyone feared us. And we were everywhere. Today, though, people think we dinnae exist, hence, we dinnae exist."

It was Dennis' turn to cock his head now. The red cap's voice had turned almost wistful, as if it was remembering the glory days of the previous millennium.

"So…you're dying off because no one believes anymore?"

"Please," said the red cap. "This isnae a children's book. You gotta believe, the power of imagination, singing songs to power Santa's sleigh or some such rubbish. It's more complicated than that. More…essential."

"…"

"Och, you probably think I'm a drunken homeless dwarf or something." The creature turned, shaking his head, and made to walk away. "You'll not understand."

"Try me." Dennis swallowed hard. "Convince me."

The red cap turned back and raised an eyebrow.

"I cannae convince you, lad. You either believe your eyes or you do not. I can only tell you what I know."

"So tell it."

"We didnae evolve." The creature, clearly skeptical, watched Dennis' face as he continued. "We werenae born. We didnae choose how we lived our lives. Men have a need to explain their world, to explain their fears, to personify what terrifies. That's what we are. A personification of fear. A reason to be afraid of the dark. Mankind believed us into being. Once enough people believed in our existence, we came to be. Belief in the powrie reached a critical mass and behold! We sprang fully formed from the forehead of mankind."

The goblin's tone was expressive, conversational yet authoritative, like a friendly university professor. "As to your statement, though, lad—no, we're not dying off because no one believes in us anymore. We're just getting old. We're dying out because we're dying out. We're old, we're sick, we're hit by motorcars, we eat bullets. Those last are most common, nowadays."

"You're killing yourselves?"

"Aye."

"Why?"

"You try living a thousand years, doing the same thing every moment of every day," the creature snapped. "It's bloody boring."

Something scuttled through the wood, and the red cap's eyes darted into the dark a moment. The red flicker sent Dennis' mind reeling a moment as the creature seemed to blur before his eyes.

I'm going to faint.

The creature, however, started to speak again, and Dennis found his mental footing.

"We are legend," it said, regaining its professorial tone. "According to that legend, we lived in the ruins of castles and murdered unwary travelers. We were nasty buggers. Robin Redcap, have you never heard the tale? Of course not. Of course not. Well, look it up. You'll see. We werenae known for anything other than fear and death. Today, all the castles are gone, or turned into museums. It isnae quite the same. People notice when their tour group comes back a man shy. They no longer shrug and break the bad news to the parents; they search and search again. Believe me. I hid in the storage closet for three weeks. And that was fifty years ago—today they'd have me on video. We cannae have that, now can we? Best to stay out of the light—but it's getting harder and harder. Every bastard and his brother has a cell phone. One slip and I'm the clip of the day on Youtube. What then?"

"I don't know. What then?"

The red cap stopped and scratched his ear with one blackish yellow talon.

"I guess I don't know," he admitted. "I'd imagine society as we know it would crumble or implode. I doubt many major religions would be pleased to learn our creation story, and I doubt many human minds could digest the fact that wee magical beings have lived alongside them for so long. Amazing, how belief works in society. A two thousand year old book is held sacrosanct, but a folk tale from the fourteenth century is called superstitious rubbish. Either way, we've kept up our end of the bargain. We're averse to being seen in daylight, letting our prey escape us, and, more recently, we're averse to cameras. If anything has destroyed the faeries, lad, it's not a lack of belief. It's the proliferation of video surveillance."

"I still don't get it. If a lack of belief has weakened you, somehow, why not give some empirical evidence, shore up the belief a bit?"

"Disnae work like that," the goblin replied. "If the fellow upstairs wants more Christians, why doesn't he start igniting bushes and such? No. Disnae work like that."

"What does it work like, then?" Dennis asked.

"It works how it works, lad," the red cap replied.

"Okay, well, why are you talking to me, then? I've got a cell phone in my pocket."

"It hasn't a camera."

"How do you know?"

"Lad, you've been here a week. I've made this hill my home. Do you not think I'd investigate the new neighbour?"

"When, while I was sleeping?"

"Aye, lad, while you were sleeping."

Dennis shuddered and felt something trickle down his esophagus like cold mercury. That thing, standing over him in the dark…

"Listen, lad, 'tis all a difficult story to explain to someone who doesn't believe." The red cap sighed and pushed his hands into the pockets of his worn, stained trousers. "Would take twice as bloody long at least, and it's not too far off sunrise. I've got to scoot away, find a place to hunker down for the day. Too bloody hot for me up here, I'll never get a wink of sleep. Come on out at midnight tomorrow and I'll tell you more."

With that, the thing stomped its foot twice and made to turn away.

"Wait!"

The red cap stopped mid-turn, arms extended. It took a second for Dennis to realize he was being sarcastic, holding and exaggerating the pose as if frozen in motion.

"What's your name?"

"What's yours?" the red cap replied.

"Dennis. Dennis Duckworth."

"Ah. Dennis. Not a bad name. Well, Dennis Duckworth, I've never been given a name. On the other hand, I've given myself hundreds of them, and none of them have taken. So go for it, lad. What's my name?"

Dennis blinked, a new habit he'd developed since reality went bye-bye.

"A name, lad. Anything. Just nothing alliterative. No Rusty or Rudy or Robin Redcap, please. Stupid cutsie names for such bloody, bastard creatures, don't you think?"

Blink.

"Eddie?"

"Och, so with alliteration off the table you head straight for assonance."

"Eddie," Dennis repeated.

"Fine, fine then," Eddie said. "Edward's a regal enough name, I suppose. That last one I especially liked, though it's a shame about that Nazi business."

"That last one?"

"Edward VIII," Eddie said. He paused and considered a moment before a soft smile came to his face. "Gave up his pre-ordained destiny to follow his heart. Quite perfect, actually. Eddie it is."

With that, Eddie again raised his right foot, stomped twice in the dirt, and bounded off. The lumpy, malformed man disappeared into the forest with the grace and stealth—and teeth—of a panther.

Dennis blinked more once before he bent over and vomited into the charred circle of an old campfire.

*

"Oh, you're still here! Lovely!"

Dennis looked over his shoulder. Through a misty haze, as though Vaseline was slicked across his corneas, he could see Gigi's bullet-shaped abdomen aimed in his direction. She had a small rucksack across one shoulder and more bounce in her step than usual.

Okay, Denny Ducky, snap out of it.

He turned back to the horizon and closed his eyes. Snap out of what? The shock, the sleep deprivation or the confusion that had kicked his brain into gray pudding?

It happened. It didn't. It did.

"Oh, it's a big day, Dennis!" Gigi lowered herself carefully to a cross-legged position just behind him. Dennis absently considered warning her about the ants, but odds were good she knew already.

"Big day. Here you go! As promised!"

Gigi held out a fistful of pound notes. Dennis reached for them, missed, reached again, and flipped through them slowly.

"There's fifty here, Geege. You already gave me an advance."

"A bonus!" Gigi's shoulders shook as though she was laughing giddily, but her stomach stayed put like it carried a stone. "For all you've done here. Did you catch another glimpse yet?"

"Of what?"

"Of the teenagers, of course!"

Oh yes. That's right. The ne'er-do-well teenagers who turned out to be a thousand-year-old midget vampire goblin.

"Well, did you see them?" she asked.

"I'm pretty sure it's just one guy," Dennis replied. "He came again last night, but I scared him away."

"Unbelievable," Gigi sniffed. "The brash little bugger. Coming night after night, waiting for you to be asleep, flaunting it like that. Deterrent! Oh Dennis you're so lovely, being here all this time, I just cannae believe it's still going on. Bugger! Well, hmm. Hmm. Maybe you'll have to actually catch him in the act, you know, get him to stop, appeal to his common decency. Threaten to call the constabulary!"

Dennis rubbed the corners of his eyes with a thumb and index finger. "Gigi, do you really use the word 'constabulary?'"

"My, Dennis." Sincere concern filled her voice. "You do not look well, young man. No! Not at all."

"I suppose I could use a shower and breakfast. Bad sleep last night."

Bad sleep. No sleep. Who could sleep? By light of morning, terror had disappeared. What remained was a dull numb throb where thoughts used to gather. For the first time, he noticed his shirt clinging uncomfortably to his armpits, glued by sweat. A mysterious rash had begun to sprout between his shoulder blades. He hadn't had a real shower since he'd arrived; clearly the occasional douse from the water jug was not enough of a hygiene regimen. Sweat gathered along the band of the captain's hat, making his scalp itch; he wore it to keep off the sun, but lately he kept forgetting to take it off, even indoors.

Gigi remained a few more minutes, unspooling long, 'lovely'd sentences that Dennis could barely untangle in his unsettled state. Her words pooled on the woodland grass as he stared over her shoulder into the distance, down the path, to where the powrie had disappeared the night before.

It didn't. It did.

The words played against one another even as Dennis headed back down the hill, over the river, and into the realm of mortal men, hoping to regain some balance.

The closest he came to that balance, however, was when he heard the familiar strains of The Smiths somewhere in the High Street air. That miserable git Morrissey wailing some nonsense about some girls being bigger than others. Dennis smiled. Morrissey was his favourite miserable git; the Smiths were probably his favourite band of all time. The familiarity of the song felt good, yet also strange. Something from home, from his normal, non-supernatural life, crossing over into his new, fucked up hallucinatory existence. It shouldn't be here, but here it was, as if to remind him that once upon a time, he had been sane.

Dennis knew the music was coming from the record shop, although he couldn't quite understand why he could hear it on the street, outside the shopping centre, three blocks away.

When he reached the shop, Dennis stood in the entrance a moment, scanning the room but retaining nothing. A voice interrupted his train of non-thought.

"Nice hat."

Abby stood behind the counter, leaning forward on her forearms, fingers laced, one eyebrow raised.

"Yeah." Dennis turned his back to her and walked to the magazine rack. His eyes began to burn slightly in the dry climate-controlled air. His head hurt. If reality was concrete, he'd brained himself on it as he'd fallen through its cracks.

"That's it?" Abby continued. "I deserve at least a 'piss off' for that."

"Keeps the sun off my head," Dennis muttered. "Other than that, I really don't fucking care." He reached one hand out and steadied himself. Abby lowered the eyebrow.

"All the rage in New York, the captain's hat?"

"Chicago."

"Oh, I see, it's a Chicago thing."

"No." His voice was flat. "No, I'm from Chicago. The hat isn't mine."

"Oh."

Again he nearly swooned; his knees buckled, but he gripped the magazine rack again until the wave of instability passed.

I am not fucking well.

"Are you drunk or something?" Abby half-smiled, the most she had ever proffered him, but it sank when he turned fully in her direction. "No, seriously though, are you all right? You look terrible."

"Why are you being nice to me?"

Now Abby blinked, and her mouth worked as if it has been turned on before the words were ready. It was barely a flicker but even in his state, Dennis could read faces.

"Look, I'm sorry for what I said yesterday."

Her neck was pale, her chin tiny and tapered, but her nose and eyes were perfect. Even her lip stud was somehow suited to the shape of her face. Dennis recognized these facts with a blank lack of interest that surprised him.

"Don't be sorry," he said. "You were right. Of course I'd heard that record. I was grasping in the dark, trying to impress you. You knew the only Americans that liked Belle and Sebastien were music nerds. Good call on your part, bad one on mine. I'm a fuckin' idiot and I've always been a fuckin' idiot. You didn't have to be such a bitch about it, though. I was just happy to find someone who seemed like-minded."

It came out in a long stream, like tap water, a monotone dribble, before he realized, against his usual instincts, he was being an asshole—but he was also telling the truth.

"I'm really not a bitch," she replied, unoffended. "I just don't put up with any shit. And you, you're full of shit."

Dennis laughed a short, weak laugh. "Pretty much. I'm impressed that you can tell."

"I'm impressed that you can stand."

"Holding onto this rack helps."

"You really do look horrible. *Are* you all right?"

"I didn't sleep much last night. I haven't slept that much since I got here." He could feel the dried sweat on him now and wondered if he smelled as unshowered as he was.

"I should go."

"Why do you come in here every day?" she interjected quickly.

"Nothing else to do. And I like music. I need to buy a Discman or an iPod or something. After I find somewhere to shower."

"What are you, living on the streets?" Abby laughed.

"No, I live in a tent. I really should go."

"See you tomorrow?" Abby asked, as he headed out.

"Most likely," he replied.

I walk in looking like a drunk chemotherapy patient in a sailor's cap, and she's civil for the first time. Women.

Dennis pulled the cap down over his forehead and made his way back up South Street. His gait was that of an unsteady crackhead, while his vision seemed dosed with LSD. The street seemed to curl upwards at its edges, to bulge and breathe in the middle. Sleep deprivation was one thing, but he'd been exhausted before. This was different. There was something about the saturation of colours. Something in the way he floated through, focusing on details without noticing his general surroundings. A young woman with light blue sunglasses perched on her hair sipped something from a straw. Dennis watched the way the muscles in her neck contracted. He watched a young man selling newspapers and noted the way he had double-tied the laces of his worn, tattered shoes. He looked at a doorway and noted a vaguely familiar "hours of operation" sign before he realized he was standing in front of the Rat and Raven. Half-sentient, he pushed the door open and stepped through.

"We're not open yet." Almost exactly the same tone as the last time she said the same words.

"You really should keep the door locked until you're open, then," Dennis said.

Margaret stepped out of the corner, wearing a denim shirt, her hair tied back. She looked uncertain a moment, and her voice sounded cold.

"Oh."

"Hello."

Margaret took a few steps forward. "You look like hell, Dennis."

"I feel like hell, Margaret. Nice to see you."

There was a long pause while Margaret studied the space on the wall behind him.

"What can I do for you, then?" she asked.

"I need a favour." He stood, steadied himself, and to Margaret's puzzlement, closed his eyes before he continued. "I realize I don't deserve one after I acted like a jerk. I'm not good with people. I'm a music snob. I don't blame you for throwing me out. Still, you're the only person I know in this town other than my employer, and I can't handle her today. She freaks me out."

Margaret studied him for a moment, trying to summarize her feelings and sum up the situation at the same time, two columns being added at once.

"You decided to stay, then."

"Yep."

"What happened with Kit Carson?"

"There never was a Kit Carson. A total lie."

"Really. I'm shocked."

She was clearly not shocked.

"So what are you doing?"

"I'm…employed by the Forestry Commission. Sort of like a security guard. I'm living in a tent up on Kinnoull Hill."

"You're *what?*"

"Living in a tent on Kinnoull Hill. Trying to ward off some vandals who've been up there lately."

"Good, honest work."

"It's all I could find."

"And you live in a tent."

"I do."

"Oh, bullshit, Dennis."

"I'm serious. That's why I came to see you." It was true, he realized, even though he hadn't realized it until that very moment. "I wanted to know if I could borrow your apartment, take a shower."

Margaret's head was shaking before he finished the sentence. She turned around dismissively and headed to the other side of the bar.

"Absolutely not, Dennis. Sorry."

"C'mon, you know I'm not going to do anything untoward. I've got a home and I've got a job. I just don't have a shower."

"So, you've come in here to charm me again, eh?"

"Margaret, there was nothing insincere about that night," Dennis lied. "And I apologized for the morning."

"Actually, no, you didn't." Margaret plunked a glass down on the bar in front of her and leaned forward. "Don't start, *captain*." Her eyes went to the cap and Daniel winced inside. "You were up to no good from the start. You had me feed you drinks all night, what with the charming questions and the charming smiles. And still I took you home, because I'm a forty-three year old widow and I'd rather fuck an asshole from Chicago than most of the punters that come into this place every week. But note that I said 'most.'"

Dennis' shoulders felt as if they were going to slide right off his torso, yet once again he found himself talking before he understood where it came from.

"You're the second person today to think I'm full of shit." Dennis leaned on the bar as another woozy moment washed over him. Margaret took it to be a pause for effect.

"And it's true," he continued, "I am. But I need to shower and feel human again. I've had a rough night. Please let me borrow your shower, then I'll come back and buy dinner. And I'll tip well. And I won't lie, bullshit, cajole or otherwise try any chicanery. I just need to spend a few hours with real human beings."

"As opposed to…?"

"There are plenty of critters up that hill. The really scary ones come out at night."

"Och, there's nothing scary up there."

"Hmm."

Margaret studied Dennis a moment.

"You're really living in a tent on Kinnoull Hill."

"Would I make that up to impress you?"

"Disnae seem likely." She continued to gaze at him "And it disnae seem likely you're going to steal my CD collection."

"Um…no, it's safe to say I won't do *that*."

Margaret pushed back from the bar. She was going to give him her keys, it was obvious, but Dennis wasn't feeling self-congratulatory.

You just look so pathetic that she's taking pity on you, he thought.

"You look so pathetic, I have to take pity on you," she said. Margaret pulled her key ring from her pocket and placed it softly on the bar. "You remember where it is, yeah?"

"I think so, yeah."

"Aye. Shampoo's in the shower but soap's by the sink. The towels are clean. Don't make a mess."

"I won't." Dennis smiled. "Thanks."

"Dennis," Margaret called as he was half-way to the door, and when he turned back, he felt a presence ahead of him and stopped himself short. In the fraction of a second before he saw Bruce McKee in the doorway, he smelled something. It wasn't a physical smell; Dennis sensed something unpleasant in the air, but it wasn't something he processed with his olfactory glands, though said glands did detect a whiff of garlic, coffee, and possibly canned tomatoes. He couldn't have explained which of his senses actually sensed it. It sent a shock through his spine and slapped away some of his stupor. He felt immediately alert, as if the thing he was sensing was danger.

"Well if it isn't our ship's captain." Bruce crossed his arms over his chest and puffed himself up to full size. "The cap your idea, Maggie? You're a fan of a man in uniform?"

"Piss off, Bruce, he's keeping the sun off his head."

Bruce McKee was plainly not used to having Margaret speak to him that way, and he stood dumbfounded for a moment.

"What're you doing here, then, when we're not open?" he asked.

"When *I'm* not open," Margaret corrected him.

"Looking for a favour from Ms…" Dennis realized he had no idea what Margaret's last name was. "From Margaret. Looking for…some advice about where to shop. On account of my luggage mix up, like I told you."

Bruce peered down his nose—which Dennis figured was his usual POV, given the length of said appendage—and snorted out one nostril, an unusual-looking feat that made the right side of his snout open wide like a blowhole.

"I don't trust you," he said simply. "And I don't like you. And there's something fishy about you being up there on that hill."

"Bruce McKee." Margaret strode across the bar and put her hands on her hips for emphasis. "You were *eavesdropping*."

Her eyes flashed inward and Dennis knew she was thinking the same thing. If he was eavesdropping, he might have heard everything. The parts about fucking and such.

"Well, Dennis," he said. "I told you'd be seeing you again. And you'll be seeing me again, again. I've got my eye on you, asshole from Chicago."

Yep. He'd heard everything.

Margaret flushed. "It's none of your damnable business anyhow, Bruce McKee, none of it. You'll not be bullying him around because you fancy me, do you understand? There's nothing happening with us and there's not going to be. Leave him alone."

"Maybe I will." Bruce turned to Margaret and eyed her directly. "Maybe I'll leave you both alone. For now. Until I figure out what in the world this one's up to."

He turned back to Dennis and snorted once more, through the same nostril.

"The Captain," he snorted derisively. "The Captain of Kinnoull Hill."

*

The doors of perception have been blown off their goddam hinges.

It wasn't just the shock of dropping head-first into his own personal monster movie. It wasn't just sleep dep. Other things—Christ, *everything*—had changed. The world was the same, but everything about it felt different, as if the little goblin had slipped him Ecstasy.

The shower had felt like warm, wet flower petals dropping gently on his skin. It almost turned him on, which disturbed him given his visions of angler fish and grey-skinned goblins. There was a floral quality to the soap, too; its aroma was a flower he could almost name. Twenty-four hours before, he wouldn't have even recognized the scent as floral, yet now it filled his sinuses completely, not too intense but complete and, simply put, un-soapy.

116

After he dried off, Dennis studied the apartment innocently, noting things he had noted before, ignoring a fleeting urge to open drawers and cupboards. He even blinked twice at her CD tower, hoping he might notice something there, but found himself disinterested, almost drowsy.

She won't mind if I have a nap, he told himself. *Hell, I can't believe she even let me in this place. She looked at me like a turd on the carpet when I walked through the door.*

He woke on the couch, bleary-eyed and thick-headed, as if he could tilt backwards into sleep again at any time. Something tugged at the top of his head, a memory, as though he'd been dreaming, though he couldn't remember any dream.

I was talking to someone, he thought, one arm draped over his eyes to block the sun that sheared through the space between drapes. *I was talking to someone in this room. I can't remember it, but I know I was.*

No one was in the room, and no one had been in the room, Dennis was sure, but the feeling continued to work its way into the base of his skull. It felt physical. It almost hurt. It wasn't just a feeling, either. It was a sound. It was a song.

I am losing my fucking mind.

*

Lunchtime at the Rat and Raven would have been overwhelming, but by dinner, Dennis felt he had a handle on some of his newfound mutant powers. He was able to smell what seemed like forty-seven different aromas in the room—he counted—and yet it wasn't making his eyes water and his head swim anymore. It merely gave him something to do. There was no need to read and re-read menus or glance over the Perth Advertiser. All he had to do was inhale to pass the time. That, or listen as conversations at the far end of the room wafted in his direction, as the smells did.

He kept his charms on slow broil, limiting it to smiles and half-decent table manners. Three or four people from his previous visit were here again, likely regulars. That night around last call—after Bruce McKee and his cohorts had left the building—he had cajoled them, impressed them with his urbane American wit and effortless banter, and left them almost convinced he wasn't simply trying to fuck their friend Margaret. It had worked—they hadn't talked her out of it, he hadn't spent the night sleeping on the mini-putt course again—but tonight he merely nodded, asked after their health, and turned back to his chicken curry.

"Everything good?" he asked, when Margaret finally came over to his table.

"Not so much, no," she replied. "And I'm not sure it's going to get better if McKee and his assholes come in tonight. I think you'd best make yourself scarce."

Dennis looked up at her. "You're joking."

"I wish I was." Margaret sighed and sat down on the chair next to him despite the patrons waiting to be served at the bar. "He's not a happy man at the best of times, and he's royally pissed now. Thinks we're on to something, which hurts his pride, given how many times he's tried to crawl into my bed and how many times I've batted him away. And…I don't know, he's getting pretty…we've got some problems, he and I. Let's just say he thinks he has leverage."

"Leverage?"

"I've had some troubles this year." Her voice took on a confessional tone. "Car trouble. Dental trouble—do you know how much a bridge costs? My God. And then staff trouble…I hired someone I shouldn't have—at his bloody suggestion, even!—and he stole from us. A lot. As a result, I'm at least two and a half months behind on the let, and he thinks that's going to make me do him favours."

"He thinks you're a whore."

"Fuck you, Dennis Duckworth." Margaret said. "He *wants* me to be a whore. He thinks I *should* be. It's different."

He scooped the last yellow-stained spoonful of white rice into his mouth and swallowed.

"So you're saying if I'm here, he might—"

"Well if he's drunk—"

"Well, well, look who's with us again!"

Too late.

Dennis looked over Margaret's shoulder and watched Bruce and his friends come into the room. This time, Bruce was at the head of the pack, and once again the room took on an uncomfortable edge, as if an electrical charge hummed softly in the air.

"Fuckin' Begbie," Dennis muttered, noting the same smell of danger he'd noted earlier.

"Not half as dangerous," Margaret replied softly, "but three times as stupid."

"It's the Captain of Kinnoull Hill!" Bruce cried with something approaching glee. "What brings you out on this fine evening?"

"Bit of food, bit of drink."

Dennis felt something rise in his throat. Something highly ill-advised. Even as the second sentence slipped out, he knew it was a mistake.

"You look like you're pretty familiar with food and drink yourself, Bruce."

As insults go, it was mild, but Bruce wasn't used to being insulted in any fashion, at least not to his face. He stopped cold, ten feet from Dennis' table, and the four friends –a stupidly grinning collection of slightly younger men who clearly fancied themselves entry-level thugs and 'real men'—almost bumped into him.

"Sorry, what does that mean, then?" The smile remained but the eyes changed.

"Nothing at all. You look like you've been after the pints a bit."

And the shape of your torso suggests it's filled with hamburgers in place of organs, but perhaps I'll keep that one to myself.

"A few drams of whiskey at home is all." Bruce waved his hand as if to fan away an unpleasant odour. "Nothing, really. Mind if we join you?"

Margaret stood and moved away without speaking to any of them. The five men gathered around Dennis in a too-tight circle, two of them pulling chairs from surrounding tables. Bruce sat across from him and leaned in with more smiles and barely-contained malice.

"So. You're here again. They must pay grandly up there on the hill. Or are you paying for dinner in other ways?"

"You mean by fucking the owner? No, Bruce, I'm not."

Bruce blinked a moment, clearly taken aback by the straightforwardness.

"You're a mouthy one, aren't you? We don't talk about women that way here."

"This, coming from someone who likes to make threats to get laid."

Oh, Denny. Shut your goddamned mouth.

Before he knew what was happening, Bruce made a motion to the lad on Dennis' left, who swiftly knocked his cap off before grabbing the back of his skull in his hands and bouncing Dennis' head off the table. Pain exploded behind his eyes like a blast of white light, and a few of the nearly closed wounds on his face shifted sideways and began to leak. A trickle of blood came out of his left nostril.

"You'll watch how you fucking speak to me!" Bruce shouted in the otherwise silent room. "And you'll apologize for suggesting that."

He spoke to Dennis, but his eyes were on Margaret.

"I'm not—"

Again, to the table, with just as much force, just as much new blood, but this time the hand held him there, head sideways, as Bruce peered into his face.

"You'll apologize."

"Stop it!" Margaret screamed. "That's enough, Bruce McKee, that's bloody well enough! Stop being such a *bully*, would you? He's done nothing. It's none of your business."

"What have you been saying to him then?" Bruce shouted back. "What have you been telling him? Have you mentioned that you're a thief, and that you're a deadbeat, and that you're a drunk? Have you? Your new boyfriend here will apologize to me for what he did. And he'll do it…"

Bruce came within an inch of Dennis' nose and smiled again.

"And he'll do it on his knees."

It happened in a flurry of elbows and hands, Bruce's goons forcing Dennis onto the floor, hands held behind his back in some lug's tight grip. Bruce came around the table to stand in front of Dennis, who was now on his knees. Bruce looked down at him smugly, waiting for the fearful apology to come.

"If you think I'm sucking your dick," Dennis said, "you're out of your mind."

The collective gasp seemed to suck the air out of the room. Bruce shook his head once, unsure of what he'd heard. When the realization arrived, it twisted Bruce's face in a way that made him uglier; only Dennis could smell the stink of aggression spike dramatically. With one swift motion, he snatched up a half-full pint glass and raised it above his head.

It never fell. Bruce stopped as if considering the damage a solid glass would do on the American's skull and played his gratification against the room full of witnesses. Bruce McKee was an important man, in some ways, but he wasn't particularly free from legal entanglements, nor was he likely to be allowed to cut open the Yank's face in front of twenty people and get away with it. He slowly lowered the glass to the table and smiled once again.

"You're a quick one, Captain, I'll give you that."

With that he turned heel and crossed over towards Margaret. His gait was apelike, mostly because while the left arm swung when he walked, the right remained posed rigidly, bent slightly at the elbow, and did not swing at all.

Bruce pushed Margaret aside with the swinging arm and stepped behind the bar. His fingers tapped at the cash register and he opened the drawer.

"What are you doing?" Margaret asked.

"Just seeing how much you've got in here," he said, thumbing through a few bills. "Getting a feeling for how long it's going to take you to pay me the rent you owe me. I'm thinking, at this rate, you're just not doing well enough."

He turned and slammed the drawer shut.

"I want it. I want all of it, in full, by the end of the month."

"Bruce, that's in a few days, and you know full well I—"

"Oh, well then," Bruce muttered sarcastically. "Let's be gracious. How about the end of next month, then?"

121

Bruce turned and headed for the door, and his lackeys let go of Dennis and trailed behind wordlessly. Dennis stood and, once standing, was unsure where to go, what to do, or how to behave. No one else in the room seemed to know either, and one by one they started to murmur amongst themselves.

Another situation well mastered, Denny.

Margaret grabbed him by the wrist and led him into the kitchen, where she proceeded to pull out a first aid kit and spit vitriol simultaneously.

"You really are a fucking piece of work, Duckworth, truly. You can't just shut your yap and nod? To you he's just another wanker but to me he's a problem. A very big problem. We're talking about my *life*, here, Dennis! He'd kick me out of here in a moment, regardless of what's happening, regardless, because…Dennis, Jesus Lord, why can't you just…I mean, I've been nice to you, and you…"

Dennis' eyes were closed as she dabbed at a wound with an alcohol swab, but he could sense that something had changed. When he opened them, he saw she was laughing quietly.

"If you think I'm sucking your dick…" she laughed aloud. "Oh, you're such an asshole, Dennis, but at least it was aimed at a fair target."

There was a pause as the wound began to sting. Dennis winced.

"You've still got me into a pile of trouble I didn't need, you know."

"Hey, it's my face imprinted on that table," Dennis said through gritted teeth.

"Oh, yes, apology *accepted*, Dennis, apology *accepted*. Bloody hell! Unbelievable!"

"Well, I'm *bleeding!*" Dennis sulked a moment. "I know, I know, he could cause trouble for you. I just…I couldn't…"

"Well, to be honest, Dennis, something like this was bound to come along." Margaret leaned back to inspect Dennis' injuries, and wiped some blood away from his eyes with a wet cloth. "He would have come for his money eventually—unless I'd gone out with him, and I'd imagine you've seen why I wouldn't do that. You've sped it up some, but it was all going to happen someday."

She looked sideways, at the floor, and sighed, her mind briefly somewhere else.

"I'll tell you this, though. If he means it—if it gets serious—you're going to help me work out a way to fix this."

Dennis didn't reply.

Margaret, I can't even work out airfare home.

CHAPTER SEVEN

As Dennis ascended Bowerswell Road, he noticed new muscles absorbing the shock of each step. Daily hill-climbing had begun to tone his calves and quads already.

Trees rustled and Dennis absently noted the direction of the wind. There was a difference between the sound of the cicadas and crickets. He could tell which voices belonged to which—and which size, and which sex. Somehow, this did not surprise him. Neither did the absolute blackness of the woods as he stepped onto the woodland path; though nighttime was brighter here, the sky tonight was thick with clouds. Dennis could feel the presence of the trees on either side, and in the dark he could still remember which fork led more directly to the summit.

In the blue-black air of the clearing, a small campfire shifted and burst in the fire pit, ripping its way through the dark with the ferocity of a concentrated sun. By that firelight, Eddie the Red Cap's face was that of a gargoyle, black crevices disappearing into the grey landscape of his loose-skinned cheeks. He sat cross-legged, his tattered tunic stained with what appeared to be blood, mud and chocolate milk. Deep in his throat an ancient tune seemed to thrum.

"Good evening," Eddie said with sarcastic genuflection. "Welcome home."

Dennis stood silently on the other side of the campfire a moment.

"What the fuck have you done to me?"

Eddie stared ahead, quizzical, something resembling a chicken leg in his left hand.

"Now, lad, is there a need to be so abrasive right off the skip?" He took a bite of the animal leg and spoke with his mouth full. "Could we be a bit more civil? Maybe exercise some manners? You dinnae want to spread that cliché about Americans abroad."

Disarming as the creature's brand of sarcasm was, Dennis did not pause.

"Screw off with the jokes. I just spent fifteen minutes smelling bird droppings. I've never noticed they have a smell before, but even worse, I could tell which ones were from different fucking birds. I didn't know there were so many genus of trees in Woodland Park, but I can tell the difference between all of them. I can tell you what kind of animals are prancing around out there in the leaves, and the whole thing, frankly, is freaking me out. So before I start asking what in hell the deal is with you, I want to know what the hell the deal is with *me*."

Eddie regarded Dennis a moment, pausing to take another bite. The curved, grey-silver nails in his mouth engulfed the meat like a piranha.

Eddie gestured towards one of Dennis' plates, piled with bits of rabbit meat. "Can I interest you in some roasted rabbit? Locally sourced, free range and hormone free."

Dennis folded his arms. Eddie shrugged off the performance and tossed the meat-flecked bone over his shoulder, over the Tower, into the abyss.

"That'll keep 'em guessing," Eddie chuckled. "They're used to dead rabbits, but not barbecued ones, eh?"

Eddie took Dennis' silence as a cue to proceed.

"You've come through the gate, lad. Things are different over here."

"Through the gate."

"Through the gate!" cried Eddie.

"Sorta like through the looking glass?" Dennis asked.

Eddie laughed. "Och, no, though I guess it feels that way. Anyhow, it's not a gate that goes sideways, it's a gate that goes up. You're not in a different place, you're on a different *plane*. You've touched the other side, laddie, and once you've done that, it stays with you. The wee beasties and pixies and all you've been told dinnae exist—well, we exist. As you've seen. It's bound to change your perception somewhat, do you not think?"

"It never crossed my mind."

"Well let's put it this way." Eddie stood up and shook his legs, one at a time, as if they'd fallen asleep. "The doors of your perception have been cleansed."

"Earlier today, I thought the same thing, except in my head, I felt they'd been blown of their hinges."

"No!" Eddie was suddenly adamant. "Dinnae think for a moment something is wrong. Dinnae think for a moment that this isn't meant to be. You're able to see things you could nae see before. You'll get used to it."

"Meant to be? Maybe. And maybe I'll get used to it. I'm not sure I'll get used to you, though." Dennis said. "You're quoting Aldus Huxley."

"Aye."

"You know it's strange to meet a thousand year old goblin that reads Huxley."

Eddie chuckled and sat back down in front of the fire.

"C'mon, Dennis, sit your arse down. This is going to be a long-ish conversation, dinnae you think?"

Dennis cautiously folded his legs beneath him. From across the campfire he stared into the thing's eyes, black marbles that flickered with fire, both a reflection of the campfire and of something else within.

"I read Huxley because I heard the Doors."

Dennis blinked.

"Aye, aye, I'm a rock'n'roll fan, too." Eddie's expression proved he was resigned to Dennis' disbelief. "Come on, lad. Televisions in windows, car stereos with windows down, books left on park benches, newspapers in the rubbish bin. I've had plenty of exposure to the world, lad. I've been alive a thousand years. A thousand years. Think about it. It's a fantasy. It's a nightmare. Either way, it's a lot of bloody time. Things only got *interesting* in the last two hundred years. Books, film, television, the internet—I cannae interact with people directly, my kind aren't known for their social graces—but I can learn by observation."

"You seem to be doing alright with the social graces," Dennis said, "though you're a bit rough around the edges."

"And you're fit for tea with the Queen," Eddie scoffed. "No matter.

I'm a bloody red cap. I can't just stroll up and start a casual conversation. Looking as I do, I'm a bit of a freak."

"Do you mean among your kind or just in general?"

"Oh, yes." Eddie drew out the vowels to make room for more sarcasm. "I'm a freak to my own and a freak to the rest of the world. I've no true kin on the entire planet, and I'm entirely alone, but yes, feel free to make light of the fact."

"Hey, man, I don't even know what I said." Dennis whined. "I was making a joke."

"Well, way to punch downward. You're a comedy master."

"Are you telling me jokes about goblins are off-limits? That you're a disadvantaged peoples somehow?"

"What I'm saying is that you're an arse," Eddie replied. "What I'm saying is obviously I'm unable to join a book club or the local gym…but I no longer fit in with the red caps either. Havenae since I started to read. Taught myself, you know. To read and write. Stowed away in the back of a classroom once or twice, at the start, but when the teacher noticed me and tried to pull me by my ear to the front to explain myself, she realized I wisnae just a naughty child. Let's just say that mayhem ensued and I never tried that again. As it was, once I put my mind to teaching myself, it was quite simple. Murder and terror takes less time than you'd think, and when that's your sole *raison d'être*, you're left with a lot of free time. I've had nothing but vacation my entire life. Gory, bloody vacation. It wasn't until about five, six hundred years ago they invented the printing press; I've no memory how I passed the time. When people started to learn to read, I'd see them doing so—often alone, often just before they became my victims, to be truthful. It became my modus operandi—I slaughtered the literate. They were wrapped up in some strange collection of bound pages; they were unaware of the world around them. It was the perfect time to strike!"

Eddie pretended to lunge forward, and opened his mouth. Dennis instinctively scrambled backward from that jaw, wide with its overlapped fangs askew and threaded with bits of rabbit flesh.

"Och, I'm sorry for that," Eddie said. "I forget how these teeth must appear to you. Anyhow, about the books—eventually I became curious. What were these paper rectangles I'd been seeing for centuries? I taught myself to read, and within a century I'd gone from illiterate to philosopher goblin. Why did we exist? The question plagued me; it plagues me still. Reading your words—the written word of humanity—took me through the gate, too, but in the other direction. I'll tell you, it was every bit as magical to me as all this seems to you. For the first time, it seemed that there were other things beyond murder, malice, and eventually, covetous rage."

"Covetous?"

"Aye." Eddie stretched one leg out and poked at the firewood with his toes. The embers ground together with a sound like Styrofoam. "Covetous. I'm talking about your remaining red caps, mind you, the ones who still exist. It was simple when our duty was to corrode your sense of safety and murder you. That, at least, lent our lives purpose. Then, along comes the modern age, and suddenly isnae so easy to slay you and escape. Aye, we're magic, but there's so many of you now. The magic only works to a point; there's so many ways we can be *seen* now. Most of us cower in hiding and *we don't even understand why.* Suddenly we've nothing to do. There's no way to pass the time. We dinnae even sleep or eat."

Dennis frowned. "You were eating five minutes ago, and you said something last night about the heat keeping you awake."

"Red caps neither eat nor sleep," Eddie corrected himself. "*I* sleep. *I* eat. *I* have been through the gate, lad. It's as if the closer I came to mankind, the closer to mankind I became. Dinnae ask me to explain it because I cannae. There's nothing especially magical about your media, but to me, it was otherworldly."

"Media made Paris Hilton famous," Dennis said dryly. "That's got to be magic."

"*Black* magic," Eddie snickered. "The dark media arts. No, what I'm saying is media is science and engineering and physics, wires and currents and pixels and radio waves. Yet to me, your media wasn't just a godsend. It was the god*head*. I devoured it, every scrap. After a while, I began to understand."

"I can't imagine why you want to learn more about us," Dennis said, "Given what you've read in the media."

"Och," Eddie said, "The media's so much inanity. That's where I learn the nuts and bolts. It's the books and films that have taught me most about humankind. I know your dark side from your light side. Don't forget, my brethren *have no light side*. Despite all the war and hatred and prejudice and terror, you are still a cheery lot compared to my kind. Through your best books and films—your best imaginings, I suppose—I can see the hopes and aspirations and good intentions. I'm especially fond of film. I sneak into movie theatres with sunglasses and a fake beard to hide these eyes and teeth. It's hard to pass for human when you've fire in your eyes."

Dennis laughed quietly. "Is it really fire?"

"Och, you idiot." Eddie slapped one knee and laughed himself, his head tossed back. The curved spikes in his mouth seemed about to snatch the moon out of the sky. "You think I've a skull full of napalm?"

"I don't fucking know." Dennis pouted. "You're a race of mythical creatures that spontaneously appeared for the purpose of murdering people. You don't need to eat or sleep. A head full of fire is about as reasonable as the rest of it don't you think?"

"There are laws, you know," Eddie chided. "Magic has its laws. I'm a physical being, I have to have a brain in my skull or I cannae function. And it wisnae spontaneous, by the way, our appearance. It isnae like someone said 'My, imagine there were creepy little men that lived in castles and murdered the unwary!' and poof, the border castles were filled with critters. I believe we appeared one red cap at a time, one castle at a time, one murder at a time. I'm not sure when we *stopped* coming, but that happened, too. It started to slow down, and then it stopped. And we all—all of us—came from you. *All* of you. We came to exist because people thought we already did."

"People were afraid of the dark, and so they invented you."

"More or less, aye."

"People were afraid of death, so they invented God. Is it the same?"

"Och." Eddie spat into the fire. "Horrible comparison. The powries were a *reason* to fear the dark. God was a reason *not* to fear the dark."

"So God exists? You've some kind of higher-plane inside line on this?"

Eddie frowned. "I have no idea if God exists or not. I'm from the other side, but not the *other* other side; after all, there are other worlds than these. I suppose you could draw the conclusion that man created a god from pure belief—I'm a walking precedent—but if it worked that way, there'd be an awful lot of gods about. And they probably wouldn't be on the best of terms with one another. Besides, if it were that simple, every bloody thing that every bloody person ever feared would be upon the earth. When's the last time you saw Samara?"

"Who?"

"The wee girl from the Ring."

"Well, the last time I watched the Ring, I guess."

"Aye. How about on the street? Ever seen her? No. But millions of people have seen The Ring and gone home at night to fear the wee lass, terrified to the point where, just for a moment, they believe she exists, that she's standing in the closet. Yet despite the film's popularity, she has not spontaneously generated into existence. As far as I know."

Dennis muttered something in the negative, embarrassed by his own confusion.

"Of course not." Eddie spat again and leaned backward on his hands, thoughtful.

"Perhaps there was a time, lad—a brief window in mankind's history—when his fears were powerful enough to create me and hundreds like me. It was the dark ages, after all. They're not called the dark ages for a lark. There was little science, little learning, little anything other than life and death, superstition and religion. Maybe back then your fears had horrible magic in them. Maybe what brought me to you is the same thing that killed your magic. Maybe with learning, you don't need magic."

"Or maybe, in our world, we've got too much to fear," Dennis mused. "There's not enough fear consensus to form anything anymore."

"Perhaps, lad, perhaps." Eddie pondered a moment. "Well, whatever it is, at least your species *has* learning. At least you *have* science. The things you don't understand today might be understood tomorrow. How did the universe begin? You're not sure, but you might know someday. What cures cancer? You're not sure, but you might know someday. The red caps? We have no science, we have no learning. Where do we turn to make sense of it all? Superstitious farmers brought us to life with their fear. How? We're not sure, and we'll never be sure—not someday, not any day.

"Consider this," Eddie continued. "People thought us evil. Back in the dark ages, people believed evil came from one place—the devil. If we were in league with the devil, it stood to reason, we could be banished by the name of you-know-whom. Now forget about losing the tooth—the reason for *that* is even more arcane, long lost in the mists of time. Just consider that I'm a nonexistent creature, utterly without religion, not in league with the devil or any other horned, claw-footed imbecile. Yet you invoke the name of the man upstairs, and sure enough, poof, I'm gone. Because I truly am in league with the devil? No. Because that's the way it is. No science. No physics. Just…the way it is."

"Jee…"

Eddie scowled.

"…pers," corrected Dennis. "You're breaking my brain a little, Eddie."

"Try being a contemplative goblin. I've had hundreds of years to think on it and I still haven't sussed it out."

Dennis felt as though his cranium were a hollow, weightless space. It wasn't the mental stress of pondering creation theories with a mythical creature, but the residual spin from having passed "through the gate." In fact, being with the red cap was almost soothing despite the mind-fuck; the afternoon had been an acid trip, but now it was more like the mild residual high of a joint smoked hours before. Eddie's voice evened out smoothly in the air, with a rough but creamy quality, the vocal equivalent of chunky peanut butter. It was comforting. Sitting with this fire-eyed, spike-mawed creature made him feel less edgy than he had felt all day.

"You still with us, lad?"

"Yeah." Dennis shook his head and squinted away the soft burn of campfire smoke. "I'm just at a bit of a loss here. Not sure what to ask a murderous nonexistent bastard like yourself."

Eddie laughed. The sound was throaty, as though the peanut butter were stuck in his esophagus.

"Whatever you please, lad. There's no secrets anymore. Not between you and I."

"I suppose not. Okay...you all started to get wiggy when the modern age came along, you say. What's that, a hundred years ago?"

"That's when it started to get strange, aye. It got much worse in recent decades, though. That's what built a wall between our nature and our reality. It's our nature to live in the ruins of the border castles and murder travelers. Those castles have closed-circuit televisions now. The travelers are on the motorway, not trudging the dark laneway by torch-light. The tourists carry cell phone cameras. Each step forward, another layer of brick atop an ever-rising wall. The higher the wall became, the more we started to wonder. Why were we here? What happens to the warrior when you eliminate war? The hunter when the game is extinct? The farmer when the crops won't grow? How do you turn to something else when you've done the same thing for a thousand years? Then there's the cap. The namesake. The bane. It's not red because we've a procliv-ity for the hue. We're to keep it wet with human blood. I've not killed a human in...many years."

"You're soaking it in rabbit blood, I suppose."

"Aye." Eddie looked away from the fire and sighed. "Truth be told, Dennis, I'd not kill a single living thing if it weren't a necessity. I've even considered letting it dry out, just to see what happens. I'm on the other side of the gate myself, as I say. I eat, I sleep. Maybe I can be rid of the cap, too. But I'd have to risk my own demise. If our caps dry out, we die. I've seen it happen. I've seen it happen *on purpose*. Suicide by drying."

"But you don't need *human* blood to wet your cap. When did you figure that out?"

"After I chose to stop killing."

"And what made you do that?"

"The realization that being on the other side gave me one other human ability."

"Which was?"

"Free will."

They were silent a moment.

"Mind you, this contemplation came after years of watching and reading and listening. I'd been nudged through the gate one Daily Mirror at a time. Perhaps it's the only reason I was capable of such philosophy. I started thinking different hundreds of years before my cursed brethren. If I could find Robin Redcap, could I make him see the world my way? Probably not."

"Robin Redcap?"

"The most famous member of our clan. He was a familiar to Lord William de Soulis, they say, which is bollocks—a red cap has never befriended a human. Until now. Robin is definitely a good example of our bad side. Met him once. Cantankerous wee prick. The least appealing of an appalling breed. Och…"

"Och" usually began a statement or rebuttal but Eddie let it waft away in the night breeze a moment.

"You must think me a snaggletoothed windbag, Dennis Duckworth," he eventually said.

"It's fine. You don't meet goblins every day."

"Aye, true. Still…I have to stop for a while. There are other things to discuss, Dennis. There's you."

Dennis chuckled, more to himself than anything. "Me? I got nothing."

"No?"

"Nope. My life story's markedly shorter. No major departures from my people, no gory past to distance myself from, nothing like that at all. Nothing like yourself."

"Nothing." Eddie sounded dubious. "Nothing in your life. Nothing at all like me."

Dennis shook his head. "Of course not."

"So your life is one of the average masses, then. No adventures, nothing unusual, all peace and calm."

"I wouldn't use the terms 'peace' or 'calm,' but until recently, yes. Nothing of note."

"Until recently," Eddie repeated.

Dennis glared back at the red cap. "Well, this isn't how I usually spend my evenings. Over a campfire in Scotland talking to a figment of mankind's imagination. But, this fantasmagorical fuckery aside, things are pretty interesting in my life right now. Potentially good. Potentially bad. Remains to be seen."

"Your present is just the nexus between your past and your future."

"That's all, huh?" Dennis stared towards the blackness of the tower and the midnight blue of the sky beyond.

"Aye."

"And so how do you live in the present if it's nothing more than a… what?"

"Nexus. The critical part. The connection. Where one becomes the other. Don't be a smartass, you know what the word means."

There was a flutter in his head, so distant it was sensed more than felt, a moth at the porchlight, harmless but unsettling. A melody.

"I'm not where I'm supposed to be," Dennis said.

"Geographically?"

"Geographically, emotionally, professionally."

"Well," said Eddie, "I'm supposed to be many miles to the south. I'm supposed to slash your throat and stop up the wound with my bloody bonnet. Perhaps being where you're supposed to be is overrated."

The moth became a swarm of them, wings like flower petals beating against his face, as if he himself had become the porchlight. New York to Glasgow. 5/4. The Random. Sylvia. They threatened to settle around his nose, his mouth, to burrow into his ears, and all the while, the melody.

Then it was gone, and all that remained in the air was the sound of embers that popped and danced into the air until they expired.

"So you're not going to relay, in any fashion, the story behind the fresh blood I can smell all over you?" asked Eddie finally, with an odd gentleness. "Or the new bandage on your forehead?"

Dennis shrugged.

"I need sleep, Eddie. I've a lot on my mind and I have to sort some things out."

"Of course you do," Eddie replied. "It's the present. That's what you do here. Use yesterday to sort out tomorrow."

"What are you, some sort of self-help guru?"

Eddie raised an eyebrow. "I suppose 'tis late for you. I should perhaps be on the move myself."

"Before you go," Dennis said, "Can I make a suggestion?"

"Aye."

"Go deeper into the woods when you get your rabbits." Dennis pointed off into the darkness beyond the clearing. "Leave less of a mess. They've sent me up here to find the 'kids' responsible for this 'sickening bout of vandalism.' Keep it up, and someday, someone's going to find you. Startle them enough, and they might blast a hole in you."

Eddie nodded to himself. "Aye. Well spoken. I'll do just that. I would like to stay here a while. The walls of the tower...they comfort me. It isnae a real castle at all..."

"A folly, I'm told."

"Aye. But..." Eddie looked momentarily distraught. "Even after your life has moved on, the need for certain comforts can linger. I'll never live in castles again, and I no longer want to live as I once did, but...the need for that comfort lingers. These walls give me comfort. Have yourself a sleep, Dennis. I'm sure I'll be speaking to you regularly from now on, though you should do some of the talking next time. Good night, Dennis Duckworth."

"Good night, Eddie Red Cap."

And in the haze of the fantastic that surrounded him, Dennis grinned. *Eddie Red Cap. Eddie Red Cap indeed.*

*

135

In their twenty-year friendship, Paul McDermott had always been the one to do the unexpected. Not unhinged, or wild, or madcap, or zany, not destructive or even impulsive. Simply unexpected. Reading the entire Hermann Hesse library was unexpected. Or the time he announced that, for the preceding three years, he had been studying fencing, and Dennis had not even known. The time he called and announced he had moved to Iowa. The time he called from a bar in Spain to say he was sitting with the singer from Pere Ubu.

These were McDermott Moments, and they could happen at any time. Of course, Paul would also make shit up, just as frequently, just to amuse himself. The time he claimed to have booked a room on a freighter bound for Madagascar, for one. It was Paul. It *could* have been true.

With tables turned, Paul proved unflappable.

"So no one stopped you," Paul said, more of a reiteration of fact than a question.

"No one stopped me."

"And no one questioned you."

"No."

"And you happened to have your passport on you."

"I did."

"And you happened to wind up in Perth."

"I did."

" … "

"Taking it all in, Paul?"

" … "

"Paul?"

"Aren't you a little old to be doing crack?"

Pause.

From the lips of any other person, the joke would have been clear—but when Paul McDermott told a joke, even his best friend had to pause for confirmation.

"Okay. Yeah. Hah. Got me."

"As always."

"Yeah, well, that's the only thing that's 'as always,' Paul. Nothing whatsoever is 'as always.' In fact, I have a suspicion that 'always' has been redefined. At least for me. I'm telling you the truth, Paul."

Omissions notwithstanding, of course. If I tell you about the goblin, you won't think it's crack, you'll think it's a cocktail of LSD and PCP.

Dennis pressed the cell to his ear, hoping to block out the shaky thunder of an approaching truck on the Perth bridge, coughing out globules of black smoke. When Dennis inhaled, he felt as though his system was thick with cancerous mucous. He concentrated on the cleaner aroma of plants that grew along the Tayside.

"So what happens now, man?"

Paul was definitely 'as always.' A rock. A fucking superstar. Whether or not he believed in magical boarding passes, Paul understood Dennis *did* believe in them, so he accepted the story without question. *Accepted without question. A good friend, that Paul McDermott, don't you think, Denny?*

Which gave him an idea.

"You should probably get back to Chicago soon, don't you think?"

"I, uh, I dunno, man." Dennis watched as the silvery Tay slid beneath him. Nothing like the rivers in Chicago, but...

...the need for certain comforts can linger.

"Things here are..." Dennis struggled for words. "Well, it's...it's kind of intense. I'm going through....something, man. Which is why I need your help. But it's not the help you think."

"You mean, you don't need money?"

"Those first messages were *completely* about money," Dennis admitted. "I wanted you to fire me off airfare so I didn't have to face my folks calling me a fuck-up yet again."

"Well, they wouldn't have believed this story of yours."

"No they wouldn't have," Dennis replied, "They wouldn't have. Only someone whose brain had been smoked into bratwurst would believe my story. So I called *you.*"

"I've got more sense in my few remaining cells than you have in that entire spongiform mess you call a brain, Duckworth. Don't forget it."

"Yeah, well, fuck you, too."

"Shut up or else I'll hang up and head straight back to Iowa," Paul threatened.

"You wouldn't do that to me, Paulie, and you know it."

"No, I guess I wouldn't," Paul eventually sighed. "So you still get the grief from the folks, even at this age?"

"Sometimes."

"You sure it's not all in your head?"

Dennis stopped a moment at the foot of the Perth Bridge. The smell of sulphur dioxide blended with the soft decay of leaves that flowed from the North Inch.

"No, it isn't in my head. It's in their eyes. I can see them thinking what a fuck-up I am."

"Well, maybe you should've used that fancy arts degree of yours."

"Look, man, that's the thing. Suddenly, finally, unexpectedly, I'm not a fuck-up. They're *thrilled* with me right now. Thrilled by what's going on with The Random. That's why I don't want to ruin it with something this…stupid. It's not that I'd need to borrow money. They'd want to know why I was traipsing around the globe when I've got an important deal on the table. I could hardly tell them the bit about the boarding pass."

"Truth," Paul said. "Truth. Speaking of The Random, caught them at the Metro last week. They were hanging out with Albini."

"Fuck you, they were not."

"They were hanging out with Albini," Paul repeated. "I heard he doesn't mind their new stuff. Same with Tusk."

"Martin Tusk?" Tusk was the head of one of Chicago's biggest independent labels, Tangerine Records. "He's *heard* their new stuff?"

Damn. Damn, this was not promising.

"Hell, I don't know," Paul said. "What's the new stuff like? They still a Fall Out Boy tribute act?"

"Are you trying to piss me off on purpose?"

"Yes," Paul said. "You seem preternaturally reserved today, man, and it's freaking me out. Someone's got to be the sarcastic bastard, and for the first time in a long time, it isn't you. And I guess the answer's no, anyway. Albini wouldn't give that power-pop stuff the time of day—plus, he thinks you're an asshole. So The Random must be doing something new. What's it sound like?"

Dennis closed his eyes and rested one hand on the bridge rail.

"Like something Albini would like, I suppose."

"Ah." Paul paused. "Of course, if Albini likes it, there's no way Universal likes it. I don't see them rushing to release something so…abrasive."

"It's abrasive but catchy," Dennis insisted. "Universal's happy with what I gave them. They want to hear some of the new stuff, though. I hoped to get home and send them some demos myself, but if people are already hearing the new stuff, and talking about the new stuff, I probably don't have enough time. Which is where you come in. I need you to drop by the office for me."

"Okay."

"Then I need you to go into my computer and open up one my folders. It's called 'July.' Ignore the other folders completely. That's the one. That's the *only one*. You got it?"

Paul hummed affirmatively and Dennis felt himself choke on another overwhelming odour.

"In my inbox there's a message with details and passwords for an FTP site. I'll forward it to you along with my passwords. I need you to upload that folder to this FTP site. That's it. Done."

What's the chemical composition of cobblestone? Or is that smell the combination of rubber and leather from hundreds of thousands of shoes?

"That's it?" Paul was incredulous.

"That's it," said Dennis

"Cool. Sure. I haven't seen the kids in your office for a while."

"Well, you're not going to see them, because I need you to do this after hours, when they're not around."

Paul didn't respond for a moment.

"You still have the key, yes?"

"Yes."

Another pause.

"They like you better than they like me, Paul. They were really disappointed when you chose Iowa over becoming my partner."

"You'll never understand that, will you?"

"No," said Dennis.

"Well, there's something *I* don't understand," Paul countered. "Considering you've got an entire staff on hand, why do you need *me* to do this?"

"Because my staff will know it's the wrong folder."

Paul laughed, though it didn't sound joyful. It was a laugh of acknowledgement; the laugh one laughs as the computer crashes when an essay is due, or a car breaks down on the way to the airport.

"The wrong folder," Paul confirmed.

"Yes."

"So the right folder, then, would contain the music Albini likes."

"Probably," Dennis said.

"So you want Universal to think they're signing a pop band when really they're signing a mathematic post-rock avant-psyche band instead."

"I'd hardly call them *that*, Paul, but that's the gist."

"And when they realize it's the wrong record," Paul said slowly, as if speaking to a child, "and your deal fails, and the band leaves you, and the label collapses, and you're living back at your parents' house hated and despised by everyone on the Chicago music scene…think your parents will give you grief then?"

Nothing could give me more grief than the nauseating perfume on the woman behind me, Paul.

"You got it wrong, man." Dennis quickened his pace to distance himself from the stomach-churning aroma. "That's not my play. This is just to hold it together until I get back. Universal loves The Random's debut. They love the demos they've heard. They just haven't heard the newest stuff, and it's a little 'out there' for mainstream tastes. I want to ease them into that. I want to be there when they hear the weirder bits. I can finesse Universal. I can finesse The Random, too, and get them to keep the weirder bits to a minimum for now. A bit of compromise on both sides and it's all good. Deal saved. Album sold. Grammy received. Houses purchased. Everybody's happy."

"So originally, you wanted me to buy you a plane ticket to come home yourself and pull this crap. Now you think your plan will fail if you wait too long, so you want me to do it for you."

"Yes."

"What if I say no?" Paul asked.

"Then I'll ask you to loan me the money to get home, so I can do it myself."

"I'd rather that's what we did, Dennis."

But...

Paul let the silence continue a few moments and then asked, "You don't want to do this, do you, Duckworth?"

Dennis stared up South Street and hitched his bag over his shoulder.

"Don't be ridiculous," Dennis grumbled. "It's important and it can't wait. That's all. By the time I can get the money and get a flight it could be the weekend, and I'm just nervous about screwing up this deal. We've known each other for a long time, Paul, and I've never asked you to do a favour like this."

"No," Paul agreed. "No, you haven't. Generally, when it comes to lying, cheating and fucking people over, you're a one-man show. I don't see why you suddenly need a sidekick."

Dennis sensed thousands of different molecules billowing through his epithelium, as though he'd turned into an animal. Yet the more aromas that blended in his nose, the more congested his olfactory glands became, the less repulsive any one smell became. His stomach, however, remained cautious.

"You're not a sidekick, Paul, you're my friend and I'm asking you for this favour. You could save the whole thing. You really could."

"Well, there's an effective spin."

There wasn't any question in Paul's tone, though. There had been questions, but Paul had accepted.

"When do you need me to do this?" he asked.

"As soon as you can."

"And how are you going to get home?"

"I don't know," Dennis replied honestly.

"Do you want me to do this, and then look into getting you the money?"

"Uh...let's just...worry about that next week."

"One more question, though, Denny."

"Uh-huh."

"This new Random material—the material you called the 'weirder bits.' Forget about Albini or Universal or all the rest. Is it actually good?"

Across the street, Dennis watched as a woman appeared in the door of a clothing shop. Paused in a drop of silence, her dark hair reflected a silver sheen in the sun. Dennis was almost certain that he could smell her shampoo. Strawberry.

"Denny?"

"Ah."

"Is it good?"

Pause.

"Yeah, Paul. It's fucking incredible."

*

Dennis was certain that, if he had never met Paul McDermott, he would think the new Random songs were atonal trash.

The cutting edge, as represented in Dennis' record collection at the time he met Paul, included The Clash, The Smiths, The Housemartins, and New Order. He considered himself hip, alternative, a lover of the obscure and a champion of the unknown. Then he went to Paul McDermott's house and flipped through the record crates. They contained significantly fewer albums than Dennis owned, but more tellingly, they contained only one artist Dennis had ever heard of—Frank Zappa. It had both humbled him and pissed him off. Hawkwind, Nomeansno, Hoodoo Gurus, Pere Ubu, Captain Beefheart, Big Black. Beside the crate, a shoebox full of cassettes by Chicago indie bands that were also unknown. Pot-smoking weirdo music, he thought, though he didn't consider Paul as much of a weirdo as he knew he should. Dennis arrived home with a handful of borrowed vinyl and puzzled over the records for days. Days later, he realized he liked this music, and he puzzled over that, too. Hawkwind sounded like hippies from outer space, Pere Ubu tracks barely qualified as songs, and each member of Captain Beefheart's Magic Band seemed to be playing a different song at the same time. It was noisy music, cacophonic, angular. It challenged him. When he began to enjoy Beefheart's *Trout Mask Replica*, he felt as if he had reached a sort of satori—he understood, and was incapable of explaining why, or how, or even what it was he was understanding. He just understood.

Robbie, Jason and Mike had been Dennis' friends since grade school. They'd played Little League together, caused shit together, gone to the mall together, listened to music together—but this music wasn't for them. They didn't understand. They understood less and less, it seemed, as time passed. To stay in the group, Dennis began to pretend that he didn't understand, either; to pretend he, too, had few interests beyond booze and chicks and making fun of other people. It was very important that he not seem too different, lest he incur possible judgments on his character. They judged him enough as it was. With each passing year, he resented his old friends more and more; their presence made him edgy, guarded, and, ultimately, unhappy. Even Dennis knew that friends really weren't supposed to have that effect on a person. They'd changed. They'd let him down. In fact, through the course of high school, *everything* seemed to change, and *everything* seemed to let him down. He wanted to tell everyone to fuck off, pretty much all the time. That's when he started to learn how to cover it up, to put on the smile, and to forge ahead. Cursing the universe became something he did under his breath; he hoped that people couldn't see it in his eyes (which, of course, they could; Dennis' pose was less convincing than he believed, and few who knew Dennis Duckworth would have described him as happy or even content).

Paul McDermott became one of the few people around whom Dennis did not act like an asshole. They used to drive through neighbouring states, often taking the Chicago-Detroit route, following favoured bands headed east, making friends with Detroit club owners so they could get in, using an array of fake I.D.s and growing half-assed beards. They didn't do it in order to drink illegally (though they did that too) but rather to see the bands play. Secretly, Dennis preferred the drives to the shows themselves; talking with Paul, listening to tapes on a ghetto blaster (Paul's car was so old it had only an 8-track player and only *Changesonebowie* and *In Through The Out Door* on 8-track, though they remained mostly on the floor by the back seat). Dennis would watch the fireflies as he drove through Michigan on starry summer nights, secretly sad when they extinguished themselves with a splash against the windshield.

It had felt good to talk to Paul again—until it began to feel strangely bad. Lying wasn't new. Asking someone else to lie on his behalf wasn't particularly new either. Asking *Paul* to lie on his behalf, well, that was something he'd never done, never dared do, never stooped to doing. It felt vaguely icky, as if he'd asked a very sweet girl to do something very sweet girls don't do. Of course, he'd done *that* before and never felt as dirty as he felt today, increasingly by degrees, as if the heat-eked sweat smelled of his own internal filth. Metaphorically and literally, he needed a shower, but he wasn't about to ask Margaret to borrow her apartment again. Not today.

Instead he'd strolled the length of the Tay on the Kinnoull side and wandered streets and highways he'd not yet explored. Occasionally, someone honked at him, perhaps because he was still wearing the bright white shirt—admittedly sweat-soaked, probably stinking—and the white cap to keep the sun off his head. Eventually, Dennis crossed back over the Perth Bridge to buy lunch. As he walked away from the till, he turned to see a familiar face.

"Well, well. If it isn't the Captain of Kinnoull Hill."

"Hello, Abby." Dennis shrank into himself and quickly removed the captain's hat.

"You look a mess," Abby said.

"Oh, you mean the injuries? Or do you mean the pungent, sweat-soaked shirt I'm wearing?"

"There's a smell? I hadn't noticed that yet." She clutched a plastic bag with a sandwich of her own.

"Oh, there's a smell." Dennis wiped his brow with his sleeve. "Captain, huh? I'm big on nicknames. I'd considered some for you, but none really worked. It's unfortunate that my new one was coined by Bruce McKee, I guess."

"That lout? Lord no. That's what they're *all* calling you now. Lord knows who started it."

"They?"

"The townsfolk. The colourful locals. Et cetera. Over at the Rat and Raven."

"Ah, you're familiar with those fine folk."

"I mostly know Margaret," Abby said.

"I mostly know Margaret as well." Behind Abby was the doorway to the shop and beyond that, a billboard poster advertising a Rihanna record. The textures and tones distracted him; he could see what elements had been digitally enhanced and could almost tell by how much.

"It's a small town," Abby said. Beneath his fingertips, Dennis could feel the cool plasticity of the laminated counter. He could sense the weight of the wood beneath the synthetic surface. Abby jingled some change in her fist, head cocked, watching him. Someone behind the counter put on some music, and much to Dennis' surprise, it was one of his favourites, an ode to his home, *Illinois* by Sufjan Stevens. The hushed, somehow porous voice filled the room lightly, with a delicate presence. The two were quiet while they both listened. Dennis and Abby could see each other's familiarity with the music; it was the shorthand of body language between music lovers. For a moment it reminded him of how shockingly alone he had been, and how little he had acknowledged the fact.

"Venison?" Dennis asked.

"Yeah, they have venison," Abby replied.

"No, not there behind the counter, in your sandwich bag. I can smell venison."

"Um…you can smell it?" She looked at him incredulously.

"With mayo, regular mustard and a very-slightly-overripe tomato."

"You can't possibly have smelled that." She pursed her lips and shook her head in dismissal.

"No, just a good guess, probably," Dennis realized this party trick was too inexplicable to perform and stopped showing off his new olfactory abilities.

"I thought you'd be the type to scoff at a mopey guy like Sufjan Stevens," she said.

"Seems too sensitive for an asshole like me? Actually, I like a lot of truly mopey shit."

"Smiths fan," she said flatly.

"Yes."

"Elliot Smith fan."

"Lonely, fragile soul, impossibly broken, ultimately doomed," Dennis said. "He stabbed himself in the heart. Surely *you're* a fan."

"I wear a lot of black, Captain, but I'm not that grim." Abby laughed. "Stabbed himself in the heart. Seems rather inefficient."

"You sound like my ex-wife."

"Why's that?"

"Talking about someone's suicide and complaining about the inefficiency of it."

"Sounds like a charmer."

"You might say she could be very matter-of-fact."

Footsteps approached and Dennis stepped sideways without looking. The customer came to the counter, and Dennis absorbed each register ring and computer blip. The computer tones were pure, like sine waves. The rings rattled and shook as if each were a pocketful of gypsy bells. The left side of the drawer was lower than the right. Plastic scraped the surface of plastic.

"You're on your lunch break, then?"

"Indeed." Abby nodded towards the sandwich that had been placed in front of Dennis. "Care to join me and eat our sandwiches on a bench like civilized people?"

Dennis nodded once and followed Abby out onto High Street. Another beautiful day, and most of the benches were taken up—some by one person, bags scattered as if to claim the bench—but one near the edge of the pedestrian course was open. Abby dashed towards it and sat down, almost triumphantly. He supposed that, on a day-to-day basis, a bench on the High Street was a pathetic kind of triumph. He sat down next to her with a decidedly less advanced sense of accomplishment.

"Ex-wife, huh?"

"Yes, I've got one of those."

"I see. Recent?"

"Ongoing."

"And you've come to Scotland to either take a break from the proceedings or to live in a state of early-life crisis to recapture some kind of youthful vigor."

"Not exactly, no. But thanks for the very nuanced analysis of my reaction to pain and suffering."

"You look like the type who's always suffering."

"You dress like the type that's always suffering."

"Touché."

They ate in silence a moment. Dennis wondered if Abby could taste the preservatives in the mayonnaise the way he could. Certainly the meat was fairly fresh; he guessed the animal had been slaughtered no more than four days prior, suggesting the shop was legitimate in its claim to only sell locally farmed meats. How he knew this, he did not know. His newly acute sense of taste and supernatural intuition grew stronger with every moment. He found it miraculously creepy.

"So, let me guess," Abby said in an attempt to restart conversation. "Your ex is a horrible witch of a woman who drove you to despair, but you love her anyway, and she's the one who suggested you end the marriage, and even though you know she's right, you're still in agony."

"About to stab myself in the heart."

"Aim well. You've probably got a pretty small target there."

"Mah. You're such a bitch."

"I just know when someone's full of crap," Abby replied through a mouthful, trying to keep her lips sealed around the chewed food. "I like to peck at them until they eventually admit it."

"Ah. Well, best of luck. I've never admitted to anything in my life. Sarcasm isn't exactly waterboarding, so I doubt you'll have any luck."

"Did *she*?"

"Did she what?"

"Have any luck. Calling you on your bullshit."

"Just how horrible do you assume I am, anyhow?" Dennis pouted as he turned away to regard the facades across the street.

"I don't know. How horrible are you?"

Dennis was quiet a moment.

"She left me because I slept with another woman, so I'm probably as horrible as you imagine."

"Another woman." Abby licked a smear of mayonnaise off her thumb. "That's original."

"I'm the type who goes back to the classics, I guess."

"The other woman is a classic for the ages, no doubt." Abby mouthed more mayonnaise from the space between her thumb and index finger. "Let me guess, there's another classic in your repertoire. You slept with another woman, but it was all her fault."

"DJ Dennis," Dennis replied.

"Come again?"

"She used to call me DJ Dennis," he sighed. "She said that somehow I always managed to take what I'd done and turn it into something else entirely, like a DJ can take two records and mix them into a hip-hop track."

"I thought that's where the analogy was going."

"And when that failed, I just flipped the record completely."

"Meaning?"

"Meaning I would throw the whole thing back at her, make it her fault."

"Was it her fault?"

"Yes! I mean, I think it was."

"You think it was."

Dennis continued to stare at the shop windows. It came back to him, the look of the storefront she had finally bought, after she left the boutique on Chestnut, when she finally had her own shop.

"When I first met her, she worked for a record distributor in Hamilton, a city in Ontario. My company had one good band, called Snack Donkey, who had this wastoid lead singer named C.K. We flew to Canada and played a showcase for her company. C.K. got hammered and fell off the stage, right onto the corner of the floor monitor. I got to know Sylvia Moran in the emergency room of a Canadian hospital at 4 a.m."

"Auspicious beginnings," Abby remarked.

"Well, they *were* auspicious," Dennis said. "The beginnings, I mean. They were bloody fucking brilliant for a while. And then…then I saw what she was really about."

"And what was she really about?"

"Herself. Her career."

Like everyone else, she changed, she let me down.

Dennis stared down at his sandwich, suddenly lacking appetite.

"Not that I'm against careers," he continued. "I'm not into the barefoot and pregnant bullshit, that's crazy regressive. But the cell phone calls at the dinner table. The endless cell phone calls at the dinner table. At the fucking *breakfast* table. And then, it got to the point where I had to ask her to put it away so we could eat a meal together and in peace, and she took it personally."

"I'm sure you asked her quite nicely," Abby said. "I'm sure you gave her a reasoned explanation of why you wanted her to put away the cell phone."

"It doesn't matter now," Dennis said dismissively. "She left, and now I'm about to be free to talk on my own goddamn cell phone all day long if I please, which I'm going to be doing."

The cell phone. The more she had sat at the table texting clients and talking to designers, the more Dennis had resented her, even as he realized she was simply turning into *him*. The moment he saw it, he started to leave his phone in the living room during meals, so he had some kind of moral high ground when he chastised her with sighs and eye-rolls. One time she looked at him, sad-eyed, as if he'd thrown the stupid phone into the garbage instead of just tossing it—quite reasonably, quite gently— onto the counter behind him.

She'd been doing what you did, Denny. Building her business. Did she bitch about JC Penny and Walmart the way you bitched about popular music and, yes, Universal Records, whose dick you're trying so hard to ride right now? Did she sell out?

They'd both faced fundamentally identical adversity. People liked Jersey Shore and Nickelback and Applebee's and Target. Both of them knew there had to be a way, there just had to be a way, for something that was actually good to make some money. To achieve a modicum of success without giving in to the machine. Sylvia designed clothes that were never going to be found in Walmart, yet somehow, she had a shop filled with people. His own mother had bought one of her goddamned dresses, could you believe it? As if she'd ever wear it, as if Elisa Mae would skip out on the town to trip the light fucking fantastic in one of Sylvia's designs. She'd bought one of Sylvia's dresses—but she'd never come to see one of his bands play. Neither Elisa Mae nor Richard had ever been to one of his shows. They didn't have that taste in music, perhaps. But they didn't have that taste in fashion, either.

"Something big on the horizon, then?" Abby asked, interrupting his reverie.

"Yeah." Dennis paused to bring himself back to the present. "Yeah, there is. You'll see my name in the liner notes while you're stocking their CDs on the shelves. And you'll be able to tell people you know me."

"Really." Abby sounded unconvinced.

"Really. I'm guessing you don't have a lot of bands come through here."

"Not so many, no."

"Why do you stay in a boring-ass place like this, anyway?'

"Perth's beautiful." Abby scowled. "And it's not *that* small a town."

Good, Denny. Good job. See? You lash out at people because you're sick of yourself. If you'd recognized that a decade ago, you'd still have friends and a wife.

Fuck you, internal critic.

150

"Have fun at work," Dennis offered blandly. "Sorry to ruin your lunch."

Abby shouldered her bag and stared down at him a moment.

"What?" Dennis asked.

"Nothing," she replied. "I'm just trying to figure out if that was a real apology."

Dennis wasn't sure, either, and she left him on the bench on High Street trying to decide if it was or not.

*

Dennis laid on the wooden bench on Kinnoull and felt the slow dissolution of the midsummer heat fading away to the west. The tower darkened against the horizon, a giant shadow that at once loomed over and sheltered the place that he now, oddly, called home. Autumn was on its way, and here in Perth it wasn't going to be a long, drawn-out affair; dampness was likely to arrive before long, maybe another month or so, or so Dennis assumed, knowing absolutely nothing about the weather in Scotland. It didn't matter. He'd decided. It was going to get damp, and it was going to suck.

For now, though, heat. More heat than this part of the nation had seen in many years. Hottest weather in Scottish history, as he repeatedly heard from people on the street—and across the street, across the bridge, behind a barn, or in a moving automobile, it seemed at times, so keen had Dennis' hearing become.

The descent of the sun was a welcome relief; that is, of course, until the winds picked up in the highlands and blew early hints of autumn across the top of the hill, which wasn't as windy as one might expect but still, it wasn't exactly sheltered.

"You're going to want a fire, yeah?"

Dennis looked over his shoulder. Eddie walked across the clearing, the setting sun shining directly on him, a bundle of sticks in his arms. The surreal quality was heightened and left Dennis unsettled. Eddie was a sight, all loose grey skin and horrific teeth, with a red glint in his eye and a reddish brown tint to his cap, freshly dipped in rabbit blood.

151

The creature sidled up to the fire pit and arranged the wood for the fire. Dennis looked out towards the fields and back; somehow, there was already a flame in the ring of rocks. *Head full of napalm indeed.*

"You've eaten, yeah?"

"I've eaten, thanks, Eddie."

Eddie, crouched on his haunches, fell backward onto his arse. "Och, what a day. Rabbits. So many rabbits to kill."

"How many'd you kill?"

"Two."

"That's not so many."

"You try it, lad. It's like I'm trying to smoke one drag when I'm used to smoking a pack a day."

"Meaning you get the urge to tear apart more living beings, I presume."

"It crosses the mind, yeah."

"How do I know you're not going to have a change of heart and rip my throat out?"

"You don't." Eddie said this without malice, but a chill burst downward along Dennis' spine nonetheless.

"Not comforting, I suppose," Eddie said. "My apologies, Dennis. I'm not going to do that, I'm just saying you don't *know*. How can you? You'll have to take it on faith."

"Faith is the reason you exist in the first place."

Eddie thought a moment, surprising Dennis with his apparent depth of concentration.

"Yes, I suppose you can call it faith," he finally said. "Well, it's just something I'll have to deal with. I cannae exactly go into town and order a burger. Though I've become fond of burgers, when I can steal them. And other foods. I've done my share of thieving, though I've mostly given it up. Difficult. Cannae imagine me with a job and a tab at the Rat and Raven, now can we?"

Dennis eyed the red cap a moment.

"Why not?"

Eddie laughed.

"No, seriously, why not?" He stared at the creature again, and Eddie stared back, unblinkingly.

"Dennis—"

"No, for real. You want to move into the human world, and the only way to do that is to behave like a human. So you find yourself some work, you do what you can do. You...get a change of clothes. Do something about those teeth—easier said than done, I suppose. Your features aren't too far off from human, you'd pass, you'd just be an odd looking dude. The grey skin, that's a problem, but there's probably something you could do. Make-up, maybe. Get rid of those iron boots. Maybe—"

"All easier said than done, considering the doing's impossible, lad."

"What do you fuckin' mean, impossible?" Dennis answered derisively. "Jesu—I mean, damn. You seem pretty bent on being difficult."

"You seem pretty bent on being an asshole, Duckworth, so who are you to judge?"

Dennis approached the fire and sat, cross-legged, across from Eddie.

"What do you know about that?"

"I hear things," Eddie replied.

"From whom?"

"From you. I hear them, I feel them. I know you're a right sonofabitch, but that you're also starting to recognize it. Must be a struggle."

"I'm not struggling with shit."

"No?" Eddie laughed again. "All right, then. You're not. Excuse me."

Silence crept over them for several minutes; only a small rustle and crackle from the fire broke the quiet void. It was almost full dark; by the time the silence was broken, the fire itself seemed to be the only thing alive on Kinnoull Hill.

"The present is the nexus between the past and the future, you said. Or something like that."

"Aye," Eddie agreed. "Where one becomes the other."

Dennis had questions, but they felt clumsy on his tongue, like a third-grader wearing an adult-sized baseball glove. The questions made him feel childish.

"Where one becomes the other," Dennis repeated. "So that means everything that happens to me happens because of what I'm doing right now. Right?"

"Your future can change in a blink, laddie. That's what I'm saying. Quicker than the type on a boarding pass."

Dennis should have been startled, but somehow it didn't surprise him that Eddie knew about the boarding pass.

"What got you thinking about this kind of thing, Eddie? What kind of philosophy books were you reading? The existentialists?"

Eddie sighed and opened his mouth to speak, but he stared forlornly into the fire a moment instead, mouth agape, his serrated jaws more than ever like the maw of an angler fish.

"It was 1925," Eddie began. "I'd already felt something in the air— something was wrong with the red caps, we were losing our way. I'd stared at these books lining the shelves in these castles for years, and never desired to read them. Who cared about what came from the minds of men? I saw the universe in every moment. What good can the thoughts of these inferior, unmagical creatures be? They were food—not the flesh, but the life, the very *life* we took fed us. You'd no more read a book than you'd try and make sense out of the twitching of an ant's antennae; it might have meaning, it might not, and who cared anyway when you were simply going to stomp on it and keep it out of your kitchen?

"Then, of course, things started changing," Eddie continued. "There was poison in the creeks. It flowed out of these new grey concrete monoliths, the same ones that spewed other poisons into the sky. Shiny metal bands had been stitched into the earth, and these great iron beasts roared along them. We were the universe, we were the earth, we knew everything, but we didn't know what these machines were. These were not beasts. These were spawned by the minds of men. Not by their fears, as we were, but by something grander, something higher. Suddenly, it crossed my mind—and some others' minds as well—that perhaps there was something, if not illuminating, at least interesting to be gleaned. I learned to read quickly. Within days, I learned: trains. These iron beasts were called trains. Then, the more I started reading, the more I was astounded. Stories. Stories! What in the world were stories? We told no stories. We simply lived. We never thought of our lives as stories, though by hell they certainly were—horror stories, adventure stories. No love stories, I'm afraid. Nary a female Red Cap exists.

"Anyhow, by 1925, it came about that I'd tear the throat out of one of you and I'd be dipping my cap in the blood pooled on the floor…but the way I'd see the body would be different. It felt…wrong, somehow."

"Like how we don't eat dogs or dolphins?"

Eddie nodded enthusiastically. "Aye, there's what I'm talking about! You were still strange creatures, but something about the books—knowing you had the books in you— kept me from enjoying the kill the way I once had. Now, at the time, I was living in a neglected old place up on the north sea, Dunnottar Castle. Built eight hundred years ago, captured once by Wallace himself, held against Cromwell for eight months before it fell. For about two hundred years, it sat there, a real sad state for a historical dwelling, a true boon for a red cap. I spent over a century there, living in its rooms, hiding in its crags, venturing out at night to—well, you know. To do things. Things I no longer choose to do.

"Then, that same year I started having doubts, they set about repairing the castle. My silence was broken by more than crashing waves—workers started tearing up, lifting, pulling, breaking, shattering, hammering, rebuilding. I thought to myself, splendid, here's a whole new herd for my slaughtering pen! They're coming my way, they're working odd hours, people might think they've simply slipped into the sea! It was perfect. It truly was. Except…"

"Except you'd been reading."

"I'd been reading!" Eddie exclaimed. "Not only that, I'd been watching. Watching this painstaking effort. The crew they hired weren't just patching here and mortaring there. It was a…*loving* restoration. They cared about Dunnottar, wanted to return it to former glories, to make it last a red cap's lifetime. It was a form of art—and I'd begun to understand how art and the human mind were related. The problem was, I was hungry.

My cap was drying out. What was I going to do? They rebuilt the Keep, and I moved back from them, living in the lodgings and barracks and stables, thinking to myself every day, this is ridiculous, lad, you're a red cap, you have to do what you have to do. Around me, the castle renewed itself, and I continued to sneak out into the night and return, not with blood on my hands, but with books in my satchel. What's the matter, then? What's your problem, goblin? Do what you have to do!

"Then I thought, what exactly *do* I have to do? *Why* do I have to do it? Humans eat and sleep and breathe to stay alive—it's biology. It's science. Killing people and dipping a cap in blood? What in the name of hell is *that*, exactly? Is it magic's version of science, of biology? Or was it just a random rule that had ne'er been questioned? Something decided by ancients long ago and ne'er challenged?

"One evening, they'd all gone but one. It was a woman—a small woman, easily taken down, easily enough blood in her to last me a spell. I remember she came in the kitchen, where I'd been pacing back and forth, anxious for everyone to leave. The temptation was so great, you see; if people were about, I had the temptation. The thought of doing it again, even once more, had become repulsive; it didn't sicken me to think of all I'd already done, because what's done is done is done. I'd not known better. Now—now I knew better. I didnae want to do it…but oh, how I needed to. I imagine it's how an ex-smoker feels when quitting. You know it's horrible, cancerous, repugnant…but oh, how hard it is not to smoke. And when someone lays out this lovely white cigarette in front of you…and practically hands you a match…and that's what it was. A lone, lovely, white-skinned woman, by herself, defenseless, coming into the kitchen to re-measure the windows for the draperies. As she entered the room I snuck into the cupboard—as I'm sure you've noted, we're good at scuttling about unseen—and her deliciously blood-filled calves were only inches from my face. I sat, and I sat, and I grit my teeth, and closed my eyes, and…"

"And you fought it."

"No, sadly, I ripped her spine right clear of her torso."

"Oh, *Jesus!*"

With a soft whoosh and tiny pop, the space that once contained Eddie was empty.

"My bad!" came a voice over the hill. "Absolutely my bad!"

In a moment, Eddie bounded back into the clearing from the woods to the west.

"Sorry, Eddie, I—"

"No, no, that wisnae delicate, wisnae delicate at all." Eddie walked back to his spot, looking sheepish. Before he sat, he picked up the thin, grayish tooth that had remained in this dimension while the rest of Eddie was whisked through another. "I deserved that."

"No, really, I was just—"

"Disgusted, Dennis, I know."

"Where exactly do you go when that happens, anyway?"

"Not far," Eddie replied. "It used to send me keening off into the darkness and I'd wake hours later uncertain of where I was. As some of the magic dims, lad, *all* of it dims…it now seems to punt me a couple hundred yards and with barely a nodding out."

"You came that far in the last…what was that, five seconds?"

"I didn't say the magic was *entirely* dimmed," Eddie chuckled. "So, yes, anyway, where was I?"

"Spines."

"Ah. Yes. Well, it was a ghastly act that haunted me for years. My past had ne'er haunted me, but this one act—made, as it was, despite my new morality—stayed in my mind. It had been one of my rather more gruesome kills. Frustration and confusion had made me seethe. I could—I can—taste the copper aroma of blood at the back of my throat. The way her weight went down limp, like a sack of wet sand. The way the red gore splashed across her dress. Even as it happened, my stomach churned. I closed my eyes and dipped my cap and ran to the furthest part of the castle, the stables, and buried myself in a corner for weeks. It haunted me years, Dennis. I swore I'd ne'er do it again. I thought, there are two ways for me to achieve this. I can either choose and stand by my choice, or I can let the cap go dry and end it all for myself."

"And you chose life, so to speak."

"Aye." Eddie sniffed at the air, cocked his head, as though listening to something, and laughed quietly to himself. Dennis didn't bother to ask.

"So, yes, Dennis, that's how I got to where I am. Not by reading Sartre or Camus, but from the taste of blood in my throat. I couldnae change my past. All I could do was change my future by letting go of the past. The past is done. It recedes. If I could change now, then I could add virtue to my past. Add kindness. Add value. Then my past would no longer be not but shame and horror. I have no idea how much longer I'll be around. I've a millennium of murder behind me, but I've added almost a century of life. I might live long enough to make the virtue balance out the shame. Who's to say?

"Doesn't work that way for you, though," Eddie added with an attempt at a meaningful glance. "You change your ways now, but you have to hope you don't get cancer or get hit by a commuter train before you're seventy-five, if you want to balance your life."

"It isn't karma I'm worried about," Dennis said glumly. "I'd just… wait, why are we talking about this? This isn't a fuckin' self-help mission here. I'm fine. You're the one who clearly needs a little help."

"Och, whatever you say, Dennis Duckworth. Whatever you say." Eddie seemed lost for a moment, in his own mind, and his face seemed to turn a different shade.

"What now?"

Eddie didn't respond immediately.

"I said the doing's impossible, didn't I?"

"About trying to look like a human?" Dennis asked.

"About, ah, integrating, is what I meant, really, the whole picture. Impossible, is what I said."

"Yes," Dennis agreed.

"Well, then, I suppose that's how you feel…?" Eddie ventured.

"About what?"

The red cap didn't reply.

*

"I'm not doing it."

At first, Dennis didn't know what Paul was talking about.

"Okay, then, the…ah…not doing what?"

On the other side of the ocean, Paul released a small sigh. It sounded as if he'd had the sigh prepared.

"*This*, Dennis. This mission of yours."

Dennis felt something clench in his stomach; it was the clench he'd felt when his credit cards were rejected, when he'd seen the boarding pass, and when he'd realized he was being beaten in a Glasgow park. One of surprise tinged with betrayal.

"C'mon, Paulie, what do you—"

"No, shut up, Dennis." Paul rarely took this kind of tone with anyone, let alone Dennis, and it shut him up.

"Listen. I went down to the label, like you asked. I waited until about nine o'clock, and I went down there. Except there wasn't no one there. Steph was there. She was responding to emails or something. I almost walked away, but she saw me through the doorway. I told her I'd seen the lights on and thought I'd come up and see who was around. So I went in, and we talked."

Dennis rubbed his temple and closed his eyes, as if he had a headache.

"About?"

"Stuff. How we've been. What's been happening. What's been happening at the label."

"Oh. And?"

"And she asked if I'd heard from you," Paul said. "I told her yeah, but I didn't know where you were, and what was up. They're starting to wonder what the hell is going on, Dennis. They're not…suspicious, exactly, because there's no way they could conceive of the bullshit plan you're trying to enact. But they know something's up. We started talking about The Random, and the deal, and the music, and she got really excited. Really, really excited. About the stuff Albini likes. About the new Random stuff."

"Oh, for God's—"

"I'm not finished," Paul rebuked. "We talked about it for a while. Then she played it for me. And you know what? It *is* good. I don't agree with the Fugazi comments she says you've made, though…there's too much Mission of Burma in there. It's like the '90s never happened, but in a good way. It's a whole new shape for old influences, and it works because those kids are good songwriters. The melodies cut through the tension in the arrangements. It's like something pretty is fighting through razor wire but somehow not getting cut. Or something, I'm not a music writer."

"So what, Paul? So…"

"So, Dennis, I'm not doing it. Have you even thought this through? Have you thought about breach of contract lawsuits?"

"By the time—"

"Bullshit. The Random doesn't want to release those old Fall Out Boy songs. Fall Out Boy have a great career, but The Random doesn't want to follow in their wake. The stuff will fall flat anyway. Universal's A&R guys are idiots. What you should do is march your stupid ass over to Martin's office."

"Martin Tusk?"

"Tangerine would freaking love this record, Dennis."

"Tangerine downsized in a major way," Dennis argued. "Tusk isn't going to buy our label and distribute the rest of our roster."

"And neither is Universal, no matter what you think. You don't need a major label, Dennis. Those days are gone. It's a quick fix and it's going to go nowhere. You want to get Martin's help to distro The Random. Make a deal with him, not Universal. That's what's best for the band, that's what's best for 5/4."

"It's not what's best for the bank account."

"In the long run, yes, it is," Paul insisted. "But that's neither here nor there. This just got me thinking about what you'd asked me to do. It's not that I give a shit about lying to some suits from the Broadway office. I *do* give a shit about lying to a band from Chicago, and I *really* give a shit about lying to your staff, because at one time, they were friends of mine. At one time, they were friends of *yours*."

"Paul, you don't—"

"Have I ever argued with you before?"

"…"

"No, I haven't. Then again, have you ever shoveled your bullshit in my direction before? No. I thought I was the one person you wouldn't try and fuck over. In fact, one night last summer, you pulled a drunken 'I love you man' moment and said, and I quote, 'Paul, I've fucked over some people, but I would never fuck you over.'"

"Paul, I'm not—"

"Dennis, shut up!" Paul yelled, startling Dennis. "Just stop talking! You're putting me in an impossible position because I know you, and I know that somehow, my refusal to do this will make you consider me less of a friend. Even though a friend wouldn't put me in this position. "

Dennis held his bridge of his nose. His eyes began to sting.

"Fine. Fine then, Paul. Whatever. Just help me get a ticket home and I'll do it myself."

"No."

At first, Dennis wasn't sure he heard him correctly, despite the fact that no other word would ever be mistaken for 'no' in this context.

"I can't do it, Dennis," Paul continued. He sounded pained. "I know it seems like a prick move, and that I'm leaving you stranded, and that you might never talk to me again. And I don't care, Dennis. I just can't care. Can't. You want to lie to your friends? Go ahead and do it. I'm not going to help you. Get your ass home from whatever weirdo trip you're on and you upload the material. You've got a couple weeks. You do it; you live with it. I'm not doing it. And by the way, if you don't call Steph, she's going to eventually get a call from Universal, and she's going to eventually pull her well-earned rank and deliver them the record in your absence, and they're going to hear the real Random music anyhow. There's a heads up for you—so I've assisted you, a little, in the scheme. Hope you're happy."

And he hung up.

CHAPTER EIGHT

When the shops were closed, and there was no more liquor to be purchased, purchased and guzzled while sitting against the wire fence surrounding the putting green on the South Inch, and when walking became too labour-intensive due to fatigue and the occasional curbside slip, and when it dawned on him that even if he still had liquor, he couldn't rightly, as a totally illegal immigrant and worker—an illegal immigrant worker!—sit on a bench and flout his transgression in public, in case the police wandered by, Dennis finally decided to risk the Rat and Raven.

There wasn't much change in his pocket, but there was enough—enough to get him a few more pints before he passed out on the bridge or, if he was lucky, made it back to Kinnoull. It didn't really matter.

He wasn't sure *what* mattered anymore. He wasn't upset that the Universal deal might tank. It was that the last person he had expected to screw him had screwed him.

Everyone did it eventually. Everyone eventually took a side other than his. It was a proven fact. Even his parents, through years of tsk tsk-ing him with their eyes and their sighs, had turned their backs on him. Oh, they were happier now, engaged him in real conversations now as opposed to simply subjecting him to mini-lectures and guilt trips, but they were only happier because he'd done something with himself. Almost. A full grown man, and still worried about parental approval. They were the ones who should have been on his side the most, and for so long, they weren't.

Paul, on the other hand, had always been on his side. *Always.* Never a doubt. All he'd asked was for Paul to upload some files, and he'd refused. All he had to do was this one little thing, and for some reason, he wouldn't do it. There was no real reason, as far as he could tell, for Paul to betray him this way, to fail him in this crucial moment, this *life-changing fucking moment*. The only reason was that it always happened eventually. Eventually, everyone failed him.

So fuck 'em. What mattered now, after several quarts of beer, was to find a way to get back to Chicago and do it himself. Paul had been right—Dennis had some doubts, and part of him didn't want to do this. Paul's refusal had steeled his resolve. Oh yes. Dennis saw the light now. He was not only right, he was *righteous*. And everyone would see.

There was no longer going to be any reward from the Council. He couldn't exactly turn Eddie in to authorities and expect to be compensated. Even if he could physically succeed, without Eddie disappearing in a puff of smoke or reverting to his nature and tearing him apart, you can't turn in an alien from another dimension. Hello, officers, your vandal is a monster spawned from the collective Id of humanity, you may not want to throw him in with the general population.

No, Dennis would have to find another way. He would have to be more inventive than he'd ever been.

He'd started to ponder the possibility of robbing a bank. Could he rob a bank? The cops here didn't seem to carry guns, and Perth was unlikely to have a crackerjack tactical unit. It was a drunken joke, but he hadn't dismissed it entirely. Tomorrow, once the hangover had faded, he'd consider his options. Now, he just wanted a couple more drinks, a few fewer brain cells, and to collapse somewhere, hopefully not in public, hopefully not landing with his teeth against the curb.

As he stumbled through the door, the room seemed to swell before him, magnified by the fish-eye lens of drunkenness. A murmur rippled through the patrons, and someone in the back actually called out, "I say Captain!" referencing a long-forgotten Captain Sensible song; he realized now that he still wore the cap.

"Dennis?"

Dennis landed hard in one of the nearest empty chairs. His tailbone would ache in the morning.

"Dennis, you look a mess."

It was Margaret, of course, looking down from what seemed an impossibly high and tilted angle.

"Dennis, you're face-first on the table. I cannae serve you if you're that drunk."

Dennis bolted upright, closed his eyes a moment, and searched for that perfect line between protesting and protesting too much

"No, Margaret, I'm just exhausted." Being drunk was easy; he was very good at it. Adept. "Sat in the sun a little too much this afternoon, I'm afraid."

"Well, then." She clearly didn't believe him, but seemed willing to suspend that disbelief. "What can I get you?"

"Pint of Gillespie's, please. Oh, and—um…how are, you know, things?"

"You mean the Bruce things."

"I do."

"They're not good, Dennis." She didn't offer more details.

"Tell him to fuck off."

"I don't think that's going to help the situation, exactly. And your being here is going to help it even less."

"You want I should leave?" Dennis asked.

"No." Margaret sighed and waved her bar rag in a circle. "Not on my account. On *your* account. You're…"

"I'm what?" Dennis was confused.

"People don't like him, you see."

"Why, because I'm American?"

"*Him*, you arse," Margaret scowled. "People don't like *him*. So, despite being a thoughtless, sarcastic mess of a human being, you've become a curiosity around here. Maybe even a minor celebrity. He'll hate you even more for that."

"A minor celebrity, huh?"

"Don't let it go to your head."

Dennis' head was too saturated to retain the conversation for more than a moment, let alone swell with ego. His pint arrived. He drained it.

He stared at the wall a few moments. A gangly young man with narrow cheekbones, like Adrian Brody with a less impressive nose, approached and leaned in toward Dennis, whose body had once again begun to lilt starboard.

"Oi, is it true you gave McKee a talkin' to?" he asked.

"It's true that you look like Adrian Brody, yes."

The man looked puzzled.

"Well, you do, you know."

"Uh…" He glanced at his friends and made a face to suggest the conversation was not going as planned. "Yeah, I've been told that. Thanks for that. But we heard you told McKee to suck your—"

"Yes, fuck, I guess so, but I also got my face flattened by a table, which kind of sucked. I think I might have wrecked Margaret's life, too, so whatever, yeah, I'm a dick."

"I didn't say—"

"Yep, I'm a *total asshole*." Dennis' tone hinted at a scene-in-the-making. It was just enough to send Adrian Brody back to his table, where he and his friends conferred and watched Dennis warily for the rest of his visit.

"Impressing more locals, I see."

"Whatever, Margaret."

"That's not my name." Abby lowered herself into the chair next to Dennis. "But judging by the wobbly marbles you've got in place of your eyes at the moment, I'm not surprised you're a bit confused."

"Oh! Yeah. Well, hey."

"Well hey indeed." Abby put a hand on Dennis' arm. "She likes you, you know. You should consider being a bit nicer to her, or taking her advice. Why don't you go home and get some rest? Are you maybe out a bit past your bedtime?"

"S'that late?"

"No, you're that drunk," Abby laughed. "You really shouldn't—"

"Don't fuckin' tell me how drunk I am."

"I'm sorry?" Abby removed her hand, surprised by the outburst.

"I said, I said don't fuckin'…tell me how drunk I am." Dennis shook his head and tried to turn away, a childish pout on his face. Being in the corner, however, there was no direction in which he could turn, other than towards the wall, which involved him craning his neck to lay his face against satiny wallpaper.

"I got a problem with that, ah, with that kinda thing," he told the wall. "Sylvia always fuckin' told me I was too drunk. So don't, even if you think I'm gonna puke on the Queen, don't tell me I'm too drunk, or *that* drunk, or *very* drunk, or in any way make reference to my *drunk*. I hate that."

"Were you too drunk?" Abby asked the back of Dennis' head.

"Wha? When?"

"When Sylvia would tell you that."

"What are you trying to do here, exactly?" Dennis turned back to face Abby, but stared mostly at the glossy tabletop, eyes slack in their sockets. "Have a conversation about my ex-wife? I'd rather that be stricken, ah, from the *agenda* too, if we can do that, that would be super. Yeah, she probably said it when I deserved it. So there's that. New topic."

"Okay."

"No, really, new topic."

"Okay!"

She sat a moment, eyes on his downcast face. When he raised his head, eyes spiteful, and spoke, she was saddened.

"You still here?"

"All I did was sit." Abby stood and leaned in towards him, closer than expected. Her shampoo, conditioner, dinner, skin cream and natural scents slashed through his liquor-deadened senses and made him swoon.

"By the way," she said, "you are really, really drunk, you asshole."

"Fuck you," he said, under his breath, several seconds after she walked away.

The room swayed again. People may or may not have been watching him—he couldn't quite tell and didn't quite care—as he stood and finished his pint in several dramatic gulps that involved more arm movement than necessary.

"Yeah, Captain!" shouted someone from the corner of the room. Dennis smiled with half his mouth, raised a hand, and bowed with a flourish. Someone laughed. Margaret scowled. Abby was gone.

The street was quiet; no cars broke the silence, no headlights passed in the distance. Dennis traced the building facades with one hand, for balance, as he wandered past windows and storefronts. One doorway appeared particularly deep and darkened. Dennis stepped in and relieved himself in the alcove.

Watch your step in the morning, guv'nah! Hah!

Warm summer air at his neck, he was reminded of the better times he'd had drinking—when alcohol brightened, instead of dulled, the edges of everything. With friends in Grant Park, watching music; on patios in Chicago, with other friends; with Sylvia. In none of these memories, he noted, was he alone.

Nor, it seemed, was he alone now; even as he'd begun to pee, he'd smelled Bruce's breath and heard the slightly irregular footsteps caused by the one arm that didn't swing.

"Oh, hey, is that Bruce?" Dennis felt the stream of urine begin to slow and continued to stare at the door. "Look, my dick's out, but that's not an invitation—"

Dennis' head jerked forward hard enough that he was certain it would smash through the glass of the doorway. Wounds reopened a second and third time and one small strand of blood trickled from his forehead, the blow blessedly diminished by the brim of captain's hat. He was able to maintain his balance, tuck his penis back into his pants, zip up, and turn around.

Four or five—or six or seven?—of Bruce's entourage stood at the curb, by a row of motorcycles and scooters, presumably theirs. Dennis had no idea which one had ambushed him mid-flow, but it hardly mattered; their sinister grins were identical. Non-descript Scottish lads of low intelligence and high testosterone counts, all too happy to join the riot. Scotland was surely no rougher than Chicago, but in Chicago, Dennis knew the neighbourhoods to avoid. He had only been beaten once in Chicago—and then because he'd been caught in an alley with the beater's fiancée.

"I've ne'er met someone with a mouth the size of yours." Bruce stepped into Dennis' considerably diminished line of vision. "It's astounding. Do you think these boys aren't looking for an excuse?"

"An excuse for what? Beating me up in full public view?"

Bruce laughed and looked around at the empty street; the Rat and Raven was the only operating establishment for blocks.

"You're really fucking things up around here." Bruce stepped closer to Dennis, even as two of the lackeys grabbed one of Dennis' arms apiece and forced him out onto the sidewalk. "I mean, well and truly. First, you start poking around where you shouldn't be poking around, if you know what I mean."

So you've been sticking your little dick where it doesn't belong, I hear.

"Then, you have the audacity to mouth off at me. At me! You've no idea what I've done to get where I am. I've built myself up from nothing. I own property. I own businesses. I have friends. People *respect* me."

"And fear you," Dennis said wearily. "Don't forget fear."

"Are you afraid of me, Dennis?" Bruce's eyes grew keen. Dennis wasn't certain how to answer the question and chose to ignore it.

"It's a bit irrational, isn't it?" he asked instead. The lads' grips tightened, though Dennis' tone was calm, even contemplative, as if he were talking to himself instead of Bruce. "I've not done much. I only insulted you after one of your boys here made me kiss the table. As for Margaret, well, that's your business, but it seems you wanted something you couldn't get. Not used to that, I suppose?"

The mention of Bruce's failed seduction brought an angry blaze to Bruce's eyes. For a moment, he looked like Eddie, until Bruce moved within inches of Dennis face and he could see the flare in his eyes only *looked* like fire.

"Oh," said Dennis, before Bruce could speak. "I get it. The manhood. Shouldn't have insulted the manhood."

The punch was swift, its motion like Anton Chigurh's bolt pistol to his solar plexus, and it knocked Dennis' breath out onto the curb. Dennis coughed and sputtered and fought the urge to relocate the contents of his abdomen, organs included, onto the sidewalk.

Bruce isn't just a talky prick with tough friends. This guy's arm is a pneumatic punch.

"You know what bugs me the most?" Bruce stepped back and half-smiled. "Not that you're American, though you're all either a bunch of poncey whiney faggots or a bunch of fat stupid idiots. Not that you fooled Margaret into bed, which, whatever, good job, I suppose. She'll have her own problems, what with me shutting the pub come September. No, what bothers me is that in another world, Dennis, I'd probably like you."

Oh, don't even say it, Fawlty.

"In fact, you're probably a lot like –"

"The fuck I am," Dennis said, and spat in Bruce's face.

Dennis saw no movement. He only saw red, black, and red again. It seemed impossible that every blow came from Bruce; perhaps it was like Glasgow again, and each lackey had an appendage in the mix.

Then, as if the violence were a cloud, it drifted away. The sounds of the storm—grunts, punches, shouts—simply wafted away from Dennis and across the street. Through swollen eyelids, he watched the donnybrook continue there. It had begun as four or five—or six or seven—men against one. Now, it appeared to be the same, with a decidedly new turn.

He's like Yoda in Attack of the Clones, Dennis mused, before he slipped downward to the sidewalk.

Dennis' pop culture comparisons had rarely been so apt. He witnessed improbable leaps, inconceivable spins and a whirlwind of movements, and though there were no light sabres, the tiny creature at the centre of the maelstrom appeared like a grey-skinned version of the green-skinned Jedi.

Eddie wore a trenchcoat, dark sunglasses, and his blood-mottled beret, and even before Dennis could focus properly, three of the five lackeys—yes, he saw, there were five—were reduced to limp, moaning figures on the pavement. The sudden appearance of the pint-sized juggernaut had shocked the crew, but now one of the two upright lads seemed to recognize that their assailant was a newcomer. Eddie stopped moving long enough for the lad to raise his fists in a classic fighter's stance, as if in challenge; the little creature met the challenge by clasping his hand around one of those fists, hosting himself upward and hurling himself onto the lad's shoulder. He swung around the back of the lad's head in defiance of gravity as he slammed two fists down on either of the lad's temples. The lad swayed a moment, a cartoon giant felled, before he tilted towards the ground.

Just as the lackey started to crumple, Eddie leapt from his shoulders and flew several yards before he alighted on the shoulders of the next lackey who was the last lad standing. Eddie repeated the temple-smash maneuver. It dispatched the final lad as successfully as it had the previous one.

Within seconds, the scene had gone from Dennis' imminent crucifixion to the aftermath of an epic battle. Only Bruce and Eddie stood, gunfighters on main street, posses felled all about them. Bruce appeared astounded, but only slightly so; his eyes darted from the boys, dazed like flies on the windowpane, to Eddie, to Dennis, and back again.

"Come on, then," Bruce said, and raised his fists.

Really? A munchkin dressed like a Black Panther just wasted five of your friends in thirteen seconds, and you're going to take him on?

At that moment Dennis realized Bruce was likely insane.

Voices arose down the road, and the excited call of "Fight! Fight!" caught Bruce's attention. As he turned over his shoulder, Eddie darted towards Dennis, grabbed his arm, and suddenly the two were…

…well, Dennis didn't know *what* was happening, or where they were going, or how they were going there. In an instant, he understood he was no longer on the High Street. Momentarily, it came to him he may have fled in the midst of an alcoholic blackout, but he somehow knew that hadn't occurred. There was a pause, in which Dennis could see the moonlight reflected off the gentle current of the Tay, and then images blurred and swayed around him. Then, as if by magic, he was on a sidewalk, half way up the steep Cairneyhill Road.

As if *by magic?*

"All right then," said a familiar gruff voice in the dark. "I'm not taking you all the way home. You need to walk some of that off or you'll have a hell of a morning."

Cairneyhill was steeper when the entire world was on an angle. Dennis leaned forward, as if into a strong wind, and trudged upwards.

"You're welcome," said Eddie.

"Hey, come on, give me a minute," Dennis replied. "I can barely concentrate on walking. But…yeah. Thanks."

"For?"

"We're really going to play this?" Dennis cleared his throat. "Okay. Thanks for saving my ass."

"You're welcome."

They walked in silence for a few minutes. Occasionally, when Dennis would waver, Eddie reached for Dennis' forearm, but Dennis pulled away.

"How'd you know?" Dennis asked.

"I smelled your blood," replied Eddie.

"From Kinnoull? How—ah, forget it. Of course you could."

They went another block without speaking. Moonlight flooded the fields by Saint Mary's Monastery. Crickets lay still beneath the pale blue light.

"I'm guessing you showed remarkable restraint back there," Dennis commented.

"Come again?"

"The fight. No spines were extracted."

Eddie rolled his eyes. "I dinnae do that no more, remember?"

More silence, save for footfalls; Eddie's a solid iron thunk, Dennis' an irregular, scrapey shuffle.

"Why'd you come help me?"

Eddie didn't answer. Dennis couldn't see him now. Despite his ability for preternatural speed, he'd fallen several steps behind.

"Eddie?"

"Yes?"

"Why?"

When Dennis turned around to look at him, Eddie was gone.

*

Alcohol tossed Dennis into a dark, dreamless crevasse, and the moment it strained its way through Dennis' system, it tossed him out again. In the distance, animals rooted and rutted in the dark; even as his head throbbed and he longed to pass back into sleep, he knew he wouldn't. He could sense his still-soddled brain beginning to reform, synapses reaching out

171

to one another like survivors of a shipwreck in the open sea, clasping together and holding on for dear life.

For some reason, as his thoughts and memories became clear, the more they were about Sylvia.

Sylvia.

Sylvia, in a hospital emergency room in southern Ontario, nervously checking her watch every ten minutes yet never leaving Dennis and the stoned, half-sleeping C.K. Dennis trying not to stare. Learning to cheat by gazing at her reflection in the window. A black turtleneck and vaguely mod haircut, entirely untrendy but somehow more stylish for it, a cross between a ska fan and an extra from Quadrophenia. Sylvia.

He remembered how he had become overtly engaged, perched on the edge of his seat, royally pissed at himself for hanging on her every word but unable to let go. It wasn't just the usual pop culture routine. They had talked about…everything. All night—until C.K. was seen and released at 10 am. He parted ways with her in front of her building, a double tall skinny cinnamon latte steaming in her hand, C.K. snoring in the back seat.

Snack Donkey got the distribution deal with Sylvia's company, and Dennis found himself courting Sylvia. He felt as though he were fifteen again, back when everything mattered. For months, he drove the nine hours to Hamilton for only a single day before he drove back to Chicago again, jacked on Red Bull and chocolate covered coffee beans. He would have driven to Canada just for one single hour, he knew, though he would hardly admit this to himself, let alone Sylvia.

I'd do it again, Sylvia, if we could be different people. But we can't be, now can we? We are who we are.

Except, of course, for Eddie, the horrific little freak who wanted to be a real boy. Dennis could hear him outside, scuttling about the firepit. His iron boots hit the dirt as if each footfall were sunk into the earth by a fence pole driver.

Outside the tent, the sky was a milky orange and red, the colour of a tequila sunrise heavy on the grenadine. Eddie crouched some yards away, near the dark wood panel that warned of DANGEROUS CLIFFS, his eyes on the bushes just beyond. As Eddie turned his head to Dennis, a small rabbit broke from the foliage and cut left. Eddie closed his eyes with a sigh, listening to dinner scamper away instead of chasing the creature, which he surely could have caught. Something was on Eddie's mind, something greater than saving Dennis' drunk ass from bullies, so Dennis kept his questions to himself.

The sun rose and a layer of fiery orange spread itself atop the treeline. Something black and fungal seemed to have taken root in his chest. A sense of regret and disappointment. He was numb. He was also completely free of ideas. He had only a few weeks to find a way home and upload the Random demos. It was an emergency now. All he had to do was swallow his pride and call Stephanie. Or his parents. Or even Sylvia. He could grovel and beg, invent stories or excuses.

Like you could have done all along.

Yes. But…

Eddie continued to crouch, his head lower than Dennis' knees, perilously close to the edge of the allegedly dangerous cliff. One nostril worked harder than the other, gaping open as Eddie squinted one eye through the brush, poised to pounce.

"Were you listening to any of the conversation last night?" Dennis asked.

"You mean before Bruce began with the beating?" Eddie replied. "Aye."

"Did he say something about shutting the pub?"

Before Eddie could answer, a loud call came from behind them.

"Deh-nis?"

Dennis started as Eddie stifled a yelp and toppled forward through the brush and over the edge of the cliff. He clutched at a cluster of weeds he'd snared between his talon-like fingernails, his cracked, ashen hands working to hold himself. A look resembling fear crossed his face briefly, before it flattened into resigned annoyance. Dennis snickered. Eddie glowered and dangled.

"Dennis, oh dear, yes, Dennis! Hellooooo?"

Gigi was the size of a small Japanese delivery truck and equally as bulbous. Her tie-dyed T-shirt was not sized for the swell of a pregnant

·

belly; it barely covered it, its globular pink underside visible beneath, taut and slick with sweat. Gigi's grey-streaked hair was askew from swatting at gnats. She was panting but looked no more tired than she had after her last climb.

"Gigi, what are you doing here?" Dennis traversed the narrow dirt trail that led from the outpost to the clearing. "What are you doing coming up here? I thought William gave you what-for last time."

"Och, aye." Gigi brushed the strands back behind her ear, adding a puff of air from her lips to the effort. "I'm too pregnant, I'm too old, I'm too old to be pregnant and climbing mountains. Och! It's fine, it's lovely to get some exercise, so long as I'm not hurting the baby, yeah?"

"Yeah indeed. Left William with the brood, I suppose."

"Aye! He thinks it's lovely, though, Dennis, it's not a babysitting task, he's their *father*, and he loves it!"

"Lovely," Dennis said dryly. "What's up? Why didn't you just call?"

"Why call when I can come to the Hill?" Gigi put her hands on her hips, proudly jutting her egg-shaped prow forward, and gazed at the tower silhouetted against the morning sky. "Oh, I cannae wait to bring the baby up here when he's old enough. This is where he was con—"

"—ceived, I've heard the story."

"Yes, yes, of course you have, of course you have! Well now. Well then. I've come up here for a couple reasons. A couple reasons, yeah? First is a thank you. There's not been a problem, a spot of blood, an unwanted fire, a streak of spray paint, nothing. You've done a lovely, lovely job."

Dennis nodded, unsure how to respond. Mission accomplished, certainly, but hardly the way he'd expected. Eddie still fed on rabbits; he simply no longer left them on the grounds. The bones and guts were scattered about, while the skins were stored in a crag on the hillside to which only Eddie could climb down. "Hate to waste 'em," he'd said. "Best to show some respect to the wee beasties. Maybe I can tan 'em and use 'em some day. Make a nice winter coat or something."

Of course, there had been some potentially troublesome teenagers one evening, and they had been deterred—though not by Dennis. They'd approached, pint tins in hand, ready to make a fire. Dennis had stepped out and asked them leave. They had laughed. Eddie interrupted the laughter with his own special brand of freakish grunting and groaning.

"What the fuck is that?" one of the kids had asked.

"You wanna stick around and find out?" Dennis had replied.

They had not, in fact, wanted to stick around and find out.

"I've done nothing," Dennis told Gigi, "but I'm glad it was effective."

"Effective, yes." Gigi breathed deeply and smiled, a forced smile, the smile of someone about to deliver what might be perceived as bad news. "Effective! Indeed. You've done your job well, just so lovely, we couldn't have asked for more…"

"…but…?"

I did my job so well that I'm no longer needed.

"You did your job so well that you're no longer needed, Dennis," she finally finished, looking down. "Maybe it's a good thing, yeah? No more tents and sleeping bags? A real bed somewhere? A real job somewhere?"

No.

Panic burst form his heart and filled him. His skin began to itch.

Not now. Not now!

He had considered himself an idiot for not calling his parents. A bigger idiot for going into Glasgow. A supreme fucking jackass for taking a ridiculous, highly unlikely job—if it could be called a job—thwarting vandalism on a Scottish hilltop. This was finally a way out, something to force his hand. He had no choice. He'd have to submit, to go cap in hand to someone, deal with the withering contempt of his wife or the deflating disappointment of his parents. He *had* to.

So why was his mind screaming *not now*?

"We just cannae afford you anymore," Gigi continued, awkwardly, he eyes fixed over his shoulder. "It's out of William's pocket, yes, you see? If I could convince the Council we needed full-time security but no, still, no. And you, well, let's face it, there was never an actual person turned in, per se. Turned away, yes! So helpful! You did such good work. But, ah, as for the reward, there's, well, there's no reward. No arrest was made, yes?

We cannae pay you another month hoping you'll run into someone, no, that's not going to work at all, Dennis, I'm so, I'm so sorry."

Something jabbed at Dennis' ankle.

"It's coming down end of August," he heard her say as he looked about his feet. "About to get colder on you, yeah? Too cold for ruffians and the like, too, I think, certainly, yes, for certain. I know you're not, well, not *legally* supposed to work, but I could put in a good word for you, perhaps? Somewhere else? Some, you know, less eccentric employment?"

This time, whatever had poked begun to press. Dennis looked down. A long, slender branch protruded from the bushes and tapped against his ankle.

"Ah, just a moment, Gigi, would you?"

Dennis walked to the bush and squatted, hands on knees. Nearly invisible but for the eyes, Eddie lay flat in the brush. His eyes flickered, and for a moment, the strange illusion of fire wavered, rippled as though the flame were being extinguished from within. When he spoke, Dennis was dumbfounded.

"Don't go," Eddie said. "Not now."

Not now.

"My, what's happening there, Dennis?"

"Nothing!" Dennis called. "Oh, nothing, just thought I heard a… wait…"

"A what?" Gigi asked. "I thought I sensed something in the brush, too!"

Dennis looked down at Eddie and up at Gigi, who tried to peer over Dennis and glimpse what he saw. She looked perilously close to moving in his direction. *Come up with something, Duckworth. You're on the make. You're in a mode. You're…oh, for fuck sakes, you're a good liar. Lie!*

And then it came. And when it came, *as* it came, it ceased to be a lie.

"You lived in ruins, yeah?" he whispered to Eddie.

Eddie nodded with an eyebrow cocked, as if to answer and mock the question simultaneously.

Dennis stood and faced Gigi, who appraised him with a queer look. "What was it?"

Dennis ignored the question.

"Gigi, the thing is, the job's not done."

Gigi had not expected that. "Oh, well, how do you mean?"

"It's the bigger picture, Gigi." Dennis stepped away from the precipice, past Gigi, and into the centre of the clearing where the walls of Kinnoull Tower rose on three sides.

Centre stage, Dennis. Now go.

"We've stopped the vandals," he began. "That was what we came to do. But we didn't do it just because they were a nuisance, or breaking the law. We didn't do it to please queasy tourists or because you're a member of PETA."

"I *am* a member of PETA."

"But that's not why you did it!" Dennis emphasized the statement with a snap of his fingers. Behind him, the Tower rose to create a proscenium arch as he stepped firmly into his performance.

"You did it for something else entirely, Gigi. You did it for love. You love this place, don't you? You love it, you love what it means to you, to your family, to the baby you're about to have, who you love so unconditionally that you couldn't bear some snot-nosed punter-in-training defiling the place where the child was made."

Gigi nodded.

"I've had a lot of time up here, Gigi, and something has become very clear to me," Dennis continued. "I, too, have come to love this place. Not just the Tower—I suppose that would be a little weird of me. No, this entire park, this place, and all the creatures I've encountered within it. I want to help you just a little more, Gigi; help you make sure this place will stand strong for another hundred years. Look."

Dennis stepped to the Tower wall and placed his fingers on one of the looser stones. The mortar around it crumbled, and the stone came loose in Dennis' hand.

"You see? Look at how easily I did that. Of course you've had restoration crews work on this place before, but how long ago? How much of a priority is it? No one important to the history of fair Scotland lived here. No one lived here at all. The Earl of Kinnoull and Lord Gray of Kinfauns, they were showing off in 1829, trying to make something that looked cool. And sure, it looks cool. But we both know it means more than that. With every passing year, with every passing hiker through the Woodland, every passing driver who glanced up from his lorry to see this stately ruin silhouetted against the sky, every view of Kinnoull Tower made it something more, something that stood as an emblem for the entirety of history and beauty and humanity here in Perthshire. Tell the Perth and Kinross Council that they need to have someone set about putting this monument right before the winter comes, and tell them you've found your man."

Gigi stood rapt at the monologue's flight into melodrama.

"My father was a mason," Dennis said. "I'm not talking the square and compass and Illuminati and pyramids on the dollar bills, I'm talking about stonemasonry. When I was a kid, they hired him to restore the Old Water Tower. That tower was the only thing to survive the Chicago Fire, and they trusted *my father* to restore it. It looks like a castle, too, a little. Call it fate, call it luck, call it karma, I believe everything happens for a reason. My father taught me everything he knew about historical façade restoration, and here I am, on your doorstep, willing to do the best job that can be done, and for next to nothing. You need the Tower. The Tower needs repair. I need a job. What do you say?"

Dennis had seen his routines work before, but rarely did he see them work so well without the benefit of darkness and alcohol. Gigi was almost breathless. She looked as though she was about to applaud. Then, as was her wont, she did.

"Dennis," she said, almost tearfully, "that was lovely. Lovely!"

Dennis leaned forward in a mock bow.

"You're right, of course. Of course you're right! This is something you could do officially, yeah? Officially and not out of William's pocket, it's like a job, a real job, minus the real papers, of course, but a real job and something…why didn't you say something about this before? How did you keep that quiet?"

Because my father actually built subway lines. I made up this water tower shit thirty seconds ago.

To Gigi, Dennis merely shrugged.

"Okay, lovely, wonderful! Yes. I am sure I can convince them. Sure of it! Let's see what we can do here. Oh, Dennis, I'm very excited. This could work out for all of us!"

Gigi fluttered in circles, inasmuch as one can describe a pregnant woman as "fluttering," before bidding farewell. She bounced up to Dennis, stood on her toes and, incredibly, kissed him on the cheek.

"Thank you, Dennis Duckworth."

As Gigi's footsteps faded down the trail, smaller yet heavier ones approached. Eddie trundled out of the bushes with an armful of small logs and fallen branches.

"That, my son, was most impressive. I especially liked the part where you quoted Ghostbusters."

"Bill Murray was the king of the improv monologue. Whatever. I was winging it. From top to bottom. And that includes every single damned word about my father, of course."

"Hence your question about the ruins."

"Aye."

Eddie chucked at Dennis' use of the colloquial.

"Aye indeed. So, then, you're hoping I've gleaned some masonry skills."

Dennis said nothing.

"Well, Dennis, your intuition is good," said Eddie. "In the last century, every bloody castle I've landed in has been crawling with lackeys brought in by the godforsaken heritage committees. Heritage committees! The scourge of Goblin Scotland. And I needn't remind of you of my days at Dunnottar. Yes. I can do it, Dennis—and a spot better than those union buffoons."

Eddie lay branches for the fire, but seemed oddly preoccupied by the act; he lay and relay branches, crossed and recrossed, trying to build a perfect teepee over a perfect log cabin. He almost seemed awkward, as if the fire was a necessary distraction.

"You asked me not to go," said Dennis.

"I know." Eddie remained fixed on the firewood.

"Eddie?"

Eddie carefully hovered over the teepee, which teetered and fell into a mere bundle of sticks. Eddie, squatting on his haunches, sighed and hung his head.

"Believe it or not, Dennis," he said, "I need your help."

"You. The guy who can teleport me out of the town centre and start a fire by winking at a pile of firewood."

"Aye, smartass, aye."

"The one who's lived a thousand years and torn the throats out of ten thousand of my kind."

"I've already conceded, Dennis."

"Yeah, but I'm enjoying this."

"Aye." Eddie seemed barely able to meet Dennis' gaze; he seemed humbled by the situation. "It seems ridiculous. Sad. Yet it's true...I need a favour of you. Which is why I was so quick to agree to this masonry project. It evens things out. Gives the situation more of a classical folkloric element, don't you think? Like Rumpelstiltskin giving the queen three days to guess his name. Like duping a kappa into swearing an oath. That sort of thing. The good old 'arrangement with a powrie' bit."

"I didn't know that an arrangement with a powrie was a thing," Dennis said, "but okay."

"Do you really think the impossible's possible?" There was a plaintive quality—a sincere quality—in Eddie's voice that Dennis had not yet heard.

"You keep referencing that and I'm only half-sure what you mean. You mean, do I think you can pass for human?"

"Yes."

"I don't see why it's impossible." Dennis crouched down beside Eddie. "I'm a bit stymied on the teeth, the fiery eyes and the bloody hat, but yeah, I imagine it's possible."

"Then, I need you to help me pass for human, Dennis Duckworth." His voice had the tone of a confession. "I thought you'd be here for a spell, so I didn't ask earlier. That's another reason I'm happy for the masonry. I didnae sense the urgency. I didnae imagine you'd be on your way."

Dennis looked at him as finally the fire began to lick at the bottom of the collapsed teepee.

"I cannae stay here forever," Eddie said. "I need to be amongst you. I need to be able to walk into Bell Memorial and read a book. I cannae sneak around town at night anymore. My kind are finished, Dennis. Either I retreat farther into the forest and disappear from the world, or I find a way to engage it. If I retreat, Dennis, it'll be no time before I'm back killing again. You're my key to the door that leads the other way."

Flames licked and crackled just below the haunted face of the red cap who had still not raised his eyes to Dennis.

"Of course, Eddie."

"Fantastic then." Eddie replied, face to the fire.

"But the price is higher than you think," Dennis said.

"My unparalleled conservational skills aren't enough for you?"

Eddie looked up at Dennis.

"My present is just the nexus between my past and my future, yes?" Dennis crouched down and held the red cap's gaze. "The nexus. Where one becomes the other."

"Aye."

"Well." Dennis felt the throb in his cranium spring back to life. "I'm supposed to be right here, at this nexus. I know it—I've always known it, somehow, or else I never would have stayed in Scotland. I would have swallowed my pride and called my parents, or the office, or asked Paul for the money to get home…but I didn't. Something stopped me. What I don't know is *why*. I'm supposed to be where one becomes the other, and here I am—but I don't know what the fuck that *means*. Basically, Eddie…I need the same thing from you that you need from me. I need *you* to help *me* pass for human."

CHAPTER NINE

Dennis didn't apologize.

In situations where he was called upon to apologize, indignation overwhelmed him; it was the source of many, if not most, of the fights he had had with Sylvia. Okay, maybe whatever he'd done that *warranted* an apology was the actual source of the argument, but his refusal to apologize was rocket fuel on the fire. He even avoided the "s" word in throwaway, casual or colloquial contexts—bumping into someone on the subway, asking someone to repeat an inaudible statement, consolation for the death of a loved one. He'd find other words—pardon me, excuse me, condolences—anything but "sorry." Sylvia had taken to calling him Fonzie, which sounded absurd and goofy, but it was never intended as funny, and never said with a smile.

"I'm not apologizing," he told Eddie now.

"Why the hell not?"

"Because I can't. I don't do that."

"Why not?" Eddie was perplexed. "You're not a sociopath. You feel remorse."

"Remorse," Dennis repeated. "Re…morse? I think I've heard that word."

Eddie sat atop one of the tower's short walls, his legs dangling, swinging his feet like a child. His iron boots occasionally thunked lightly against the stone.

"Careful, there." Dennis pointed to Eddie's feet. "Any cracks you make are yours to repair."

On the ground beneath the goblin's feet lay the detailed notes about every crack, crevice and loosened bit of mortar in the tower walls. As

Eddie's boot heels connected with the wall, a miniature landslide of debris fell onto the powrie's papers, obscuring his oddly slanted yet curiously legible handwriting.

"Don't change the subject," Eddie chided, as he stopped kicking.

"You can't just wave a magic wand over this and have it all shored up in a snap?"

"Och, you arse, no. I'm magic, not a miracle worker. Some things have to be done with shovel and stone, lad. This is one of them. The magic will come in how fast it happens. How well. Trust me. I'll earn you your money. Now get back on topic."

"Yeah. Well, I..."

"Remorse. You made an infantile joke about never having heard the word."

Of course you feel remorse, asshole, answer the man. Thing. Whatever.

But answering the man, or thing, meant admitting there was something for which he should feel remorse.

"Think hard, yank." Eddie was impatient. "A slight gnawing feeling in the pit of your stomach. A tiny bit of doubt about your actions."

"I know what remorse is, Eddie."

"Do you?" Eddie asked, not rhetorically. "I used to slaughter people as part of my daily routine, and I feel remorse. You're barely even able to repeat the word without turning it into a shitty joke. What about Margaret? Do you really not give a shit that you've ruined her livelihood by pissing off Bruce McKee, or do you just not allow yourself to feel badly?"

"Self-reflection has never been one of my strong suits," Dennis replied. "Self-reflection isn't even a suit I own. Not even buried at the back of my closet."

"In that idiom, 'suit' refers to playing cards, not menswear, genius."

"Whatever."

"Do you think that maybe if you let the shields down a moment, and allow something to get through to that craggy heart of yours, that might change?" Eddie said. "Here's what I've seen from you so far. When you fail, you say someone else has let you down. When you err, you say you meant to do it. Let's proffer an example. Your wife."

"Ex."

"Soon to be."

"Fine. What about her?"

"Why'd she leave?"

"I cheated."

"Why'd you cheat?"

"I was unhappy."

"And who's fault was that?"

Dennis shook his head. "That's not fair."

"Not fair!" Eddie cried. "Dennis, as far as I can see, you can feel remorse but you rarely do because you're too damn quick to absolve yourself of blame."

"The Margaret thing is my fault," Dennis allowed. "I mean, her debt is her fault, but I could have kept my mouth shut."

"Aye, you could have."

Dennis looked out over the patches of green in the distance. "Yeah. That's…"

"It's what?"

Don't be so dramatic, Dennis. You hate to admit to people you're wrong, but Eddie isn't people.

"That's something," Dennis continued. "I never meant to do that. I failed to think. I wasn't thinking about how it might turn out for her, I was just pissed at the prick. I…I'm probably sorry for that."

"Probably?" The goblin threw up his arms in exaggerated exasperation. "Are you for real?"

"I am. I *am* sorry for that."

There it was. No spinning the record around, no remix. The reality sank into him as he allowed himself to dwell on this fact for the first time. One of the reasons he refused to accept blame, he quickly discovered, was self-preservation. The feeling that grew in his stomach was like concentrated nausea, and he had never allowed it to grow before. Now, here he was, intentionally cultivating the sensation. It felt horrible.

"What does it mean to be sorry?" Eddie asked. Dennis looked at Eddie for the first time since the conversation began. "What does it really, truly mean, Dennis?"

"A regret." He spoke slowly, as if a universal definition was his to create. "To be sorry for something means if you could hop in the Tardis and go back, you'd not make the same mistake again. A feeling of sadness for something you've done that you wish you hadn't done. The genuine desire to make amends."

Eddie smiled, his silvery grey teeth meshed together in a slanted jumble.

"Can you grow a beard, Eddie?"

"A what now?"

"A beard. Facial hair."

"I…I don't know." Eddie was clearly taken aback by the sudden shift in conversation. "I don't shave, of course, but…well, if one's never grown in by now, one's not likely to grow in later. So I have sincere doubts."

"That's too bad." Dennis approached the powrie. Red luminescence shifted and flowed gently in Eddie's eyes, as though they were tiny monochrome lava lamps. "You could have grown it out to help hide those teeth. It would also have hidden some of the grey pallor. Someday, maybe, you can replace your teeth, but it's a big job and a lot of surgery. So, where to start? I think with clothes. A new wardrobe. You can still sneak in and out of places?"

"Of course."

"Well, then. I'm going to write you up a list, and you're going to go for the five-finger discount. Then we're going to take a look at something you've never seen."

"And what's that?"

"Your feet."

Eddie straightened both legs into the air in front of him. "Bye to the boots, then?" he asked.

"You can't wear iron footwear in the real world. Bye to the boots. And add to the list a grooming kit—you need to trim those talons back into something resembling a human fingernail. And a shower. Your hair…I don't even want to think about your bloody hair. Your literally bloody hair."

185

Eddie smiled again.

"Well, Dennis Duckworth, you've changed the topic yet again—"

"No," Dennis said. "I just need an emotional break. Regret is new to me. At the moment, I can only process one regret at a time."

"Oh." Eddie grinned. "Well, that's unfortunate, you poor, wee delicate flower, because what we just did here? That was simply the lesson. After this, there's the homework. You're going to write me up a list of clothing items. Then you're going to make a list for yourself."

"A list of what?"

"What in hell do you think? A list of regrets."

*

It was a surprisingly long list, and a surprisingly miserable night.

If this is price of self-reflection, I don't want to pay it.

An electric lantern illuminated the tent with an eerie white glow; in films, it was the quality of light that emanated from E.T.-concealing government tents and, fittingly, portals to other worlds. By this eerie light he spent hours staring at his homework.

The list was an excuse for meditation; a word Eddie had purposefully avoided as he wisely knew Dennis would scoff at the concept. Yet Dennis knew what was up. He had admitted guilt and a desire to make amends. He recognized the hole forming in his stomach wasn't an alcohol-induced ulcer. It was remorse. The list would help him meditate on remorse.

He should have known it would suck.

The names on the list were people towards whom he had, as they had said, "a genuine desire to make amends." The more he added to the list, the deeper and colder the hole in his stomach became. The more he stared at the page, the more he realized what an asshole he had become.

By 4 a.m., the list, and accompanying notes, read as such.

- Margaret (for fucking up her shit)
- Abby (for being a dick)
- Eddie (for having to save my sorry ass?)
- Mom and Dad (for being so grumpy over the yrs)

- ~~Sylvia~~ (for you know)
- 5/4 staff (for screwing up—maybe)
- Paul (already apologized!)
- ~~Sylv~~
- Various girls since forever (for, well, you know)
- Various everybodys since forever (for being a general prick)

The list was as finished as it could ever be without itemizing names and transgressions, a task that would take months if it were even possible.

Yet despite being finished, the list wouldn't let him sleep.

You never wanted to blame yourself.

Was that Sylvia's voice, or was it the list talking?

No, I didn't blame myself, he sort-of replied. I learned how to blame others.

So why in hell are you trying to change now, Denny? Don't you think it's a little too late?

Maybe. Maybe it is. Or maybe that mystical little bastard was sent here clean out the pipes. Let me have access to normal human feelings. I hate that snaggle-toothed little bastard for making me...

Making you figure it out for yourself? For tricking you into nurturing this horrible sensation in your stomach?

Yeah.

And so the list sat on his sleeping bag, face-up and somehow expectant. There was too much blank space. There were words left out. Not names—by God, if he were actually to write down the name of every person he could remember, the list would swallow him whole, drown him in blue ink. Yet there it sat.

What do you want from me, list?

The list, of course, said nothing.

You want me to figure it out for myself, too, don't you, list?

The list gave him a meaningful look that said you know full well that's what I want.

Dennis picked up the pen again.

A genuine desire to make amends.

I could never do it. Never in a million years. It's too much. It's too hard.

He was reminded of the film Unforgiven. He was no William Munny, with a past filled with carnage and lawlessness; he also had no Claudia to set him right. Besides, Eastwood went on a murderous rampage at the end of that movie, so the movie proved his point. He was who he was. A person can't change. They can't. I can't.

Still, he pressed the pen to paper. Beside Abby (for being a dick), he wrote: Apologize.

It was weak, but the list was encouraged.

Beside Paul (already apologized!), he wrote:

apologize again.

Beside 5/4 and mom and dad, Dennis wrote nothing. He had not truly done anything to the former, and could not begin to summarize the ways in which he owed some kind of recompense to the latter.

Beside Various girls since forever (for you know) and Various every-bodies since forever (for being a general prick), he wrote:

Live long enough to make one balance out the other. Start small.

The page was fuller. It seemed almost finished.

He erased the two crossed-out references to his wife and replaced them with question marks.

My wife. My ex-wife.

Dennis told people he'd married Sylvia because she was gorgeous, smart, and willing to move to Chicago—she wanted to start a career in fashion design, or get into the vintage business, and Chicago seemed as good a place as any, though ultimately she wanted to move to New York. Dennis' contempt for New York bordered on legendary, but he had promised he'd consider it.

Dennis had never intended to consider it. He had never intended to even attempt making peace with New York City. He was who he was; he was a proud Chicagoan, a proud enemy of the Big Apple, and his stubborn position only set harder over the next nine years.

If they couldn't move to New York, Sylvia reasoned, she could simply make her name in Chicago. She had probably felt as though he'd married her under false pretenses; occasionally, as the years progressed, her temper ran hotter, her fuse, her patience and her libido shrinking.

You're the one who caused that, Dennis.

He hated that, in the end, the decision to separate was hers; that the fault, ultimately, was his. But what was he supposed to have done? Put up with the endless cold shoulder? Wait until she was asleep and yank his own chain? Fuck that. She had done what everyone else had done. She'd changed on him. She'd changed the rules on him. She'd betrayed his trust. She'd let him down. He had trusted that Sylvia would remain Sylvia, that their relationship would remain strong, and she'd changed. After years of supporting Dennis and his world of lesser-known musicians, she'd wanted success and fulfillment of her own. Day after day, it got worse, until he'd gone to another rock show and found another twenty-two-year-old. The odds of getting caught were infinitesimal.

Infinitesimal, he soon learned, was not the same as non-existent. The girl was a college co-op student at a design studio. It wasn't the studio where Sylvia worked, but it was still the same industry. Within a few weeks, Dennis came home to Sylvia, eyes drawn into pursed holes, fists balled tightly at her sides.

"I hear you've been sticking your little dick where it doesn't belong."

She changed on me.

I'm sure you asked her quite nicely, Abby had said. I'm sure you gave her a reasoned explanation of why you wanted her to put away the cell phone.

Oh, Abby, it had nothing to do with the cell phone. It was me. I'm an asshole, and I don't know how to act like normal, pleasant human being, least of all with the people I care for.

Dennis made no mention to Abby of how he had felt when Sylvia made business deals by candlelight meant for dinners, not deal-making. No, of course he hadn't. He hadn't told her because he'd done no different in the early days of 5/4, and she knew it. Instead of being a hypocrite, he'd chosen to be a quietly simmering son of a bitch. He chose to compete with Sylvia instead. Wonderful choices, these had been.

Sylvia. He crossed it out, rewrote it, crossed it out again.

I can't do this one.

The last name was Margaret. It leapt off the page at him. He had brought his assholery transatlantic. Being a jackass was one thing; causing a near-stranger with whom he had slept irreparable damage…amends were not enough. Apology was no good. Ideas raced through his mind. Kill Bruce? Turn the city of Perth against him? Call the police? Rob a bank and give her the money to pay him? Of these, somehow, the bank robbery was the least insane. At least it was possible. But so was…

Beside Margaret, he wrote two words, and the list was satisfied enough to let Dennis sleep.

*

Regular people—those who had not been "through the gate" so to speak— would have found the aroma of eggs wafting across the clearing to be incongruous or downright weird. Dennis thought the same, but for different reasons.

Who taught the little bugger to cook eggs?

Despite being hunkered inches over the skillet, red flame dripping upwards around the blackened pan, Eddie showed no signs of being warm. Dennis, on the other hand, stood sweating in the warm morning breeze. One hand picked at an errant thread on his new jeans, and every few seconds, he shifted his weight from one foot to the other, as if pacing in place.

"You sure you know how to do that?" Dennis peered into the frying pan. "It's not like your people have had to cook, traditionally speaking."

"Traditionally speaking, you have ne'er known when to shut your gob," Eddie grumbled. "So, if I'm going to break with tradition, how about you do the same and shut it?"

"You sure you don't want me to do that?"

"Oh for Christmas' sake!" Eddie smacked the bottom of the skillet against the rocks that ringed the fire pit. "I'm bloody magic, remember? I'm quite sure I can manage a pan of scrambled. I'll poke your eyes out, you ungrateful bastard."

Eddie poked the air with one finger, a gesture intended to be threatening, but without the two-inch long fingernail and its flesh-piercing pointed curve, the threat was decidedly less ominous. While still thick and yellowish, like ancient bone, the nail—all his nails—had been cut, filed and buffed enough to resemble a human fingernail, albeit one with a questionable fungal infection.

"You found a grooming kit last night, I see."

"Found, yes, at the Tesco, if you can call that finding." Eddie curled his fingers and inspected his cuticles. "Hell of a job, this was. Like trimming shale, it was. Had to be done, though, and made a shower much simpler."

Where once there was a straggly, greasy frenzy matted with congealed blood, there was now a tamed ponytail of freshly washed grey hair.

"By god, that shower made a difference." The red cap held up a hand mirror he had tucked into the pocket of his tunic. "Except I look like Billy Connolly. However, with the proper eyewear…"

Eddie slipped on a pair of black plastic-framed sunglasses, hiding the red flicker of Eddie's irises. Those who had never spent time hanging with a goblin—which Dennis figured was most people—would at least mistake Eddie for an unhealthy, poorly aging dwarf. So long as they thought him human, Eddie would be pleased.

Dennis stepped back and placed his hand on his chin in an exaggerated pose of contemplation.

"Well?" Eddie prompted.

"Well…you're not there yet. But it's a start."

"It's not a start!" Eddie growled. "I started decades ago. This, Dennis, is the end. The last steps!" He stomped the ground—presumably to emphasize "steps"—and the solid weight of his iron boots pummeled the ground like sledgehammers.

"You might need to lighten up in the loafers, though."

"I can keep 'em quiet." Eddie looked down at his footwear. "I found my way into the Tesco, not a sound. Can we just let the boots alone?"

"I don't care if you can prance about gracefully like you're in the Royal Ballet," Dennis replied. "They look crazy. You don't have to be a fashionista but you shouldn't look like a renaissance faire reject crossed with an old-timey strong-man."

"A what now?"

"Iron boots? Works the leg muscles? Forget it, it really isn't important." Dennis smelled the sharp smoke of burning eggs, and stepped past Eddie to remove the skillet from the fire. "What's important is that you look human—but like a human today, not a human from several hundred years ago. That tunic…"

Eddie rubbed his tunic with two fingers and looked downward as he spoke. "I quite like it. Rabbit hide, you know."

"Look, maybe tomorrow you can hit the High Street and pick up some clothes."

"In the children's section?"

"If you have to, yes."

"Another snatch and grab under the cover of darkness, then."

Dennis stared at the creature momentarily.

"Neither of us has the money to buy you an entire wardrobe."

Eddie balled his hands into fists and beat them against his hips. "Och, I know, I know, Dennis. I'm…I'm impatient is all. You're not telling me anything I don't already know."

"You said you needed my help," Dennis said, feeling defensive.

"Aye! Stealing clothes in the night isn't something you can help me do. What I need are the little things, Dennis! None of the books I've read or movies I've seen has, for example, taught me how to ride a bus."

"You get on and sit down."

"Very funny, you wanker. No! Where does it tell you to pay? Do you give money to the operator or put it in a machine? Do you pay up front or when you reach the destination? Do you pay for return trips or only for one-way? Do you pay different fares for different distances?"

Dennis shrugged. "Different systems in different places, actually."

"Aha! You see, until now, I'd hadnae known that. Now, what about bigger things? I know how money works, but how do I get myself a job? What am I qualified to do? How good is my magic? I can't magically get myself a national insurance number."

"You're not supposed to exist," Dennis said, "and according to the world and the government and society, you really don't exist, Eddie."

"Aye. Nothing you can do about that. I don't expect you to hack into the public files of the United Kingdom, or mastermind my fake identity. I just need help with the ordinary business of living."

"What you need is to shut up and listen, then."

The red cap lowered his shoulders and raised his head, which gave his thick, stumpish neck a disconcerting length.

"You've been to the Bell Library, you said."

"Aye."

"Right." Dennis stuck his hands in his pockets and cocked his head. "In the dark of night, skipping past the security cameras. You probably don't turn on the computers, the cameras would see that, too. You probably have to prowl the stacks in the dark and grab books at random, looking over your shoulder the whole time. I understand you're impatient, and that you think you know how to dress yourself, but you've got your priorities all wrong. The first thing you need to do is fit in. I'm your fuckin' Henry Higgins, champ. So against your goblin morals though it may be, go on down and steal yourself some goddamn clothes. The sooner we have you looking more normal—or even less horrifying—we can set about this ordinary business of living you speak of."

Dennis grabbed two plastic plates from a mesh bag that lay beside the fire pit, scooped half the eggs onto one plate, and held it up to Eddie.

"And let's face it," he said. "Goblin or human, there's nothing ordinary about living anyway."

*

"Look at this guy," said Dennis.

Eddie turned his head over his shoulder and smiled.

"Only taking stock, lad, only taking stock. The real work will begin later. I've yet to gather the supplies I need."

"No, I meant really look at you," Dennis clarified. "I'll be damned."

Hands on his hips, Dennis stood with his head cocked to one side as he regarded the red cap. He was not dressed for the heat that continued to bake Perthshire. Instead, he wore dungarees—which Dennis, being American, thought of as bib overalls—and a long-sleeved T-shirt underneath. His new habit of taking showers—Dennis knew not where, nor did it matter—had shown that Eddie's skin was also less gray than previously thought. Though he still appeared ashen, it was less corpse-like than before. From these few meters away, Eddie's frame was child-like, but close up, in a best-case scenario, Eddie would have to pass for a human dwarf. His proportions were not those most people associated with dwarfism though. The dungarees somewhat disguised this fact.

"How does it feel?" Dennis asked.

"Odd," admitted the powrie. "My clothes were rags, but there was a certain comfortable quality to them. These are so restrictive! Sometimes it feels like a form of bondage torture. How do you put up with it?"

"We're a race of masochists."

"Aye, I can believe it. So, I took a skip through the boys' section and came up with these. Hides the frame, I thought. Do you think it succeeded?"

"Aye. You look like a little kid."

"Great!" Eddie sounded genuinely pleased. "I know I'm shaped like a wee lad. It helps to know what I look like to others. If I'm going to call myself a dwarf, I'll have to explain why I dinnae look like one. I'll have to tell people I'm a proportional dwarf."

"A what now?"

"Many dwarfs suffer achondroplasia. The proportions are different."

"Achondrowhatnow?"

"Just trust me, Dennis. I've had a few years to do the research. Oh! And, also, I found shoes. They look about right, though…we've no idea what size my feet are going to be."

"We have no idea what your feet are going to look like," Dennis said. "I'm just hoping you actually have five toes per foot."

"What do you expect, talons?" Eddie frowned. "I'm not a bloody eagle. Can we just get this o'er with?"

He gestured to his left, where there sat a small upright trolley, its chrome surface rusted in the ringlets around the soldered joints. Strapped to the trolley were two canisters—one green, one blue—affixed with dials, gauges and hoses.

"The torch?" Dennis asked.

"No, it's a nitrous tank." Eddie smirked. "Thought we'd get right messed before we burned off my boots."

"You are a testy one today," Dennis replied as he rolled the tank closer to the red cap. "Are you nervous?"

Eddie said nothing but he reached up, absently, to touch his bloody cap.

"Well, good job. I guess the torch was harder to find."

"Yes, and that's not something we're going to keep." Eddie crossed his arms. "All of these items were strictly borrowed. There's hundreds of pounds of gear here—and I mean pound sterling, not weight. I had to purloin it from a smaller company, owned by a regular private citizen, and if it's not back by the time he's home…"

"You have an over-developed sense of guilt for a homicidal goblin."

"Watch your sarcasm lad or you'll catch a glimpse of that homicidal goblin," Eddie warned, without much malice. "Yes. I feel guilty stealing from a young fellow starting up his own shop."

Eddie hopped up onto the wall, his feet dangling.

"A genuine desire to make amends," mused Dennis.

"Aye, lad. And you'll have some amends to make if you remove anything more than the boots and a few stray hairs."

"That's…" Dennis looked at the tools below him. "That, ah, shouldn't be a problem."

"What's the matter?"

"This is an oxy-acetylene torch."

"Aye."

"OA torches are shit with iron. We oughtta be using an arc-air torch or something."

"But can you still do it?" Eddie demanded. "I want this over and done with."

Dennis turned the oxygen knob a few times and turned the acetylene knob a fraction of one turn.

"I've used these things before," Dennis said as he eyed the torch. "I know I don't look the type, but I've done a bit of work, yeah."

A pair of goggles dangled from the cart handle; Dennis fitted them over his face. "I lied about my father being a stone mason and a restorations expert, but he actually did help build the El—the trains in Chicago. He started on the Skokie Line when my folks moved to Chicago in '62, and he worked on the Logan Square Line and the Dan Ryan Line. He worked on railroads before that. He'd tinker in the garage all the time, and I picked up some stuff along the way. But this kind of torch will ignite the carbon in the iron. We don't care about a clean cut, but it'll be slow, because it'll cause the iron to melt."

"Onto my flesh."

"I can do it more quickly because we don't give a shit about the cut looking good—but yeah, it might happen."

"Och." Eddie pressed his hands against the wall, moving his legs forward as if to jump down. Dennis pressed a hand to Eddie's knee to keep him seated. A surge of warmth travelled up his arm as he did so, and his already-overdeveloped senses surged momentarily; he had the sensation of barreling forward though a tunnel towards some brilliant yet horrible unknown.

Dennis yanked his hand away.

That felt like Frodo putting on the One Ring. Note to self—don't touch the goblin.

"You'll be fine," Dennis managed momentarily. "This iron's barely a quarter inch thick. You're not scared, are you?"

Dennis had assumed the red cap would be immune to pain—having forgotten his complaint about the paranormal tooth extraction—and was amusedly surprised when Eddie closed his eyes and grit his otherworldly teeth.

"Do it."

"Do you have a light?" Dennis asked.

Eddie simply glanced at the torch and a ten-inch flame erupted and spewed black smoke. Dennis turned one of the knobs until the black smoke all but disappeared, then another until the flame became a narrow blue-white cone of heat. He waved the torch over the toe of Eddie's boot, back and forth, pre-heating the metal, before he finally pressed a lever to begin cutting.

"I can't really pull back much, Eddie, so yeah, it might hurt."

"Och, it's not going to hurt me," Eddie replied unconvincingly, his eyes still closed. "I just don't want to see the scars you're going to leave."

"A mouth full of spikes and you're worried about the aesthetics of your feet."

"Pay attention, damn you!"

Dennis paid attention. Cautiously, he moved the torch from the rounded front of the boot's toe, over the top towards the ankle. Flame spewed as the carbon in the iron caught fire; sparks scattered across Dennis' knees and shins. A red-hot globule of metal dripped sideways from the ragged, molten crevice in the metal.

"Just leave it!" Eddie suddenly cried, leaning forward to grasp Dennis' cutting wrist. "I'll crack it open myself. Leave it!"

"There's not nearly enough of a gap for you to get your fingers into," Dennis replied, voice raised over the hiss of the torch. "I have to do some of the other side, at least, so you can get some leverage. You're not that strong, Eddie. Physics will still play a role, you know."

"You, sir," said Eddie, his voice tight between clenched fangs, "are a bastard!"

Eddie grunted, inhaled deeply, and maneuvered to face the opposite direction, draped over the wall on his stomach. Dennis aimed the flame towards the front of the boot again, and slowly pulled upward, extending the existing fissure backward, melting a line through the sole.

Over the hiss of the machine melting metal, Dennis thought he heard voices, but wasn't certain; he couldn't smell anything beyond chemicals and molten iron.

"Aaaaaah!"

Eddie kicked his foot backward in an agonized reflex. As Dennis realized what happened—he'd lingered too long in one spot whilst listening for sounds in the forest—the red-hot iron boot connected hard with his jaw. The torch leapt sideways from his hand, snuffed out the moment he let go of the control, and fell harmlessly into the dry grass, but a few driblets of molten iron sprayed across the browned turf. Tiny tufts of fire erupted immediately, but Dennis didn't notice them, blinded first by the pain in his jaw, and then by the more alarming smoke that rose ominously from somewhere around his waist.

The molten iron had ignited the front of Dennis' pants. He gaped in horror, without noticing two young boys had emerged from the forest to witness the ass-end of a little person thrashing in a prone position over a wall, sparks flying from his flailing foot, and patches of flame surrounding a man who lay on his back, desperately smacking his groin with open palms and making a pained, strangled exclamation with each slap.

The boys said nothing.

"What are you doing?" Eddie shouted.

"I'm on fire!" Dennis shouted back.

Eddie twisted around and jumped to the ground, where he crouched and beat the flames in the grass.

"Put it out!" Dennis shouted.

"Put yourself out!" Eddie shouted back. "You don't want my hands on your genitals, I'll tell you that!"

So Eddie stomped and smacked at the fires and Dennis padded down the flames on the front of his jeans as the two boys tumbled and leapt down the pathway in Woodland Park.

"Did you see its teeth?" shouted one.

"Did you see its eyes?" the other shouted back.

"My goddamn dick is on fire!" screamed Dennis.

*

When the fires were out, and neither Kinnoull nor Dennis' privates had sustained heavy damages, Eddie dropped to his behind and crossed his legs. Fine as the gap in the metal was, he managed to work his fingers through it to pry the boot apart, face crumpled into a tight ball of strain, lips pursed, a low, extended groan emanating from his throat. It rose and rose until it became an exclamation of victory; the boot snapped away in two pieces and fell to the side. There, exposed to air for the first time in millennia, was Eddie's left foot.

"Not much to look at," Eddie remarked after a silence.

For all intents and purposes, it was a regular foot. Its flesh was as grey as the rest of him, and its nails, like Eddie's fingernails, were thick, yellowy, and longer than looked comfortable. Dennis had expected withered, fungal horrors, but the magic that created Eddie chose, in its apparently random manner, to take good care of the creature's feet.

"Could use a wee pedi," Eddie mused.

"After a few hundred years in iron boots, you're looking pretty good." Dennis crouched and gestured a little further up Eddie's leg, where a charred black hole, at least a centimeter in diameter, burrowed into the ashen flesh.

"That hurt?"

Eddie regarded it, as if he'd not noticed before, and shook his head. There was no blister, no bubble, no blood, merely a hole, as if a cigarette had burned through.

"A minor injury, considering," Dennis said.

Eddie grunted but otherwise made no reply.

"We've got another one of those to come off." Dennis picked up the boot, now split open from the heel, like a used-up iron cocoon from which something had recently been freed.

"Wait a moment, will you, lad?"

"We can't wait a moment." Dennis returned the eyewear back to his face with a snap. "Let's finish the job now, before the trails fill up for the day."

"It's just…"

"It's just what?"

The red cap sat still, his eyes wide, searching the flesh of the arch of his foot.

"I've never seen my feet before," he said. "It's a bit strange to discover new physical parts of yourself after so much time."

He stared out across the Tay and the fields beyond and smiled.

"Aye, Dennis. A bit strange."

*

By the time both of Eddie's boots were peeled back and cast aside—the second with significantly less drama than the first—all the red cap was interested in doing was walking throughout the forest park.

"I've sensations I've never had before!" Eddie bounced from the wall to the grass to the fire pit, making a plume of ashes rise and float in the morning air. "I want to feel everything beneath my toes!"

Dennis could understand the desire, theoretically speaking, but was puzzled into silence by the sudden exuberance of his normally grumbly, unflappable friend.

"You go do that," he told him. "We're done with you for the day. Now, you wanna get to work on this tower again or what?

The expression on the goblin's face told him no.

"Some fuckin' fair trade we've got happening here," Dennis whined.

"What's your rush, lad?" Eddie stood on his left foot, stroking the top of it with his right foot. "I've a lot of work to do, but I'll have it done in a day or two. Your work, on the other hand, is gonna take a lifetime."

"My work, Eddie, is in Chicago. I've got things I have to do, and I need to be home in time to do them."

By Labour Day, to be precise. The sooner he was home, the better.

"Not that work, idiot. The other work. The work you'll need to put in so the world doesn't see you as a purulent boil on society's arse."

"Wow, thanks Eddie." Dennis was genuinely wounded. "I didn't realize the world thought me purulent."

"Your feelings, not mine." Eddie then leapt five, ten, twenty-five feet in the air to land on top of the tower walls and then the stack, a look of lunatic glee in his eyes.

"Hey, it's a nice day out!" Dennis called to him. "There's gonna be hikers!"

"Och, I'll hear 'em a mile away," Eddie replied. "Literally!"

"I never said I felt like an ass pimple," Dennis added.

"You thought it!" A moment later Eddie landed in the grass in front of Dennis with a soft poof. "You're not much for self-reflection, you've said. It's my task to remind you how you really feel inside. And you feel like a cancerous bulb."

"Like hell I do."

"It's okay, Dennis. It's okay to hit rock bottom, as long as you know it and try to climb back up. And it's okay to fail at it. Did I let one eviscerated spine set me back? No. And here I am, toes free in the grass, for the first time in my ancient life."

Dennis glared.

"I'll get on the work as soon as you get on yours," Eddie chided. "Start with the easiest one. Shorten your bloody list."

*

The list. Every time Dennis felt anxious about returning to 5/4, Eddie reminded him about the list. Once he got thinking about the list, everything associated with Chicago felt like a decades-old song you longed to drop from the set list. It was a big hit once, but you were more interested in playing the new stuff.

Dennis rummaged through his things, donned one of the few new T-shirts he owned thanks to Marks & Spencer, and doffed the captain's hat once more in defiance of the raging sun. When he set out down the trail, Eddie was perched in a tree, massaging the bark of the limb with his toes.

"Brilliant!" Dennis heard Eddie remark behind him. "Bloody brilliant!"

Eddie played with new sensations like it was Christmas morning. Dennis' heightened senses were less novel but continued to spin his head sideways nonetheless. From a hundred feet away, the false cheer of the HMV's florescent lights pinned his eyeballs to the back of his skull; with his newfound sensitivity, Dennis had to squint until they were bearable. Then, something stranger; even in the swirling cloud of aromas that surrounded his head, he could smell the combination that constituted

Abby's scent—shampoo, skin, soap, and just her, that combination of odors bodies emit but people no longer register.

Never, ever tell her you can recognize her smell, Dennis. That's just plain creepy.

Abby glanced at him when he came into the shop and quickly averted her eyes. It wasn't until he approached her directly that she spoke, even though she never removed her eyes from the wall in front of her.

"What do you want." Not a question, but a provocation and dismissal all at once.

"I wanted to apologize."

Abby sniffed. "Yeah, well, say it and move on, then."

"No, I mean really apologize, Abby."

Abby tilted her head in his direction. The look in her eyes made him wish she'd look back at the wall.

"I'm sorry I yelled at you for telling me I was drunk." After fifteen minutes' rehearsal, the words came easily, but not without effort. "It's a self-defense mechanism. It's…not something I understand, but it's something I do. Jesus, everything I do is a self-defense mechanism. I'm sorry I got mad about you bringing up my ex-wife, because really, who gives a shit. I'm sorry about telling you to fuck off."

"I didn't know you told me to fuck off."

"Oh." Dennis looked at his feet and up again. "Maybe you were already gone by then."

"Well, I called you an asshole, so tit for tat on that one." Abby half-smiled, but her eyes were suspicious. "What's brought this on, Duckworth?

"I'm not sure what you mean."

"Why are you apologizing?" Abby suddenly returned to her former self, less steely yet somehow equally distant. She leaned over the countertop and fixed her quizzical gaze on him as ManagerMan called to her from the back room.

"You told me that you never admitted wrongdoing in an argument." Abby waved an indifferent hand towards her manager as she spoke. "You told me about DJ Dennis, master of the remix. Apologizing is admitting you were wrong."

"Yes," Dennis agreed, "it is. I am admitting I was wrong."

Abby leaned farther across the counter, inches from his face now, her smell—*creepy*, Dennis—overwhelming him. ManagerMan called again; this time, Abby didn't even bother with a hand gesture.

"I'm going to get you in trouble," Dennis said.

"You might," Abby replied. "Not likely. I think my boss is afraid of me."

"I'm a little afraid of you myself."

It was difficult to detect, but Abby laughed at that.

"So yes," Dennis managed, "I admit I'm wrong. Because I was wrong."

"That's it?"

" … "

"That's it?"

"Well, no, of course that's not it." Dennis paused. "I'm also doing it because…because I, uh, I like you, and care about your opinion. I was hoping we could be friends."

Abby's eyes widened almost imperceptibly, and Dennis would have heard the change in her heart rate if he'd been less preoccupied with his words.

"Friends."

"Yes," said Dennis. "You know. Show in the '90s. I can be Joey and you can be Phoebe."

" … "

"Maybe you didn't watch that one."

"No, I know it. It was just a terrible joke."

"Sorry," Dennis almost whispered. "I'm just a little embarrassed and I tend to react to embarrassment with anger or crappy jokes. Anger isn't working for me, it seems, socially speaking—so there are bound to be plenty more of these terrible wisecracks."

Abby's eyes changed again, but Dennis wasn't sure what this new look meant.

"That sounds a bit more self-reflective than I'd expected out of you, Dennis. Have you been seeing a therapist?"

"I wouldn't call him a therapist, but he has worked a little magic."

"Elizabeth Wojcinski!"

Abby's head rotated so slowly it was almost unsettling, and when she faced her manager, Dennis could almost feel slivers of ice bounce off the man.

"Really? Would you like to call me by my middle name, too, so you can sound more like my mother, then?"

ManagerMan slunk away.

"Good Lord." Her head rotated back at a normal speed. "I should be getting back. He's clearly not pleased. Afraid of me yes, but perhaps not afraid enough to not fire me. So. Friends. Why?"

"Because of your sparkling conversation and obvious appreciation of my company. And…"

"Yes?"

"There's one more thing."

Abby sighed, her entire face falling slack in disappointment. "Oh. Oh God, you want something."

"Yeah. Yeah, it's true, I do. But it's not for me. It's for Margaret."

Abby's facial muscles returned to their previous positions.

"Margaret?"

"Yeah. Well, you know, I've …put her in a bad position."

"You pissed off the biggest asshole in Perthshire, aye, but Margaret got into his debt on her own. It's not entirely your fault."

"Yes, well, be that as it may." Dennis took a moment to collect his thoughts. "I…I thought of a way to help her out."

Abby cocked her head. "Go on."

"Well, it's…it's kind of a stupid idea, and it might not work, but I'll need your help."

"A terrible plan that might not work, you say?" Abby raised an eyebrow, but her eyes grinned. "Count me in."

CHAPTER TEN

The stink of petrol flooded the trail to Kinnoull Tower, pooling in puddles along its red needles and brown earth, thickening the air between the trees. To Dennis, it smelled as though a heavy lorry had driven to the top, where it had continued to rumble and sputter fumes that flowed back down the hillside and into his sinuses.

The rumbling and sputtering, however, did not come from a vehicle. In the clearing, Dennis could see large swaths of the tower walls had been draped with a rough brown fabric. Several large bags of sand and lime mortar lay open at the foot of the farthest wall, around the base of a large gas generator, painted green on top and rusted brown beneath. He recognized the apparatus it was currently powering—a forced-action mixer, like the ones he'd seen during some of his father's home repair escapades.

Above it all perched Eddie, impossibly defying gravity; he clung to the vertical surface like Spider Man. After a few moments Dennis realized the goblin's toes had a firm grip on a miniscule protrusion, while his right index finger gripped the tiniest of cracks. In the other hand, he wielded a trowel. His jeans were rolled up to mid-calf—a gummy, blistery blackened-red burn still visible on his leg—and his grey T-shirt was covered in mortar dust and sand.

"Oi!" Dennis shouted over the ruckus.

"I know, I know you're here, give me a second!" Eddie dabbed a small amount of mortar into a niche between stones, leaped backwards, landed on his feet beside the generator, and snapped it off with one hand.

"What do you think? It isnae bad for a day's work, aye?"

"You've…it looks like you've done half the tower!" Had Eddie been human, Dennis might have not believed a moment of it.

"Aye, that's about right." Eddie pointed upwards with the trowel and wiped his other hand on his pants. "The thing of it is, Dennis, it's not as simple as I'd expected. These were Victorians built this. A 19th century interpretation of what a ruined tower might look like. I'm used to real masonry—in real castles, hundreds of years older."

Dennis lifted the edge of one of the damp sheets of fabric and ran his fingers along the edge of wet, grey stone surrounded on all sides by lime mortar. "Jesuuuuuh, I mean, jeepers, Eddie—you cut new *stone?*"

"Aye, of course!" Eddie frowned. "D'ye think I'd leave it half-arsed? Hardly have a quarry nearby, so I've had to be a wee bit huntery-gathery with it. Luckily, it's mostly repointing work, lad—filling up the gaps. Maybe do some turf capping, but I'm not convinced the Council wants that look. Important to retain the look, disnae matter otherwise."

"And all this?" Dennis gestured to the fabric.

"Hessian!" Eddie tugged lightly on one of the pieces that draped the wall. "Stops the mortar drying out too quickly. If it dries too quickly, it falls out, white and crumbly. See, lime mortar doesn't dry out and harden—it carbonates. It's a *chemical* reaction, not a *drying* reaction, so—"

"Zzzzzzzzzz."

"Sod off. I'm explaining it to you."

"Then get to the point."

"I'll get to the point, and then I'll take that point and use it to gouge out your eyeballs, you impatient bastard."

"Easy, little fella."

Eddie shut his eyes and held his breath a moment.

"Okay, sorry about the little fella business," Dennis laughed. "What does it all mean?"

"It means this'll cure hard in a couple days, but it's a managed curing process."

"Managed curing process!" Dennis laughed again. "The red cap is overseeing a *managed curing process.*"

206

"As a matter of fact," Eddie said defensively, "yes, I am."

"Where in the world did you get the water?"

Eddie tossed a thumb over his shoulder towards several enormous barrels tucked behind the wall.

"Those must weigh—"

"One thousand kilograms per cubic metre," the red cap said with a dismissive wave.

"Eddie, how in the name of all that is holy did you get it *up* here?"

Eddie smiled. "Now isn't that something you'd like to have seen?"

Dennis smiled in return. "Yes. Yes, it is."

The two stood a moment, silently regarding the sun on its downward arc. A fine sheen of gold and silver reflected off the damp sackcloth.

"It all came from the same yard," Eddie said as he continued to stare into the horizon. "Seems the proprietor of said yard had a minor disagreement with the missus, and in order to set things right, he's taken her to Toulouse, though, really, why Toulouse, I've no idea. I've got six more days to finish up and return what amounts to four-fifths of his business investment. Sadly, I can't replenish his materials at this time."

"Maybe you can cut him a cheque once you've been paid," Dennis said dryly.

"Maybe you can teach me how to open a bank account," Eddie replied.

"Maybe you can find yourself that elusive national insurance number."

"There are going to be complications, aren't there, Dennis?"

"You can't open a bank account without identification," Dennis said. "Eventually we'll have to get you some. I don't know how or from where or from whom, but some day, you will…"

"…spring fully formed from the forehead of forgery," Eddie concluded.

Dennis smiled and nodded his head towards the tower. "Don't go too fast, now. They'll never believe one man could do it all so quickly."

"I'll keep it at a human pace," replied Eddie. "An extraordinarily competent human, but human all the same."

"Thanks. These days, any form of competency will look good on me."

"*Nae borra.*" Eddie wiped more grit from his hands. "Though this plan of yours, this plan to help Margaret…it makes me question your competency."

"What's wrong with a benefit concert?"

"You need a performer."

"I've chosen a performer."

"You've chosen a performer?"

"Yes."

"And…?"

"Ah," said Dennis, "yes. Well. Um…I think we should approach Kit Carson."

"Kit *Carson?*" Eddie looked aghast.

"Bad choice?"

"Best choice I can imagine since he had the biggest single of the spring and then completely went to ground, making him twice as famous. The thing is, he's a practically a child, with depression and anxiety issues, and, as I say, he's gone to ground. You can't get him because you can't *find him*. Aye?"

"I checked out North Inch," Dennis continued as if he had not heard. "If we keep it modest, their Council's not opposed to us going ahead."

"Dennis—"

"Now we've got to get about making posters—"

"—Dennis, for the sake of all that is holy, do you know where he is?"

"What was the question again?" Dennis seemed sincerely confused.

"Do you know. Where. He. Is."

"Not remotely, no."

"Ah." Eddie nodded. "Well. At least you're tilting at the biggest of windmills. Idiot."

"It's not a windmill," Dennis insisted. "Listen, Eddie, when all these supernatural shenanigans began, I pulled Kit Caron's name out of my ass. That was where I said I was going—to work with Kit Carson. If boarding passes and violent punters and accidental trains and notices on the Tesco bulletin boards and bloody goblins could bring me to this point, if they're all connected somehow, then…it's the only sensible choice. It's as though fate wants this to happen."

You don't believe in fate.

No, but he also didn't believe in goblins, and he'd helped one remove his iron boots all the same. Goblins and boarding passes and unexplained music in his head...all of it so surreal, a big box of crazy that he had come to accept. It was surreal, but it wasn't unreal. It was *real* real. With that logic, the box of crazy became a *toolbox* of crazy, with which he could draft and develop various feats of mental engineering to suspend his disbelief. Was it unlikely that he could find Kit Carson? Yes. What it unlikely that the boy would play even if he found him? Absolutely. Yet given the events of the summer, the term "unlikely" had become relative.

"Listen," he replied. "If we go through the usual channels, it's a definite no-go. But...you. You do have certain...abilites."

"Dinnae even start, Dennis. I'm a red cap, not a superhero private eye. I cannae find him. But you, master of every situation, have an alternative plan."

Dennis squinted. "What did you call me?"

"The alternative plan, Dennis. What is it?"

"We find him," said Dennis.

"We find him?"

"We find him," Dennis repeated.

"..."

"Then, when we've found him, we skip the famey-fortuney crap. If he's hiding from his publicists and the press, we act like he's a regular person, and we go *in* person. We make a personal appeal."

"A personal appeal."

"Yes. He knows Margaret, she used to teach him a while back."

"So, two strangers pulling into his drive and asking him to play for free for the benefit of a former teacher, this is the best approach."

"Former substitute teacher."

"*This* is the best approach."

"I'll admit, it's a long shot."

"I'll admit you're an idiot." Eddie stalked away, towards the generator, and slapped it back on again with the palm of his hand.

"What are you doing?" Dennis shouted over the noise. When there was no response, he followed Eddie to the generator and turned it off again.

"What are you doing?" he repeated.

"Getting back to work," the red cap replied. "Hoping you'll come to your senses."

"So you won't help me find Carson?" Dennis asked. "The magic little creature won't have a little faith in the unlikely?"

Eddie stared at Dennis a moment, amusement stirring in his eyes. "I didnae say that," he said. "I've plenty of faith in the unlikely."

"You just aren't sure you have faith in *me*."

"Forgive me, lad, but you're right." Eddie sounded reluctant to admit it. "Every time I think about this plan, I think about your half-baked scheme to land your band a record deal. I can't help but think this scheme is headed in the same direction. But I'll go with you, lad. I'll go. On one condition."

"Oh, this should be good."

"You take me into town tomorrow," Eddie said.

"Okay."

Eddie looked up at Dennis, his eyes searching Dennis' face for sarcasm.

"No, that was a serious okay, Eddie. We'll go into town. By daylight. Wear sunglasses and keep your mouth shut, and I think you'll be okay."

"You dinnae think I'll terrify the locals?"

"I think you'll pass for human," Dennis replied.

Eddie nodded sharply, as if concluding a business deal, and turned back to the tower and the work at hand.

*

"Look at that," grumbled Eddie as they passed their reflection in a shop window. "We're in need of a whimsical soundtrack."

The window revealed a harsh reality—they looked ridiculous. The Captain of Kinnoull Hill and his tiny friend. He removed the captain's hat and marveled at how his hairline had begun to reposition itself, moving ever-so-slightly up and away from his wide-set eyes. Beside him, the

Gollum-hued, nearly thousand-year-old creature and emergent Scotsman sported Ray-ban sunglasses, the ancient suggestions of blood and gore stained into the fabric of his cap.

Dennis loomed a full head-and-torso above the goblin, whose cap and sunglasses made him resemble some sort of poorly outfitted 1970's undercover policeman or an unconvincingly disguised whistleblower. To Dennis, the loose, greyish skin on Eddie's face—ultimately not so different than that of an elderly man, though decidedly ashen—appeared looser and greyer than the wizened knees of an elephant. The dichotomy between his height and his visage was so great, even Dennis was taken aback by the unlikely sight. Beneath the sunglasses, the flicker of fire was invisible, but the cap itself was a stinking, blotchy mess; if someone were to lean in too close for a whiff, Dennis would be helpless to explain the odour, like rusty iron and rotting flesh, that wafted about Eddie's head and attracted the more-than-occasional insect.

"Whimsical soundtrack," Dennis repeated. "More like a sad trombone."

For his part, Eddie was entirely unconcerned about how he looked. He was concerned with how he behaved. Every simple step they took—getting on the bus, counting out change, using the public restroom (red caps, it seemed, also needed to pee)—required a softly-spoken sentence of explanation, followed by some mild assurance, and completed with a louder, slightly more exasperated reassurance. Eddie knew Dennis was as tense as he, and forgave him the exasperation.

At one point, Dennis leaned towards Eddie as they approached an intersection.

"Okay, this is a stoplight. Red means stop. You're—"

"Oh, red means stop?" Eddie placed both palms against his cheeks in mock surprise. "I assumed it meant to immediately start stabbing your neighbor."

"Funny."

"I'm improvising."

"Your improv needs work." Dennis massaged the back of his neck, rigid as oak from pretending not to look at Eddie, at others, into mirrors, et cetera.

"Your textbook needs an upgrade," snapped Eddie. "I know what a bloody stoplight is."

The duo crossed, ordered venison sandwiches at the sandwich shop, and sat on the same benches where Dennis had sat with Abby on a day that now seemed long ago.

"Listen," Dennis said. "Maybe it's just as easy if I go about my business and you just wander through the streets yourself."

It was a bluff, and Eddie sniffed it as such, but he felt the cold hand of fear close around the base of his spine. Eddie gazed about the square, already filled with an early lunch crowd. Once upon a time, they would have *been* lunch.

"I dinnae think that's a step I'm ready to make."

Humility and wonder. How new are these emotions for him?

"Then again," Eddie continued, "just mimicking your movements, your actions, your interactions—seems to nudge me in the direction of being human. A surly, sarcastic and pathetic excuse for a human perhaps, but—"

"Careful. I'm the only sensei you've got."

Eddie said nothing.

"Hurry up and finish your sandwich, little fella."

Eddie stopped mid bite. "Do. Not. Ever. Call me. Little. Fella."

Dennis grinned. "I told you I was an asshole. Now hurry up. We've got one more place to go."

"Another errand?"

Dennis swallowed his last bite and stood.

"You'll see."

*

Red flowers lined the edges of the strikingly green lawn of the A.K. Bell Library. Though his eyes were shielded by sunglasses, Dennis saw, from the shift in the wrinkles on Eddie's forehead, that the creature's eyes had flown open wide in recognition.

"The library!"

"Of course," Dennis said, pleased at Eddie's surprise. "You didn't think we'd skip the library, did you?"

"I've never seen it in the daytime." Eddie's voice was distant, as if floating away.

"Good afternoon, Dennis," said Meaghan Behind The Counter, whom Dennis had stopped thinking of as a rolly-polly little bat-faced girl, and now simply thought of as Meaghan.

"Afternoon, Meaghan. You're looking sparkly this afternoon."

Meaghan Behind The Counter blushed and clutched at the line of sub-rhinestone stick-ons that bejeweled her sweatshirt. "It's a bit sparkly, I know."

"Do you like it?"

"…yeeees," Meaghan replied cautiously.

"Then sparkle away."

As usual, Meaghan flushed, but this time, something was different. Not for her—she heard the same casual flattery she heard every week. This time, however, Dennis' sentence lacked its usual thick sediment of sarcasm.

"Your usual?"

"Yeah, an hour of internet, please."

Dennis glanced about for Eddie, but the goblin was gone, lost among the stacks, where Dennis guessed he might remain for the rest of the day; he'd have to scout him out when it was time to leave. Once Dennis logged into his computer, though, he felt the creature's presence by his side.

"So," he said to Dennis, "this is the fabled Internet."

"Says the fabled creature."

"So much information."

"So much to ignore."

"If your books are the best and worst of you," Eddie said solemnly, "then the internet will be the extreme best and extreme worst. Can I—"

"Git!" Dennis swatted Eddie's hand away from the mouse. "We'll come back, buddy. I want to get this Carson stuff out of the way first. Check some of the message boards, see if anyone's got a real idea where he might be."

"As far as you know, he's on the other side of the ocean," Eddie sulked, still wounded by the rebuke. "Or in Vladivostok, or on the bloody moon."

"It doesn't matter. It has to happen. We have to find him."

"Hello, Mr. Carson." Eddie's voice elevated to a pitch of mock cordiality. "We would be honoured if you'd come home from Fiji to play our benefit on the North Inch for some woman you barely remember!"

"He's not in Fiji."

Eddie and Dennis looked over their shoulders at Meaghan, looking sheepish.

"Sorry, I don't mean to eavesdrop or intrude, but he's not in Fiji."

"Ah."

"He's at home with his parents." Meaghan reddened under the intensity of Dennis and Eddie's unblinking stares. "He's...he's just taking a little time off. One song, one viral video, and suddenly he's the big heartthrob superstar and you know, he just wants to play music, and I suppose he..."

"Got spooked," offered Eddie.

"Yes."

Despite all his talk of having faith in the unlikely, it was this conversation that struck Dennis as the unlikeliest of all events.

"And you know all this because...?" he asked.

Meaghan looked down at her bejeweled bosom. "I'd rather not say. I probably shouldn't be telling you any of this and I don't want to get people in trouble. I shouldn't have been eavesdropping, either."

Thank God you were, thought Dennis.

"It's okay, Meaghan, your secret's safe with us. We're glad you told us. We really need to find him. We wanted to put on a charity concert, something small, something local. Something that might help him ease back into public life again, too. Something for everyone, if you will. That's what we're looking to do."

"What's your charity?" asked Meaghan.

"Ah...the..."

"Friends of the Rat and Raven," Eddie said.

"Animal rights, then?"

"Yeah, sure," Dennis replied.

"He really likes any charity that involves children and the arts," Meaghan said. "Musical instruments for children, that sort of thing. For the right cause, he might just do it."

"Thank you, Meaghan," said Eddie, "you've helped us immensely. If you've time, perhaps you can help us convince him!"

Meaghan shook her head stiffly. "No, no, I can't do that. I haven't the power. You'll have to convince the father. It isn't Carson. It's his father.

"Bankfoot," she added in a half-whisper. "It's not even a twenty minutes' drive."

The bell at the front desk dinged, and Meaghan closed her eyes in relief.

Dennis started to ask another question, but before he opened his mouth, she was off.

*

The car park at the foot of Kinnoull was a narrow strip of asphalt, deep enough for one automobile to park perpendicular to the road. There were only a handful of spaces, and as the sun disappeared behind the hill, the day's hikers retired to the city below. Dennis and Eddie crested the Cairneyhill Road and saw what Eddie had found in the night.

"A Citroën?"

It was a 1987 model at best, rust-laced and dent-adorned. Its trunk, tied shut with red wire, was plastered with pro-John Major bumper stickers.

"Bah!" Eddie spat into the dust at the side of the road. "You wanted a Range Rover?"

"No, this'll do," Dennis replied. "Actually, this isn't too bad."

"It's going back tomorrow, you covetous fathead." Eddie picked a fleck of rust from the rear driver's side bumper. "I've 'borrowed' enough for the sake of us, don't you think?"

"Sure. You wouldn't have had to borrow *anything* if you'd just agreed to, you know, magic me up there the way you did the night you saved my ass."

"And when the Dunlops call the coppers to have you arrested for

215

harassment and/or trespassing, you can explain to them why we came twenty mile on foot."

"Driving it is, then."

"And I'm driving," Eddie muttered hesitantly.

"What!?" Dennis laughed and held out his hand for the keys. "Okay, and when the 'coppers' pull us over because they can't see a person in the drivers' seat, you can explain to them why you're driving without a license."

"It's a manual transmission."

Dennis let his shoulders fall in an exaggerated pose of frustration.

"You know I can't drive standard. You did that on purpose."

"Of course I did it on purpose!" Eddie bounced from one foot to another like an excited child. "Dennis, I developed a taste for it last night. More fun than I would have expected. You'll not regret it. I'll not do anything stupid."

"It's not stupidity I'm worried about, it's legality. You have no human identity, let alone a driver's license."

"There's a child's booster in the back," Eddie said as he pushed past Dennis and into the driver's seat. "Pass it to me and at least I'll be able to see the road."

"Then you can't reach the pedals."

"Well, dammit, which is more important?"

"A bit of both would be good."

So Eddie pulled the Citroën smoothly out of its parking spot and began to coast down the hill, feet barely able to rest tip-toe on the pedals, eyes barely above the horizontal line of the dashboard.

"Hey," pondered Dennis aloud. "Why in hell do you drive a stick shift?"

Eddie said nothing, and continued to say nothing, the entire length of the A9. They drove in silence for nearly ten minutes, along the A9 headed north. In truth, it was not a silence, but an absence of words; Eddie tapped his fingers on the wheel, hummed, and occasionally giggled to himself as the car rattled and shook along the asphalt.

"You're loving this, aren't you?" Dennis said.

216

Eddie nodded and continued to hum to himself, a sound at once guttural and gurgly at the back of his throat, like a kitten's growl. When Dennis finally recognized the tune, he laughed aloud.

"Are you humming 'Born to Be Wild?'" he asked. "You know that's about motorcycles, not cars, right?"

"Shut up and let me enjoy the freedom of the open A9, Duckworth."

"'Born To Be Wild'," Dennis continued. "You weren't born, you were conjured."

"I wisnae conjured." Eddie frowned. "I was believed."

"Believed?"

"Believed into existence."

"That statement doesn't really explain itself, Eddie."

"Well, I've ne'er given the semantics of it much thought, lad."

"Too bad they didn't have cars back then. Did they even have wheels?"

"Och, shut it."

"Did you saddle up a dinosaur like Fred Flintstone?"

"I'll slap you back to the Jurassic if you don't stop with the age jokes."

"Since when are you sensitive about age jokes?" Dennis stared out the window a moment. The Scottish countryside rolled past, peaceful like a river, like the Tay itself, gentle. "Is it because you're, uh…coming over to our side?"

"What on earth are you talking about?"

"Well, I mean, you're old and it doesn't matter that you're old. But you want to become human."

"As close as possible for a creature like myself, yes."

"Humans die."

"I know." Eddie stopped tapping the wheel. "I've dispatched a few myself, thanks for the reminder. While you're at it, why don't you just give me a nice paper cut and pour lemon juice on it?"

"Wow. Reaching back to old Billy Crystal movies for jokes. Timely. No, you twit, I meant…everybody you know, starting with me and ending with whomever you encounter for the rest of your life, is going to die."

"Who says I'm not going to die?" Eddie asked.

Dennis glanced at his driver, perched forward on his seat as if in anticipation of the road, and laughed. Eddie glanced over quickly and returned his eyes to the road.

"Who says I'm not going to die?" Eddie repeated. "Theoretically, red caps don't die of old age. Theoretically, we also don't eat, watch Rob Reiner films, wear sneakers and let humans live peaceably without raining down violence upon them. The only way we're supposed to die is if this dries out."

Eddie pinched the edge of his cap lightly between his thumb and forefinger. It was the only accoutrement that remained from his previous wardrobe; Eddie now dressed like a casual preppie, which seemed the best he could do in the children's section at Marks and Sparks. He kept his scraggly mop in a ponytail and tucked it under the cap, which worked well enough, but the cap continued to be damp to the touch at best, glistening with gore at worst.

"This stinking, blood-soaked cap." Eddie sounded disgusted. "Ugly, unsanitary, smelling like the death rot of the ages. I want to be done with it, but I'm afraid. Then again…I've started to wonder if I haven't already started dying."

"What do you mean?" Dennis felt something akin to alarm at the red cap's tone.

"I don't know if I ever believed, in any real sense, that using rabbit blood would keep the magic alive," Eddie confessed. "I still dip it in blood, but out of…I don't know. Trepidation? Tradition? Ritual?"

"Do you feel…I don't know, weaker?"

"Do I appear weaker?" Eddie scoffed. "I'm as sprightly as the day I was believed."

"You really need to stop saying that. It doesn't make sense."

"But what am I supposed to feel if I'm dying?" Eddie said. "I suppose I'll not know until the time comes that I die. Red caps don't think much about their own demise, so I don't know what that will feel like. I can't imagine it."

"Most of us feel immortal until we're dying," Dennis said. "It's not a concept we can wrap our heads around, either."

"Well, then, there's something we all have in common, humans and goblins alike."

They pulled off the motorway and glided down quiet, tree-sheltered streets until they came upon a short laneway. At the end of it sat a blue-grey cottage, nicer than the suburban homes in Perth proper yet still distinctly weathered in that now-familiar Scottish way, almost begging for the first frost so it could lay comfortably under a light snowfall with a tendril of smoke rising from the chimney. Dusk had fallen, and they could see clearly through the wide windows into the warmly lit living room. Idyllic seemed too harsh a word.

There were no visible signs of life, but through another window, they could hear the faintest tinkle of dishes in a sink.

"Well, this is it, then," said Eddie.

"Indeed," Dennis agreed.

"You think it'll work?"

Dennis stepped out of the car. "Will it work? Hell, no."

"Laddie, it's not too late to abandon ship!" Eddie scurried along behind Dennis, whose determined stride belied his pessimism. "Wait until you get paid for the restoration, give her the—"

"I'll be too late, Eddie." Dennis mounted the front steps, onto a tiny porch lined with herb pots, half of which were filled with damp cigarette butts. "Margaret will have lost the pub, and I'd have no money to get home. I have to get home, Eddie."

"Why are you obsessed with home, Duckworth?" Eddie leapt up the steps behind Dennis.

"You know why."

"Of course I know why, you beetle-headed git. I'm being rhetorical. It's your asinine plan to cheat your way into a record deal. If you think befriending a powrie on a hillside in Scotland was unlikely, that has nothing on what you've got up our sleeve."

Dennis glowered. "You have a better idea? I've screwed enough people. You made me make a list, remember? A sorely incomplete yet still painfully lengthy list. I can't let everyone down. I have to get home and save

219

this deal. I can do it. I *will* do it. It's my last chance."

"Och," Eddie spat. "There's no such thing as a last chance, Dennis. Not if you're willing to take the next one."

"We're standing uninvited on the front porch of Scotland's newest young, handsome, enigmatic singer-songwriter, who just happens to have disappeared from the public eye," Dennis replied. "Don't talk to me about taking chances. Remember, don't talk. And don't smile."

Eddie observed his reflection in the darkened glass of the screen door. "They're going to think me just lovely."

"They'll think you're old and unpleasant," agreed Dennis, "but if you smile at them, they'll run screaming from the room."

Dennis rang the doorbell.

You can do this, Dennis. You've sweet-talked plenty of people.

It occurred to him that his sweet-talking stakes were usually not so high, and usually didn't involve the futures and livelihoods of others.

CHAPTER ELEVEN

"Susan!"

The voice sounded as though it came from the bottom of a bucket of phlegm. A hideous, boggy cough followed, which in turn was followed by a series of drier coughs like machine-gun reports that caused Eddie to wince in sympathy.

"I've my hands in the dishwater!" Clearly, this was Susan, and she directed her words to the visitors on the stoop. "One minute, one minute!"

The wooden door swung inward with a soft sigh of air, and Susan appeared. She was possibly in her fifties or sixties, in a navy dress with small white and red polka dots. Her long, greyish brown hair sprang from a part in the middle of her scalp and cascaded downward to her shoulders. She did not smile warmly, but she smiled, which was encouraging.

"Sorry about that." Susan eyed Dennis quickly and decisively, but her eye lingered, somewhat puzzled, on the diminutive lad in the red cap and sunglasses despite the passage of dusk. "Can I help you?"

"Yes," Dennis replied. "You're Mrs. Dunlop, I presume?"

"Yes," Susan replied, more cautious now.

"Mrs. Dunlop, my name is Dennis Duckworth, and this is my business partner, Edward."

Eddie stuck out his hand and pretended to cough into his other hand as he quickly said, "Excuse me. Call me Eddie. Pleasure to meet you."

Susan did not reach down to shake Eddie's hand.

"Mrs. Dunlop, I need a moment of your time." Dennis felt his heart rear towards the top of his chest like a frightened horse pounding its

.

hooves against the inside of his ribcage. He fought it down. Nerves? After all these years?

The futures and livelihoods of others. In jeopardy because of you, Denny.

"I know it's highly unpleasant, unorthodox and likely unacceptable that we're on your doorstep this evening, unannounced and uninvited." His words unspooled breathlessly. "As a result, I won't be too surprised if you're unwilling to speak to us. Still, we had to try. Mrs. Dunlop, we want to talk to you and your son about a performance at our fundraiser."

A look of disgust and possibly horror contorted her face. She quickly looked over her shoulder, into an unseen room of the house, as if to ascertain if anyone else was listening. "I'm sorry, gentlemen, but that's not something we can do. Now please leave, and please for the love of God *do not tell anyone we are here.*"

"I know, I know, not something that you do, not something that's done." Understanding agreement, even tone. "Carson is recharging, regrouping, and doesn't want to be bothered. I get it—I run a small record label in Chicago, and I know how the pressure of sudden success can overwhelm you. Why, I'm working with a band *right now* that will have to face the same thing. The problem is, Mrs. Dunlop, we're in a bit of a spot. A good friend of mine is in a much bigger spot. She's going to lose everything unless we're able to help her. There's precious little time, and there's precious little else we can do but help her out."

For a moment, Dennis was sure she was going to simply slam the door shut, but there was a strange hesitation in her demeanor now, as if she wanted to hear more but knew she shouldn't.

"Mr. Duckworth, I just don't think so…this is…my husband is ill, and Carson is—"

"The show would be in Perth on the North Inch, September 5th," Dennis pressed on. "We'll be donating a large amount of the proceeds to charity, one of which supplies musical instruments to underprivileged children in Glawgow—"

"Well, he'd love that, yes, but—" Susan cut herself off and frowned as though confused; as though she wanted to be angry but was too flummoxed by the ambush to feel the emotion. When it was clear she was not going to continue, Dennis spoke again.

"Yes, of course it is. We thought that, at least, might entice him. It's truly only an hour or two of his time we're asking, Mrs. Dunlop. We'll set it up. We'll do it all. We'll even send a car. One hour, acoustic, on stage, weather permitting, pay what you can with a suggested donation, and—"

"You're out of your minds!"

It was the father. His voice was swampy; he sounded like an angry bog creature with terrible emphysema. "Be off with you!"

"If I could just speak to Carson—"

Dennis raised an arm, as if to push Susan aside. It was more subliminal suggestion than actual motion, but a protective instinct took over Susan's demeanor as she stepped backward, planted her feet and placed her hands on the doorjamb.

"Don't you dare try and come into my home! Get out now before—"

"I'm sorry!" Dennis threw up his hands and stepped backward. Eddie remained where he was, unmoving. "I wasn't—we've just—we don't know what else to do, and thought if Carson might at least hear our story and maybe help us out—"

"Off!" Mr. Dunlop exclaimed, his voice clear. "No one speaks with Carson! They speak with *me*, and I'm saying sod off!"

How did you ever pick up women, Denny? Your powers of persuasion are hopeless.

"Mr. Dunlop, I haven't had a chance to explain—"

"I don't give a damn!" Mr. Dunlop's cry seemed to dislodge an entire lung. The ensuing cough was low and mournful; he sounded like a sad sea lion. "Don't make me get off of this couch! Get off!"

"Fine!" Dennis screamed. Anger, familiar and as insuppressible as a smoker's taste for nicotine, rose into his cheeks and inflamed his head. "Fuck you, Dunlop!"

"It disnae need to escalate to this." Eddie's lips barely parted as he spoke.

"Apparently it does." Dennis spun about and stared down at Eddie. "I knew this was a horrible idea. I couldn't let it go. I couldn't let it go!"

Dennis looked to the sky above Eddie's head and cried, "*I'm supposed to be the master of every situation!*"

"I've news for you," Eddie replied solemnly. "You're not."

Dennis pounded down the steps and towards the driveway.

"Don't feel badly," Eddie said after his friend. "Nobody is!"

Over Eddie's head, Dennis watched Susan in the doorway. She hesitated a moment, picking at a seam on her dress, and then stepped quietly out of the house, holding the screen door until it gently closed. Susan approached them as they stood in the driveway. She widened her eyes and tilted her head a few degrees, indicating the far side of the Citroën. The trio stepped between the overhanging trees and the automobile.

"Listen, now." Susan spoke quickly and quietly. "This is a strange and horrible time. Our son was having panic attacks, he's had to go on medication, we've had to move our home, you have no idea. No idea. No one's found us until you. Everyone wants to know, why? Why did this lad disappear when he was about to become famous? Or more famous, that is? You have to understand. They've been looking for us, and when they don't find us, they make up stories. Saying Carson's on drugs, saying he's ill."

"Is he ill?"

Susan glared at Dennis. "No, Mr. Duckworth, he is not ill. He is merely a confused young man with a hormone-besotted brain who has made some life choices that were, shall we say, not the ones his father had hoped he'd make. Alan wanted none of this. Alan wanted Carson to be a chiropodist. Alan is protective, more protective than you'd imagine a father would be, more protective than Carson needs. He's been that way since Carson was a child. Carson wanted to play music, and the two argued over it. Alan used to play music, and it never went anywhere, it only led to heartbreak for him. They argued for years until Alan finally saw that Carson was different than him. He agreed Carson could give it a try. The second it had an effect on his personality, or on his schooling, or on his anxiety, though, it was to be over, that's what Alan told him. And Carson agreed to it."

Susan glanced back at the house nervously.

"Oh, he'd be furious to know I was speaking to you," she said. "Furious. But we've had our disagreements on the issue too."

"You and Alan?" asked Eddie.

"Yes. This has not been Carson's decision. This is Carson acquiescing to his father. Carson didn't disappear. His father disappeared him. And I understand what Alan means to do, and I understand what he says, but it disnae seem right."

"Isn't he eighteen?" asked Dennis.

"He's nineteen," Susan replied, "but you have to understand their dynamic. You've an overbearing father and an anxious son who needs to please. He could be thirty seven, he'd still be living in our back room if his father demanded it."

"What would you have happen, Mrs. Carson?" Eddie asked softly.

"I don't know, " she sighed. "It's all been mad. He'd sing and play guitar in his bedroom every day. Since the age of ten. Ten! But no one cared. A few videos on Youtube and suddenly somebody cares. Alan helps Carson record a song, helps him get it released, and suddenly *everyone* cares. Because of 'On The Horizon,' there's a contract to pick up the album, to do some more recording. He was supposed to spend his summer in a studio, he was supposed to start doing all this press and these TV appearances. He'd never been so confident and happy in his life. Then, when it was no longer a promise—when it all became reality—Carson just, well, he was a little frightened, that's all. Wouldn't you be?"

They nodded.

"I think he'll be fine." Susan stared off towards the house. "I think Carson will be fine. I think they need to try it again."

"You think he should play our show, don't you, Mrs. Dunlop."

"Aye, Mr. Duckworth. I do." Susan turned her eyes back to them "But if Alan doesn't, you'll not convince Carson to cross him. I'm sorry."

Dennis nodded to himself and bit his lower lip. Susan left them by the car and went back towards the house.

"We came so close," he said to Eddie.

"Aye, lad. We did."

"I don't know what we can do," Dennis said dejectedly. "Maybe we should go pay a visit to McKee and try to talk to him ourselves."

"That's a terrible idea." Eddie said as he opened the car door. "Visiting Bruce McKee is a *remarkably* terrible idea."

"Bruce McKee?"

They looked up to see Susan stopped at the foot of the stairs.

"Yeah," Dennis replied. "You know him?"

Remarkably, Susan smiled. She dashed over to them, her voice low. "Say all that again."

"What all that?" asked Dennis, confused, but Eddie had caught on.

"That's a terrible idea." Eddie half-shouted, walking directly towards the open front window. "Visiting *Bruce McKee* is a terrible idea."

A sound issued from within; again, the grief-stricken sea lion.

"We…don't have any choice?" Dennis half-asked, realization dawning on him more slowly than it did Eddie. He stepped towards Eddie, near the window, and turned to look at Susan, who winked in his direction. "If Kit Carson can't play then we'll have to ask *Bruce McKee* if he'll come to his senses."

"Bruce McKee," lamented the sea lion. "Susan, did they say Bruce McKee?"

Eddie and Dennis both held their breath.

"Aye," Susan said as she opened the front door. "They said Bruce McKee."

"What about Bruce McKee?" Alan Dunlop asked.

"I don't know," she replied, smiling at Dennis and Eddie. "I should think you'd have to ask *them*."

Pause.

"Let them in."

"Alan—"

"Just a—" Cough, cough, cough, phlegmy expectoration, hopefully into a tissue. "Just a moment. Let them in."

Dennis' shoulders felt as if they'd been freed of all their tendons as he felt his entire body slump in relief.

"Thank you, Mrs.—"

"Susan will do, Susan will do."

Susan led them through the dim kitchen into the equally dim but warmer glow of the living room. Varying hues of brown and creeping vines of knick-knackery clung to every tabletop and shelf, which surrounded the room like the walls of a canyon. In the centre of the cluttered room sat an ancient, timeless-looking couch, shaggy with cushions and afghans. In its centre, protruding from a mound of grey cotton blankets, was the head of Alan Dunlop. The head was reddened, tear-streaked, chapped and bleary-eyed, to match the unearthly, Lovecraftian croak that was Alan's voice. His nose appeared ruddy and swollen, his eyes waterlogged, and his lips hung open as though his jaw had gone slack. No wonder he was cranky.

"Ugh," Alan sniffed. A small wicker wastebasket at his feet overflowed with crumpled tissue. Alan dabbed one at his nose as he spoke.

"What's this got to do with McKee, then."

Dennis approached Alan, who nodded him in the direction of a chair—a safe distance from the plague-ridden man.

"Mr. Dunlop, again, I'm really sorry to—"

"McKee," insisted Alan. "You want me to listen or not?"

"You want it short or you want it from the beginning?"

Alan sniffed again, a low, sluggish burble of phlegm. His expression told Dennis he wasn't happy about being seen in this state, so Dennis tried not to stare too intently.

"Okay." Alan took a breath, wheezed, and continued. "It's like this. Bruce McKee is the lousiest human being I've e'er known. Him and his smug face and his stupid motorcycles. He's said and done a lot of things to a lot of people, from here to Aberdeen, and a few of these people are my friends. Once, a long, long time ago, I was a musician myself, and he caused a stir at one of my concerts. Punched someone in the eye. Another time, he purchased a beautiful parcel of land that I'd come to cherish. It's a petrol station now. There are petrol stations and Tescos and parking lots…well, again, here to Aberdeen. He's a sorry bastard with a bad attitude and he's ruined enough of my beloved countryside. You might say if there was a downfall at hand, I'd at least want a personal stake in it."

Dennis smiled. "Sounds like you truly dislike him."

"If I used the word 'hate,' which I try not to do, I'd use it in this instance."

"Well," Dennis said as he leaned forward, "then you're going to want this from the beginning."

Dennis didn't tell it from the beginning. The beginning, for him, was a shape-shifting boarding pass that connected Dennis, Margaret, McKee, Eddie and, now, Alan Dunlop. And hopefully, before he left this house, Kit Carson.

"Margaret!" Alan hacked hard when her name arose, his swollen face bouncing atop the blanket mound like a bobblehead. "Och, not Margaret. Margaret used to be Carson's teacher for a short spell. Margaret's lovely. Go on."

So Dennis went on, admitting his culpability outright so as not to appear the hero in the situation. Alan made no further remarks until Dennis was clearly finished.

"Well." Alan sat back, cinched the afghan around his neck, and closed his eyes. A liquid rattle came from his chest like a wet shiver.

"Alan," Susan stood near the doorway, an inscrutable glimmer in her eye. "You can't mean to use your son to get back at Bruce McKee, can you?"

Dennis squinted at Susan, unsure where she was taking the conversation.

"I wouldnae do that, no," Alan huffed, irritated by the suggestion. "No, of course not. But what of the rest of it, then?"

"Well, what of it, Alan?"

"All that you've said about Carson making his own plans and leading his own life. You know, the thing we've been arguing about for, oh, six months now. That wee thing."

"Yes, well—"

"Well, this might be exactly what we've needed. They said it's to benefit music education for children and that they were trying to help Margaret. It's local, it's low-key—correct, gentleman?"

"Your son's too big a deal to put on a poster," Dennis said. "The Inch isn't Wembley. I was thinking we'd say it was a special mystery guest and leak rumours that it was Kit Carson. Enough people would show up based on the rumours, but not so many as would show up if it was confirmed. It's also an escape hatch—you change your mind, it was only a rumour in the first place. No harm, no foul."

"There you are then, Susan. No reason not to put this to him, and let him decide for himself."

There was a moment of silence in the room. Fresh bubbles crackled and popped inside Alan Dunlop's chest. Susan stared at her husband expectantly. Dennis was about to speak when Alan and Susan's eyes rotated in the same direction, towards a doorway behind them, where Kit Carson stood.

*

What's the big deal? He's just a kid.

Dennis meant it both literally and figuratively. Carson Dunlop was nineteen, but appeared a mature seventeen at most. He stood, resting on one leg, the other slightly akimbo, clad in grey track pants and a matching grey T-shirt. There was nothing athletic about the athletic wear; it was the uniform of someone whose idea of a marathon involved video games or the Lord of the Rings trilogy. The finest blonde hairs traced his face, the stubble of one who needed to shave perhaps three, four times a month. His hair, usually fashioned into that flop-mop so common with popstars his age, stuck up and out in different directions, like rage-fuelled bed-head. His eyes blinked with the uncertain focus of one freshly awakened.

"I thought you were having a nap, son." Susan's voice was soft, as if speaking to someone fragile.

"Yeah." Carson rubbed one eye and stifled a yawn. He looked Dennis and Eddie over once, quickly, and cocked his head sideways. "Who's this?"

"This is Dennis Duckworth and Eddie, ah…" Alan looked at Eddie.

"Eddie will do," Eddie lifted his fingers but left his arm at his sides, resulting in the smallest of waves, as if afraid he might spook the boy.

"They're here to talk to you, actually," Alan said. "You've talked about wanting to get back out there, and these gentlemen have a fundraiser they'd like to talk to us about. It sounds like something you might like. Come on out. Let's have a wee chat."

"I'd rather not," said Carson. His mother looked crestfallen immediately, while his father attempted to refashion a mild scowl into something more sympathetic.

"Oh, son, it's no big—"

"I'd rather talk to them on my own," Carson clarified.

This latest turn appeased Susan, but the difficulty of controlling his facial muscles appeared to have increased for Alan. The smile he held was the blank-eyed, awkwardly open-mouthed smile of a fourth grader told to smile in a school photograph. Carson, clearly his father's intellectual equal even in this sleep-addled state, caught both parents' reactions and let them settle a moment before he continued.

"We talked about this," Carson insisted gently.

"Well, yes, we did, but—"

"We talked about my choices being my own choices."

"Yes, we—"

"We talked about the next move being one hundred percent mine."

"Well, certainly—"

"Let me talk to them myself."

Alan's resolve cracked and fell apart, and the scowl fell across the rest of his face. "Son, this is important. If you think you're well enough to do this we can consider—"

"*I* can consider, Da, remember?"

Alan was quiet then, and he raised his shoulders slightly in what might have been seen as an acquiescent shrug.

"All right then."

Carson looked over at Dennis. "Okay. Come on in to my office."

Dennis and Eddie crossed the room, following Carson through a small sky-blue bedroom, remarkable for its unremarkableness. Desk, chair, bed, dresser, photographs gathered in a collage on the wall. Dark balls of denim and white clusters of cotton piled in one corner, otherwise, a spotless floor.

Carson opened what might have been a closet door to reveal there was, in actual fact, an office behind the bedroom, though it was immediately clear to Dennis that it was an office, a studio, a safe space and a sanctuary combined. Four guitars lined one wall, vertical on their stands, in front of amps and outboard synth gear. Carson moved a plastic milk crate full of cords, placing it beside a desk covered in scraps of paper, impenetrable lyrics jotted on scraps, surrounding a laptop plugged into several pre-amps and other bits of equipment. Carson sat in the swivel chair and gestured for Eddie to close the door. Dennis sat on the couch beside the door.

"You still write lyrics on paper," Dennis said.

Carson regarded Dennis, his eyes as inscrutable as his handwriting.

"It seems kind of old school."

"I guess you're right," Carson replied. "All the biggest teen pop stars road-test their lyrics on Facebook these days. If rhyming 'moon' with 'June' gets the most likes, then 'moon' and 'June' it is."

"Burn," whispered Eddie.

"Not a bad studio for goofing around in, either." Dennis pretended to ignore Carson's sarcasm.

Carson sighed and blew his hair, which had been slowly dripping downward into its usual flop style, off his forehead.

"I'm in. You don't have to make small talk. I'll play the show."

"You don't know the first thing about it yet,"

"Yes, I do. Meaghan told me already."

Dennis and Eddie looked at one another.

"Meaghan from the library?"

"Meaghan Campbell, yes."

"And how do you know Meaghan Campbell?"

"She's my girlfriend."

" ... "

"What? Are you suggesting there's something wrong with my *girlfriend?*"

"Easy, champ." Dennis raised both his hands in mock surrender. "I said nothing. I'm just…Meaghan continues to take on new dimensions for me, that's all. Didn't think she'd be dating a pop star."

Carson rolled his eyes so dramatically that his irises actually disappeared for a moment.

"She told me the day she first talked to you," Carson continued, now looking down at his hands as if he thought he was holding a phone. "This is already a done deal. She thought that sending you out here would maybe get you to crack my dad. Everyone else just tries to phone. He screens our calls. After we moved, no one knew where we were. Someone would have found us eventually but Meaghan seemed to think what you had to offer was a better idea, more father friendly. If another industry weasel or music journo showed up at my door, Da would have sent them packing."

"Wait." Eddie would have grinned, if not for fear of exposing his maw. "So that means…*you* used *us*?"

Carson dropped the non-existent phone and regarded Eddie, one eye squinting at him.

"Yeah," he said. "Thanks. Listen…it's been…kind of mental, you know? You have to understand where I come from. I'm not popular."

"But you're—"

Carson somehow doubled the arc of his eye-roll as he waved Dennis into silence.

"I love music, mate. I love playing, I love writing, I love all of it, because I've been doing it all since I was wee. I took music. I listened to what people thought was weird music. I'm seven stone soaking wet and my voice sounds like—"

"Teddy Pendergrass," offered Dennis.

"*Please.* Everyone says Bill Withers now. Bill Withers sounds nothing like Teddy Pendergrass."

I'm arguing old soul singers with a child, marvelled Dennis.

"Point is, I wasn't a talent, I was a misfit. If there was a prank to be pulled, it was pulled on Carson. If there was a joke to be made, it was at the expense of Carson. I was bullied."

"And you got through it," Eddie said.

"No," Carson insisted. "I *blasted* through it. I said to myself, if they think I'm odd sitting in the music room for two hours after school, I'll sit there for four. And that's what I did. If I was too afraid to talk to people, too afraid to stand up for myself, I'd do what I *could* do and then, one day, when I'd made it, they'd see. That would be my *fuck you*. But then, when the time came to show them, the whole thing showed *me*."

"Showed you what?" asked Eddie.

Carson glanced at the invisible phone again.

"That it's horrifying becoming something you've never been. I had hundreds of thousands of people like my first Youtube video. I play my first show in Glasgow and instead of it being in some dodgy basement club, it's at the O$_2$ Academy, and suddenly there's all this *weirdness* to everything, and you think you're somehow a fraud. Everything's different, and people at school ask daft questions, and people on the street recognize you, and then you come home and…"

He raised both his hands, palms up, as if to show something, but clearly he meant for Dennis and Eddie to understand something.

"And?" Eddie prodded again.

"And *this*," he replied, a certain amount of *you know full well what I'm talking about* in his tone. "Mum's fine, but she never could argue with Da, she gets too upset. Him, he's over-protective, doesn't want me in music because he failed at it and thinks I will too."

"Is that fair?" Eddie, again. "Do you really think your father feels that way?"

"Yes, and it's worse than that, I think," Carson replied. "I think he's a wee bit jealous. His first show in Glasgow was in one of those dodgy clubs with the jakey clientele. His last show in Glasgow was no better."

"Surely jealousy isn't his main concern," Dennis said.

"No." Carson agreed. "No, it's just one of a million concerns. My father is always very concerned about *something*."

Dennis nodded.

"He worries about you," he said. "Maybe all his other issues make him a pain in the ass to deal with, but at its root—"

"I know." Carson looked back and forth between Eddie and Dennis. "I know that. And he had good reason. There were a few panic attacks, a few breakdowns. Questioning everything I'd worked for, listening too closely to the voice that said *they were right*. So I took some time to stay here and think about it. And I'm ready now."

"Ready for what?" Dennis asked.

"At the moment? Ready to play a fundraiser in Perth. Isn't that enough?"

CHAPTER TWELVE

Along the A9, Dennis sat with his head back, staring out the window. The car seemed silent despite the rickety clatter of the engine and the rubber on the asphalt. Dennis' mind was still for the first time in…days? Weeks?

"Well here we are," he said.

"I'd think you'd be right chuffed," Eddie replied.

"Chuffed?"

"It means—"

"I know what it means. Yeah. The word works. I *am* chuffed. What luck. What amazing luck."

"Luck, is it?" Eddie glanced sideways.

"…"

"You don't really think so, then."

"I'm not sure, Eddie." Out the window, the Scottish night was deep blue. The boughs of the trees were alive with shadow.

"It doesn't get fully dark here in summer," Dennis noted aloud. "It's like the day sinks down towards dark, nestles up against it, but never really embraces it."

Dennis stared out the window a few moments longer.

"I'm good at pretending everything's fine," he said eventually. "When everything goes to hell, my attitude is fuck 'em all, I will survive, don't let the bastards drag you down, et cetera. The problem is that even when things turn around—when things are actually good—I'm still just as angry. When Universal called and this whole deal started to happen…it never really felt like victory. There was always something nagging at me—behind it, beyond it, just out of my grasp. Getting Carson on board…this feels different."

235

"There's something to be said for purity of intent," Eddie replied, after a moment.

"Trying to assuage my own guilt is pure?"

"You're only trying to save the Rat and Raven because you feel guilty?"

Dennis' silence answered the question. *No.*

"Purity of intent," Dennis continued as the blue sky deepened towards a black it would never reach. "I think I used to have that in my life."

Eddie snickered. "You mean, you weren't always a bitter son of a bitch?"

"Maybe not when I was a child," Dennis replied, as though Eddie had not meant to be facetious. "Once I became a teenager, though, the bitterness started to fester. I surrounded myself with some pretty big assholes, and like begets like, I suppose. My life wasn't so bad. No real hardships. I was never as smart as I wanted to be, never as popular as I wanted to be, that kind of whining. Talking to you, Eddie, I feel kind of pathetic talking about unhappiness."

"Forget about my life," Eddie scolded. "It's apples and oranges and a waste of our time."

" ... "

"Go on."

"You're asking me to start up with this self-reflection thing, and you know I suck at it."

"Laddie, at the risk of sounding like an annoying self-help guru, the answers you seek are within you. So get in there, for land's sake. Just start talking out loud, and some sense will hopefully come of it."

Dennis sighed.

"Something's bothering you," said Eddie.

Dennis' laugh was more like a sarcastic quack.

"You didn't see any, uh, similarities there?"

"The lad's sarcasm reminded me of someone I know, indeed," Eddie said.

"He's a teenager," Dennis said. "I'm an adult. And I'm kind of an asshole."

"I'm aware of the lede, lad."

"Fuck you."

"And he proves it yet again!"

"Okay!" Dennis exclaimed. "You want me to talk, let me talk."

"Apologies. Continue."

"I'm kind of an asshole," Dennis repeated. "And I know it. I just don't understand why there's so much anger in me. Sometimes when people talk to me, it feels like they're kicking sand into my eyes. It's just painful and annoying. So I act pained and annoyed. I can muster up some surface charm. I'm good at that, but not for the long term. Look at Abby. She was trying to be nice, maybe even willing to be a friend, and I *still* had no self-control. It takes so much fucking *effort* to think about how to behave. It's so much easier to just be myself."

"Except you don't like yourself."

Dennis didn't respond to that.

"I've always had a sarcastic sense of humour," he said. "That's how it started, I think. The meaner the joke, the funnier it was. I ran with a group of guys in school—Robbie, Jason and Mike. They were all right guys, but at the same time, they were bastards, in the way thirteen-year-olds can be bastards. We created a yearbook for our grade eight class, and somehow—dear Jee...bus..."

"Jeebus is okay to say. Thank you."

"You're welcome. Dear Jeebus, I don't know what our teacher was thinking. The yearbook was *awful*. Cruel, brutal, racist, sexist—hell, it wasn't even really a *yearbook*, it was some photocopied pictures and essays and poems and things we thought were funny. Caricatures of the teachers. The fat teacher got six chins. The Japanese teacher's picture looked like it was straight out of World War 11 propaganda. In one segment, we 'predicted' the futures of our fellow classmates. The one Muslim kid, of course, was going to travel in the desert. One heavy girl was going to grow up to study the hippopotamus. That kind of stupid shit. The kicker, though, is that we didn't think we were being mean. We thought we were being *funny*."

Eddie seemed to understand, and Dennis continued.

"Some wild animals protect the young and weak in the pack," he said. "Humans aren't so noble. Once we got to high school, I started to develop…empathy, I suppose. I felt bad about hippo girl and desert boy and the countless others we'd laughed at. Empathy made me the weakest of the group, and the group turned on me accordingly. They made fun of me for everything. The size of my forehead—"

"You do have an impressive forehead."

"Thanks, asshole." Dennis smacked Eddie on the side of the head. "The size of my forehead. The fact that I had pimples. The fact that my dad worked on the trains. The fact that I never had a girlfriend—especially that last one. Merciless."

"Far more unfortunate souls have been abused in far more egregious ways, Dennis," Eddie replied. "It doesn't always lead to sour misanthropy."

"What did I tell you? Let me talk."

"As you wish."

"I remember one time, we went to the roller rink. You know roller skating?"

"Popular in the '70s," Eddie said.

"Yes, it was. This was more mid '80s. The last days of disco. Tracing the outlines of the circle to the strains of 'Let The Music Play' by Shannon, maybe a little Chaka Khan or Cameo. We'd go every Friday. Most of our time was spent playing arcade games, but occasionally we'd get out on the rink. I wasn't the best skater around—none of that backwards stuff, fancy moves or anything—but I was fairly steady on my feet, and that's about all you could ask for.

"Now, when Robbie, Jason and Mike thought I was getting too big for my britches, they'd insult me. 'Hey, Denny, that girl we were talking to yesterday? She told us she thought you were a loser.' I never entirely believed their nonsense, but it hurt anyhow. They'd also create nicknames and hurl those as insults. Dennis the Forehead. Permutations of that, like Denhead. Neither funny nor clever, but when you're thirteen, it hurts anyway. They also employed some alliterative brilliance—Larry Loser, Perry Pud, Denny Dickweed. Believe it or not, they didn't come up with the last one first."

"They were clearly budding geniuses," Eddie remarked.

"Yeah, well, I'm the only one of the lot who went on to college, but that's another story. Anyhow, the worst insult, the worst nickname, the one that humiliated me more than anything in the world, was in regards to…"

Dennis touched his forefinger to his thumb and made a stroking motion in the air.

"Leave the bathroom unlocked one time?"

"No!" Dennis finally turned in his seat and looked at his travelling companion. "That's the thing! Maybe I was too enthusiastic about my buddy's dad's Playboy collection. It's irrelevant, though. Nothing humiliates a teenager like a jerkoff joke, so that's where they went with it. They nicknamed me Spanky."

Eddie seemed to hiccup.

"Did you just *laugh* at that?"

"Aye," Eddie said with composure. "Aye, I did."

"See, that was the problem. Even *I* kinda want to laugh at it. Kinda. But you can bet your ass those guys were monkeys behind the bedroom door too. Dammit, we were *thirteen*. Yet they called *me* Spanky. Why?"

"Because you let them," offered Eddie.

"Maybe. Yeah, maybe. Anyway, it doesn't matter why. One Friday night, we're at the rink, and I spied this girl. I can't remember a thing about her, but I was thirteen, so what does it matter?"

It did matter, of course. Her name was Cindy. Cindy something, something that started with an "M." Dennis remembered most of his crushes, even though the crushes of a thirteen-year-old virgin boy, frequent but fleeting, usually dissipated within hours after the object of his unrequited affection had left the room. He knew now that it was merely a confused biological and emotional response, grappling with sexuality and attraction and everything all at once, but he could remember how every one of those girls was very important in that moment. As fleeting as those crushes were, the fact that they were interchangeable didn't make them disposable, not to Dennis.

"So that night at the roller rink, I decided to go talk to this girl. Robbie, Jason and Mike mocked me. They told me I'd never have the courage to approach her, and normally they would have been right, but I went to the bathroom and talked myself into it. I looked at myself in the mirror. Breathed. Shook a little. Then I left the bathroom, strode across the lobby, right up to her. She watched me approach, and right when I stopped in front of her, she said, 'Hi, Spanky.'"

Eddie winced.

"Yeah," Dennis agreed with Eddie's expression. "I was mortified. I said nothing, just slunk away. Then I got angry. I went over to my friends—who were howling, of course—and shouted at them. I lost my shit completely. What kind of friend tells a girl to call me that? What kind of person thinks that's funny? They just kind of stood there, smirking. Maybe Robbie was uncomfortable. He *did* end up being the least of the assholes in the end, but he was still an asshole."

As they coasted around a bend, the blue-black shadows of hills on either side of them retreated and they were left with a view of the moon reflected in the Tay. Dennis kept silent and contemplated the reflection, a ghostly white shimmer on the calm water, until the hills caught up with them and overtook his view once again.

"After that, I got…harder," he continued. "I'm not saying it was some kind of pivotal moment. I'm not saying 'from that moment on, my life was never the same' or some ridiculously simplistic shit like that. I'm saying from then that was the direction I went. At one time, I wouldn't make jokes if I thought they were too mean. That began to change. It was horrible, but it worked; the guys began to laugh with me again. They went easier on me, because, well, I was smarter, my comebacks were sharper. Soon they left me alone– not because they admired me, but because they were afraid of what I might say in return. Afraid of the humiliation. By the end of high school, if someone made a wisecrack about me, people would get this nervous look on their faces. Widen their eyes and shake their heads as if to say 'don't start with this guy, you'll regret it.' And then, if the person didn't stop, I'd launch into it. Reduced people to tears sometimes."

Dennis looked down at his own invisible phone. The Citroën reached the bottom of the Cairneyhill Road. A rabbit hopped lightly through their headlights; Eddie braked and they watched it, washed out and white in the glare.

"This Carson kid. He's treated badly, and he decides he'll show 'em. I didn't do that. I *joined*'em. I grew arrogant, angry...terrible mix for a kid."

"Not a splendid combination for an adult, either, lad."

"I guess there's a reason everybody hates me." He heard the whiny undertone in his voice. It was the sort of statement people make when fishing for consolation, yet even as he spoke, he knew no such consolation would be forthcoming.

"Well, there were at least two who didn't hate you."

"Paul and Sylvia."

"Aye. It would seem."

"I suppose I've crossed them both pretty badly, haven't I?"

"I suppose you have."

The rabbit was long gone, but the car still idled on the Cairneyhill Road.

"Eddie, I'm going to walk the rest of the way."

"But it's dark," Eddie replied, as if to be polite.

"Since meeting you—going through the gate, as you said—I've been able to do crosswords in the closet. And it never gets dark here, in Scotland, in summer. Not really."

Eddie smiled as Dennis got out of the car.

"Hey, by the way," he said over his shoulder, "You're right. That cap is right funky. Ripe. If you're going to keep it, you need to at least Febreeze that sucker."

"Febreeze?"

Dennis laughed. "Never mind."

Eddie turned the car around, a swift and sure three-point turn, and headed back down the hill.

He's taking the car back, Dennis thought as he pulled out his cell phone. *Conscientious little bugger.*

"Hey. Me. Mess—"

Click and clatter, and a voice.

"Yep."

"Paul, it's me."

"…"

"You got a minute?"

"Sure."

"…"

"I said I got a minute, not an hour, Dennis."

"Oh, yeah." Dennis stared at his feet as he walked, phone to his ear. "Paul, do you remember how we met?"

"Uh…"

"It was in the hallway at Schurz, in our first year. September. We'd just started high school."

"Yeah, I remember."

"We started talking because I was wearing a Smiths T-shirt. You asked what my favourite album was."

"Yeah. You said *Meat is Murder*," Paul said.

"I never would have said *Meat is Murder*, are you crazy?"

"You said *Meat is Murder*."

"I said *Hatful of Hollow*, and you agreed."

"*Hatful of Hollow* isn't an album, it's a compilation."

"Whatever," Dennis replied dismissively. "Do you remember what happened next?"

"…"

"Robbie, Jason and Mike came around the corner. And they cheered 'Hey, Spanky!' And you looked at them, like they were amusing chimps, and you asked them why they called me Spanky."

"And they looked confused," Paul said, as he abruptly recalled the long-forgotten moment.

"They did!" Dennis laughed. "They couldn't believe you'd ask them that! And then they acted like you were stupid, and said obviously it was because I liked to spank it all day and all night. And do you remember what you said? You said, in this dry, incredulous, sarcastic way, and I quote, you said, 'Uh-huh. And you guys *don't* whack off.'"

"Yeah, well, I'm pretty sure they did whack off," said Paul flatly.

"Of course they did. So they wandered down the hall, even more confused, grumbling. And I said 'hey, what do you think of *The Queen is Dead*?' and we argued about that a while. But do you remember what I *didn't* say?"

"No."

"I didn't say thank you," Dennis replied.

"Dennis, are you in a twelve-step?"

"No."

"Are you sitting in a running automobile in a closed garage?"

"No."

"Are you—"

"Paul, I was just thinking about that day, and I wanted to say thanks. I also wanted to say I'm sorry."

There was another pause.

"Please, man, step down off the ledge. Come back inside."

"Paul, for real" Dennis pleaded and laughed simultaneously. "I'm not suicidal. I've just…had an epiphany, if you will."

"Epiphany."

"Yeah. No. Okay, nothing so extreme. I guess I just realized it was wrong for me to ask you to be part of my whole scheme with the Random. I'm doing it because I think it'll save the deal, save the band, save the label, and make us all a pile of money. Even so, it's still dishonest. It's a lie, and I shouldn't ask you to lie for me."

"Remember when you fucked that girl," Paul said, "and Sylvia called me?"

"Yes."

"I texted you," Paul said. "While she was on the landline, I texted you and asked if I should lie for you."

"I remember it," said Dennis. "I said no, don't, go ahead and tell her what you know. I'd never asked you to get involved with my bullshit, and I shouldn't have crossed that line now. I only did it because of this weirdo situation I'm in. Hence, I'm sorry."

Crickets whirred and chirped like a noise orchestra all around him. A few gnats flew into his ears, but they no longer bothered him as they once had. On the phone, the low-intensity static hum rose and then fell when Paul spoke.

"Accepted, pal. Thanks."

Thanks, Eddie.

"So, what now?" Paul asked. "You still trapped over there? You…you still need me to help out?"

"No," Dennis replied. "Thanks, but no. I've got a plan. I should be home the day the demos are due. You'll see me on September 7th, and I'll have just completed the deal that makes Chicago music history."

"So, no Tusk."

"No. Tangerine Records is fine but the money's gonna come from a major label like Universal."

"Major labels haven't mattered in years," Paul replied. "They haven't a goddamn clue what they're doing. What if it just doesn't work out, Denny?"

"I don't know," Dennis replied. "Maybe I can stay here and start a career in event management."

"What?"

Dennis considered a moment. He could explain Margaret, the concert, McKee, Kit Carson, all of it, without mentioning Eddie—but it would be like describing the plot of Star Wars without mentioning Han Solo.

"Never mind," Dennis said. "Never mind."

CHAPTER THIRTEEN

The motors began to roar shortly before 3 a.m.

In his half-sleep, Dennis connected the sound to the generator Eddie used to power his restoration equipment, and he half-dreamed puzzled questions to himself. Why was the generator on? Why did it sound more distant? More like motor scooters?

Motorcycles.

Dennis stumbled into the clearing just as white lights cut through the dark and bleached wide circles into the sides of Kinnoull Tower. Two scooters—a Vespa and a Piaggio—burst out of the forest trail, each with two passengers astride. These were followed by a racing bike, the kind of bike favoured by aspiring roughnecks with something to prove. The scooters slid sideways into the clearing and stopped while McKee drove his bike threateningly towards Dennis, who was too tired and bewildered to flinch, even as the light ground glass into his eyes and caused him to squint into the headlamps. McKee braked five feet in front of Dennis, skidding another few feet before the motorcycle stopped.

"Fer chrissakes, it's true!" someone exclaimed as the gang dismounted. It was only the second time he'd heard any of the lackeys speak. Dennis glanced at the still-burning bonfire, where he and Eddie had cooked dinner before they'd headed to Bankfoot. It should have been embers by this hour, yet it burned hot. Eddie was somewhere nearby.

Bruce and the others set their bikes on kickstands and stepped towards him. With the glare of headlamps extinguished, Dennis could see two flecks of red flame flicker at the top of the tower stack. Relief settled his stomach and steeled his resolve. Eddie was watching. Eddie wouldn't let him die.

"Unbelievable." Bruce looked about, his posture too loose for him to be sober.

"Unbelievable!" he repeated, with forced incredulity. "You actually do live up here. You actually do live in a tent."

"I actually do, yes."

"I see your little ninja friend isn't about," said one of the others. He had pulled a steel bar out of one boot. Another held a cricket bat.

Eddie might not be quick enough to make a difference, Denny.

"He's about," Dennis said calmly. "Just not here at the moment."

"What is he then, your little bodyguard?" Bruce stepped up to Dennis. Dennis glanced past him at the others. Many of them sported sizeable shiners and bruises on their cheeks. "Your little ass man, perhaps? Your special little friend?"

"Really, Bruce?" Dennis asked. "Gay jokes?"

Bruce shoved Dennis then, hard, and before he knew what was happening, one of Bruce's feet was firmly planted on Dennis' neck. Dennis coughed, but the expulsed air had nowhere to go. His lungs throbbed as his chest bucked.

"I don't give a fuck what he is," Bruce said. "If he were here, he'd be drinking down his just desserts."

"Since…when…do you drink…dessert?"

Bruce stomped again, squeezing a strangled croak out of Dennis' throat. One of the lackeys stormed past quickly; something flashed and sparked beside him and as flame began to rise, Dennis realized the lackey had set fire to the tent.

Bruce applied more pressure onto Dennis' neck and leaned down towards him. For the first time, he noticed the hunting knife in Bruce's hand, a dull glow in the moonlight.

"A benefit concert?" Bruce looked down, his eyes heavy-lidded and dull.

"Word travels fast," Dennis managed. "I only signed the headliner tonight."

"Oh fuck you, you bastard." The eyes spun in their sockets, flipped immediately from dull to manic. "I've friends in the government! I know you've applied for the permit for the North Inch. There's already rumours you've tracked down Kit Carson, which is obviously utter shite. It's your fault Margaret's in a spot, and you're trying to help her out of it. I was really looking forward to watching her grovel, but instead, I get to watch you grovel, which will be much more fun, given what your little friend did to my crew."

"Crew?" Dennis croaked. "What are you, an emcee or a break dancer?"

"Do you know what's going to happen here, Duckworth?" Bruce smiled an unpleasant smile, lit demonically by the rising flames of the tent a few yards behind them. "Your little friend isn't around for us tonight, but you are. Hence, you're going to pay his debt as well as your own. An eye for an eye, so to speak. And speaking of eyes, your little friend almost took out a few of those belonging to my crew here."

Bruce leaned closer and rested the tip of his knife directly on the soft divot beneath Dennis' right eye.

"Maybe I should repay all those favours in one?"

Through the delicate skin, he could feel the tip rest against the bottom of his eyeball.

"Put the knife down, bastard!"

Despite the blade poised to pluck out his eye, Dennis allowed himself a series of blinks.

This is where Eddie saves my ass…except that wasn't Eddie.

The long barrel of a rifle crossed Dennis' line of vision to rest against the back of Bruce's head. The moment the muzzle connected, Bruce raised both hands slowly and allowed the knife to fall to the dirt.

"Boys!" he shouted. Said boys froze in their tracks.

"Stand up. Get up, now!"

As Bruce's foot released his windpipe, Dennis coughed. He rubbed at the skin above his bruised larynx, trying to swallow against tissue that had already begun to swell. Bruce rose carefully, as though his joints were made of glass.

"All of you! Stand in the middle there! Now!"

Gigi held the rifle at her eye, the other narrowed in a Clint Eastwood squint. The barrel ended mere inches past her impossibly swollen belly, which resembled the front end of a zeppelin where it protruded from her sweater. Gigi ushered Bruce's crew into the centre of the clearing with a sideways motion of the gun, and something whooshed past Dennis in the dark, something unseen that dragged a snakelike darkness behind it. Flames began to hiss. It was Eddie with the hose he had used to dampen the hessian, trying to put out the fire. No one seemed to notice.

"Bruce McKee, as I live and breathe." She sounded like a flustered and frustrated Sunday school teacher. "You've the devil's nerve and twice his ugly, you have. What are you up to?"

"It's none of your concern, Gillian." All of Bruce McKee's entourage now held their hands aloft. It looked like villains rounded up by a cowboy hero, but for the fact that the hero was a cowgirl and approximately eleven months pregnant.

"Gillian." Bruce spoke as though to an unreasonable child. "Put the gun down."

"Put the gun down?" Gillian scoffed. "You're threatening Council employees with knives and lighting the place on fire and driving unauthorized motor vehicles into Woodland Park in an intoxicated state! Right? Yes! That's what you're doing! You're a menace, yes, right? A menace and a scoundrel and a right bastard son of a bitch! Now get the hell off my property!"

"This isn't your prop—"

Click.

"She's insane," said one of the crew, dumbstruck.

"Get on your bikes and be off with you all! And don't let us find you here again!"

Bruce's gang looked embarrassed by Gigi's scolding. They made their way to the scooters, never turning their backs on the weapon, lowering their hands only when they mounted the vehicles. Bruce, however, lowered his hands, moved briskly towards his motorcycle, and turned around. Gigi raised her gun higher, but Bruce didn't seem to notice. He looked directly at Dennis.

"This isn't finished," he said.

"No," Dennis agreed. "It probably isn't. With bullies like you, it never is."

Dennis and Gigi stood in silence until the roar of bikes had faded. Dennis could hear the change in sound as the tires hit asphalt at the end of the Woodland path. Gigi likely could not.

"Oh." Gigi sighed and plopped down heavily on the bench. "Oh."

"What are you doing up here, Gigi?"

"I was out for a drive," she replied. "I cannae sleep, with this heat, with this belly, it's difficult, so I drive up the Cairneyhill sometimes in the night, just, you know, to get out of the car and stroll for a bit of exercise, and the gun, well, hah!"

Suddenly, she aimed the gun above the tower and fired. The snap that hit the air was modest, empty with the sound of wind, and there was no odor.

Dennis chuckled. *Of course. A pellet gun.*

"I know, horrible how I scared them!" Gigi smiled sheepishly. "I keep it in the car, you know, just in case. And this case was just such a case! I saw them on their way up the hill and knew something was amiss. He was here to cause you trouble, oh dear, yes, I knew it. There's stories, Dennis. They call you the Captain."

"So I hear."

"Yes, well, anyone in town would recognize that beast of a bike McKee rides," Gigi continued, "so when he passed on his way up here in the dark, I thought, no, what can he be up to? Oh, what a horrible, horrible man! What have you done, Dennis Duckworth, to make him so angry with you? Mostly he's simply snide and cruel, he's not usually this fired up, resorting to knives and arson."

"He's trying to prove he's a big man by hurting someone I like," Dennis replied. "I'm trying to stop him and he doesn't like it."

"Ah. People doing the right thing," Gigi sighed. "Nothing gets under the skin of a bully more than that, I suppose. Oh, Dennis, your tent—"

She gestured towards a misshapen, smoking lump in the dark, and suddenly realized, though it was quite apparent, that the fire was out.

"Who…"

"Don't worry about it," Dennis said. "It seems he got most of it out."

"He?"

"Oh. Yeah, my…assistant, Eddie. The fellow I hired to help with the restoration. He…he's here somewhere. Maybe—"

"I'm here," Eddie called out of the dark. "Just cleaning up this mess. Hello, Mrs. Gent. Nice to meet you."

"Nice to meet you, but…" Gigi stood and stared into the blackness. From her hip she took a flashlight, dangling from her belt, and shone it on the tower. "Dennis! You—the Council hasn't approved this yet! I haven't—you can't—there's CDM to consider—"

"Sorry?"

"Construction design and management regulations! They're sticklers for that kind of thing! They need to—ah—but…"

The closer she got to the tower, the longer the pauses in her protestations became. With her flashlight in one hand she pulled back some of the hessian and inspected the work in uncharacteristic silence.

"My lord, Dennis, you've…this is…what lovely work! What lovely, lovely work! Absolutely lovely! It…it looks so good! So authentic!"

She skipped over to another piece of the damp cloth, pulled it back, and shone her light behind it.

"Oh, Dennis *I am thrilled!!!* And so *fast!* This work should have taken a week at least, but here it is, mortar setting, stones in place…Dennis, this is fantastic!"

"Thanks, Gigi, but it's Eddie you really have to thank. He's a whiz at this kind of thing."

"Eddie!" Gigi shouted into the woods. "Come here a moment you lovely young man! I want to say thank you and hello and meet you, yes!"

Eddie slowly emerged from the woods. The moon was bright, but the dim still hid most of Eddie's features. She seemed to regard him as quite regular, despite the fact the fire glowing in his eyes still shone. It was, in fact, about all that Dennis could really see.

Maybe she can't see it.

"I'm not such a young man," Eddie said, fist over mouth, "but a pleasure to meet you all the same, Mrs. Gent."

"Oh, you're…" Gigi searched for words. "Oh, you're a lovely man, and probably younger than you think! I didn't expect—"

"Me to be so tiny?"

"No! I did not expect you to be so tiny!" Gigi clapped her hands, Eddie glanced at Dennis, and Dennis nodded as if to say *I told you she does that.*

"Mister…"

"Eddie will do, ma'am."

"Eddie, I cannae thank you enough! I mean, yes, still, there's a problem, the Council will be dismayed, no, perhaps not, but irritated, they'll complain and shout about processes and procedures and policies but then if one, just one of them, sees the work you've done, then, oh, then they'll be so, so impressed, they'll forget all about it! I know it! And if not, I'll talk them through it!"

Then, pleased with her kind words, Eddie forgot himself and smiled. Dennis caught it and froze, noting the flash of uncertainty that passed through Gigi's eyes.

"Oh, Gigi!" Dennis exclaimed, placing a hand on her shoulder to distract her. "I'm going to ask a lot less than a regular mason would, too. They'll be very pleased. Very!"

Gigi remained silent. Her head was at a slight angle, as though she believed she had have seen something and was deciding whether or not it was a trick of the moonlight.

"Right, then," she said, turning to Dennis as Eddie bolted for the safety of the woods again. "What was that?"

"Cost. Cost will be low, quality high, I promise. I just…I'll need to get paid by September 6th. The first Monday in September. I have to get myself a flight from Glasgow Airport that day. Is it possible?"

"Aye," she grinned. "Even if I have to advance it myself! I don't mind. We'll do it. I cannae be more grateful, Dennis Duckworth, this is just so lovely…"

She took one long look at the tower in the moonlight.

"I'll be back tomorrow to have a real look. For now, though, this adventure seems to have exhausted me. I best get back to the car. I'm so sorry about the tent. So sorry! Dennis, you'll be all right, yes?"

"Yes, I will," Dennis said. "Will you?"

Gigi laughed. "I ran up that trail, Dennis, ran up it in record time! Four days overdue, and still I can run if I need to!"

"You know," Dennis chided "You shouldn't be running anywhere in your condition. Four days overdue! Most women would be sitting by the hospital doors."

"Hospital?" Gigi laughed again. "Posh! Home birth, lad. With a lovely midwife. I call her and she comes to my home, that's how it works. If I called her, she'd come up to Kinnoull! In fact, giving birth up here... it would be..."

"Lovely?"

"Indeed, lovely! Thank you, Dennis Duckworth! Thank you, Eddie! See you in the morning."

As her footsteps faded down the trail, Eddie approached and stood beside Dennis.

"Well," Eddie said. "She seems lovely."

"Indeed." Dennis breathed deeply and exhaled slowly. "Did you manage to save my stuff?"

"I'm sorry, lad," Eddie replied. "The clothes on your back and the ones in your suitcase are all that survived."

Dennis' clothes had lain in one corner of the tent, waiting to be folded. The only clothes in the suitcase, of course, were the captain's whites.

"She almost saw the teeth, didn't she?"

"Not almost," Dennis replied. "She saw something. She just decided it was a trick of the light."

Eddie slowly paced a circle around the campfire pit. "She'll be here in the morning and, if I may say, she's not the type to allow me to stand silent. She's not the type to trust a man who doesn't smile. Add to that the fact that she saw something, whether she believes she saw it or not..."

"So don't be here."

"I must be here," Eddie replied. "There's work to finish. I want to show her how it's going to go. I want to…earn you your money, Dennis. And so, I think, it's time."

Eddie stopped and seemed to brace himself. Abruptly, he took a deep breath and shouted.

"Jesus Christ!"

The *poof* was followed by *whuuuuup* as air rushed in to fill the vacuum left by Eddie's disappearance. Dennis watched as a single tooth fell to the ground, thin as a needle.

Somewhere in the distance, Dennis heard the voice again. Then again, far on the other side of Kinnoull, perhaps down the Cairneyhill Road. Then, again, maybe a hundred yards to the east. Then again, from down by the motorway. Again, from the river. Again. And again. It was quiet, then loud, muffled, then clear, it surrounded him, a circle of curses. Once, Eddie appeared just to Dennis' left, only to exclaim "Jesus Christ" and disappear, leaving another otherworldly tooth in his wake. It went on for what seemed like minutes, the voice like the voices of many men, random men taking the name of the Lord in vain across the hills and valleys of Perthshire.

Dennis began to grin, and smile, and chuckle to himself in disbelief.

Finally there was a moment's silence to herald Eddie's return. He marched across the clearing and stood in front of Dennis in the moonlight, where he threw his head back to reveal his now-empty mouth. Every last fang was gone.

"Dennisssh," he said, "I dink dis wiw make me shound punny."

There was another silence but it was interrupted quickly by laughter; the type of laughter that causes people and goblins alike to double over and hold their sides in joyous agony. Eddie attempted to speak again, and each time, they both broke out in fresh giggles. Eventually they sat down from the strain of it all and the giggles grew apart, allowing them to catch their breath.

"I dink I wiw need dendures," Eddie said.

*

"You haven't had a haircut in what—a thousand years?"

A copy of the NME lay unopened in Dennis' lap. He had been much more interested in observing the reactions of his friend who sat like a child in the relatively enormous barbers' chair, apron tucked into his shirt, hair dark and flat against his scalp. Dark and flat and *short*.

"Och, you be making fun of me again," scoffed Eddie, eyes closed.

The barber, a short but broad-shouldered man whose Orkney accent was all but indecipherable, snorted and stopped clipping. "Aye! A thousand years! You'd almost think so!"

They'd chosen a haircut not unlike Donald Sutherland's, which seemed age-appropriate, to replace the shaggy Billy Connolly look. The barbershop was but one stop in another tour of Perth and its human world, Perth above ground, Perth in daylight. Dennis paid their way through poster printing, busses and lunch, but Eddie actually performed all the transactions as Dennis watched. All the while, Eddie talked, and when he ran out of subject to talk about, he began reciting poetry and lines of film dialogue. With every word, he carefully considered the placement of his tongue, finding alternate ways to approximate his Ts, Ds and Ls. With that mouthful of spikes, the red cap hadn't used his tongue as a human did, and it took him little time to regain most of his diction. It might also have been magic; Dennis could never tell.

"You're from around here, then?" the barber asked Eddie. Eddie, who lacked a surname, an origin, and any stories related to human life, prepared to wing it. He continued to keep his eyes shut. The barber either did not notice or did not find it weird.

"Och, no," he replied casually. "Born in Edinburgh, but I've been all around the country. Spent some time in the north, spent some time in the south."

The answer was entirely true, use of the word "born" notwithstanding.

"What brings you to Perth, then?"

"My friend Dennis here," he replied. "He has me working on a restoration project up on Kinnoull."

"No." The barber lowered his shears and regarded Dennis. "So you're the infamous Captain?"

"At your service," he said, pulling the captain's hat from his duffle bag and placing it on his head.

"Well!" the barber remarked, as he continued to clip. "What a pair the two of you make!"

"I don't doubt it." Eddie grinned his now-toothless grin.

"No wife, then?"

"No sir. All my life I've either scared women away or, well, let's just say I was no good for them."

"Family?"

"You might say I'd an enormous family at one time," Eddie considered, "but we didnae amount to much. Troublemakers, really. Today they're dead, dying or living a life I want no part of."

"You mean the Captain here is your only friend in the world?"

"You might say that," Eddie replied. "You might indeed say that."

When the haircut was complete, Eddie quickly slipped his sunglasses back on and paid. It was Eddie's task to pay for anything, with Dennis' money, of course, to navigate streets, to talk to shopkeepers. Dennis tagged along, largely in silence, unless Eddie had questions. Dennis oversaw every exchange of words or currency with the anxiety of a nervous father watching his child barrel down the driveway without training wheels for the first time.

There was a vague grey sky and the occasional non-committal drift of drizzle—weather Dennis would have expected here, but had rarely seen. Eddie pulled his own cap out of a small plastic bag he'd tied to his belt and pulled it low over his ears.

"You had that off for twenty minutes," Dennis noted.

"Longest it's ever been off my head," Eddie agreed. "Apart from the time the wind tossed it out into the north sea and I had to swim for it. That was only ten minutes, what with the undertow kicking up a fight."

"How do you feel?"

"Not a damn shade different," Eddie admitted. "Just…not confident yet."

"Well, it looks pretty awful. The more I look at it, the more it looks like what it is. Blood-soaked. And let's not talk about the smell."

"It's the heat."

"It's the rotting blood, Eddie. It even attracts flies."

"Do you think he saw the eyes?" Eddie asked.

"I don' t know," Dennis replied. "But…you know, you looked right at Gigi, and…"

"And?"

"And she didn't seem to notice the eyes."

Eddie considered a moment before he spoke.

"Maybe it's fading," he mused.

"I still see it," Dennis countered.

"Well then." Eddie paused a moment. "Maybe she sees it, but her mind dismisses it. After all, you met a goblin. She thinks she met a wee little human being."

"Maybe, if you're lucky, that's what will happen with everyone."

"Maybe."

They strolled along the interlocking stone, past the Woolworth's and benches where he'd eaten lunch with, then summarily offended, Abby. Dennis squinted, the fine mist gathering on his eyelids as the drizzle began to cascade like mist from a waterfall.

"What if you're right, though, Eddie?" he asked. "What if it *is* fading?"

"What do you mean, Dennis?"

"Well, just…" Dennis sighed, wiped his eyes, and stared up into the mist as they walked. "Don't you ever feel like you're betraying your nature? You had a huge family, you told the barber, and here you are, forsaking that history. I don't know…the end of magic seems sad to me."

Eddie waved an impatient hand in Dennis' direction.

"Dennis, the end of the red caps won't be the end of *magic*. We're not the last ones standing, you know. Not one of the last ones—but one of the worst ones. We're a sorry lot, Dennis. We don't live in families, we live alone. We don't socialize or arrange football matches on the Inch on holidays. Our collective history is one of murder and destruction and horror. That's all we have, Dennis. A shared history of murder. I suppose, to a race without magic, it might seem like I'm renouncing something irreplaceable, something valuable."

"You're giving up membership in a pretty cool club," Dennis offered. "Sorta."

"Bah!" Eddie made a sour face. "You've peeked through the gate, lad, but you're still a thousand miles away from me, no matter how improved your sense of smell might be. There are beings and worlds far beyond your imagination. Not all are evil, I assure you. I cannae cross into them, and I dinnae see them, but I…I feel them. You might say, I know who I am and where I am from. It's bigger than being a red cap. It's more than being a goblin. You're the one who should be having a crisis of faith."

"Me?"

"Aye, *you*, lad." Eddie slipped one finger into the corner of his mouth, marveling again at the disappearance of his fangs, at the smooth, fleshy ridge that remained. "Cannae be easy, trying to reign in that galloping tongue of yours."

"So what does that mean?"

"There's a lot of freedom in being an arse. You're never wrong. You can cheat on your wife, you can lie for financial gain. Surely part of you feels like you're…giving up membership in a pretty cool club, no?"

"Fuck you, Eddie," Dennis sulked. "That isn't funny."

"I'm not trying to be funny. You're forsaking a history, too—but one of your own making. It's going to be tempting to just give up and go back to being an arse."

"Well, maybe I'll land The Random this record deal, and maybe I'll find a way to cross the rest of those names off my list, and maybe that'll make me happy. I feel like being happy is the key. If I'm not a miserable fuck, I won't act like a miserable fuck."

"Chicken and egg, Dennis. Chicken and egg."

They passed through downtown and headed across the Perth bridge. The Tay was grey under the clouds. Wind picked at Eddie's collar and smacked it against his chin.

"Think it'll rain tomorrow?"

Eddie remained silent.

"I think it's going to rain tomorrow."

"Welcome to your new world, Dennis. You've the meteorological precognition of a cow or an arthritic knee."

Every few feet, the red cap seemed to quicken his step. Clearly he was not used to walking in lighter shoes, and occasionally forgot his own strength.

"Slow down. You're walking too hard."

"What in hell does that mean? How does a person walk too hard?"

"A person," mused Dennis.

"A person," Eddie replied. There was a hint of satisfaction in his voice. *Person.*

*

The scuff of boots on dirt reached Dennis' ears long before she emerged from the trees, yet he still felt slightly thrown by her arrival.

"Ah. Um…hey."

"Hey back." Margaret stood, one hand swatting at gnats around her left ear. "Thanks for the cordial welcome, Captain."

"Oh, yeah, sorry," he said. "Wasn't sure how to greet you. I can't exactly say 'welcome to my place' because it isn't exactly my place, though, I guess it is, …for now."

"Roomy." Margaret stepped into the clearing and turned 360 around the ruins. "Airy. Lots of light."

"It's not easy being the award-winning house on the block. Visitors come through at all hours. They're good, but sometimes their horses leave droppings."

Margaret suppressed a snicker.

"I used to live in a little humble little nylon job in the trees there." Dennis gestured to the blackened smudge on the forest floor. "But a few nights ago, Bruce McKee burned it down, so now I live there."

He nodded his head backwards at the tower, where he and Eddie had fashioned a lean-to of sorts from wood, rabbit fur and leftover hessian fabric. The rest of the hessian had been removed from the walls, and now the tower stood in all its restored glory. He and Eddie had carefully brushed the stones and made them come alive as if in high definition. Only the rusty metal band around the stack had been left untouched. "Looks better rusty," Eddie had noted, and of course he'd been right.

"McKee actually did that?" she asked.

"Don't underestimate how much the man dislikes me." Dennis crossed to the fire, where a frying pan was positioned above the flames. He removed the lid and poked at its contents with a stainless steel spatula. "Sorry, give me a moment. You like fish, Abby told me."

"I'm Scottish."

"Aye. Well, I guarantee you, it'll be the most…succulent sea bass you've ever had."

"Succulent?"

"I went with my second choice of words." Dennis finished turning the fillets and covered the pan again. "My first was 'fucking excellent,' but that seemed a little crass."

"Are you always so careful with your words?" Margaret stretched her arms behind her back, which Dennis took to be a sign of discomfort. He brushed off a blanket that had been placed by the fire and motioned for her to sit down.

"I'd suggest your whole problem with McKee is that I am not so careful with my words," Dennis sat on a second blanket, purposefully placed beside—but not too close to—Margaret. Margaret was only here because Abby had cajoled her, and because word of the fundraiser had trickled in through the doors of the Rat and Raven. It didn't matter that Dennis had a genuine desire to make amends; he was still the one who'd made amends necessary, and he did not know how much value his reparation attempt would carry.

"Careful with my words," he mused as a pop and burst of steam came from the pan. "Sometimes, maybe. I'm more of an…improvisational sort. It's all about getting into the right character, and then letting that character say what he needs to say to, uh, complete the scene."

"All the world's a stage, then."

"As Rush and Shakespeare would have you believe."

"And you're living in the limelight."

"Maggie, you do *not* know the lyrics to a Rush song. I can't even deal."

"I do. Canadian classic rock doesn't make it across the pond that much, but Rush and Max Webster are a few that I know."

"And now you out-obscure me on music! Who in fuck is Max Webster?"

"It's a they, and never mind," said Margaret. "Back to Rush. Isn't there a line in that song about insufficient tact?"

"The heart of my problem. Right there."

"You might say I agree," said Margaret.

"Well, I've said and done some things to some people here and there along the line."

"And you're coming clean now because…?"

"Because someone I recently met suggested it." Dennis removed a piece of fish and some rice from the pan and placed it as carefully as he could on the plate. A small chunk of fish broke apart and landed back in the fire. "You know, I could tell you all about what an asshole I am, if you have the time. Maybe you'll get a good laugh out of it. Maybe it'll do me some good."

"So I'm your confessor, then," Margaret said with mock solemnity. "And here was Abby, suggesting this was some kind of date."

"Is it a date?" His surprise was genuine. "I assumed you had mustered up a grudging tolerance for me, at best."

"Tolerance may be an overstatement, actually," Margaret replied. "Then again, I've been here three minutes, and you've neither insulted my taste in music nor cost me my livelihood, so perhaps there's hope."

Dennis closed his eyes, smiled, and shrugged. "That's the best I can expect. We started off well, but my proclivity for dickish behavior got the best of me. Assuming the comment about the Commitments soundtrack can be forgiven, and assuming that all goes well tomorrow and I right what I've turned upside down…can we start fresh?"

"I don't know," Margaret replied. "I don't know you. I know you're an American music business player who likes to talk shit and live on a hill."

"What do you want to know?"

"Why in hell are you living on a hill?"

Dennis managed to get his own piece of fish onto the plate without losing any of it; as Margaret hadn't touched hers yet, he switched their plates, giving her the whole piece of fish.

"Nope," he said.

"Nope?"

"Nope," Dennis repeated. "I'm not gonna answer that one yet. You have to think I'm halfway normal before I prove I'm halfway insane. Ask me something else."

"Fine," she replied, though now the only question she wanted answered was the one he hadn't answered. "Tell me about something easy, then. Something non-intrusive. What do you do?"

"I'm a music industry weasel."

"I know your species. I was asking about your breed."

"Record company owner."

"Ah. One that I would have heard of?"

"You know much about Chicago record labels?"

"Tangerine…"

"Yeah, yeah yeah." Dennis waved his hand. "The competition. We're called 5/4."

"I hang my head in shame."

"You shouldn't. No one knows us yet. Small office in Wicker, a couple of small bands, and one that's about to make me a boatload of money, if all goes well."

"What led you to the music business, then?"

Dennis reached behind him and retrieved a bottle of red wine and two glasses.

"I was into music like every other kid," Dennis said as he poured the first glass. "Ozzy, Zeppelin, whatever, that kind of thing. In high school I met a guy named Paul who introduced me to all kinds of sonic weirdness. He…opened the doors of musical perception, I guess."

"Awkward paraphrase, but go on."

"Exceedingly awkward, but apt. That's when I realized that music was…" Dennis fought for words to fit a concept he'd never verbalized before. "I don't know. To me, a movie's a movie. Stray too far off the map and it stops being a movie, it becomes some kind of weird artsie experiment. Music is music. You can take a Gregorian chant and a shitty rap-metal song, both are music. You can even combine the chant and the rap-metal—it would probably suck, but you could do it. And it *could* be amazing, theoretically. Either way, it's still music. There's no need for linear logic, like in film or novels. It's more visceral, more immediate than visual art, at least for me. Visual art always enters through the eyes and heads straight for the brain. Music… music goes for the head and the gut at the same time. I dunno, I haven't written a dissertation on the subject or anything. I just loved music—but I wasn't a musician. I wasn't much of anything, really. I was a good student but sure as hell not a great one. I didn't exactly go for the career track, either, so when I graduated, I really couldn't think of much else to do."

"Where'd you go?" Margaret asked, as he passed her the glass.

"University of Chicago. God, just saying those words out loud stirs up some dusty memories. Coming out of high school, university was like a music festival. It was Glastonbury. You paid a stupefying admission price, but the event lasted eight months. There was always a horde of students sitting on the grass, waiting for busses, bustling in and out of buildings. Even studying seemed like a joyous social event. Well, not at the time, but now, retrospectively."

University hadn't been the frat-boy filled beer keg of a time he'd expected. It was something different, richer, and had little to do with the things he'd studied. He'd majored in English, and had forgotten the names of at least half the books he'd been forced to read. His minor was in Business, full of the theories he'd tried and failed to implement at 5/4, leaving him with only a vague understanding of how it was all going to work. Instead, he'd forged ahead as though using the Force; he'd built 5/4 on love of music and intuition, not his business education.

University was where he and Paul had finally settled into a true groove, their friendship revolving around tea and weed and beer and bands and long road conversations; a time when suddenly there was no Robbie or Jason or Mike. For the first time, there was no more human baggage. Outside of high school, Robbie and Jason and Mike had disappeared, as if they were no more. Dennis no longer felt forced to associate with them simply because they'd always associated. He felt free, and the only association he chose to carry forward into this freedom was Paul.

"I was free to make a new life and meet new people there," Dennis said, shaking off the reverie, "but in the end, I didn't make any friends. Or, should I say, I made a few and lost them fairly quickly."

"Such scintillating conversation," Margaret said dryly. "Your ex-wife, your sad, lonely existence in school…any dying pets or parents I should know about?"

"I'm sorry, did I talk about my ex-wife?"

"No, Abby told me a little, though. Don't worry, nothing detailed. And what's with the apologies! I think I might have preferred the old, unrepentant Dennis."

Dennis laughed. "No, I don't think anyone prefers the old, unrepentant Dennis. I'm in the process of destroying him. I'm…well, let's just say, the present is a nexus."

"A nexus?"

"Yeah. The point at which one becomes another. Where your past and future intersect. I'm trying to move forward in a new way, but I'll still be the old guy."

"Jesus, you have been doing some soul searching, haven't you?" Margaret strained to filter the incredulity from her voice and replace it with soft humour. She was almost successful; some of that warmth, the warmth Dennis had noticed that first afternoon in the pub, began to glow in her face. "Are you always this introspective?"

"No," he replied, "it's part of this new leaf I'm trying to turn over. Good deeds, introspection, not being a douchebag. These sorts of things."

"And part of this is the concert."

"Part of this is the concert."

"A concert to save the Rat and Raven."

"Exactly."

"Which is going well."

"Indeed."

"And was it you that leaked this rumour that it's going to be Kit Carson?"

"I didn't leak a rumour. I leaked information. It's being treated as a rumour."

Margaret squinted her eyes a moment before they snapped wide in astonishment. She straightened her back and leaned forward.

"You did not!"

"I did!" Dennis smiled, knowing he looked self-satisfied but feeling he deserved to be.

"How on earth did you find him?"

"I had an inside tip. From that girl Meaghan who works at the library."

"Meaghan Campbell!" Margaret laughed "Of course!"

"You knew they were an item?"

"Dennis, Perth's not that small a town, but it's not that big, either. And you could spit on the library from the Rat and Raven."

Margaret raised her glass and sipped. She closed her eyes and let the wine sit on her tongue a moment. Dennis watched her as subtly as he could. When she opened her eyes a few seconds later, she seemed suddenly concerned about something.

"Bruce," she said flatly. "He's 's not going to take this laying down. He's going to do something."

"What? Throw stinkbombs? Burn down the Inch?"

"Dennis, he burned down your *tent*. He held a *knife* to you."

"I didn't tell you that."

"Word gets around. Let's face it, he could do anything. Kidnap Carson, maybe. Light the bushes on fire. Conjure up the rains. Actually, that may be a real problem."

"He's a shaman?"

"No, you arse, rain. They're calling for thunderstorms now."

"The first full-fledged rain forecast in a month is now for tomorrow?"

Dennis pretended to be incredulous. "Until yesterday they've been calling for another sunny day."

"That's the way it goes."

Much to his own surprise, Dennis was unaffected by thoughts of Bruce McKee and rain.

"So, you're a city boy," Margaret said, taking a moment to sip her wine. "Did you have much experience in the great outdoors before you started living in the woods?"

"None," Dennis laughed. "Tried camping once or twice, with the ex. Didn't take to it."

"She wanted to go camping, you didn't, you went, and you hated it. Correct?"

"I don't really think I should be talking about my ex-wife right now," Dennis answered.

"Why not? I thought I was your confessor."

Dennis smiled. "I'm not sure I want to talk about her. Where would I start? I met Sylvia, just out of school, after I founded 5/4. She was different, and she made me different, too. When I was around her, I changed—and it was good. I used to drive a whole day, to Canada, to be with her. I drove to *Canada!* We'd talk for hours, and the jaded sociopath inside me never made an appearance. It couldn't last, though. The jaded sociopath has ruled most of my interpersonal relationships. It was only a matter of time before the sociopath snuck across the border and into my marriage."

"So, you weren't Dennis the Asshole when you were with her."

"Not at first," Dennis replied. "But eventually, yes. I stopped being fun. Sober, I was sullen. Drunk, I was antagonistic. In groups, I was combative. One on one, I was worse."

"You sound like a delight."

"Oh, don't get me wrong, I could be a charmer, but you can't consistently charm the person to whom you're closest. Eventually you have to be yourself. Not surprisingly, the more I became myself around her, the more she spent time at the studio—she's a fashion designer—and I started giving her grief about all the time she spent there. She stopped sleeping with me. I got indignant. I slept with someone I shouldn't have slept with. End of chapter."

They were quiet a moment, staring off over the hills, looking at the way the world spread out beyond their line of vision, how it met the sky in front of them, open, unbroken. The sky here seemed wider than back home, as if there was more space on the horizon, more *horizon* on the horizon, all of it encompassed by brilliant blue. It was impossible to explain the illusion, considering Chicago had its own expanses to witness. Chicago was on the edge of the world, or at least it seemed so to a ten year old staring out across the shimmery expanse of Lake Michigan. Years later, at the University of Chicago, Dennis would tag along with friends to the beach at Oak Street, ostensibly to play beach volleyball, but he never had any interest in the game. Dennis just liked to be near the water. In New York, you probably never noticed the river, steaming with puke and bile; in L.A., you probably went to the beach as Californians did, with sun block and beach towels and impossibly toned abs. Chicago was more vibrant and alive than either town, and surrounded with the kind of water that made Dennis feel at peace. Still lakes and quiet rivers.

"When she first married me, Sylvia worked at a small boutique on Chestnut," Dennis said aloud, more to himself than to Margaret. "I would hop on the El at Damen and take it to meet her at Starbucks. We'd take coffees to the corner that overlooks the river, where the tourist boats glide beneath the bridges. I loved that spot, but never had a reason to hang out there. I wasn't in the habit of hanging out alone on the sidewalk. With her, though, it became a daily ritual, even in rain and even in winter when the city earns its nickname. Her face would be bitten and reddened by cold, and we might only last a few moments, but in summertime the coffee break would expand and fill the hour. Sometimes I jogged back to the shop for a second cup—mine black no sugar, hers double tall skinny cinnamon latte. We'd just lean on the cement rail and watch the boats. She was always on the lookout for new boat names that made her smile. There was a boat called Summer of George, a reference to Seinfeld; we both liked that."

Margaret watched Dennis as he spoke. He seemed, however slightly, to be a different version of himself—softer.

"Sylvia had this favourite hair band," he said. "I don't mean a hair metal band, I mean, you know, an actual band you put in your hair. An orange one. She was very particular about it—it was carefully placed to give her that vaguely mod look that worked so well on her. She wasn't a flashy beauty, Sylvia, but…I don't know, her looks had more power. She didn't clamor for stares or cat-calls. Men almost never turned in her direction; instead, they kind of pretended they weren't watching her. She'd be wearing whatever ensemble she had tacked together from the remnants of other wardrobes, old clothes refitted, her eyes almost, you know, black but…"

Luminous, he didn't say. She was a breathtaking beauty, the kind that surpassed a man's libido and stilled his heart. The kind of beauty that made men sigh. Dennis said none of these things to Margaret. He didn't mention that, after he'd destroyed the relationship completely, he began to see those dark eyes as black holes, collapsed stars that would pull you into the crushing nothingness at the event horizon, reduce you to atom spray.

"After she found me out, she threw me out," Dennis continued. "I still took the El from Damen Station every day for six weeks, went to the coffee shop, stood at the same corner. I had always loved that spot, before Sylvia came into my life, and I went back to reclaim it. But I never could."

Here atop Kinnoull, there seemed to be enough space on the horizon for him to pour it all out, to let it gush out of him like water from a broken main, and it would barely make a puddle on the world. For the first time, he wanted to open the sluices, to just let it all drain away, be done with it. End of a chapter, yes, but it had been an unsatisfying conclusion. Too much bad blood. Too much awful.

I don't deserve another chance, and I'm not sure I want one. The well is poisoned. Best to let it go.

And for the first time, he truly believed that.

*

Beneath the hessian covers, underneath a tarpaulin made of the same material, Margaret slept. She'd been led gently into slumber by wine and night air, and Dennis had promised her no harm, no sketchiness, nothing of the sort. For whatever reasons, she'd believed him.

In his hand, the cellphone.

"She's asleep," Eddie whispered out of the dark.

"Out cold," agreed Dennis. "I put her there about two hours ago. She'll be ok."

"Of course she will," Eddie said, then added, "I'm looking out for you both."

"In case McKee comes back?"

"In case of anything."

"I appreciate that."

"What are you going to do now?" Eddie asked. "You should probably get some sleep. Big day tomorrow, no?"

"Yeah," Dennis said absently, his thumb poised above buttons.

"Ah," Eddie nodded. "Well, get to bed when you can, then."

Eddie left Dennis alone. In his hand, the cellphone, ringing across the ocean, and then, her voice.

"Hello?"

"…"

"Hello?"

"Hello, Sylvia."

"…"

"Please don't hang up. I'm not calling to scream and shout."

"Oh, what a relief." Her sarcasm cut through the miles of air and atmosphere, bounced off satellites without losing its edge. "What do you want, Dennis?"

"Hmmm. Yeah. I don't know, Sylvia. A few things, I guess."

"And they are?"

Dennis closed his eyes, in order to think better, but he only saw flashes—Sylvia wearing a black and white checked dress, one of her own creations, smiling at the bridge, drinking coffee, laughing. Dozens of hairstyles, outfits, weather conditions, times of day, but always the bridge, and always laughing.

"Remember the night we drove back home from your parents' house, and we came along Highway 3?"

"You mean, instead of taking the 401?" she asked.

"Yeah, the night we took the long way and drove along Lake Erie. Do you remember that?"

"I do," she replied cautiously, as if it were a trick question.

"Yeah. Remember how we stopped on a side-road and lay with our heads hanging out the open door, upside down, and there was that meteor shower?"

"Dennis." She sounded impatient. "I don't know what you're trying to do here—"

"Neither do I," he admitted, "but what I'm *not* trying to do is excavate sweet memories, dust them off, and use them to convince you to take me back. After the last little while, I think it's clear we shouldn't be together anymore. I betrayed you, and then we both let anger take over. And that led to suffering."

"You left out the hate part, Yoda," she said. "Anger leads to hate. *Hate* leads to suffering."

Dennis smiled. "I know. I left that out intentionally. I don't hate you, Sylvia. I mentioned Highway 3 to remind you of a time when you didn't hate me."

She was quiet a moment, and now the silence seemed softer.

"I don't hate you, Dennis," she said eventually. "I just hated the way you let yourself fall down that well. You let that bitterness take over every part of you. I saw it in you, it was there all along, but I never thought it would enter our marriage."

"Well, it entered," Dennis replied. "It entered and devoured it, and started to devour me, finally, after all these years. So I've started to get rid of it. I don't know how successful I'll be, but I'm trying."

"You started seeing a therapist?" she asked.

"Uh…yes. He's a bit unorthodox, but his results have been spectacular so far."

Dennis stared at twinkling stars and sailing headlights.

"I'll be back in Chicago soon," Dennis said, "and maybe we can meet for coffee, talk about how we're going to deal with all the details. We've got things to split up, things to sort out. Maybe…maybe we can avoid the lawyers after all. Maybe we can do this like adults. I know you were always capable of that, but maybe it's something I can do now, too. Then you and I can leave this all behind, and all this will just be a shitty tail end to an otherwise pretty good time. The good times will outweigh the bad. Eventually."

This time, her silence seemed filled with quiet surprise.

"Why now?" she asked. "Why are you trying to make peace now?"

"Because," Dennis said, "It's only now that I realize I'm sorry."

She began to cry then, a gentle sound, soft not because she was trying to stifle it, but because they were a different kind of tears—tears of sadness, tears of relief, tears of love, the kind of tears he'd denied her by making her so angry and bitter. He started crying too, for the first time in years, his emotions overflowing, reaching the surface unsoured for the first time. His heart felt as if it would break, possibly explode, but he knew that if it did, the sallow ichor it once contained would drip harmlessly to the ground, instead of poisoning him as it once would have done.

"If you're not in Chicago," Sylvia sniffled after a moment, "where the hell are you?"

Dennis laughed, interrupting the flow of tears. "You wouldn't believe me if I told you."

"I wouldn't have a few minutes ago," she said, "but now I might."

"Okay. Well, I'm sitting on top of a hill in central Scotland. In fact, I'm living on top of a hill in central Scotland."

"Living on a hill?"

"Aye. In a lean-to."

"Dennis!" Sylvia laughed. "You hate sleeping outside!"

"Yeah," Dennis sniffled and sighed to himself. "Up until a few weeks ago, I really did."

CHAPTER FOURTEEN

Dawn came to Kinnoull as though it had nothing but glad tidings to share. The sky was clear, the air crisp. Orange hues flowered out across the countryside, petals of light and colour laying on hills and settling into the valleys. It was going to be a beautiful day for a concert.

Yet despite all available evidence, Dennis knew it was going to rain.

"Ready for today, my friend?" Eddie stood over the fire, as a familiar aroma floated up over his shoulders towards Dennis. Dennis rubbed a pebble of sleep out of the corner of his eye and nodded.

"As I'll ever be." He stared into the horizon, his face as dark as the thunderheads he was unable to see but knew were coming.

"I know it looks nice out, Eddie, but—"

"It's Kit Carson, lad," Eddie interrupted. "As long as a typhoon hasn't blown in from the coast of the Philippines, you'll have an audience. Stop worrying and sit down to breakfast."

"Purloined bacon and eggs. The fruits of our illegal labours."

"No!" Eddie leapt up. "No, laddie, not this time. I had to occupy myself during your wee date last night, so I went into town."

"By yourself?" The news startled him.

"No, lad, with my wife and kids. Of course by myself!"

"How did it go?"

"It went well," the red cap replied. "Nary an unfortunate moment. A few funny looks, as I suppose any little person is wont to receive, but compared to being invisible, a few curious glances is nothing. Seems a fair price."

Dennis suddenly imagined what parents felt like on the first day of kindergarten. It was somehow a bittersweet moment.

"You're leaving tomorrow," Eddie said solemnly.

"Aye."

"You've got a ticket?"

"No." Dennis approached the fire and crouched down to look down at the delicious sizzle. "No, I'm going to fly stand-by, or whatever they call it these days. Grab the first available flight out of Glasgow."

"Sleep in the airport?" Eddie asked. "You sure you want to do that? You talk in your sleep, you know."

"Everyone tells me that!" Dennis stood up again. "I never gave a shit, but now that you mention it, what do I talk about?"

"You always say the same thing," Eddie replied.

"Really? What do I say?"

"*I am the master of every situation,*" said a voice behind them.

Margaret came towards them, her freshly opened eyes squinted against the morning sun. "I heard you say it last night. It's the same thing you were muttering the night we...ah...*met.*"

Dennis frowned. "It's from a fortune cookie."

"It's what I've heard you say," Eddie agreed with Margaret. "Every night, it seems, since you've arrived. At some point you say that in your sleep. Some nights it's a murmur, other nights you shout it aloud."

"Well." Dennis paused. "How about that. I used to believe I was the master of every situation. Now, not so much."

"Well," offered Eddie, "I do not think it means what you think it means."

"Fortune cookies and the Princess Bride again," Dennis smiled. "As always, it all comes full circle."

"I don't believe we've met," Margaret said as she approached Eddie. "You're Eddie, the master of restoration Dennis told me about, yes?"

"Yes." Eddie stood, doffed his cap, and placed it back on his head with some uncertainty. "Pardon the headgear, it's in need of a good wash."

"Nothing to pardon." Margaret regarded him a moment. Her mind seemed caught somewhere else—a déjà vu, a lapse in consciousness—and then it was gone.

Dennis, oblivious, took over stirring the eggs.

The three of them ate cross-legged around the firepit, where they chatted together in the morning sun. Eddie honed his biography, much fleshed-out with brief references to family and upbringing, some details gleaned from reading, some details observed, a millennium of experience, a millennium of examination, all distilled into a story so simple it rang truer than the truth. Dennis marveled at him. It was as if Eddie, though not a real human, had a singular understanding of things, things of which women and men could only grasp the edges, and as a result, these truths only hovered on the edges of their consciousness. Every tale he told, though nothing more than fiction, was intuitively true. True to something other than the facts of history. As if Eddie were some kind of Jungian archetype of mankind, in a little, wrinkled form.

As Eddie began to brew the coffee, twigs snapped to the south. Out of the trees stepped Abby, beads of sweat beginning to form on her temples and forehead. She approached the group with a grin, as though neither her presence on the hill nor present company was in any way unusual. Margaret insisted she join them for coffee. Abby crossed the clearing and sat cross-legged on a swath of hessian that had been laid around the fire pit.

"Dennis."

"Abby."

"Are you ready?"

"Ready as anyone could ever be. I would figure you've not met Eddie."

"Eddie?" she turned to the goblin and extended her hand. "You...you are clearly the one they're calling—no offense intended, I didn't make it up—the wee Jedi."

"The wee Jedi!" Eddie clapped his hands together once, with obvious delight. "No offense taken. That's a fabulous nickname. I'm a bit wee, after all."

"Big enough to have put the fear of God into Bruce McKee," Margaret replied. Dennis felt his stomach drop at the G word, his head filled with a sudden intense panic. It took a moment for him to realize that Eddie remained, thoughtfully mashing eggs between his bare gums. No whoosh of air spirited him away across the hills.

The red cap saw something in his friend's eyes, and smiled at Dennis.

"I've no teeth," he whispered at Dennis, unheard beneath the continued discussion. "I guess you can't have one without the other."

It made little sense, but at the same time, perfect sense. *Whatever the reason, thank the G word. Sudden teleportation might prove difficult to explain.*

Dennis turned back to the topic at hand.

"So…how mad is he?"

"Oh, he's enraged." Margaret sounded pleased. "Utterly furious. You know what you've done with this fundraiser? You've made my situation public. I don't enjoy airing my dirty laundry in the town square… but now, people will be a might suspicious if McKee tries any funny business. If I pay him back—which, thanks to you, I surely will—he cannae try to find a loophole, or illegally shut my doors. If the Rat and Raven closes, he'll be in the hot seat."

"Well, I sure as hell didn't help with your creditor relations," Dennis said. "It was the least I could do. And again, I'm sorry."

"Least? You're putting on a concert in the park with an extraordinarily popular singer! If this is the least you can do, I can't imagine the most. Where did this come from? Come to think of it, where did *you* come from?"

"Chicago"

"Hah hah. I meant this new Dennis Duckworth. You've made yourself scarce."

"With Bruce McKee out there, I thought it best if I went to ground."

"It didn't really work so well," Abby said. "He rooted you out."

"I'm still here," Dennis said. "No new injuries, just a few charred clothes."

"Well, thank you, Dennis," Margaret said. "Remember, though, Bruce won't let this slide. He's up to something, I can almost guarantee it. Be wary."

"We're wary," Eddie said. "but what could he possibly do now?"

Another series of footfalls snapped and crunched out of the nearby wood. The quartet looked up to see the monstrously sized Gigi. Her legs were bowed, as if struggling to bear the enormous sphere of flesh above them, and her lips curled inward with strain.

"Gigi!" Abby ran towards the woman, who had stopped to rest, hands on knees. "What are you doing here? Are you okay?"

"She's involved in, uh, all this," Dennis said. "She's our employer, I guess."

"Oh, yes, and…lovely work!" Gigi panted. "Have you seen it? Have you seen?"

"Enough of that." Margaret said briskly as she approached the pained woman. "Why in the name of God are you hiking up that hill? Your doctor would slap you silly."

"Och, doctors!" Gigi panted and grimaced. "My midwives, yes, they might protest, though, that's true, oh I'm such a horrible client for them, I know! Coming up here in this heat. But Dennis and Eddie deserve to be paid, and I know Dennis has to get back to Chicago, and I'm just so grateful, he's been so lovely, he and Eddie both, just lovely, and I thought, I thought I'd better come up here today and give him this."

Gigi pulled an envelope from her back pocket, thick with pound notes, and passed it to Abby. Eddie stared at Gigi intently, mild concern on his face.

"Can you pass this to him, love? I don't think I can walk for a moment."

"Why didn't you just wait and give it to me at the show, Gigi?" Dennis protested.

"Oh, no!" Gigi replied. "No, no, I might not be around by this afternoon."

"What do you mean?"

"She thinks she'll be in labour," Eddie said. "I've news for you, Mrs. Gent. You're already in labour."

"Ah, just some early contractions, that's all."

There was no audible gasp at this statement, but a flurry of curses and mild admonishments instead.

"How far apart are they?" Eddie stepped forward, his demeanor suddenly authoritative, his gait so assured that he seemed to sprout a foot in height.

"Oh, I don't know," Gigi replied. "You might call it frequent."

Eddie's eyes flitted about the tower until they landed on a pile of clean, dry hessian. Abby followed his gaze and didn't wait for instructions.

"Wait, what?" Dennis stood a moment, uncertain as Abby laid hessian down on the grass in front of Gigi. "What are we doing? Shouldn't we be getting her to the hospital *right now?*"

"Ladies," Eddie motioned to Abby and Margaret, "Make sure she's comfortable. Gigi, lassie, you should page your midwives and let them know about the change of venue. And perhaps your husband! Dennis, a word?"

Eddie led Dennis around the tower and out onto the precipice of the lookout. Dennis noted his bright, clear sky had a ruffle of darker cloud forming at its edges, but pushed the thought from his mind.

"Dennis, we can't get her to the hospital."

"But surely there's some time—"

"There's no time. And…there's another problem."

"What?"

"Another problem," Eddie repeated gravely. "Inside her. Don't be concerned about the baby, it's healthy, it's just…not properly on the slide, if you follow."

"So…"

"So, I can…" Eddie stopped.

"Magic that up a bit?" Dennis suggested.

Eddie looked over his shoulder quickly to survey the progression of the situation.

"I'm not a wizard, Dennis, but yes, I've certain abilities. With living things, even babies, I hold a certain sway. I cannae snap my withered fingers and make it all come up right, but at least I can try and get that baby swung 'round. But by that time, she'll be fully dilated and ready for the child to make its way into the world. If he's dropped too far, I cannae help, so I need to go and fix it. Now."

"So, you're like, the baby whisperer or something?"

"Stuff it," Eddie said as he grumbled his way back to Gigi. "Baby whisperer. Always with the jokes."

"Gigi, lassie, forgive me." Eddie knelt down beside Gigi, whose face was as bewildered as it was pained, as though surprised that childbirth was the end result of the pregnancy. "I know it isnae the most comfortable situation, but believe it or not, I've ushered others into this realm."

"Realm?" she panted.

"Er, world, yes, world. What I'm saying is, dinnae fear this wee stranger inserting himself into this moment. I promise I can take good care of you and yours. Your midwives will never make it here in time; nor would you get home in time, or to a hospital, or wherever you were planning to be."

"You mean, my little man will be born on Kinnoull?"

"Aye, ma'am, it looks that way."

"Oh, that's…" Her face contorted into a grimace and the word came out as an agonized, guttural growl. "*Luuuuuuvleh.*"

"Have you phoned your midwives?"

"Aye."

"Husband?"

"Ooooh, dear… William!"

Gigi began a frantic phone call, overflowing with pauses, stutters, grunts, groans, and, unimaginably yet inevitably, a few lovelies. Margaret scoured the fireside for dish soap and a bucket of water that sat nearer the tower.

"Scrub for at least a minute," she suggested to Eddie, "It's that antibacterial stuff."

"Eddie," said Dennis.

"Oh, I know, William sweetheart, I know, but I'm fine, really I'm fine!" Gigi shouted behind them, her words boosted by a wave of pain. "Call Cynthia and pick up the girls and bring them here, love!"

"Didn't you notice your water break, Gigi?" Abby asked, folding some hessian into a makeshift pillow.

"Oh, yes, dear, my darling—yes, I noticed, Abby, it broke in the car!—no, dear, I was talking to—yes in the car—don't you mind that, now, those seats are leather, we've other more important—"

"Eddie," repeated Dennis, as Margaret brought the water and soap.

"Yes, lad?" Eddie replied distractedly.

"Eddie, you're going to need to wear something clean around you, maybe a hessian apron." He pointed directly at Eddie's head. "And you're going to need to take that off before you scrub up."

Eddie felt at the edges of his cap, and even as he did so, a fly or two was disturbed and buzzed circles around his face. Eddie sighed.

"Right, then."

Eddie jumped to his feet, marched quickly to the tower, and out onto the lookout, as Dennis followed.

"Eddie? What are you doing?"

"That's enough of this, then!" He removed the cap and held it, arm tucked inward as if he were about to toss a Frisbee.

"Eddie!" Dennis was alarmed. "Don't get rash. Just take it off and put it on again later!"

Eddie closed his eyes a moment, as if uttering a benediction.

"No, Dennis," he said. "If ever there was a time to be done with it, now's the time to be done."

With that, he snapped out his arm and released the cap. It flattened as it hit the open air, curving off into space, high above the trees, pre-ternaturally high, to the point of improbability. It sailed, caught by the wind or by magic or both, and had anyone been looking they would not have seen its final descent unless they had the keenest eyes—the eyes of a red cap, for example, or someone who had been touched by one. And so it was that both witnessed the cap as it slapped directly onto the slow-moving surface of the River Tay.

"Let her sink and be gone," Eddie said, "and let what must come my way come my way." With that, he turned heel, ducked past Dennis, and headed straight for Gigi, who lay on her back, panting, distressed, and yet somehow smiling.

*

278

The arrival of young master Gent took an astonishingly short ninety-two minutes. The minutes travelled in loops, extended themselves through long stretches that crawled by with great difficulty, only to spin and turn in another direction, burning through a quarter-hour without pause. Margaret and Abby acted as assistants, caregivers, and coaches, while Eddie mostly crouched in front of Gigi. For one long, breathless moment, he lay his hands on her lower torso, fingers splayed, and seemed to be talking to himself.

"Oh," Gigi gasped, "Do you feel that, Eddie? It's like he's doing back-flips! Gymnastics! Tumbling and such!"

Eddie responded with an 'aye' and a smile. At that moment, Dennis knew everything was going to be all right.

Gigi pushed for a mere twenty minutes before the rumble of an engine approached and an ATV broke into the clearing. William Gent bounded from the machine before the engine could die, and before the two consternated-looking young women in the trailer could regain their composure from the bumpy ride. As William approached, he looked equal parts terrified and elated.

"You, my friend, are here just in time." Dennis smiled.

"It's a miracle," Gigi gasped.

"Miracle, magic, coincidence, serendipity, whatever." Dennis stepped sideways to allow William room. "It's all the same damn thing."

"Thank you," William said aloud to no one in particular as he knelt at his wife's side. "Thank you, thank you, thank you."

And, at that very moment, as the midwives approached, Gigi released a great cry, and the child was born. Seconds later, it wailed up at the sky and out into the river valley below. Eddie cradled the child a moment before looking up at a dazed but somehow smiling Gillian Gent.

"I just realized," she said breathlessly, "that you've the same name. Eddie, meet…Eddie."

The elder Eddie smiled. His eyes watered, and for a moment, Dennis thought the creature would cry. He didn't; he quickly passed the newborn to one of the midwives, who set about the business of cleaning up the child and allowing a slowly calming William to cut the cord.

"He was born on Kinnoull!" Gigi beamed at her husband. "Isn't it lovely?"

"My dear," he replied, "it's the loveliest thing in the world."

*

"We're going to have to move her soon," one of the midwives said to William, pointing at the sky. A heavy grey blanket had rolled over the western horizon.

"It doesn't matter." Abby touched Dennis on the sleeve. "It'll be okay. If it rains, it'll pass. It'll clear up."

"I knew it was coming."

"Still," Abby continued, "We really should get the hell out of here. It's late."

Dennis felt the bottom of his stomach give way. "Jesus! Carson's supposed to be here in fifteen minutes. I...can we just..."

"Go!" Gigi cried from behind them. "Just go! You've all done more than enough already! I'm well taken care of, Eddie's well taken care of—Eddie Junior, I mean—oh, if I'd not already chosen the name, I'd say you were his namesake, Eddie Senior! I'd say you were his namesake!"

"Actually," Dennis said under his breath, "the truth is, he's your namesake, Eddie. I named you after the baby."

Eddie's hair was damp, flattened against his head in a ring where the cap had rested. Now, the cap was either at the bottom of the Tay or headed out to sea.

"That," he replied, "truly *is* lovely."

*

The thunder grumbled closer to them as they crossed the Perth Bridge, four abreast, like some kind of fellowship on its way to join a great battle. They walked the short distance to the North Inch, where a very healthy-sized audience had begun to gather, especially considering showtime was forty-five minutes away. The sound crew had built the stage and, presciently, suspended some blue tarp over equipment in case of rain.

280

Meaghan Campbell, after a bubbly explosion of thank-yous and hugs one afternoon on High Street, had offered to help take donations; she'd recruited some friends, along with ManagerMan and Italian Girl from the record shop. As Dennis and his group approached, they felt the first soft yet enormous drops of rain splash against their heads and watched Meaghan look up to the sky, crestfallen.

Dennis donned his cap, which matched the uniform—his only uncharred clothing. As he walked through the crowd, some young kid, far too young to remember the Damned or Captain Sensible, actually yelled "I say, Captain!"

To which he replied, naturally, "I say wot?"

"Good luck!" The boy gave him two thumbs up in the nerdiest manner possible, to which Dennis replied with a salute and a smile that wilted quickly—as soon as the boy looked away, in fact—as the rain thickened and swelled. A gust of wind caught the audience's attention; people looked about nervously, uncertain what they wanted to do. A great number of the faces were young, but the curiosity about Kit Carson had clearly expanded far beyond his Youtube demographic; anyone in Perth who had a passing interest in the gossip seemed to be on the Inch. A passing interest, however, wouldn't hold them through a rainstorm.

"Get up there and start talking," Abby suggested.

So Dennis climbed onstage with Eddie at his heels, Margaret and Abby standing at the foot of the steps. The rain began to pound harder, and people began to scatter towards their cars, the trees, the buildings off the Inch. Dennis tapped the mic, safe and dry beneath the tarp-protected stage, and the sound guy became the second person to give him a thumbs up that day.

"Good afternoon everyone!" Dennis said. There was little response; disconcerted by the sudden downpour, people had scattered—but, he noticed, they hadn't exactly left. Some sat in their cars, but no engines turned over; they walked towards buildings, but their eyes were back on him. So, in case they were still listening, he spoke.

"Welcome to our end-of-summer benefit!" A small smattering of applause, separated by thunder, raindrops and distance. The remaining audience members were tucked neatly under umbrellas of varying sizes, colours and, depending on the age of the holder, heights.

"I see you're sticking around, hoping the rain will abate," he continued. "The weather reports are vague, but we're certain this isn't even going to last more than a couple more minutes."

He eyed Abby and Eddie and concluded, based on no more than a powerful, through-the-gate sort of hunch, that they all shared this belief.

"I know it's first instinct to find shelter and most of you have," he continued. "Except for those of you with the umbrellas, good thinking—but don't even think about leaving! Then you'd all miss what you came for."

A small smattering of applause again, though it was more concentrated and vigorous as people tucked their umbrella handles under their chins to free up their clapping hands.

"You've got a lot of faith for no reason, Captain," came a voice from the crowd. One of the umbrellas, a wide black one, dislodged itself from the group and floated towards the stage. Beneath it was the familiar, doughy form of Bruce McKee.

"It's going to get rained out and you're going to be stuck with nothing," McKee said.

"And you didn't have to do anything," Dennis called back, away from the mike, shouting in to the rain. "Imagine that."

"God's on my side, it seems." McKee puffed out his chest.

"I wouldnae be too certain about that." Eddie stepped out from the wings.

"Ah, the wee Jedi!" McKee sounded gleeful. "Finally, you show your face. You'll not get out of here except in handcuffs, for what you did!"

Eddie glanced askew at Bruce, the way one might regard and simultaneously regret regarding a drunk vomiting on the sidewalk. Dennis could sense the discomfort and indecision of the audience, but he knew what choice they would likely make if the rain continued. In fact, if the weather worsened, they would have to call it off themselves, for safety and liability reasons.

"I think it's done, Eddie," Dennis mumbled.

Eddie appeared not to hear. He stepped into the wings on stage left and removed his sunglasses. Deep in his dark eyes, a pinprick of red light pulsed, invisible to everyone save Dennis.

"There's one more thing we can try," Eddie called to Dennis over the increasing volume of rain smattering against the tarp.

Dennis crossed the stage, and Eddie led him down and behind the rigging. They stood in the rain a moment, hidden from the crowd, before Eddie closed his eyes and opened his mouth slightly, head pointed upwards towards the gunmetal sky. His jaw began to work, as though words were passing through them, but if Eddie spoke aloud, the sound was surpassing this world and heading straight into another.

"You've got to be kidding me."

Eddie's eyes opened and one eyebrow shot upward.

"Now is not the time for skepticism, lad. This is what you might call our Hail Mary."

Dennis stepped up beside the creature.

"And now you follow American football?"

Eddie did not reply, and, in spite of Dennis' own previous warning to himself—*don't touch the goblin*—he rested one hand on Eddie's shoulder. Immediately, his vision darkened and flashed, darkened and flashed, again and again, until finally the world around him settled into a place somewhere between light and darkness. The sound of the scattering, dampening crowd went from murmur to muffled roar. They were blanketed by rain and cloud, and now Dennis could hear Eddie's voice surrounding it all as he murmured in a language that was neither English nor Gaelic.

The clouds did not relent.

I cannae do it, came Eddie's voice in English—not to his ears, not exactly, but directly into his brain. *I dinnae have the power, Dennis.*

Neither do I, Dennis thought, knowing the red cap could hear him. *But you have to shut up, now, and keep trying.*

Dennis did his best to shut out the luminescence of the world as seen through Eddie, to forget that Bruce McKee stood twenty yards away, and to align his focus with Eddie's, to direct it at the sky above.

This is ridiculous, I know, Dennis thought at the sky, *but I've seen boarding passes change and goblins fry up eggs. So gimme a break.*

Suddenly, he felt a great weight, as if something, somewhere, had accepted his challenge. It was no longer Eddie trying to alter the forces of nature, it was Eddie and Dennis together. Eddie could feel the added force, as if someone had picked up one end of a particularly heavy object that he'd previously carried on his own.

That's it, lad, Eddie didn't say. *We're not making something happen here. I need you to understand that. I'm…asking, really. Begging and pleading. With your hand on my shoulder, you're asking with me.*

Eddie then continued to murmur, and Dennis thought he could hear a contemplative voice, muffled and distant, respond in kind. There were no true words, but its tone was neither good nor evil. If Dennis had to describe its tone, he would have used the word 'bemused.'

Then, silence. No more voices, from the beyond or from the crowd… and no more raindrops tapping away on plastic.

"Did we—"

"We didn't do a bloody thing," Eddie said. "Don't flatter yourself. Someone took pity on us is all."

"Who?" Dennis asked after Eddie, who was already half way up the side-stage steps. Dennis felt dazed, one step sideways from reality, almost depersonalized. He followed Eddie to the stage and from there he could see, above the crowd in the far distance, that the darkness of the clouds on the horizon was underlined by a bright white line. Behind that line, pushing the line forward as perfectly horizontally as a rising curtain, was a streamer of brilliant blue. He felt something flash down his spine, like the sparking flame on a cartoon fuse; it reached the bottom and puffed out into smoke. His mind and body came back together and everything felt as it had before, save for the blue sky ahead and the look of contemptuous disbelief on Bruce McKee's face.

"Oh, for the love of God." He looked simultaneously irritated and spooked, an unusual combination of expressions.

"That sky, McKee?" This time, Dennis spoke into the microphone.

"Five minutes away, if that. And if you need more impetus to stay put, then let me tell you now, finally, that you are going to enjoy the show very much. I can now confirm what you've only been guessing!"

A murmur broke across the audience, but swiftly swelled into an extended wave of cheers and whistles.

"That's right everyone," Dennis shouted over the din. "Today, here in Perth, it's the much-anticipated return of Kit Carson!"

Bruce turned to look over his shoulder. His jaw dropped as if he were a cartoon character; Dennis expected his tongue to loll out and land in the puddles on the grass. The crowd was already beginning to swell again, as the cheers receded into excited chatter.

In minutes, the clouds abated, as though wiped out of the sky like a puddle off of a countertop. The line of blue proceeded forward and suddenly there were no clouds. The grim grey sky was pushed over the horizon as though the forces of evil were in humiliated retreat. People began to stream back onto the Inch, mindful of the puddles but not particularly concerned; many wore Wellington boots, and others simply let their feet smuck and pull against the mud and wet grass.

"I don't know how we did that," Dennis said.

"Laddie," replied Eddie, "I barely know that myself."

Dennis smiled and stepped down off the stage, but not before he noticed McKee, umbrella up as if in defiance of his bad fortune. He was trying to look through his briefcase, which he supported on one knee while standing on one foot. He refused to close the umbrella, for unfathomable reasons, and as he tried to stand on one foot, sort through a half-supported briefcase, and hold the umbrella all at once, Dennis watched him teeter, then topple completely, into a thatch of soupy wet grass beside him. A small string of curses erupted; mothers nearby glared with disbelief. McKee scrambled to pick up his gear, finally acquiesced to the improvement in the weather conditions, and closed his umbrella. He was, however, still fighting to find something in the briefcase.

"He's up to something," Margaret said, as Dennis joined her at ground level. "What's he looking for?"

"I don't know," Dennis said, "but it doesn't matter. This is happening. You're keeping the Rat, Margaret, and he knows it."

The crowd continued to trickle onto the Inch, and now, just moments after the downpour, cars were pulling into the adjacent lots. Crowds of old and young alike streamed across the bridges now; some people were wet, obviously caught in the recent rain, and others touted closed umbrellas or rainjackets over their arms, beaded and glistening in the newly returned sun. The staging company's workers went back to work, securing the tarpaulin and firing up the sound system.

For all his time in Perth, Dennis had met few people. Of those he had come to know, one fifth were in the hospital, one fifth hated him, and one fifth was not even a person per se. Yet here he was, returning waves, giving handshakes, and more than once marveling over the fact that so many young people—if two counts as "so many"—would continue to make Captain Sensible references. An elderly couple approached to tell him how much they appreciated what he was doing for Margaret; it turned out to be her aunt and uncle. Young kids smiled and darted for freedom, passing beneath their parents' outstretched arms. Legions of teenagers milled about, but only a few seemed curious about the nutter who lived up on Kinnoull Hill and dressed like a sailor.

One of the stage crew started to strum the acoustic in front of the microphone when Margaret tugged on Dennis' sleeve. McKee was mounting the stage steps, a clutch of papers in one waving, gesticulating hand.

"Seems he's found what he was looking for," Margaret noted.

"Stop it," Bruce said to the sound person, waving the papers directly in over the strings of the guitar. "Stop it, there's no need."

"Ladies and gentlemen," Bruce said to the expanded crowd. "Ladies and gentlemen, I'm sorry to be the bearer of bad tidings, especially now that the sun has come out, but today's concert will not be taking place."

A low boo rose from the audience.

"Now, now, this isn't my doing." Bruce looked sorrowfully out onto the Inch. "It seems that today's host, the fellow you all know as the Captain of Kinnoull Hill, didn't fill out his paperwork properly. This concert is illegal and will be shut down by police within minutes if we don't disperse of our own according. It's all here in section—"

"You're full of shite!" bellowed a brave voice from the audience.

"Now, sir, please, watch your language, there are families present." Bruce's tone was appeasing, but a steely look came over his face.

"You *are* shite!" came another voice from the other side of the stage, and the audience laughed.

"Watch your tongue, lads," Bruce snapped, "or I'll come down there and watch it for you."

"Oh, threatening kids now, are we?" called a woman from the very front—directly in Bruce's line of vision. "Why don't you come on down and threaten *me*, then, McKee?"

Margaret tugged on Dennis' sleeve and whispered in his ear.

"They've been terrified of him for years," she said, "but they've never faced him all together."

Dennis felt Eddie's presence beside him.

"Should I go up and look at those papers?" Dennis asked without looking at him. "Clearly they're fake. Abby crossed every T and dotted every I."

"No," Eddie said, his eyes on the crowd. "No, just…just watch. Something's happening."

"Ma'am, I'm not going to threaten anyone," McKee was saying into the microphone, his steeliness softened, replaced by a combination of uncertainty and simple, pathetic red-faced anger. "I'm just saying that if we don't—"

"Elizabeth Wojcinski filled out those forms right in front of me," said a small middle-aged woman in a plaid skirt, her courage bolstered by the courage of others. "I'm a city clerk, I checked them out for myself, and there was nothing wrong with them. Nothing!"

"Well," McKee said, rooting through his forgeries, "Right here, it says, clearly, that there must be a public—"

"It's all lies, Bruce!"

In the crowd, a constable stepped forward. "No one's called upon me to shut anything down."

"You're off duty," protested Bruce.

"No, I'm not!" shouted the officer. "I'm on duty, you blasted git!"

Another ripple of laugher in the face of Bruce McKee. The crowd was emboldened, nearly brazen. Bruce crumpled into himself, his uncertainty melting into confusion, his red-faced anger only redder and angrier.

"You don't even work for the town, what are you doing up there?" called a gentleman who must have been eighty. "Who elected you to speak for us? Why are you even here? Get out!"

"Why you can't—"

"Where's the Captain?" someone cried. "Captain, shoo the pest away!"

And now the entire crowd swayed against the man on stage. Their angry rabbling suddenly found a rhythm as a chant arose, Captain, Captain, Cap-tain. Voices joined and pivoted around this chant, Cap-tain, Cap-tain, until Dennis, smiling (but not too much—he wouldn't put it past Bruce to clean his clock even in front of an audience) took the stage.

"Mr. McKee," he said, audible in the microphone, "the people have spoken."

"Oh, you little fuck," he said, stepping directly to Dennis and pressing his face forward, his blood-bloated crimson cheeks so close Dennis could feel flicks of spittle as Bruce spoke. "This show is not happening. You'll not make me an ass in front of the entire town. You'll not get away with any of this, you fucking bastard. Your show is done. He is not coming. He'd be here already if he were. He's backed out. You know it and I know it.

"Bruce!" Dennis gaped at him theatrically. "*Who's* not coming?"

"Kit Carson!"

The audience screamed in delight.

"But he's not coming!" Bruce said to them. "I told his father, you and your family come anywhere near the Inch today and it'll be lights out for you!"

"You…found the Dunlop family and threatened them?"

"What?" Bruce replied mockingly. "Did you not think I'd have a back-up plan?"

"No," Dennis replied. "I just didn't think you'd be stupid enough to say that in front of a live microphone."

With that, they both slowly turned their heads towards the audience. Not everyone had heard the statement, but clearly, some had. The murmur in the crowd had a serrated edge to it; faces were angry or in various stages of disgust and disbelief.

Dennis cupped the microphone and whispered, "You'd better get the hell out of here."

"What for?" Bruce was, unbelievably, indignant.

"Because you're going to get your ass kicked by the entire township," Dennis replied. "You just told them you sabotaged the show, are you that clueless? Go while you still can."

"Go while I still can?" Rage and disbelief contorted his face; powerlessness sank his shoulders. Never had Dennis seen a furious man look so weak.

"It's ok!" Eddie yelled from the side stage. "Look! He's here!"

Dennis looked offstage to see the entire Dunlop family in the wings. Carson had his back to him, opening his guitar case, but Susan and Alan scowled in Bruce's direction.

Dennis grabbed for the microphone, but Bruce snatched it from the stand first.

"Looks like you just made them angry, Bruce," Dennis smirked.

"Shut up."

"Give me the mic, you moron," Dennis said.

"No," insisted Bruce.

"Punch him!" someone cried. "Lay a beating on the bastard!"

"Yes, yes, yes!" cried the crowd.

Bruce glared, his eyes now barely a pair of beads at the back of his crater-like eye sockets.

"Here's the thing." Dennis was contemplative and soft-spoken, but he was certain his words were finding their way into the microphone, as the audience hushed. "When I first got to your country, I was attacked and beaten in a Glasgow park by a group of punks. You, you're worse by far."

The audience listened.

"Someone out there wants me to punch you in your smug little rat face," he continued. "I'm not one for violence. You've beaten me up twice—or should I say, you've had your boys do it—and I still have no desire to kick your ass."

Bruce snorted.

"Then again, if I send you out there now, the fine people of Perth might just kick the living shit out of you."

There were more than a few shouts of agreement.

"See?" Dennis said with a smile. "It's either them or me. So remember—this is for your own good."

Dennis swung as hard as he could, struck Bruce on the jaw, and sent him across the stage. The microphone thunked to the stage floor as the audience roared.

"Eddie!" Dennis felt pain shoot up his arm from his throbbing hand, but he was able to ignore it.

Eddie's face poked out from between the curtains.

"What in the name have you done here, bruiser?" Eddie asked.

"Just get him somewhere far away before this crowd kills him, would you?"

Eddie stepped lightly across the stage, grabbed the dazed and agonized Bruce by one hand and dragged him backstage.

"Ladies and gentlemen," Dennis said to more cheers, "the pre-show is over. We're going to be sending out the donation boxes in a moment. Remember that all proceeds go to Kit's favourite charity, the Music and Youth Project Glasgow, and to the Save the Rat and Raven fund, which, really, is the best way for you to metaphorically kick Bruce McKee in the groin."

More laughter.

"Now, stick around a little while longer, enjoy the sun, and enjoy Kit Carson!"

Dennis poked through the curtains where Carson sat on a stool, regarding his feet. His parents stood on either side of him, regarding him quietly.

"You okay, Carson?"

Carson looked up, somewhat stunned.

"Yeah, I'm okay," he eventually replied. "It's just…there's a lot of people here."

"It's all right," Dennis said. "Remember. All you have to do is give them what they came for, and all that they came for is you and your music."

Carson half-rolled his eyes, but said nothing.

"Was that McKee just now, Da?"

"Aye, indeed it was."

"And was the crowd calling for you to punch him?" he asked Dennis.

"Aye, indeed it was."

"And you punched him?"

"I had to do something," admitted Dennis.

Carson looked back at his feet again, shook his head like a wet dog, and chuckled.

"Well," he said. "You were right, Da. He really is a douchebag."

"It doesn't make me happy to see him suffer," Alan replied, almost convincingly.

"You know what'll make me happy?"

Alan shook his head.

Carson closed his eyes and breathed deeply before grabbing his guitar from the stand beside him.

"This." And with that, he stood, smiled, and headed for the stage.

CHAPTER FIFTEEN

Kit Carson played for fifty-two minutes that afternoon, beneath a beaming sun and a spotlessly blue sky. It was the biggest crowd on the North Inch in many years, though attendance estimates vary.

When people talk about that day, no one remembers exactly how much money was raised for The Music and Youth Project Glasgow, despite Carson's heartwarming speech before performing "On The Horizon." No one remembers exactly how much was raised for the Save the Rat and Raven fund, either, except for Margaret Donleavy. She would tell you it was £2,714.38, some of which she immediately transferred to Bruce McKee, the rest of which she, too, donated to MYPG. People donated far more than the suggested minimum that day, their generosity engendered by the smiles, the hellos, the spirit, and perhaps because, in a less humanitarian yet nonetheless satisfying way, some enjoyed seeing Bruce McKee get a sock in the chops.

What people remember most is that the afternoon felt magical, otherworldly, as if everyone there had been touched by an unseen power. As if something had stepped across a bridge—or through a gate, perhaps—and smiled on them, made them feel some kind of providence they could never explain. You just had to be there.

For Dennis Duckworth, from Chicago, and Eddie the Red Cap, origins unknown, the magic was literal. They stood and listened and cheered and clapped with the rest of the crowd—Kit Carson's music wasn't Dennis' bag, per se, but he could appreciate the songcraft—right up until the moment Carson strummed the first few chords of something familiar.

"This is something new I've been working on." The audience hooted briefly in appreciation, as they did for almost every sentence Carson uttered into the mic.

"I started playing it in my bedroom earlier this summer, when I was thinking about how much I wanted to come back and play for you all."

He paused for the cheers to subside.

"I got a wee bit overwhelmed by how you all responded to my music," he continued. "It was sudden, too, which made it even crazier. So part of working that all out in my head was writing this song. It's about how hard it is to think you're one thing and then find out you're more than that. It's about how the past and the future exist together in only one place, and that's the now."

"Well I'll be damned," whispered Eddie softly.

"This is called 'I Can Change.'"

"Of course it is." Dennis looked down at Eddie as the chords fell into familiar grooves in his brain. "Of course that's what it's called. Eddie. I know this song."

"Aye, lad." Eddie's eyes were wide with wonder. "And I'm not surprised in the least."

"You've heard this, too, haven't you?"

Eddie nodded. "For months now. Comes to me from nowhere. Like it's implanted in my brain, coming to my ears from the inside."

"Yes." Dennis listened as Carson began to sing.

"You told me once you weren't where you were supposed to be." Eddie continued to smile. "Do you still feel that way?"

Dennis paused, although he knew the answer. He understood that boarding passes and violent punters and accidental trains and notices on the Tesco bulletin boards and bloody goblins were all simply parts of the journey. They didn't bring him here. What brought him here was the music—or, more succinctly, whatever or whomever it was who had sent him the music.

"No. I think quite the opposite now. I'm supposed to be here. No idea why, and it doesn't make any goddamn sense, but there you go."

"Och, Duckworth," Eddie replied with a grin, "don't go looking for sense now. It's beyond our ken. Accept the madness and take your next step accordingly."

"Well," Dennis said aloud, more to himself than Eddie. "I think I've been doing that since I first encountered your hideous mug."

Eddie ignored him, and began to hum along himself. Dennis looked over the smiling faces in the audience and, at that moment, locked eyes with Meaghan Campbell, whose face was positively alight. She somehow widened her smile, and Dennis returned it.

"Thank you," he mouthed.

Meaghan shook her head and mouthed the same back at him.

*

"He looks better today." Dennis smiled down at the tiny, fragile creature in Gigi's arms. "He looks cleaner. Less like a stewed prune."

"Och, you're horrible, Dennis Duckworth, truly horrible!" laughed Gigi. She lay on the orange velvet chesterfield of the Gent living room. The impressively hefty newborn lay on Gigi's once-prominent stomach, deflated to a soft rise beneath a baby blue yukata. The living room was not unlike Gigi's office—somewhat bewildered, mostly crooked, populated by piles of boxes and dog-hair encrusted blankets. The floor resembled Sanibel Island in Florida, with children's toys instead of seashells. Somewhere beyond, they could hear the high squeals of children and, just a notch below, William's winded oomphs and ughs as they children pelted him with pillows.

"I am horrible," Dennis agreed. "Though I did bring you a lasagna."

"That was Margaret," Abby reported, "*Margaret* made you the lasagna."

"But I brought it!" Dennis mock-protested.

"Yes, and thank you, it's lovely!" Gigi smiled. "One less meal for poor William to cook while I rest! If you can call it resting, it's not truly, not resting, but lovely, oh, you all took such good care of me, you're all family to me now, I swear it, I think of you as family. Oh, you're all so lovely."

With that, Gigi began to cry, and Margaret patted her hand.

"Gigi," Dennis said, "I have to go. I have a flight to catch."

"You're leaving us so soon?" Gigi asked.

"No choice, I'm afraid," said Dennis. "My deadline has come. Besides, the work on the tower is done. There's nothing left for me to do up there, which means I've nowhere to stay and no job. I've both of those things in Chicago—and I need to get back."

"Oh, I understand, Dennis," said Gigi. Eddie Gent burst into tears a moment later, his young vocal cords surprisingly resilient. Eddie Red Cap reached out, touched his hand, and the boy was quiet again. No one noticed but Dennis.

"If you ever come back, I'm sure, I'm quite sure, that we can find you more restoration work," Gigi said. "That was the quickest, most professionally done work I've e'er seen in my life."

"Well, Gigi, I've got an admission to make," Dennis looked over at the baby who, impossibly, seemed to be watching the red cap, despite being far too young to see such a distance.

"I didn't do anything," Dennis continued. "It was all Eddie—my Eddie, of course, not yours. I did literally nothing. If there's anyone who could use the work—and I know he's looking for work—it's this gentleman right here."

"Aye," Eddie said, staring at the child, "I'm available any day you need me."

"Oh, where can I find you, then?" Gigi asked.

"Don't worry." Eddie smiled but didn't break eye contact with the child. "I've a way of appearing when I'm needed."

*

Dennis had no luggage. His carry-on had melted into the nylon of his tent, and the whole mess had been gathered up hastily and stuffed into garbage bags. The camp, what little there was of it, was gone. Eddie had returned the borrowed items in the night, without incident; the hessian and other materials had been removed, revealing a tower that, at first glance, looked pretty much the same as the old one, but would stand longer and stronger than the old one ever could have.

"Your train's already on the platform." Abby, Margaret and Eddie stood in the entrance of Perth Station. "You'd better move on through. Here." With that, Eddie held up a ticket, out of nowhere, which Dennis took; when Dennis turned briefly to Abby, Eddie vanished.

"Yeah," Dennis said, puzzled. "Well…"

"Email me when you get back," Abby said, giving him a quick hug. "And send me some of these records. Surely you've got something half-decent on that label."

"Surely."

"Pleasure to have met you, Dennis Duckworth."

"Indeed."

Margaret stood a few feet closer to the gate. Dennis approached her, unsure of himself.

"You don't have to try and say anything," Margaret said. "We're…well, I don't know what's going on between us, but whatever it is, it probably doesn't warrant a—"

"But it does," Dennis interrupted. "It does warrant a…something. Because I like you, Margaret. I always have. It doesn't matter that you own the Commitments soundtrack."

Dennis laughed and continued. "Anyway, you helped me, and I screwed up, and, I think, made it right. And I'll be back."

"Not for me, I hope." Margaret seemed almost horrified, but Dennis recognized a reflex when he saw one.

"Not just for you." Dennis held the captain's jacket across one forearm; he tugged at the pocket that held his wallet and his passport, the only personal items he had left, though he thought of the jacket and cap as his own. "I can't say you're not part of the appeal, I admit. I can't say that when I come back, I don't want to see you again. Immediately. But no, it's a more practical reason. The Dunlops want me to come up with some ideas about bringing Carson to the U.S."

"Snack Donkey, Random…and Kit Carson?"

"I didn't think you had heard of 5/4 Records!" laughed Dennis.

"There's this thing called the Internet?" Margaret joked. "Yeah, your bands are pretty good. Not sold on this Random band, though. Too much like Fall Out Boy."

"They used to be like that," Dennis agreed, "but not so much anymore."

"And you're going home to get them signed, then."

"Yes, I am. I'm going home to finish something I began, and I've left it far too long."

"Well."

"Well."

They stood a moment, quiet, and then Margaret kissed him, furtively, on the cheek.

"You'll get in touch when you come back, then?"

"I'll get in touch when I get home," Dennis replied. "You know. Just so you know I got there okay."

"I'd like that," Margaret said. "I really would."

"Talk to you later, then," Dennis said softly.

"Talk to you later, then," was Margaret's soft reply.

With that, Dennis stepped through the gate, and onto the southbound platform. The sun was blocked by the overhang, but the heat was still pressing, tight. It reminded him of the oppressive summers in New York City, except that here, in Perth, he liked it.

"I suppose it's Labour Day back home."

Eddie reappeared beside Dennis as unexpectedly as he had vanished. It failed to startle Dennis anymore.

"It is Labour Day, yes."

"So you've a busy day tomorrow."

"I do. I've got—"

"To finish something you began," Eddie completed the sentence. "Yes. I've only one question for you, though, Dennis."

"Yes?"

"Which thing are you finishing? You've begun more than one."

Dennis didn't answer.

"Thank you for the endorsement, back at Gigi's house." Eddie scratched at his scalp unconsciously, unfamiliar with the sensation of having his head exposed to the air. "I admit, I didnae see that coming."

"You need a job."

"Aye, it's true," Eddie grinned. "And you've found me work I'm able to do."

"Eddie, I didn't find you anything, you found it yourself. You didn't even need me to help make you human. You already were. Not so much on the outside—there you're still a total freak show—but on the inside… "

Dennis reached up and touched the captain's hat, its white now streaked with brown and grey, its brim weathered and warped.

"Sod off," Eddie spat, but his eyes were smiling. "You had the opposite problem. You were a soulless ghoul when I met you. And that's coming from a fellow who used to vivisect folks with his teeth."

"Well, thank Christ we met each other, I guess."

Dennis looked sideways at the goblin, who did not disappear at the blasphemy.

"You're such a dick," grumbled Eddie, "but yeah. Thank…och, I still cannae say it."

Dennis laughed and removed his hat.

"The Captain is dead; long live the Captain," Eddie said.

"I prefer to think of myself as demoted. Maybe to chief steward or purser or something. I'll leave you to steward Kinnoull from now on."

"You'll be back, lad."

"Sure, but next time I'm living in a hotel room."

"Well, I may have an apartment in town myself."

"How will I find you?"

Eddie grinned his toothless grin. "Don't bother. I'll know when you're back."

"I suppose you will," Dennis agreed, as the train began to spit and hiss. "Goodbye, Eddie Red Cap."

"Goodbye for now, Dennis Duckworth."

Dennis stepped up the stairs, into the train, and turned at the last minute to look at his diminutive friend below on the platform.

"Oh, Eddie, before I come back, do something for yourself."

"What's that?"

"Get yourself some teeth."

"Och!" Eddie waved Dennis away. "Off with you, you bastard!"

And on that, the doors of the train slid shut.

EPILOGUE

Dennis Duckworth owned a little red phone book. Its pages were dog-eared and ink-smeared, and the little gold telephone embossed on the cover had been worn so badly it was more like a constellation of gold flecks which merely *suggested* a telephone. It was his back-up, in case of emergencies—emergencies such as a cell phone ground into a marble floor in New York, for example. The phone book lay open on his lap as he thumbed numbers into his new, uncrushed cell phone. Dennis knew some of these numbers by heart; often, they were numbers he knew he'd never call. He input them anyway. You never knew.

Jet lag pulled at his shoulders and chin, but Dennis fought it valiantly. He'd been unable to sleep past five a.m.; Steph had been shocked to find him in the office when she arrived at eight.

"Dennis!" Steph looked at him as if something was amiss. "What—"

"Well, hey, the deadline's today." Dennis grinned at her from behind his desk. "I told you I'd be here to meet it. I just sent the files off to New York. Now we wait."

"No, not that," she said. "Why are you wearing that hat?"

Dennis wore his usual black ensemble—jeans, black shirt, blazer—but atop his head sat the captain's hat. He reached up and touched the brim thoughtfully. "I wanted a little magic today," Dennis said. "You might say this is my good luck hat."

"You look like something you'd find in a box of licorice all-sorts."

Steph waited for the sarcastic rejoinder but received only laughter instead. She stared at him in puzzled wonder for rest of the morning.

Now it was afternoon, and Dennis programmed numbers dutifully, until he reached the "M" section of the phone book and stopped to dial the first number he found. He already knew it by heart.

"Hey. Me. Mess—"

"Hello?" Paul said, interrupting the answering machine.

"You need to change your phone message," Dennis said.

"I'm thinking of changing my message to the opening theme from the Rockford Files."

"Older, yet somehow fresher," Dennis said. "I like it."

"You're back."

"Yeah."

"You deal with The Random?"

"Yes," Dennis replied. "I sent it off this morning."

"They're going to hate you," Paul said simply.

"Who?

"Everyone."

"Why?" asked Dennis. "It's not my fault they started to sound like Fugazi. If Universal doesn't sign them—which they won't—it isn't my fault."

"So…you…"

"Sent Universal the proper files," Dennis finished. "The new Random songs, not the old ones. Yes."

There was a moment of silence.

"I'm proud—"

"Oh, shut up, for God's sake," Dennis laughed. "Just because I made an ethical decision for once? Anyway, I can't talk, I just wanted you to know I was back and that we should hook up for beers after dinner."

"Sure. You're at your office?"

To Dennis' right, an office door swung open. Martin Tusk smiled and waved as if to beckon him into the room, festooned with posters and framed records—not exactly gold records, but framed nonetheless. Big Black. Jesus Lizard. Slint.

"No, I'm not at the office," Dennis replied. "I'm just out finishing something I began."

Acknowledgements

First, I'll thank the people I've undoubtedly forgotten. If you're going to go unnamed, you deserve the top spot.

Thanks to my wife Teresa Caterini, my son Jordan Tennant, my mother and brothers for their support.

Thanks to my early readers (Greg Vickers, Jan Steinberg, Sherri Vanderveen, Jaime Krakowski) for their thoughts and suggestions.

Thanks to The National Trust for Scotland, Association for Preservation Technology, Perth & Kinross Council, the Forestry Commission Scotland and others who assisted in my research.

Thanks to Iain MacKinnon for the Gaelic translation.

Special thanks to my publisher Aimée Dunn and everyone at Palimpsest Press, designer Dawn Kresan for the cover, and to Noelle Allen of Wolzak & Wynn for pointing me in their direction.

Apologies for any liberties taken with the geography of Perth. Likewise, apologies for any liberties taken in regards to the state of Kinnoull Tower. Perth & Kinross Council and the Forestry Commission take fine care of it, and to my knowledge, they haven't needed help from any goblins.